Out on the
Sound

R. E. BRADSHAW

Titles from R. E. Bradshaw Books

Rainey Bell Thriller Series:
Rainey Nights (2011) (Lambda Literary Award Finalist)
Rainey's Christmas Miracle (2011) (Short Story)
Rainey Days (2010)

The Adventures of Decky and Charlie Series:
Out on the Panhandle (2012)
Out on the Sound (2010)

Molly: House on Fire (2012)

Before It Stains (2011)

Waking Up Gray (2011)

Sweet Carolina Girls (2010)

The Girl Back Home (2010)

Out on the Sound

A Decky and Charlie Adventure

R. E. BRADSHAW

Published by
R. E. BRADSHAW BOOKS

USA

•R.E.B.BOOKS•

Out on the Sound
2nd edition

R. E. Bradshaw
© 2012 by R. E. Bradshaw. All Rights Reserved.
R. E. Bradshaw Books/Sept. 2012
ISBN-13: 978-1442135857

Website: http://www.rebradshawbooks.com
Facebook: https://www.facebook.com/rebradshawbooks
Twitter @rebradshawbooks
Blog: http://rebradshawbooks.blogspot.com
For information contact rebradshawbooks@gmail.com

Acknowledgments

During Christmas vacation in 2009, I sat down with my better half and wrote <u>Out on the Sound</u> in fourteen days. After years of wanting to write, I finally did it. I never intended for anyone to read the novel, other than friends or family, but I got the bug and continued to write three more novels before August of 2010. I published the four novels on Amazon without a professional editor, a mistake, but it proved to be a good move in the long run. Readers found me, encouraged me, and my fate was sealed. I became a fulltime author in the fall of 2010 and have not looked back.

I did take to heart what the reviewers said about my first four, which was basically, "Good stories, great characters, get an editor. I listened and hired an editor for my subsequent releases. I am reissuing <u>Out on the Sound</u> and the other original four after having an editor go through them. I did, however, make a conscious effort not to change the books. I know that I could go back and make them better, but that's where I was when I wrote them, and something tells me to leave them alone. I hope that I have improved in my writing and that I can always look back fondly on those first four that changed my life.

<u>Out on the Sound</u> will always hold a special place in my heart. Not only was it my first novel, it was the book that launched a dream. I have many people to thank for making this dream come true. The readers are at the top of the list, but the one person that I owe everything to is my wife. She has stood by me, encouraged me to quit my fulltime teaching job and follow my dream. I could never write about romance, if I had not had the most fantastic love in my life.

This book is a testament to that love, twenty-five years into this relationship and going strong. I wish for everyone a person to stand with them through thick and thin, encouraging the following of dreams, and the pursuit of happiness. So, it is to her, my Deb, that I say thank you. Thank you for being my Charlie.

R. E. Bradshaw

PS. I am frequently asked where I came up with the pen name R. E. Bradshaw. Rebecca Elizabeth Bradshaw was an ancestor of mine. Her nickname was Decky. I used that name for the main character in <u>Out on the Sound</u>, who happens to be a writer. When you get to the end of the book, you'll see how R. E. Bradshaw became an author of Lesbian Fiction. I was a fulltime teacher in a public school in the reddest state in the Union. I needed a pen name. It all just fell into place.

PART I

Love isn't something you decide to do,

...the heart wants what it wants.

1

First, there was the touch, not much of a touch, just a simple brush of skin on skin. Decky locked eyes with her, surely seeing the same surprise she felt from the jolt of the touch. She played the afternoon over in her mind, but it always came down to that one touch.

It began like all the other tournaments, when the Merle's Furniture women's softball team played in the Memorial Day Invitational. They pulled up and piled out of cars, trucks, and SUVs. Even a few minivans were represented, one belonging to the oldest member of the team, complete with three little blondes dressed as batgirls.

When Decky walked up to Mother Margie, as she was known, the older woman was supervising the girls unloading the van. "Don't forget that new bat in the back, girls. I think there's a hit or two in that one."

"Good morning, Mother," Decky said, cracking a smile.

"Well, good mornin' darlin'." Margie stopped giving directions long enough to give Decky a quick hug and a peck on the cheek, before going back on duty. "And don't forget my ukulele this time. Last time y'all had to run back and get it. I didn't get it till the fourth inning."

The girls looked at each other and then caught Decky looking at them. Decky mouthed the words, "Good job," to the girls. They giggled and went back to gathering the equipment. Mother Margie was old school. She still wore the same high top black leather cleats she had always worn. Of course, the steel cleats had been replaced with rubber, but still, she had them repaired every year. She also carried that old holey ukulele everywhere. No one had the heart to tell her how irritating the sound could be sometimes, but Decky had to admit it drove the other teams crazy.

Mother Margie was the heart of the team. She was on the very first roster and had been responsible for keeping a very competitive team together year after year. She raised her own kids and half the county's young women on these fields. In fact, it was Mother who brought a fourteen-year-old Decky into the world of competitive softball. That was twenty-three years ago.

Decky could still hold her own, although no longer the athlete of her younger days. It took a lot more training to stay in shape, but it was worth it. The thought of retiring from softball was way down the road, but changing to the old lady league crept into her mind on an occasional Sunday morning.

Today she felt young and alive. Who wouldn't? The sun was coming up on a beautiful Carolina blue sky, which held only a few wispy clouds wafting in from the coast. Decky took in the combining aromas of freshly mown grass and leather. Cleats clicked on pavement all around her, as the girls of summer began to take the field. I love this, she thought to herself.

Finding a warm-up partner, Decky joined the dozens of women tossing balls back and forth. Decky could hear the snap of the glove as the player behind her caught the ball from her partner. That snap meant the partner was throwing pretty hard. Decky perked up. Having been hit before, she took a quick peek at the pair.

Closest to her was a short, blond, athletically built woman, standing with her gloved hand on her hip, obviously about to make a point. The woman's partner was a teenage girl, who looked like she had just left the farm, all arms, legs, and freckles.

"Hey," the woman called out. "The purpose of this activity is to warm up and stretch the muscles. It is not about showing everybody how hard you can throw." She tossed the ball back to the teenager with a little zip on it. "Besides, you'll thank me when you are my age." She laughed at the girl. "Now go find someone else to pound on. I'm done."

Decky laughed too, as she watched the small blond woman walk over to a cooler and grab a bottle of water. She didn't realize she was still watching the woman until a ball came dangerously close to her head. Suddenly aware that she had been staring, she quickly threw the ball to her partner, who was now looking at Decky with that "What are you doing?" look on her face.

Because so many teams wore similar uniforms, it wasn't until the bottom of the first inning that Decky noticed the blond woman playing centerfield for the other team. This time Decky could see her from the front. Although the distance made it hard to see her features, Decky could tell this was an athlete. From what she had said to the teenage farm girl earlier, she must be close to my age, Decky thought. Decky had always admired the athletic body in all shapes, sizes, and colors, but she particularly liked to see a woman her age with a toned body. Mainly because she knew how hard it was to stay that way.

The other things she was feeling, that part of her that was attracted to women, she had never explored. She chalked it up to natural urges, but nothing more. She liked men, always had and always would, as far as she knew. The two things she loved in life, other than family, were theatre and softball. How could she do either of those things and not be around gay people?

Decky remembered her mother freaking out when she was fourteen. "You lie down with dogs, you get up with fleas," her mother had stated emphatically. "You keep playing ball with those dykes and you'll end up like them."

"Mom, I play with them because they are the best players, not because of who they choose to sleep with. Everybody that plays softball is not gay."

"I hear things. I know what goes on, on those trips," her mother quipped.

"You only know what other people make up."

"I don't want a gay daughter!"

"I don't want to be your gay daughter!"

"Decky, quit day dreaming and grab a bat." Margie's voice broke the memory and just in time, Decky thought. "You're on deck."

Where did that unpleasant memory come from? Fortunately, the batter before Decky lined out and the sides changed, so she didn't have to bat while she felt so distracted. She tried to shake it off and succeeded until the third inning, when Decky let the blond centerfielder back into her mind. Actually she appeared, after turning a line drive to right field into a double, standing sixty feet away from where Decky waited at third base.

"All right Charlie, come see me down here," the third base coach called out to the woman on second.

Decky could now see clearly that this was a very attractive woman around her own age. She was sneaking a look between each pitch, and when the woman caught her looking, Decky even managed to smile back at her.

Decky, who prided herself in being the most competitive person she knew, could not believe how this woman was invading her mind, but she was.

What in the hell is wrong with me? Concentrate, before you end up wearing a line drive.

The ball came off the bat with a crack. More from instinct than ability, Decky fell to her right and stopped a sure base hit. Hopping up, she looked back the woman on second and let the ball fly to first where the runner was called out. The look back had not worked well, in fact not at all. The blonde left second as soon as Decky let the ball go. The first baseman threw to the shortstop now covering third, but the little blonde was fast, very fast. She slid under the tag with ease.

Cute, athletic, my age, and fast. My kinda girl.

Decky couldn't believe she had just thought that. Wait, did she say it aloud? The blonde, who was dusting herself off, smiled at Decky.

"Nice slide," was all Decky could manage as she bent down to recover the woman's hat.

"I think I have a half acre down my shirt," the blonde said with a touch of country twang, brushing off the front of her shirt.

Decky handed her the hat and as she did, they brushed fingers ever so slightly. They locked eyes for a second.

"We're gonna score now, Charlie. Let's go," the third base coach said, saving Decky from saying anything else.

Decky tried to act normal. The next batter grounded out to the pitcher, giving Decky time to recover her wits and somehow manage to make it through the rest of the game without losing her mind. Her team won by a run and proceeded through the winner's bracket, making it to the Sunday games. Decky did not see the blonde again – Charlie, that was her name – but she thought of her often.

Mother Margie was holding court at the minivan. "We have to play that bunch from the first game at 10 a.m. tomorrow. Let's get here by 8:30, okay? Darlene, you make sure Brandi gets here on time. I'm holding you responsible, 'cause Lord knows she ain't."

Decky was only half listening. As soon as Mother pointed out that they would be playing Charlie's team again, her heart began to palpitate uncontrollably. She knew her name was Charlie and that was all. What was happening to Decky? Why was she so excited at the prospect of seeing Charlie and fearing it just the same?

"Hey Deck, you wanna grab a beer?" It was Brandi, a big ol' gal with a good heart and not much brain, but God, could she hit a softball.

"No, thanks, I think I'll head home and put this old body to bed."

"God, I hope I never get old enough to turn down beer," Decky heard Brandi say to Darlene as they walked away.

"I remember thinking like that too," Decky said to herself, as she hauled her tired body into the Expedition and turned the key. She caught herself in the rear view mirror and paused there, remembering that second when Charlie touched her and the electricity shot up her arm straight to her heart.

What in the hell was that? She sighed and put the car in gear.

#

There were good things and bad things about living around the people with whom you grew up. You could count on folks being there when you needed them and when you didn't. This was one of those times.

As Decky rolled down the wooded driveway towards the sanctuary of her home, she almost relaxed, but then she saw the glint of brake lights through the trees.

Oh, God! Not tonight.

The backup lights flashed on briefly, as the still moving car was slammed into park.

"Mom."

The sound left Decky's mouth in a sigh. She slowly pulled into the garage, lowered the overhead door, and stepped out through the side entrance to see Elizabeth Anne Bradshaw, Miss Lizzie to county folk and Lizzie to a precious few, waiting impatiently by her front door.

Thank goodness she had remembered to lock the door or she would have walked in on her mother cleaning her house, which was never, in her mother's opinion, clean enough.

"Where have you been? Your daddy has tried to call you. I tried to call you. Your son called and did not even know where you were."

"Is something wrong?" Decky asked only because that's what she knew came next.

"Well, no, nothing's wrong. It could have been and we wouldn't have known how to get up with you. Where's your cell phone? I haven't heard from you in two days."

"Momma, I called and talked to Daddy yesterday." Decky stepped around her mother and opened the door. They went into the kitchen, where Decky's golden retriever, Dixie, greeted them with much ado.

"That dog ought not to be shut up in the house all day," Lizzie said as she took off her jacket and plopped down on a stool at the kitchen island.

"She wasn't shut up all day. The twins come over and let her out twice a day when I'm not here. I've told you that." Decky opened the door to the deck, which Dixie took as her chance to escape. "Coward," Decky said to the dog, who smiled back over her shoulder, then headed for the steps to the beach. She left the door open for Dixie's return, but Decky doubted she would until the coast was clear.

"I can't believe you gave those little heathens a key to your house. Rebecca Elizabeth, do you still have on your cleats? Lord, you ruined my floors, now you'll ruin yours."

"It's slate. That's why I put in slate. Normally, I would have come in from downstairs and taken them off in the mud room, but since you were waiting at my front door, I thought it would be rude."

Decky sat down opposite her mother with a thud. Deliberately placing her dirty shoe on the stool seat beside her mother, she started taking off her cleats.

"I tried to raise a dainty girl, but no, that wasn't Decky Bradshaw. Look at you. You are thirty-seven years old and you are still out playing softball."

Decky dropped her cleat to the floor and said softly, "Your mother played until she was fifty-two."

"I do not want to argue about this again, Decky. Your son called and said if I saw you to tell you to call him. So I am delivering the message."

Lizzie was in one of the down loops of her bi-polar disorder that she, of course, denied she had. Therefore, Decky chose not to start a fight by reminding her mother of the invention of the voice message, and tried to smooth things over.

"I appreciate you going out of your way. Do you want a glass of water or a coke?" Decky moved toward the refrigerator, but Lizzie was already on the go.

"No, your daddy is waiting for me and I've been gone a while. I stopped at Bobbie's to talk about the motel before I came over here. Call that sweet boy. I still can't believe you let a seventeen-year-old go off to Alaska like that."

Decky bristled, but did not take the bait. "He'll be fine, Mom. He's becoming a man now and he needs his space."

Lizzie had, by now, put her jacket back on and was almost out the door, but she had to say it. "If he had a daddy that was worth a damn, he wouldn't need to go to Alaska to become a man."

Dixie looked in through the deck curtains and saw the expression on Decky's face. She quickly stepped back into the shadows and tiptoed away. Decky, contemplating the appropriate response, reached up and pulled off her ball cap. Holding the hat in one hand and rubbing the back of her head with the other, she looked down, flashing for just the tiniest second on her moment with Charlie. Looking up at her mother, Decky forgot what Lizzie had said.

"Well, thanks for stopping by. I love you. Give Dad a hug," and with that Decky skillfully maneuvered her mother out the door.

Lizzie looked back through the door at her daughter with a puzzled expression. She waved and walked down the steps, shaking her head from side to side. Decky knew her mother was talking to herself as she watched her get in her car and leave. When she could no longer see the taillights, Decky placed her back against the door and slid to the floor. Dixie padded over and licked Decky in the face.

"It's okay, baby girl. She's gone." Decky hugged the big dog to her and whispered in her ear, "Momma had the strangest thing happen today. Let's start up the hot tub, grab some wine, call your brother, and then we'll talk about it."

#

Decky left a message for Zack on his voicemail, then after soaking the soreness out in the hot tub and two glasses of wine, Decky set the alarm and crawled into bed. She thought long and hard about the woman named Charlie and the impact she was having on her. It made no sense. Decky was around gay women all her life and never felt like this. Of course she had the occasional adolescent crush, but wasn't that normal? In addition, she was jumping to conclusions about Charlie, just as everyone had always jumped to conclusions about Decky herself.

Whatever it was would have to wait until morning. It was after midnight and she had to get up in time to do a good stretching warm up. Maybe she would hit the hot tub again in the morning, if she were still aching. Dixie climbed up on her side of the bed and put her head on the pillow opposite Decky.

"Good night, sweet girl. Sweet dreams."

Decky had just closed her eyes when she thought she heard the doorbell.

"Good Lord, who in the world is that," Decky said to Dixie, who for some reason, and totally out of character, did not appear to care that someone was ringing the doorbell.

Decky stumbled down the spiral staircase to the foyer. Blinking her eyes several times, adjusting to the lights she had sworn were turned off, Decky froze in her tracks. There on the other side of the door was Charlie. She smiled at Decky and then pantomimed unlocking the door. Decky, still frozen, realized she had been gaping at the woman on the other side of the door for some time. She snapped out of it and opened the door.

"I'm sorry. Come in. It took me a minute to recognize you." Decky stepped back, allowing Charlie to pass.

"I know it's late, but I wanted to know if you would be at the game tomorrow. Oh, I'm sorry. You must think I'm crazy. My name is –"

"Charlie. Your name is Charlie. I heard your coach call you that." Decky was still in a state of shock, recognizing a familiar longing beginning to well up inside.

"Yes, well, I wanted to make sure you would be there, that's all." Charlie looked around. "You have a nice house. Can I see it?" She headed for the spiral staircase. "What's up here?"

Decky thought to herself, what an odd time to visit, but if Charlie wanted to see the house, she would show it to her. She wasn't sure of much, but she knew she didn't want Charlie to leave.

"It's the master suite," she heard herself say, but Charlie was already halfway up the stairs.

By the time Decky reached the top of the stairs, Charlie was already standing between the French doors that led to the balcony. She must have opened them, Decky noted.

Charlie turned to Decky. She was framed in the moonlight with the white curtains billowing around her. Decky thought she looked like an angel.

"My God, Decky, this is beautiful." Charlie turned again to look out at the water.

Without knowing why, without caring, Decky stepped up behind Charlie and placed her arms around her waist.

"You are beautiful," Decky whispered in Charlie's ear.

Slowly, Charlie turned in Decky's arms until their lips were so close, they could feel each other's quickening breath.

Decky woke with a start. Dixie was inches from her, breathing right into her face, and the alarm was blaring. She pushed Dixie away, cut off the alarm, and swung her legs out of the bed. Sitting on the side of the bed, she nuzzled Dixie.

"Girlfriend, I have never had a dream like that. I do believe I am going over to the dark side." Laughing, she and Dixie headed down the stairs to start the day.

2

Dixie barked out her last goodbyes as Decky pulled out of the garage. Once the garage door was shut, Decky knew she would promptly cuddle up on the couch and wait for the twins to come. Decky, however, was not so relaxed. She worked out for twenty minutes and soaked in the hot tub for ten, but she still felt tight. It was sexual tension and Decky was on familiar terms with it, by now. Although she tried desperately, she could not stop flashes of her dream from playing repeatedly in her head.

"God, you need to get laid," she said to no one and flipped on the CD player. Emmy Lou Harris sang out loud and proud from the speakers. By the time Decky pulled into the parking lot at the fields, she was feeling much better. Brandi walked over to her window just as Decky was helping Emmy Lou finish up.

"C'est la vie, say the old folks. It goes to show you never can tell."

"I don't know how you listen to that country crap," Brandi said with a sneer.

"I don't know how you can walk around with an earring in your nose, so I guess we're even."

"Well, I see Decky's feeling chipper this morning," Mother Margie said, yanking the van door open. "Watch your mouths girls. I got a vanload this morning and more comin' on that bus there. Seems the Sunday-school class would rather praise the Lord out here, than in church."

With that, the entire county all-star twelve-year-olds, and a few stragglers, unloaded out of the van and the small church bus that just pulled up. Margie leaned into the open bus doors and said to the man behind the wheel, "Come back and get them about five. I'll probably have had enough of them by then."

"All right Mother, y'all play good now."

The bus pulled away as a few of the girls ran by Brandi slapping high fives. One of the twelve–year-olds was asking Brandi about her nose ring.

"Oh good Lord, would you look at that, Decky. Brandi is playing show and tell. Let me go nip this little thing in the bud right now. Hey you, Ashley – Amber – Blondie, com'ere."

Mother was off again to lead another child down the right path.

Decky warmed up, stretched, and watched everywhere for a certain little blonde. As the team took the field for the first inning warm up, Decky searched the opposing dugout once again. No Charlie. Decky was happy to see her friend Brenda coming to coach third for the other team. Brenda and Decky had played sports with and against each other all their lives. Brenda was now the softball coach at the local University, where her husband coached baseball.

"I see Mother Margie brought the cheering squad this morning," Brenda said as she hugged Decky. "It's been too long since you've been over for a party."

Brenda and her husband, Chip, were famous for their seemingly endless summer parties. After any game, a party was going down at BC's, as it had come to be known. You never knew if it would be three people or three hundred, but it was always legendary.

"Yes, it has. I've been staying close to home lately, but I do feel the need for some backyard badminton." These games were also renowned.

"Okay, I'll hold you to that." Brenda smiled and patted Decky on the back.

Decky kicked at the dirt, like she was clearing away debris, but what she was really doing was trying to ask a question without giving her emotions away. Finally, she took a deep breath and said, "I saw you had a new centerfielder yesterday."

"Oh, yeah, that's my friend from college, Charlene."

"I thought her name was Charlie," Decky said, and immediately wanted to take it back. She sounded too interested.

"Well, yeah, we call her Charlie." Brenda studied Decky with a puzzled look on her face. She shrugged it off and continued, "Charlene, or Charlie and I go way back. She just took a job, teaching math at the University. Chip and I are just thrilled to have her back in the gang again. You should come over tonight and meet her. I'm sure you two would hit it off."

Decky was stricken. When Brenda said come over tonight and meet her, Decky stopped breathing. She was still stuck somewhere between reality and a dream, when Brenda grabbed her arm. "Are you okay?"

"I'm fine. I just felt a little sick there for a moment. Shouldn't have eaten that extra piece of bacon, I guess."

Decky moved into defensive position as the first batter took her stance. She was glad to be able to lean down and rest her hands on her knees for a moment. Brenda was still looking at her with concern at the end of the inning. Luckily, nothing had been hit to the third base side, so no harm done. Decky was just glad to be heading to the dugout when Brenda stopped her.

"Are you sure you are okay?"

"Yeah, I'm fine. I just need a little water."

Brenda looked her up and down, apparently deciding she was overly concerned, she went on, "Well, get in there and get some water and perk up. I really want you to meet Charlie. She had to take her friend to the airport this morning, but she'll be here later."

"Batter up!" Decky heard the umpire say, which was exactly what Decky's stomach felt like. Thank God Brenda returned to her dugout and Decky finally reached the water cooler at the end of the bench. She collapsed near Darlene and Brandi, who were arguing over some trivial slight perceived by one or the other. These two young lesbians were not role models for prospective lesbians, she thought. Decky needed to talk to someone.

Is this some kind of mid life crisis? Jesus, I'm only thirty-seven. This isn't mid life already? Did Brenda say "her friend"? What did that mean? Was she the lesbian lover, going back to wherever they came from to get the rest of their stuff? Why leap to that conclusion? It could be a man. A boyfriend. Why didn't Brenda say boyfriend?

Decky looked up from staring at the dugout floor, just in time to see Brandi remove the nose ring and fling it at Darlene.

"You can take this back, too. I don't belong to you anymore," Brandi said, as alligator tears rolled down her face.

Decky couldn't help it. She burst out laughing. She knew she shouldn't, but the image of Darlene leading Brandi through a pasture by her nose ring had flashed in her crazed mind. Decky laughed even louder when Darlene got up and stormed out of the dugout with Brandi hot on her heels. The alligator tears were now streaming down Decky's own face and try as she might, she could not regain her composure.

Mother left her post as third base coach, to see what was going on. "Decky, what in the hell did you do to those girls?"

There was no way Decky could stop laughing long enough to tell Mother what had just transpired. One of the other women, who also found it amusing, relayed the events.

Mother stared at Decky, who was now gasping for air. "I do believe you have lost your mind, Decky."

Decky, finally able to breathe again, said, "I know."

To Decky's relief she did not have to talk to Brenda again, because she moved over to coach first. The laughter had been exhausting, but somehow cleansing. There were no little blondes named Charlie anywhere in sight. It was a beautiful day and she was playing softball. Soon Decky was in the zone and having a great game.

Decky was five feet eight inches tall, every inch solid muscle. With short strawberry blonde hair, blue eyes, and still a hint of freckles underneath tanned skin, she looked much younger than her age. She had the kind of androgynous good looks that turned heads no matter what the gender, and an extremely mischievous boyish charm.

She had been "strong as an ox" all her life and then someone introduced her to the weight room. Decky never tried to get bigger muscles, just stronger, faster muscles for quickness in the field and thunder in the bat. She swam almost every day, which helped keep her lean and flexible. Decky stepped into the batter's box in the bottom of the seventh inning, down by one, with a runner on second and two outs.

Fouling off two pitches, with rockets just outside of the third base line, Decky stepped out of the box and removed the batters helmet, wiping her hair back from her forehead. Brenda was out of her dugout moving the outfielders to shade left field. The right fielder moved over behind the second baseman. Decky grinned and hoped for an outside pitch. Lo and behold, the pitcher threw the perfect ball to hit to right field, and hit it she did.

Decky crossed the plate before the ball got back to the infield and the game was over. She felt great. She loved this game.

After the game, the shaking hands tradition began at home plate. Decky gathered her things and got in line.

"Good game." "Nice hit."

On and on through the line, until there she was again. Charlie stood at the end of the line, smiling and shaking hands. When Decky arrived at Charlie's outstretched hand, she actually dropped her bat. Instead of shaking her hand, Decky bent to retrieve the bat.

"You better hang on to that. I saw that last hit. Very nice."

"Thank you," Decky said, fumbling to gather herself. "See ya'."

Decky turned away and headed for the nearest exit. Inside a voice shouted, *"See ya'. That's what you came up with. Why didn't you shake her hand?"* Another scared little voice inside said, *You saw what happened the last time she touched you. It's official. I am losing my mind. I have started answering myself.*

Decky did not look back. If she had, she would have seen Charlie staring after her.

#

Decky's team run-ruled the next opponent, ending the game in five innings, ahead by ten runs. It wasn't really a fair fight since their best players, the King sisters, were Pentecostal and their mother refused to let them play on Sundays. It was always a problem, but they never went out and found someone to fill in on Sunday. It was like the team took pride in saying, "Yeah, we lost, but if the King sisters had been here, it'd be different."

I guess we'll never know.

She gathered up her things and headed over to watch the end of the game between Brenda's team and the team from Tidewater. Sitting in the stands, surrounded by so many people she knew, Decky was nervous that someone would see her watching Charlie, so she worked very hard at not looking. When she realized Charlie was coming into the on-deck circle, she excused herself to get a drink, only to stop and watch her from behind the stands. She remained there for the rest of the game.

The Tidewater girls were big, but slow. These large fields kept the homeruns down and with some really fine defense Brenda's team pulled it off, sending the giants packing. Now Decky's team had to play Charlie's team for the championship.

Wherever Decky's head was, it wasn't on what she was doing. Walking from one field to the other, Decky stepped off the curb wrong and rolled her ankle, the same ankle that had given her trouble all her life. The same ankle that she had taken the brace off, after the second game, and had not yet replaced.

It was decided that Darlene would drive Decky to the hospital emergency room, where they would check to make sure the screws that held Decky's ankle together were still in place. Darlene was chosen, because she and Brandi were still fighting and it was her turn to sit out. Mother had decided a long time ago that fighting lesbian couples would not be on the field at the same time. It could be dangerous.

And just like that, Decky was gone from the ballpark, rushed off to the hospital. Decky tried to relax while Darlene drove her SUV like a wild woman.

"Darlene, you don't have to speed. I'm not bleeding."

"I want to hurry up. There's a party after the game at BC's and I got to get there before Brandi gets drunk."

Decky closed her eyes and tried not to think about anything. It didn't help that every time she closed them she saw Charlie standing there in the moonlight.

After two hours in the emergency room, Decky was finally released with yet another pair of crutches and a promise to stay off her ankle for ten days. The screws were in place, but it was a severe sprain. The pain meds hadn't kicked in yet. Darlene was waiting, pacing outside the emergency room doors.

"I thought they were never going to let you out of there. Brandi called and said everybody's already at BC's," Darlene said, breathlessly.

"Oh no, Darlene, can't Brandi come get you at my house? I really don't feel like going over there." Decky might as well have been talking to the moon.

Darlene continued, "Brandi has been drinking already. She said she only had one beer, but I could tell she's had a lot more than that. I have to get over there, you know what she gets like when we've been fighting and I ain't around to corral her."

Decky moaned as she climbed into the passenger seat, saying, "When have you two not been fighting?"

Darlene got in. She thought about what Decky said and then answered, "I know we fight a lot, but I do love her. She is still real immature and me being two years older means I got to look out for her. She can be real sweet. Relationships with women can be complicated. I guess it's hard for you to understand, being straight and all."

"Okay Darlene, let's go save your damsel in distress. Off to BC's." Decky popped another Loratab and cried out, "The lovelorn and the cripple, to the rescue!"

#

Darlene drove slower on the way to BC's or the meds had kicked in, Decky wasn't quite sure. Darlene related that the game had been won with one of Margie's patented long ball outs, scoring Brandi from third. Decky didn't really listen. She knew she was heading straight into a mess. A mess she had made for herself. For all she knew the woman had built up some static electricity sliding and the shock was nothing more than that. The attraction was all in her head. Decky's son was not living at home for the first time in seventeen years. Maybe she was just lonely. She could not react, no matter what happened. *God, Charlie could be straight or worse, married.* She knew absolutely nothing about this woman except her name, she taught math, and she could play softball.

She couldn't deny that Charlie was attractive. Attractive, hell, it made her twinge inside just thinking about her. There she was, standing in the moonlight again. The abrupt stop jarred her back to reality. Darlene was looking at her when Decky opened her eyes.

"You dozed off there. Must be some killer meds. I called ahead and they cleared a parking spot for us by the door, so you don't have to walk too far. Here they come." Darlene pointed out the windshield.

Women of all shapes and sizes poured out of the house. Two large women insisted on carrying Decky, although she argued she was fine on crutches. They scooped Decky up, carrying her in through the house and out to the deck by the pool. Brenda waited next to a lounge chair with a pillow and a bag of ice .

"My Queen, your throne awaits." Brenda curtsied, and then pecked Decky on the cheek.

Decky was embarrassed, but loving it, because Brenda could make her laugh no matter what was happening.

"This seems like old times with me and you," Decky said, as Brenda tucked the ice around her ankle.

"Been there and done this. What can I get you to drink, oh crippled one?"

"I don't think I should drink alcohol on these pain meds."

"Oh hell, I was an army nurse in a former life. A glass of wine won't kill you."

Decky laughed. "But it might make me pass out."

"Chip will get you home. He's not drinking again, some new diet. He turns forty this year and he is scared to death of getting old."

"Chip will never get old. He's Peter Pan."

"And I'm Tinker Bell. I'll bring you some cheese and crackers and a glass of white wine. I think that's the color with pain meds. Looks better coming back up anyway."

"Brenda, you do have an unusual way of looking at things, practical, but unusual."

Brenda situated Decky by the pool where she could be in the middle of the party, but out of the way if things got rowdy, which they sometimes did when the men came or the "young ones" were in attendance.

The "young ones" were the girls under twenty-five. When the young ones attended, clothes sometimes became optional and throwing people in the pool the absolute perfect thing to do. Decky knew, because she had been a "young one" once.

Whether it was the pain meds or the ongoing questioning of her sexuality, something made Decky gaze around at the inhabitants of this gathering. Over by the grill, Chip stood with a couple of his coaching friends. Decky dated one of the guys briefly. Briefly was how Decky always dated. Most of the "young ones" were around the badminton court, marked out in Chip's "award winning" grass field that he called his backyard. Brenda swore that baseball coaches had a love affair with grass. The older players were seated near Decky on the deck. She spoke to different people as they stopped by her chair or sat down next to her so she could repeat once again how "it" happened. All the while, she watched women interacting with women. Even in these times, only a few of the female couples were out – out in the open, for all to see. Small communities didn't take to their teachers, cops, nurses, and doctors being gay. Still, here they were.

Decky watched closely, more closely than ever before, as the games played out in front of her. Hands brushed thighs slightly. Smiles and winks passed among the women. Straight women flirted with gay women and vice versa, presumably because it was safe. Decky didn't think it was too safe anymore. She may have passed the point of no return, but wait, she hadn't flirted with Charlie. Had she? She only noticed her. So what? She had noticed good-looking women before. She noticed that good-looking hunk over there by Chip, too. She dated him, bedded him, and then only called now and then, for old time sake or a quick romp in the hay. He saw her looking at him and smiled back, tipping his beer her way. How could she be gay? She liked having sex with men. She wasn't even sure what women did in bed.

"Oh shit, I hadn't thought about that," she blurted aloud.

"I'm sorry. Did you say something?"

Decky looked up into the biggest blue eyes she had ever seen. There was Charlie, standing over her, hand out, holding a glass of white wine. She was beautiful, more beautiful than Decky dreamed. She had showered and changed clothes. Without the ball cap, her golden hair hung down to her shoulders like silk. She wore a white tank top tucked into lightweight white pants that pressed against her skin when the wind blew. Over the tank top, she wore a large white sheer shirt. Tan and sculpted, she looked like a model on the cover of L. L. Bean.

"I'm sorry, did I startle you? Brenda told me to bring you this, but I'm not sure you need it. You look a little out of it."

Decky stared just a little too long.

"Are you okay? I know you can talk, I heard you talking to yourself."

Decky blurted out, "What did I say?"

"I don't know. I didn't quite catch it. Do you want this?" Charlie offered the glass of wine again.

"I guess it won't hurt, according to Nurse Brenda." Decky sat up and reached for the wine.

Charlie laughed lightly. "Oh, she pulled that past life army nurse thing again. She almost killed me in college. Are you sure you trust her?"

Decky responded quickly, "Do you trust her?"

"With my life," Charlie said.

At that exact moment, Decky touched Charlie's hand as she passed the wine glass. It was more intense than before. This time Decky knew Charlie felt it too. The smile, the blush, it was the same for both of them. Then the touch was over and neither one knew what to say.

Right on time, Brenda arrived with a tray of goodies from the kitchen. "I see you've met."

"Just now, but I'm afraid we haven't been formally introduced," Charlie replied.

"Dr. Charlene Warren, I should like to introduce to you Rebecca Bradshaw, or Decky, as she is affectionately known."

Charlie and Decky exchanged nods. Decky even managed a, "Pleased to meet you." There was no way in hell she was going to shake her hand. This seemed to be okay with Charlie too, but then Charlie began to speak. She spoke with an educated nuance embedded in the kind of southern drawl that draws you in, a storyteller like Dolly, Emmy Lou, and Reba. Decky was absolutely captivated.

"Decky, what an unusual nickname. I mean Charlie is an unusual name for a girl, but I am named after my father Charles. That's how they came up with Charlene, with the hard Ch sound. Momma said, you don't say Sharles, do you? When it turned out I was a tomboy, it was shortened to Charlie. But now 'Decky', there has to be a story there."

"My brother is only ten and a half months older than I am. He couldn't say Becky. It came out Decky. It just sort of stuck."

"You see, Decky, I knew you two would hit it off," Brenda interrupted. Obviously being sarcastic, she added, "Unfortunately I have to worry about Charlie. She's such a shy and shrinking flower, I was afraid she'd find no one to talk to."

Charlie motioned for Brenda to take the chair next to Decky, while she lowered herself down onto the lounge chair with Decky. Decky instinctively slid over to make room for her.

"Sit down Brenda, so we can entertain Decky here with our escapades from long ago."

Decky listened for two hours as the old friends talked about their wild days back at Duke. She laughed with them and at them, but mostly she looked at Charlie, which was convenient because as the conversation went on they had somehow gotten closer. Charlie's back was now pressed against Decky's abdomen, as Decky curled around her. It felt natural. It felt tingly. It felt like home.

#

Soon the party started to wind down; after all, it was a Sunday night. Brenda yawned and Charlie took the cue. "Well, I guess we ought to see about getting this cripple home."

"I'll get Chip," Brenda said through another yawn.

"No, I'll take her. He's in the middle of a man session in the kitchen. Just send him after me in a few minutes. If it's okay with you Decky, I'll come in and make sure you're settled."

Decky's heart leapt in her chest. "Sure, that'd be great." She was sure her voice had cracked.

After the goodbyes, they made it to the car without much trouble. If Decky's ankle was hurting, she couldn't tell. The pounding in her chest had all her attention.

From behind the wheel, Charlie asked, "Okay, which way do we go?"

Decky couldn't believe how dry her throat was, when she answered, "End of the driveway, take a right. It's straight on for about ten minutes, then a left."

"Hang on. Let's just get moving in the right direction to start." Charlie focused on getting them headed down the road and then said, "We spent so much time talking about Brenda and me, we didn't talk much about you."

"I really enjoyed the stories. That Brenda is a one of a kind." Decky began to relax into the buzz from the pills and the wine. She reached for the radio.

Charlie touched her hand gently. "Don't turn that on. I really want to hear about you. Brenda says you were a teacher and now you are a successful, brilliant writer."

"I should have her write my press releases," Decky answered. "Okay, I'll tell you about me, but it isn't as glamorous as it sounds. I used to be a drama teacher. I wrote a couple of historical, fact based, fiction novels. The books did okay in print. I sold the movie rights for one of them and made a shit pot load of money. Invested well, quit my job, and now I write articles and novels for a living, with a little genealogy thing on the side. You need to turn left at the next road, up there, by that abandoned looking house. It isn't, you know."

"What isn't?"

"That house isn't abandoned. People actually live there." Decky was prone to distraction, because of her ADD. It made following conversations with her sometimes difficult.

Charlie was quiet while she maneuvered the big SUV through the turn. They were headed down Aydlett Road, a dark and winding path through the swamp. Charlie looked so tiny behind the wheel, Decky thought it was cute and let out a laugh.

"What are you laughing at? You didn't take any more of those pills did you?" Charlie looked serious.

"No, I just thought you looked kinda tiny driving this big ol' truck."

Charlie snapped back playfully, "I'll have you know I was driving trucks before I could walk, to hear my daddy tell it. They tied wood blocks to the pedals so I could reach 'em. I grew up on a wheat farm in the panhandle of Oklahoma. Everybody worked."

Decky couldn't resist. "And next you're going to tell me you walked miles to school, with icicles hanging from the hem of your dress."

Charlie feigned a deeply hurt ego. "Damn, how old do you think I am?"

"Well... if you graduated from school with Brenda you are thirty-seven, maybe thirty-eight, unless you are a child prodigy or something. I know that out-of-state tuition at Duke makes you either rich or incredibly gifted. I know you teach math and I have seen you play softball. I have to ask myself, what kind of math?"

Charlie was intrigued. "Does it matter?"

Decky nodded yes, as if in deep thought.

"I teach mainly Calculus and Trig, beginner to advanced."

"Take the left fork in the road and keep going till the road runs out." Decky took a single breath and continued. "Then I say your daddy is a rich wheat farmer, with a little oil on the side. You come from people who settled on the Cherokee land. Built up from nothing. You worked on the farm, because you wanted to and your mother would rather have you out in the fields than under her feet."

Decky looked the small woman up and down. "You are in the younger range of a big family, maybe even the baby, after life got softer. You carried that with you so you worked hard to prove that you were one of them. The ones who couldn't go to college, already with families of their own, pinned their hopes on you. You excelled both on the field and in the classroom. Did you ever think of the naval academy?"

Charlie shook her head no, and continued to listen intently.

Decky went on, "Well, you would have made an excellent candidate. Do they have a height requirement? Never mind, I know you are touchy about that "tiny" word. Duke University came calling. You had a family meeting and it was decided that you would accept the scholarship for the tuition and the family would pay your expenses. All of which, you have probably paid back and more, by now."

Decky stopped talking. She looked at Charlie, who was staring straight ahead.

"I'm sorry; did I say something to upset you? It's what I do. I read facts and make up stories to go with them."

Decky was desperately trying to think of something else to say when Charlie turned to her. "When you are done reading my bio, would you tell me, do I turn right or left at the water or do we just drive right in?"

Decky had been so focused on Charlie, she did not realize they had arrived just a few feet from her driveway. "Turn left at the mailbox, the lane will light up as you go through, motion detectors."

Decky could see the look on Charlie's face as they approached her house. The same look appeared on everyone's face when they saw Decky's house lit up at night. With some cheap software and expensive lights, Decky had rigged the second floor living area to glow blue when a car approached at night. The light appeared to come from an unearthly source. A fact that caused a few phone calls to the police with sightings of strange lights in the woods when she first moved in.

"It's a lighting effect sandwiched between two panes of glass. It's all digital. I can change the colors and even frost them over so you can't see inside. All the windows in the house do that. Saves on curtains."

Charlie gushed, "Wow, that is the coolest thing I have ever seen. You must have made a large, 'shit pot load' of cash on that movie deal."

Decky laughed at Charlie's candor. "Yes, yes I did."

When they pulled into the garage, Charlie put the car in park. It was quiet for a moment, and then Decky asked, "How close was I, on the bio thing?"

Charlie turned to her, saying, "You hit it right on the head. Right down to the parents who missed Planned Parenthood classes, but you didn't say what my scholarship was for, brains or brawn?"

"I figured it had to be brains." Decky grinned. "Like I said, I've seen you play softball."

Charlie leaned over and punched Decky in the arm. "My momma told me not to beat up on cripples, but I think she might let me make an exception in your case."

Decky flinched. "Ouch. Did you know your accent gets thicker when you talk about Oklahoma?" Charlie punched her again. "Ouch."

Once they were out of the truck, and Decky was a safe distance from Charlie, she reflected on what she had learned about this woman, in particular, and women in general. The first lesson she would take away from dealing with women was don't pick on a woman who grew up with lots of brothers, because they were mean.

Charlie stepped up beside Decky, who was waiting on the stoop leading into the main house. Charlie looked at the crutches and then up at Decky. "This is a big house. There has to be a lot of stairs to climb."

"Well," Decky began, "we can go through this door into the mud room and climb a stairway to the next floor, or we can go through here." She opened a door onto the pool area.

The humidity and pool vapors hit them immediately. Decky leaned back so Charlie could pass into the room. As she did, Charlie brushed up against Decky's chest. Decky felt the breath catch in her throat. She prayed she had made no audible sound.

Charlie walked further into the room, taking it all in. "This is so... absolutely perfect."

Decky beamed with pride. She had designed this house and picked out every piece of trim and embellishment. It was a labor of love and she was always pleased to see others enjoy what she created. Here in this room, Decky had surrounded the space with Dutch doors, painted white, encasing large window panes. A few wicker pieces were here and there. Outside, close to the house, was a raised stage made of hardwood. The deck above made up the roof of the stage area. The view looked out over a willow-lined backyard, which Decky illuminated with a remote control. The lights exposed a luscious green lawn leading down to a dock on the Currituck Sound.

Charlie chuckled. "Chip did your grass, no doubt."

Decky called back from the corner of the room, where she had taken up residence on a tall stool at the wet bar, "My, you have an eye for great works. I'll have to tell him you noticed."

Charlie took in the tropical flowers lining the walls and hanging everywhere. Down the middle of the floor, running the length of the house, was a heated lap pool. The pool and floors were made of a combination of Italian marble and blue slate. The floor was lit from beneath the baseboards. The results were dazzling.

"There's a sauna behind the stairs back there," Decky called after Charlie, as she disappeared around the corner.

Charlie reappeared. "I could live in this room. You have a full gym in here including a shower and toilet. This place rocks."

Decky laughed.

"No, really, I could live in this room," Charlie repeated.

"Come on." Decky probed around in the bar. "I hid the key here somewhere."

"Those spiral stairs don't look easy to climb with crutches," Charlie noted, taking in the wrought iron stairs that seemed to spiral on forever. "Is that a painting?"

"It's an illusion. A trompe d'oil." Decky found the key and was unlocking a door just off the wet bar. "The stairs appear non-ending, but it's just a painting. You'll see when you get upstairs."

"You might have to lean on me to get up there," Charlie remarked, still looking up the stairs.

"As much as that would please me, I think I'd rather take the elevator." Decky stepped into the doorway she just unlocked. "You may join me if you wish."

As much as that would please me... you may join me if you wish. Who in the hell was talking? Nobody talks like that, well, except people in your books. This is not a book, Decky. Act normal, please act normal, and for God sakes don't go into actress mode.

Charlie, stepping into the doorway, broke up this inner monologue. "You have a goddamned elevator in your fucking house!"

It was something about the way the words rolled off her tongue in that drawl. Charlie didn't usually talk that way, Decky thought, but then again she could be a chain smoking, sailor-mouthed old broad. She had only known her a few hours. Charlie giggled with glee as she jumped into the elevator with Decky.

"I don't usually use words like that to express myself, after all I am an educated Dukie, but Jesus, I know somebody with a goddamned elevator in her fucking house and this certainly wasn't built for your grandma."

Decky was enjoying this. "Well as you can see, I have spent an incredible amount of time on crutches." Decky began shutting the door. "I decided if I was truly going to live out my life in my dream house, I wanted to be able to get around comfortably, even when I get old. You can fit a wheelchair and one other person in here." She inserted a key, turned it, and they started to rise.

When they reached the second floor, Decky slid the door open and waited for Charlie to exit before hobbling out. This was her masterpiece. The center section of the house was supported by the massive iron structure containing the spiral staircase and the elevator shaft. The structure allowed for a free flowing floor plan with arches to the outer walls replacing all the inner walls in this part of the house. Decky's son Zachery had a suite of rooms that were along the front of the house, which included an office for Decky. Those rooms were in a separate closed off portion on the main floor.

Charlie stood still, taking it in. Decky, whose foot had begun to throb, headed for the couch. "I have to get this ankle up, before it swells anymore."

Charlie responded, "Oh yeah, how about some ice? Just point, I'll get it."

Decky pointed to Charlie's left. She watched as Charlie started toward the kitchen area. She almost laughed aloud when Charlie stopped, took a step back and then forward again.

"Decky, your base boards light up just in front of where you walk. No more broken pinkie toes. You actually put quite a bit of thought into this. I don't want to gush like some backwoods hillbilly, but this technology is amazing."

"It's all out there; you just have to adapt it to the environment. It's theatre in your home. It's entertainment." Decky was gushing now.

"It costs a butt load of money," Charlie countered.

"I was smart about it. I researched and did a lot of the work myself, or at least made sure it was done right. I get much of my energy from the solar panels on the lighthouse facade over the third floor and under the slate you'll find around the property. Besides, it's really cool and I was forever leaving lights on."

Charlie had continued past the kitchen island to the massive refrigerator. "Did you get a big enough refrigerator? How many bodies do you think that will hold?"

Decky didn't answer. She was thinking about the sailor-mouthed broad again when Charlie saw the look on her face. "I was only kidding, Decky."

Decky laughed at herself and then at the look of triumph on Charlie's face as she rounded the corner, heading for the couch with a kitchen towel and an ice bag. She had managed to find one of the ice bags Decky kept on hand in the freezer.

Charlie helped Decky get comfortable and then went back to the kitchen to make some coffee. Decky used her remote control to change the lights and frost the windows for privacy. She even lit the fireplace to a glow and turned on some music, all from her back, on the couch. She knew there was a reason she built this house with all these gadgets. It was to seduce women. Damn, had she really done that?

She was lost on that train of thought when Charlie called from the kitchen, "I called Chip, and told him not to come till in the morning. You shouldn't be alone, on painkillers and gimpy. He said he'd come by early, before he goes to work. By the way, where's your dog? I see the food bowls."

"I called my mom from the hospital and she came and got her from the twins. They're my neighbor's boys. That's all anyone ever calls them, including their mother. Anyway, the twins look after Dixie when I go out. They have a key to get in. That's why I hide the elevator key. I caught them playing on it once. My mom doesn't even have a key to my house. It makes her furious, but after you meet Miss Lizzie, you'll know why."

Charlie entered the den area where Decky was lounging. Over-stuffed furniture, made for teenage boys to lie around on, was scattered about. The glow from the fireplace lit this side of the room. Charlie handed a cup of coffee to Decky and took the seat directly across from her. From this vantage point, she could see the entire room and out onto the decking that encircled the whole second floor.

"This is so romantic. It's like something out of Architectural Digest." Charlie put on her best southern drawl. "Why Decky Bradshaw, is this how you seduce all your women, feign injury and helplessness to lure them up to your trap?"

My God, she knows. How could she know? I didn't know until a few minutes ago.

Before Decky could think of an answer, Charlie saved her. "Lord, I don't know a woman who would turn down a go at this place."

The words were out of Decky's mouth before she knew what was happening. Had some strange force taken over her brain? Was she channeling Rudy Valentino?

"You're the first."

"I'm the first to turn it down? Hold on a minute, I'm still thinking." Charlie laughed and took another sip of coffee.

Shit, Decky thought, Rudy's doing okay so far. "No, you're the first woman I have tried to seduce with my house. Really, you're the first woman I have tried to seduce in my life."

Charlie gulped and almost choked on her coffee. She stared at Decky so long that Decky began to think Rudy might have read this all wrong. Decky started to believe that, when Charlie stood up and without saying a word, walked back into the kitchen.

"Hey, that's not fair. It's not as if I can run after you. I'm sorry. I've never done this before, honest. Come back and fight like a man."

When Decky saw Charlie's face, she knew that joking hadn't been the right way to handle this at all. She looked like she was about to cry, which Decky desperately prayed she would not do.

Charlie spoke softly. "I think I know what happened here. Brenda and Chip decided their lonely, recently broken hearted, lesbian friend needed a romp in the hay and since you were looking to switch teams, I'm sure Brenda the matchmaker told you I'd be an easy mark."

"Wait a minute, Charlie. Brenda doesn't know anything about this."

"Don't try to cover for her, I know she meant well."

Decky pleaded, "No, really, she –"

Charlie put her hand up and Decky stopped talking. "You are a great person, but sleeping with a woman for the first time should be special for you, and quite frankly I am not interested in being your experiment into the dark side."

Decky couldn't help but chuckle and that turned into a full-grown laugh. Charlie, looking puzzled, finally said, "Why are you laughing? This is not a joke. You can't play with people's emotions."

"The dark side. I called it that this morning when I was trying to figure out why I dreamed about you. I told Dixie I was going over to the dark side. Funny, isn't it?"

"I guess so. You dreamed about me?"

"That's what I've been trying to tell you. I never laid eyes on you until yesterday. I didn't know you were a friend of Brenda's until this morning. I nearly threw up when she asked me to come to the house to meet you this evening. I only came because Darlene dragged me there. I figured fate was taking over and I had better take my chance while I had one, if I had one. Hell, I wasn't even sure you were gay and I know I'm not, at least I wasn't."

Charlie contemplated this and then stared Decky directly in the eyes. "Let me get this straight, you see me, a total stranger, and for some unknown reason you decide to give up the heterosexual life and take a stab in the dark at a woman you don't even know for sure is gay?"

Decky nodded in agreement.

Charlie continued, "Can you tell me what about me caused you to think I might be a willing participant?"

"When I touched your hand, something happened. I never felt anything like that before," Decky admitted.

"When did you touch me?"

"When I handed you your hat, at third base. I thought for a second you felt it too, I guess I was wrong."

Decky closed her eyes and leaned back into the pillows. She heard Charlie stand up and walk out toward the deck doors. She knew the doors had been opened when the fresh breeze crossed her face.

Then ever so softly, she heard Charlie say, "You weren't wrong."

Decky stood up, without the crutches, a fact she regretted almost immediately. Hopping on one foot, she turned to see Charlie framed in the moonlight streaming through the French doors, white fabric billowing around her, just like in the dream.

Charlie asked, "Do you mean it? This isn't some research project for a book? You are not just some straight woman wanting to give it a try just once?"

"No, ma'am." Decky almost stuttered. "I... I swear my intentions are honorable, well not real honorable, but honest anyway. By the way, how am I doing on the seducing part?"

"What's on the third floor?" Charlie asked, pointing up.

"The master suite."

"Does the elevator go up there?"

"Yep, it sure does." Decky was trying to suppress a grin, but couldn't. "The reason I asked about my seduction technique, is well, in my dream you were standing there just like that, and I walked over and kissed you. Well, actually I woke up just before I kissed you, but I was sure going to kiss you, I know that."

"So, you don't know what to do next." Charlie was playing with her now.

"Oh, I think I know what to do, I just can't get to you," Decky said while hopping in place, having left the crutches on the couch.

Charlie took a step forward and Decky almost died right there. Charlie kept coming and Decky kept breathing to her utter amazement. When she was just within reach, Decky could stand it no longer. She reached out and pulled Charlie to her. When they finally kissed, every fiber in Decky's body exploded. She heard herself moan and felt her knees begin to buckle.

Charlie pulled away only far enough to look into Decky's eyes. When she leaned in and breathed on Decky's neck, Decky felt the world start to close in.

Charlie whispered, "Still got that elevator key?"

#

Sometime late in the night, Decky lay there with Charlie's head on her chest. She could close her eyes and relive it moment by moment. They had crashed into the elevator, desperately clinging to each other. Decky had barely shut the door, when Charlie ripped the snap buttons on Decky's uniform top open in one quick move. Decky slid the big white shirt slowly off Charlie's shoulders and then losing all semblance of control, yanked the tank top over her head. They were on each other like bees on honey. The rest of their clothes were gone by the time they hit the bed.

Decky had pulled Charlie on top of her. "I'm not sure if I'm doing this right. You really are the first woman I've ever touched like this."

Charlie had looked down with a smile. "You are doing just fine."

Charlie stirred on her chest, breaking Decky away from her waking dream. Decky thought to herself, she's going to wake up and freak out, but she didn't. Instead, Charlie leaned up and kissed Decky, which was her mistake. Decky was like a person who had been lost in the desert with no water. Now that the water was here, she wasn't going to stop drinking until the well ran dry.

3

The sun was just coming up, but Decky could wait no longer. She could feel Charlie's deep breathing, as she lay spooned against her. Her left arm no longer had any feeling and Decky had to use the restroom, really, really badly. She slowly slid her now useless limb from under Charlie's head and sat up. Her ankle throbbed like a freight train, which also happened to be pulling into the station in her head. Decky rubbed her eyes and temples with her one good hand, as she tried to shake the life back into the other. She was seriously considering permanent nerve damage, when the familiar tingle of nerves snapping back to life emerged.

Slowly she lowered her feet to the floor, bracing for the rush of gravity and blood. She let out a short gasp as the pain changed from throbbing to stabbing. It would subside. This was all too familiar territory. Under normal circumstances, she would have crutches. These were far from normal circumstances. She abandoned the crutches on the first floor, near the couch. Lust had taken over as the most powerful painkiller she had ever known.

Using furniture to steady her, Decky hopped from piece to piece until finally reaching the French doors that hid the bathroom from the rest of the floor. The master suite was an open floor plan like the main living area downstairs. Unlike the second floor, the third floor of the house was round. Divided into thirds, one third of the floor was closed off for the bathroom and walk-in closet. Decky arranged the sleeping area on one side with a library and reading area on the other. Both areas looked out over a deck that was accessible through huge glass doors that slid back into the walls. The Aspen planking on the floors continued out the doors and onto the deck. With the doors open and a breeze off the water, the result was the feeling of being in a tree house far away from the world below.

Decky, who had finally reached the toilet, was giving her bladder some much-needed relief. When the fog began to lift from her brain, Decky had a sudden realization. There is a naked woman in my bed. My crutches are sprawled across the floor, where anyone could look in the front door and see. No telling what else they left flung on the floor down there. At the moment, Decky couldn't be sure. It was all such a blur.

Oh, my God! Momma!

Decky reached for the phone and dialed her mother. She wasn't worried about it being too early. Her mother rose at the crack of dawn every morning. A fact Decky could attest to, due to the numerous mornings she had been awakened by the phone ringing.

"Hello, darling, how are you?" Decky's mother thought caller I. D. was the greatest thing ever invented, and had taken to answering the phone with the authority of someone who was in the know.

Decky had always had trouble lying to her mother. She felt as though the woman had special powers to know when mendacity was in the air. In reality, her mother was just naturally suspicious and guessed right sometimes. She drew in a deep breath and got it out as fast as she could.

"I'm okay, a bit swollen and sore. I was wondering if Dixie could stay with you today. I don't need to be getting up and down to let her in and out. I'll come get her tomorrow. Is that okay?"

She was going to fry in hell. Dixie could let herself out, if the door to the deck was unlocked. Decky had added a handicapped style push plate to one of the doors on the second floor, so Dixie could push it and let herself in and out. There was a naked woman in her bed and she was naked on the toilet, lying to her mother.

The other end of the phone was oddly quiet, then Lizzie's voice came back. "I'm sorry hon, what were you saying? Your father was telling me you should let Dixie stay today so you won't be bothered with her."

"Oh, that would be great. I really appreciate it. I'll come get her tomorrow."

"Do you need me to bring you anything? I know you don't like to be fussed over, but I don't mind bringing you something."

"No, no. I'm great. Just need to keep my ankle up and ice it."

"Well, if you need anything just call. Love you. Bye bye, now."

Wow. It was over just like that. Decky now had twenty-four hours to figure out how to handle Lizzie. She had been gay less than eight hours. She wasn't quite sure what all that entailed, but Decky was sure that life would never again be as it was before Charlie. She hobbled over to the walk-in closet. She remembered a pair of crutches left there from the last episode with her ankle. Grabbing the crutches and some towels, she made her way to the sink. She looked in the mirror.

Well, I don't look any different. There's no red flashing sign saying Lesbian on my forehead.

Under the sink, Decky located an old two-gallon plastic bucket. With bucket in hand, she crossed to the large cabinet by the shower. Opening the top doors revealed a wet bar, complete with ice machine, which she used to fill the bucket. Like an old pro, she crutched to the shower door with the bucket securely in hand. Placing the bucket on the shower floor, Decky stepped in, sat down on the ledge, and let the multiple shower heads beat down on her tired, sore muscles. When the bucket was full of water, Decky plunged her now multicolored, swollen ankle into the frigid slush. She gasped at the shock, but held her ground. She'd been here before. Well, not exactly here. Not in this state of mind, with all this shit to deal with.

Calgon, take me away.

Leaning her head back, she closed her eyes and within seconds, Charlie was in her arms. She held her close as Charlie's body released time and time again. With each jolt and catch of Charlie's breath, a strange sensation crept across Decky's chest.

"This is fucking amazing, literally."

"Decky, are you talking to yourself again?"

Decky's eyes popped open. There on the other side of the glass shower door stood Charlie, draped in a bed sheet, looking even more beautiful than she remembered.

"I'm sorry, did I wake you?" Decky said, as she tried to stand, then gave up and leaned back against the glass.

"No, I guess I heard the water running, because I woke up needing to potty. I hope you don't mind."

"No, go right ahead." Decky giggled, turning around to give Charlie some privacy.

"I already did. Why are you laughing?"

"You said potty, only moms say potty. I didn't expect you to say – Hey, how long have you been standing there?"

"I have umpteen nieces and nephews. I say potty and I've been here long enough to see that you were in deep thought. Are you okay? I mean in the light of day things sometimes look different." Charlie stared at the floor, as if afraid of what might be coming next.

Decky opened the door to the shower. "Well, I did have one question. All I know about 'coming out,' as they say, I learned from 'Ellen.' So, when do you get your new toaster?"

Charlie met Decky's gaze, seeing the grin on her face and the want in her eyes. When Decky extended her hand, Charlie dropped the sheet, stepped into the shower, and was all at once enveloped in the warm water and Decky's hands all over her body.

#

After the shower, Decky dressed quickly and headed downstairs to start the coffee. Charlie, still wrapped in a towel, sat on the bed talking to Brenda. Charlie was evading Brenda's questions, with the excuse that Decky was going to help her look at some real estate offerings, since she couldn't stay with Brenda and Chip indefinitely.

"Well, it's obvious she knows houses. Have you seen this place?" Charlie was saying, as she waved at Decky, who was descending in the elevator.

After recovering a few items of clothing from the elevator and the mislaid crutches by the couch, Decky started the coffee. By the time Charlie came down the stairs, Decky was seated on a stool at the kitchen island, sipping her first cup of java. Charlie had found one of Decky's old three-quarter-sleeve baseball undershirts and some sweats. The shirt, thin from wear, was too big and so were the sweats Charlie wore rolled up at the waist. Her hair was pulled back in a ponytail. Decky couldn't get over how Charlie seemed to look different each time she saw her. Each look was unique, fresh, and no less attractive. What she really marveled at was the way her heart pounded each time Charlie walked into view.

"Decky, if you are going to stare at me and say nothing every time I walk in a room, we may have a problem."

"Good morning, Charlene. Would you care for some coffee?"

"That's much better. How about some breakfast? I'm starved."

Decky started to get up from the stool, but Charlie waved her off.

"Stay there. Just tell me what you want and where it is. I think I can handle the rest. I'm quite the cook."

"Oh good, I was afraid I would go out and find a lesbian that couldn't cook and there we would be, the two of us, together, starving."

"You are really quite the smartass, aren't you?" Charlie came over to Decky, stepping between her legs, pressing in close. "Now what do you want to eat?"

Decky grinned. Charlie, exasperated, said, "For breakfast! I have created a monster."

Breakfast was finally accomplished through much flirting and innuendo. They worked side by side, Decky chopping and preparing, while sitting at the kitchen island, with Charlie at the stove. They decided to eat out on the deck, with Charlie insisting that Decky put her ankle up with ice, while Charlie did the serving.

Decky hadn't realized how hungry she was. The omelet was either the best she had ever eaten, or she was near starvation and hadn't recognized it.

"Damn, girl. You can cook!"

"Momma said she couldn't help us catch a man, but she could sure show us how to keep one. It doesn't seem to apply to women or at least in my case anyway."

"Maybe your luck will change," Decky said, just before taking in another mouthful.

Charlie put down her fork and looked out over the Sound. She took a deep breath and started to speak. "Decky, you and I have just complicated our lives in ways you may not yet fully understand. You especially have much to lose if this keeps going."

"I am not a child. I came into this with my eyes open. If you remember, it was my idea."

Charlie met Decky's eyes. "That's today, last night, just you and me in this bubble you've built, where nobody knows. At least you don't have a real job." Decky started to take offense at the last remark, but thought better of it as Charlie continued, "What about your son, your parents, your friends? They will find out. Are you ready to face that?"

"To quote a great southern icon, 'I'll worry about that tomorrow. After all, tomorrow is another day.'" Decky laid the southern drawl on heavy and for affect.

"Be serious, Scarlet." Charlie seemed to be trying to make a point, but it was hard for her to stifle a laugh.

Decky wasn't quite ready to let go of the rush she was experiencing. "I am being serious. Let's just live in the glow of the moment, this moment might be all we get."

"That glow you're feeling is just hormones. We're coming up on forty. It's supposed to be our sexual prime. It too shall pass." Charlie smiled as she proceeded, "You are too much the romantic and quite dramatic, I might add."

"Decky Bradshaw, you are a complete hopeless case of pure shameless romanticism, I believe Dr. Jones said to me in undergrad."

"Wow! Way back then, and yet you haven't been jaded by age and experience."

"Of course I'm jaded. We all are, if we've lived at all, but not now, in this moment."

"Decky, you don't understand. I am just trying to prepare you for the moments that come after this."

"Charlie, I know how hard this is going to be. Believe me, you have no idea what I'm about to face. However, for the next several hours, it's just you and me in this 'bubble,' as you called it. We can waste the day worrying about tomorrow or spend it like there is no tomorrow. We have a choice."

Charlie stood up and walked to the deck railing. With her back still turned, she said softly, "What are your intentions here, with me, I mean?"

"Come here and I'll tell you."

Charlie didn't move. "No, I can't let you touch me right now."

Decky sat up straight in her chair, pulling her injured ankle off of its resting place and onto the floor. "Ouch! Why not?"

Charlie wheeled on her. "Because we're like magnets – like fucking bunnies – because I can't control myself when you touch me!"

Decky laughed, loudly. "Like fucking bunnies, that's good."

"Stop laughing," but Charlie was laughing too. "You know it's true. What could possibly have come over two well educated women, in their late thirties, to cause us to behave this way?"

"You said it was hormones earlier," Decky quipped.

Charlie was pacing back and forth in front of the table. "Oh no, this is more than hormones. I mean I can understand you, it being your first time with a woman. You are a very quick study by the way."

"Thank you."

"The first time is like, wow, what have I been doing wasting my time with men."

Charlie was on a roll now. Decky could only sit and watch as Charlie gathered the facts and tried to solve their dilemma like a math problem. The professor was at work.

"But me, I've had sex with women, not a lot, but enough to know that this is different. Hell, my last relationship ended because I supposedly did not like sex enough. Judging by last night, I'd say that is a completely false accusation."

Decky chimed in, "I would have to agree with you."

"So all things being equal, the only variable in this equation is you. After what I've just been through, I will not allow someone to have that much control over my emotions again, not without some ground rules."

"Okay," Decky leaned in closer. "What are they?"

"Last night notwithstanding, I do not sleep around. I don't do open relationships. So if you think that in a couple of weeks you'll start looking around for some more fish to fry, tell me now. It would be okay, I mean, we could just go our separate ways, no harm done." She only paused long enough to catch her breath. "Listen to me. Now you're going to think I'm one of those psycho lesbians who latch on to you like a leech. You know the old joke, 'What does a lesbian bring on the second date?'"

"A U-Haul," Decky answered.

"See, even the straight girl knows that one." Charlie stopped pacing and leaned on the back of the chair she was once sitting in. She hung her head down with a moan. "Oh, I don't know." She lifted her eyes to meet Decky's. "You're different, this feels different. I am afraid to let this happen, whatever it is."

Decky sat back. She looked at Charlie for a long time before answering, "You are right. I am new at this, but newness aside. I have been in relationships before. I have even had my heart broken to the point I never thought I would feel that way again. This is different, and not because you are a woman, but because I think this is what it was supposed to feel like all along."

Charlie sighed. "This has all happened so fast. I swore I would not do this again."

Decky stood up and hobbled on one leg and a crutch until she was facing Charlie, but not touching her. "You're not doing it again and neither am I. We are doing it right for the first time, together."

"Can I trust you, Decky Bradshaw?"

"With all your heart's desires."

"That sounds like a line from a play." Charlie smiled up at her.

"It is, but it's still true." They were being drawn closer.

Charlie was teasing her now. "Got any other lines?"

"If you kiss me once, you'll never stop."

"Oh, that's a good one."

The space between them disappeared, the magnets having gotten too close. Decky sat down on the edge of the table and pulled Charlie to her. They melted into a tender kiss, immersed in the emotions of the previous conversation. A longing, profound in both women, was being fed for the first time.

Charlie finally put her hands on Decky's chest, pushed back, and gasped for air. Both of their chests were heaving now. "Air, I need air."

A breathless Decky could only nod.

Charlie put her head on Decky's chest. They stayed like that until the heavy breathing subsided. Holding Charlie felt so natural. It was as if this was the piece Decky had been missing her whole life. Decky wanted to say something. She wanted to tell Charlie that she had already decided she would never let her go, but how would it sound? Would Charlie think she was crazy? The words kept screaming in her head. The only way to stop it was just to get it out.

Decky kissed the top of Charlie's head. Gently placing her hand under Charlie's chin, she turned her face up to hers. They looked deep into each other's eyes. Decky began, "I have to tell you something. I know it's going to sound crazy, but I need to say it."

"Uh-huh," Charlie waited.

"I have only known you for a few hours, and yet, I feel so at home with you. It's like I have always known you. I can't explain it. I know that two days ago, I did not believe in love at first sight, but I have to tell you, if this isn't love then I don't know what it is. So there, I said it. I'm already in love with you, Charlie."

Charlie had the most serious look on her face. She was biting her lip while studying Decky's face. Her eyes darted back and forth, as if seeking a clue to the truth. Decky was about to panic, when Charlie finally sighed and spoke, "Oh, hell. I'm already in love with you, too."

Decky smiled so broadly it hurt. She bent to kiss Charlie, but Charlie placed her fingertips against Decky's lips. Decky thought Charlie looked as if she were about to cry, causing a pain to flash across Decky's chest. God, she looked so helpless.

Charlie cleared her throat. "Please God, Decky, don't break my heart."

Decky took Charlie's hands in hers and pressed them up between her breasts. "I promise you, your heart is safe with me." Then she grinned, that boyish grin that seemed to melt

Charlie's fears away. "Your heart is safe, but the other parts of your body are in danger of a severe ravishing."

Charlie said nothing. She merely pulled away and started into the house. Decky watched Charlie as she made her way toward the spiral staircase. She was on the second step when she turned to Decky. Slowly she peeled the shirt over her head. Without a word, she crooked her finger at Decky and disappeared up the stairs.

#

The lovemaking was slower, not so frantic. Decky took the time to explore Charlie's body more thoroughly. She found that the small of Charlie's back and the base of her neck were favorite places. When her hand was in the small of Charlie's back, as they moved in rhythm together, she felt wholeness long absent from her life. When she kissed Charlie's neck, small sounds of pleasure emitted from her, which pleased Decky immensely. They slept tangled together for several hours. Decky woke to see it was one o'clock, as her stomach growled loudly. This sex stuff sure made you hungry. Charlie stirred and opened her eyes.

Decky smiled at her. "Your eyes are so big and blue when you wake up. They have the look of childlike wonder. I bet you were a beautiful baby."

Charlie smiled and yawned. "A hungry baby. And so are you, judging from the sounds coming from your belly."

"Lunch then, but first I need another shower. Care to join me?"

"No," Charlie pulled the covers from Decky, pushing her toward the side of the bed. "You go first, or I'll never get anything to eat."

Decky hobbled up from the bed. She was laughing as she headed for the bathroom. Assuming an air of superiority, she called back over her shoulder, "You're probably right, considering you can't keep your hands off me."

Charlie threw a pillow at her.

#

When Decky made it down to the kitchen, Charlie had cleaned up the breakfast dishes and was in the process of making a salad. "I found this stuff in the fridge. I hope a salad sounds good."

"It does. How about adding some shrimp? Add Thousand Island, Captain's Wafers, and you have my favorite lunch. How did you know?"

"That sounds great. Sit down. I'll take care of it." Charlie spun around in a circle. "Where are the shrimp?"

"I keep shrimp in packages in the freezer, the one in the pantry. They are already cleaned and seasoned. All you have to do is drop them in the steamer for a few minutes."

Charlie followed Decky's pointing finger to the doors at the back of the kitchen. The double doors to the pantry were carved to look like a live oak, with its characteristic wind twisted tree trunk and limbs. Stained glass formed the leaves, sky, and surrounding beach scene. Upon closer inspection, Charlie could see that names were written on each leaf.

"Is this your family tree?" She asked Decky.

"It's part of it. Genealogy is a hobby and sort of a side business. The tree on the door represents my father and mother's first ancestors to settle in the new country, beginning in the 1600's."

Charlie read a few names and dates aloud, adding, "It's beautiful." She turned the brass handles and entered the pantry.

Decky called out to her, "It's a very southern thing to do."

"What is?" came from inside the pantry.

"To trace your roots. To prove beyond a doubt that you are a true Southerner, who gave up family in the Great War, and have remained true to the cause. It's even better if you can go back to the Revolution. A membership in the Daughters of the American Revolution can go a long way in social standing."

Charlie emerged from the pantry with a freezer bag and a package of sourdough bread. "And are you?"

Decky bowed at the waist, drawling in her best Southern accent, "You have before you a true Southern Belle and a dues paying member of the Dare County D.A.R. By the way, you're not from one of those families, in Indian Territory, who sided with the Yankees? That would definitely throw a wrench in things."

"Oh Lord, no! My family came from Georgia. Burned out by Sherman. I know, because my daddy carries a deep seeded grudge, handed down through the generations."

"Sounds like we would get along. Although Sherman was a brilliant military strategist."

"Don't ever let my daddy hear you say that."

"I'll try to remember. Tell me more about your family."

"Well, Momma and Daddy have been married for fifty-two years. They are both seventy-two. You were right; I am the baby in a family of six boys and four girls. The oldest, Mary is fifty-one, married with three grown children; Bobby is fifty, and has two blond girls in college and is on his second blond wife; David, forty-nine, married with two boys and three girls; John, forty-seven, also married with four, two and two; Debra, forty-six, Andy, forty-five, Jimmy, forty-four, Joseph, forty-two, and Francine forty-one, all have wonderful marriages and three kids each. Then there's unmarried, childless, poor old Aunt Charlene, who sticks out like a sore thumb in the family photo album."

"Wow! How do you remember all that?"

"You should try remembering all the kids' names. And now the kids are having kids."

"Do you all get along? With that many people, some personalities must clash." Decky was enthralled. She had a brother she couldn't stay in the room with more than ten minutes, and a mother who could make the Pope cry for mercy.

"Yes, we all get along quite well. I am closest to Francine, Franny we call her. Momma said Franny adopted me like a pet when I was born. She's always been there for me. She's the only one in my family I told about being gay. She's okay with it. She thinks it makes her cool to have a lesbian sister. I think she watches too much Oprah."

"I like Dr. Phil myself."

Charlie continued to work on lunch while they talked. Decky removed a bottle of white wine from the wine cooler under the island. Charlie brought over two wine glasses from the rack over the sink and Decky poured the wine. Charlie talked and chopped vegetables, taking the glass from Decky's extended hand without stopping either one. To Decky, the whole scene was as it should be. The two of them moved fluidly together, like two people who were very familiar with each other. Anticipating moves and words so frequently, Decky thought it almost dreamlike. The little voice repeated in her head, *Please don't wake up, don't wake up.*

"Okay, now all you have to do is watch the shrimp while I take a quick shower." Charlie was saying, when Decky stopped listening to the voice in her head and rejoined the room. "Where did you go? Your mind was somewhere else."

"Nowhere. Hey, come here a second before you go." Decky held out her hand for Charlie to take.

Charlie hesitated. "I'm coming right back, I swear."

"Just come here a second."

"Are you going to kiss me? Because I really need a shower and the lunch is almost ready. Like you said I can't keep my hands off you, and I would truly hate to overcook the shrimp, it being your favorite and all." She was laying on the Okie accent pretty thick when she batted her long lashes at Decky.

The bottom of Decky's stomach hit the floor. Her knees went weak and she knew that if this woman ever batted her eyes at her she could have anything she wanted. She knew that for a fact, like Gettysburg was the key to who had won the war.

Still Decky proceeded, "I promise to only touch you with two fingers."

"Where?" Charlie took a step back and lowered her gaze, one eyebrow questioning.

Decky laughed. "On the arm."

Charlie moved in closer, but not too close. Decky reached out with her forefinger and thumb, promptly pinching Charlie on the arm. To which, Charlie responded by smacking Decky's hand and jumping backwards.

Rubbing her arm, Charlie gushed, "What in the hell was that?"

Decky smiled. "I wanted to make sure I wasn't dreaming."

Charlie reached out and pinched Decky on the arm. "You are supposed to pinch yourself."

"Ouch," Decky held up her bruised ankle, "but I'm already wounded."

Charlie pinched her again.

"Okay, it's real, it's real."

They started to laugh, exchanged a quick kiss, and then Charlie was off to shower.

#

It started to rain after lunch, cooling off considerably. A soft drizzle set in for the afternoon. Rain frogs could be heard singing through the open deck doors. Decky selected her chick music CD for the stereo. Bonnie Raitt crooned from the hidden acoustic system. She set the window glass surrounding the room to allow the soft gray light from outdoors to filter in through blue frosting. The baseboards emitted a soft blue light upward on the walls.

Countering the cooling effect of the light from the windows, she set the ceiling lights, which were LED's concealed in the coving, to an amber glow, and added the reading lamps at each end of the couch. Light from the small fire in the fireplace radiated from the hearth. A touch of rose on the floorboards and the picture was finished. Decky had been a theatrical scenic and lighting designer at one point in her career. The lighting in this house was a source of pride and endless hours of fun. The effect isolated the couch where she and Charlie spent the bulk of the afternoon wrapped up in a lightweight down comforter, searching Internet real estate sites on Decky's laptop. A giant plasma screen descended from its hidden compartment in the ceiling, in front of the picture window that looked out over the deck and Sound. When they found a house that looked promising, Decky would put the image up on the big screen, while Charlie got up to take a closer look.

"Maybe I should build a house. I sold my house in Louisiana, so money isn't the issue. What about land? Maybe a waterfront lot, what do you think?"

"I've got plenty of land out here. I could extend the lane and you could build on the next rise over."

"Oh, I couldn't do that. There's a reason you plopped yourself in the middle of this dense little oasis alone. I wouldn't want you to give that up and regret it later."

"I have a cottage another mile down the main road. It's on the water. The land floods quite often, but the house is on stilts. It's small, a vacation house really, nothing special about it. I liked it though, or I wouldn't have bought it." Decky couldn't believe it had taken her this long to think about it.

"We've been looking for hours and you just remembered you had a cottage on the water. Are you trying to sell it?"

"Well, not until a minute ago, I wasn't. We use it when guests come in, or Zack has a party he thinks I don't know about."

"So you're not interested in selling it?"

"Not to just anybody, but I would sell it to you. I really think you should live in it for a while. It will give you time to look around, buy some land if you want to build, or buy the cottage if you decide to. Like I said, it floods, it can get pretty muddy."

Charlie sat down between Decky's one leg propped up on the couch and the other touching the floor. "Are you trying to tell me I need a four wheel drive to get to it?"

"No, I just want you to have all the facts."

"When can I see it?"

Decky snuck a hand in the small of Charlie's back. "I'll take you tomorrow. Are you busy?"

"I don't start teaching summer school for another week, so I'm available all day. I planned to use this week for house hunting anyway."

Decky pushed a button on the remote control and the plasma screen disappeared into the ceiling. She closed the laptop and set it on the coffee table. "Okay, we're done with that, now what do you want to do?" She had now begun to rub her hand up Charlie's back, inside her shirt.

"Well, I think I know what you want to do. My God, you're insatiable," Charlie said, unable to help melting into Decky's chest.

The first notes of Allison Krauss's 'When You Say Nothing At All' came through the speakers. Decky, remote still in hand, turned the volume up. "I want to dance with you."

Charlie sat up. "But you're crippled."

"I can lean on you."

Charlie stood up and walked to the center of the room. Decky hopped over with one crutch, placing one hand in the small of Charlie's back. Charlie's arms went up and around Decky's neck as she pressed her body in close. They swayed back and forth without moving their feet, as the resonance washed over them. Sometimes they looked at each other or exchanged a sweet kiss, but mostly they just held on. The outside world would soon come calling, but for now, it was just the two of them and Decky was in heaven.

The phone rang just as the song was ending. Decky sighed and reached for the receiver on the table. It was Brenda, checking on Charlie. Charlie took the receiver and walked out onto the deck. Decky guessed she needed some privacy, so she busied herself emptying the last of their second bottle of wine into the glasses. She hobbled into the kitchen to dispose of the empty bottle.

She was studying the selections in the wine cooler when Charlie set the phone down at the island. "She knows," Charlie said matter-of-factly.

Decky looked up from the cooler. "What does she know? What did you tell her?"

Charlie headed back to the couch. "I need a drink."

"Charlie, tell me what she said."

Charlie came back with both glasses and handed one to Decky, insisting, "You're going to need a drink, too."

Decky unconsciously took a drink and waited for the rest of the story.

"I didn't have to say anything. She said she knew what was going on over here. She said she had never seen two people so attracted to each other and we weren't fooling anybody. Evidently, after we left the other night, we were quite the talk amongst your friends. She even said some of the locals were a little upset that it took an outsider to finally get you in bed."

Decky's mouth was open, but no sound came out.

Charlie took a drink and eyed Decky, before she continued, "Brenda insists that we 'not shut ourselves up in your fortress.' We are summoned to dinner tomorrow night. I reminded her of your ankle, but she said she had seen you walk on worse, so no excuses."

Decky thought about it, then making up her mind she spoke, "Well, I guess it's settled then. We are a couple and I am out of the closet, ready or not."

"Are you ready?" Charlie asked with genuine concern.

"Well, the hinges are still smoking so I don't think I can climb back in."

"No, I think you have basically burned that closet down." Charlie added.

"Okay then, tomorrow night we introduce ourselves to the world."

"Not the world, just Brenda and Chip."

"You obviously haven't been to dinner at Brenda's lately. It's never just Brenda and Chip."

"At least your first trip out will be among a more accepting crowd."

"Do you really think it's going to change things that much?" Decky was rationalizing now. "I've been around gay people all my life. I never judged them, or even really thought that much about it. They just were and I wasn't."

"Decky, listen to yourself. You called gay people 'them.' You grouped them and by grouping them you set them apart, labeled them different. Now you are one of 'them.' You'll see it's quite unsettling to be labeled, just because of who you choose to love."

"Oh hell, these people around here have thought I was gay for years, so it shouldn't be too much of a shock to them that I really am. I will tell the truth to those that matter. I don't think it's going to be easy, Lord knows just keeping my mother out of this is challenge enough. Lizzie's going to have a stroke or worse, if she finds out."

"It's not if she finds out, but when. You can't hide this from your family."

"But you said only your sister knew you were gay." Decky was confused.

"I said my sister was the only one in my family I told I was gay. The rest of them, well, we just don't talk about it. It seems to work for them, so I don't have a problem with it."

"So your mom knows, you just don't talk about it, and that's okay with you?"

Charlie finished off her wine before answering, "Momma told me once that you couldn't find love, it found you, and when my love found me, she only wished me many years to enjoy it. I think it was her way of saying she wanted me to be happy. She has made it her policy not to ask questions she really doesn't want the answers to. So, that's about as close as we ever got to having 'the conversation'."

"Do you think your mom would adopt me?" Decky flashed her best grin.

"I think my mother would adore you."

"You know, usually when I have a problem, I like to think about it while I'm swimming. I have some of my best ideas underwater." Decky grabbed another bottle of wine. "I think this might be a three bottle day." She started toward the elevator.

Charlie followed with the glasses, protesting only slightly, "You know, I don't think us in the pool naked is going to help you think."

"No, but it might give me some new ideas. Underwater ideas."

They mounted the elevator together as Charlie went on, pretending badly to not have noticed the innuendo, "I'm starving again. I need a snack. I can't remember eating like this, ever. Thank God we're burning off the calories."

"I know what you mean. The fridge behind the bar has cheese, fruit, and yogurt, with some Gatorade and other fluids. I got on a health kick after I quit teaching full time. I had always said that only rich people could afford to be healthy, so I had to put up or shut up."

"That's why you built the gym and the lap pool."

"No, I built them because I am naturally lazy. I knew if I had to drive somewhere to work-out or run around a track, it wouldn't happen." Decky slid the elevator door open. "Now, it's just part of my daily routine. I spend so much time sitting in front of a computer, I have to exercise. I have a healthy fear of blood clots. I might as well tell you, I'm a bit of a hypochondriac."

"You and everyone else. We're bombarded daily with images from drug companies. I'm afraid they put subliminal messages in them. You know, negative thoughts can cause cancer." Charlie looked at Decky and burst out laughing. She could tell Decky had never thought about that before. "Jesus, Decky, I was just kidding. You really are a hypochondriac."

Decky was still thinking about the drug companies controlling her thoughts, while she set about frosting the windows and pouring the wine. Charlie walked to the other side of the bar and began rummaging in the cooler. Decky hopped around the bar and stood behind Charlie. They ate standing in the open cooler door. They didn't bother with taking the food to the bar. Decky sucked down a large bottle of water. Between the alcohol and the sex, she was dehydrated.

When their needs for nourishment and hydration had been met, the feeding became more playful and soon they were stuffing fruit in each other's clothes.

"No fair, I can't chase you," Decky cried as Charlie ran to the other side of the bar.

"I've seen you motor on along when properly motivated," Charlie said playfully.

Decky feigned indifference to Charlie's obvious flirting. "I've always said you can't motivate people. They have to motivate themselves."

Charlie stepped back from the bar so that Decky could see her from head to toe. She slowly slid the sweats from her waist and let them fall to the floor. The baseball shirt she was wearing hung down just far enough to make Decky want to see more. Charlie still said nothing when she stepped forward, grabbing Decky's open bottle of water from the bar. Before Decky knew what was happening, Charlie turned the bottle up and slowly poured it down the front of her white shirt. When she was done, she threw the bottle at Decky.

Decky was in shock. She hadn't thought it was possible for Charlie to be sexier with clothes on than off, but my God. She was frozen to the spot, unable to do anything but stare. Then Charlie dipped her chin and gave a 'come hither' look that caused an explosion in Decky's chest. Charlie crossed her arms in front of her, about to take her shirt off over her head, when Decky finally spoke.

"No." It was more a croak than a word. Charlie stopped taking her shirt off and instead ran her fingers through her hair, down her neck, and then pressed the wet material tight to her breasts, before settling her hands behind her on her hips.

Decky was beside herself. Her legs were like jelly and her hands trembled on the crutches she had somehow managed to stick under her shoulders. Charlie wasn't finished, but Decky almost was. When Charlie turned around and slowly, ever so slowly, slid her underpants to the floor, Decky's blood was rushing so fast she could hear it. She looked down to see her heart beating through her shirt.

Decky looked back up just in time to watch Charlie step into the Jacuzzi attached to the end of the lap pool. She kept her back turned until she reached the center of the tub, then she slid down into the water. Charlie emerged from the water facing Decky, with the now soaking shirt clinging to every curve of her body. Then and only then did she speak. "Miss Bradshaw, have I motivated you?"

Decky blurted out, "Hell yeah, I'm motivated, but there seems to be a problem."

"And what might that be?"

"I can't walk. I can't feel my legs."

"Do I have to come get you?"

"No. Just stay right there, I think all the blood rushed to my heart. I'm sure it will make its way back to my legs eventually."

"Is there anything I can do to help?" Charlie wasn't really trying to help. Decky could see that. Charlie was enjoying Decky's predicament. She dipped her chest in the water again, kind of a bobbing peepshow.

That's it, Decky thought. *If I have to crawl over there, I'm moving now.* She didn't even stop to take her clothes off when she got there. She dropped the crutches and hopped down the steps on one foot and then it was on. Wet clothes flew from the water in all directions, all except the baseball shirt.

#

Decky finished swimming a few laps in the pool with a float on her ankle. There was no way she could do her normal distance. She couldn't have done it with the banged up ankle, and she sure couldn't do it after all the recent activities. She had time to think while she swam. Zack would have to be told, and soon. Cell phones had made the grapevine so short she'd have to hurry.

Zack was an unbelievably cool kid. Raising him had not always been an enjoyable experience, but he had turned out all right. He was intelligent, although his grades did not reflect it at times, a major bone of contention for a while. He was off to music school in Boston this fall, but right now, he was working on a science expedition, studying whales in Alaska. If being a student came as easily to Zack as music did, he might be a marine biologist. That was a big if. He called it his fall back plan.

Zack was not going to have a problem with Decky's new lifestyle. He would love Charlie. He would probably say something like, "That's cool." That's just the person he was. Decky envied his ability to glide through life. She associated this ability with his love of jazz music. He had an old soul. He should have been a flower child.

Satisfied that Zack would not be a problem, she turned her thoughts to bigger fish. Daddy's reaction would directly reflect how much shit he had to put up with from Miss Lizzie. Robert Charles Bradshaw was a religious man, but he loved his daughter. Decky knew a few debates over the good word were coming, but they would be debates not dictates.

It would all go back to the same argument they always had. Decky believed the bible was written by men, to control men. They could agree that men had compiled the books that made up the old and new testaments. That's where they would part ways. Decky had read enough literature to recognize the creation myths and their constants. The same stories played out in history, long before Jesus walked this earth. It made it hard for Decky to believe this one book and only this book contained the keys to God's wishes and demands.

That there was a God, Decky had no doubt. She just didn't have a conventional way of looking at the whole religion thing. She had faith in a higher power, having looked to it for guidance in times of turmoil, but she didn't buy the judgmental, white haired old guy watching your every move. Decky's faith was in the power of free will bestowed upon us all. It's what people did with that free will that mattered. The decisions made, not what people thought about what you wore to church last Sunday, were the true mark of one's character.

As far as the bible thumpers went, it also says kill your wife if she wears the wrong kinds of fabrics together. If you wanted to get specific, it doesn't say a word about women lying with women, probably because men wrote it. That was something Decky would never understand, the way men acted over two women in bed together. Now that she had actually been to bed with a woman, she thought, well guys, the joke's on you, because those gals can get along just fine without you.

So checking her moral compass one last time, Decky took stock. Could something that felt this right, so absolutely as it should be, be wrong? If the way Decky felt about Charlie was simply a chemical reaction, a scientific mix of pheromones and hormones, it also was a once in a lifetime chance. The odds that two people, born in different states, thousands of miles away from each other, and who reacted this way to each other, would come in contact was astronomical. It was a fucking miracle and Decky was going to go with it. *You don't mess with mother nature.*

The jukebox in Decky's mind started playing, "If lovin' you is wrong, I don't wanna be right..." She was singing it when she hopped up on the side of the pool.

Charlie threw a towel at her. "Well, you're just a regular ol' little dolphin aren't you?"

Decky caught the towel and grinned, that one dimple smile Charlie seemed to be quite fond of. "Thank you."

Charlie was seated at the bar, nibbling on cheese. She wore one of the terry cloth robes Decky kept in the downstairs shower. Charlie's left ankle rested up on her right knee. Decky could see the soft blonde hair she had grown to know and love peeking out at her. Charlie seemed very comfortable in her nakedness now, as if they had crossed an unspoken boundary of trust.

As Decky dried off and hobbled over to the nearest stool, Charlie went behind the bar, retrieving another robe she had placed there earlier. She handed the robe to Decky with one hand, while stuffing a Wheat Thin coated in smoked Gouda cheese in her mouth with the other. She reached into the cooler for a bottle of cold water for Decky and then picked up the crutches. Charlie brought the crutches to Decky, kissed her on the cheek, and sat down opposite her. Throughout the entire process, Charlie kept a running monologue.

"I have to tell you, you have the best body of any woman I've ever been with. And that whole watching you swim naked is something I could get used to. It's very beautiful in a 'Greek statue in motion' kind of way."

Decky toweled her hair. "I'm flattered."

"You should be. Not many thirty-seven-year-olds have asses like that."

"You're thirty-eight and your ass is perfect."

"Yeah, but I was born with a perfect ass. No kidding. My mother has this picture of me lying on my stomach at three months and everybody always says, 'What a cute little ass.' Of course it has been displayed prominently in our house since it was taken, so everybody in town has seen my ass." Charlie belched.

Decky was afraid she would fall off the stool. She was laughing at Charlie. "God, you're funny."

Charlie's foot slipped off the bottom rung of the stool. "I also think I'm a little drunk."

Decky looked at the now empty wine bottle on the bar and then back at Charlie. "You finished off that bottle by yourself?"

"Well, you were doing your dolphin thinking thing, so I was doing my drinking thinking thing, okay."

Decky reached over and helped Charlie steady herself. "So, did you come up with anything while you were thinking and drinking?"

"I was kind of distracted by your tight ass going up and down that pool."

"Sorry."

Charlie put both hands on Decky's shoulders. "I know I'm drunk, because I never, I mean never, talk like this."

"Do you normally do wet tee shirt strip tease acts?"

"I have never done anything like that in my life, either. I'm not exactly sure what happened there, it just sort of came out of nowhere."

Decky was really enjoying this. "It's okay really, I don't mind. If the urge ever strikes you again, feel free."

"Okay, I have another ground rule."

Charlie was trying to be serious, so was Decky, but it was really hard with Charlie weaving back and forth.

"I'm listening. Let me get you a coke. I think you need a little sugar and some real food." Decky hopped around the bar. "Here, have another cracker."

"Look, I know I'm drunk, but I have to say this. Sometimes I can be, let's say, a little more uninhibited than others. I am all about having fun at these particular times, but don't ask me about it later. I know it sounds weird, but it's just a thing with me. I will fuck your brains out, but let's just not talk about it… Oh my God, listen to me."

"Your secret is safe with me. You know, I suspected that under that homecoming queen exterior lurked the soul of a sailor-mouthed old broad. Come on, let's get upstairs and get some food in you and some dry clothes on you."

Charlie started laughing. "Well, now that's a switch. You've been taking my clothes off every chance you've had since I got here."

To Decky's utter amazement, they made it to the elevator and into the kitchen without falling down. She got Charlie situated on a stool and quickly started making sandwiches. She handed Charlie two Advil and a coke with the sandwich. Decky sat down beside her with her own sandwich, watching to make sure Charlie ate. After a half a sandwich, Charlie started to come around.

"While you were swimming, did you have any ideas about how you were going to deal with this, us, out there in the world?"

"I did think about it. I decided Zack would be okay with it, Daddy will get over it, and well, there's my mother."

"She can't be all that bad."

"You haven't met her."

"Well, then maybe I won't have to."

Decky had known this moment was coming, but she still hadn't fully prepared for how she was going to broach this subject with Charlie. "I'm not sure you'll be able to avoid meeting her, as a matter of fact, I know you will meet her on Friday, at the new-faculty luncheon."

Charlie perked up. "And you know this because…?"

Decky could see no way around it. She was going to have to tell her eventually. It would be better than Charlie being blindsided with it. "My mother is on the board of regents at the university. As a matter of fact, her name will be one of the ones on your check."

Charlie dropped the sandwich and spit out the bite she had just taken. "You have got to be shittin' me."

"Bigger than life. Elizabeth Bradshaw, right there on the middle line."

"When exactly were you planning on telling me this?"

Decky slid her stool back a little. She really thought Charlie might hit her. "I hadn't thought that one all the way through."

"That's an understatement." Charlie was really panicked now. "What were you thinking? Oh, dear God. I'll never find another job and my career will be ruined. Brenda knew, too. She didn't think to warn me either. Am I the only one thinking here?"

"Come on Charlie, it's not like I'm some young-thing student you have the hots for. What can she do to you, snub you at faculty receptions?"

"You are unbelievably naïve." Charlie got up and walked toward the deck. "You have insinuated that your mother is nosey and judgmental. She is exactly the kind of person I have been trying to warn you about. I've dealt with her kind before. One day, everything is going along fine and the next you find yourself being fired because of 'budget cuts.' Except you know it's because some idiot in the community decided you might unduly influence the young women you're teaching. They don't even have to be sure you're gay, it only takes a rumor and a determined zealot."

Decky followed Charlie. "I wouldn't let her do that to you."

"You think you can stop her?" She was crying now.

"Jesus Charlie, I'm sorry. I didn't think – – "

"That's the problem. You didn't think and now look at the mess I'm in."

"We are in … the mess we are in."

"Decky, I love to teach. I'm good at it. At one time, that was taken away from me because of a rumor that wasn't true. Luckily, I found a new job and moved on, but that one instance has haunted me my entire career. How will I defend myself against something that is true?"

"As far as I know, being gay is not a reason to be fired from the university system. Everyone around here knows Lizzie is a pain in the ass. Who knows, most people will probably relish in her misery and rally to your side."

"I hope you are right, but as far as I can tell, the good ol' boy attitude of don't ask, don't tell is alive and well in this little part of the world."

"Come on, there are lots of gay people teaching out there."

Charlie was starting to look a little green around the gills. She glared at Decky, desperate for her to understand. "Yes, but how many of them are lesbians that just happen to be fucking a member of the board of regents', here to fore, straight daughter!"

With that, Charlie hung her head over the railing and threw up.

Decky went to her and held her hair up out of her face. "Go ahead, it'll wash off, and you'll feel better."

"No, I will not feel better," Charlie said, as she began to sob. "Oh my God, what have you done to me?"

Decky's mind raced. What could she say to make her stop crying? She would rather Charlie screamed at her. A mad Charlie had to be better than this, because the crying one was tearing Decky apart. *For God's sake, say something Decky.*

"Oh no, Charlie. I didn't get you pregnant did I? I mean, of course I'll do the right thing." She fell down on one knee. "Charlene Warren, if you'll have me, I'll marry you and raise the child with you."

Charlie started laughing, softly at first, then a full-fledged belly laugh. "Decky, you are stark raving mad, do you know that?"

"I mean it. I mean to do the right thing here. Your happiness is my only concern."

Charlie turned around, looking down at Decky. "Do you have any more little tidbits you think I should know about? As you can tell, surprises are not exactly my cup of tea."

"That's it. No more surprises. Cross my heart." Decky crossed her heart.

"Then get up from there. I need to lie down for a minute, but first I want to brush my teeth."

Decky scrambled to her feet and followed Charlie into the house. After a few steps across the floor, Charlie turned around. Decky stopped short, not sure if the storm had really passed.

"I think it's best that your mother doesn't know I know you, at least for a little while."

"If you think I'm going to tell her, you're nuts. My policy with her is it's best to ask forgiveness, than permission. When she finally figures this out, there'll be hell to pay, and that's not a check I'm in any hurry to write."

"Sounds like you are afraid of her."

"No, I'm not afraid of her. I've just been dealing with her Tennessee Williams in drag personality for so long, I know this is going to be a wild journey. She's a bit bi-polar," Decky said, knowing full well that was like being a bit pregnant. "We catch her on the upswing, it won't be so bad. We catch her on the way down; let me tell you, it's a long ride to the bottom."

Charlie turned toward the stairs again. "This just keeps getting better and better."

#

Decky tucked Charlie into bed. Decky could see that she was exhausted from all the spent emotions of the day, not to mention the wine. She kissed her sweetly on the cheek, as Charlie sighed and slipped into sleep.

Decky sat in the reading area on the third floor. She did not get in the bed, because she knew she probably would not let Charlie sleep. The wireless computer system she installed allowed Decky to access the main CPU from any area in the house. She had a laptop or tablet in nearly every room. She never knew when an idea would come, so she was prepared to sit down anywhere in the house to write.

Decky spent an hour answering emails, her ankle in or out of a bucket of ice every twenty minutes. Her editor needed to know if she was closer to completion of her next book proposal. Decky had spent the last two years gathering research for the book. She was a stickler for detail, a fact that had won both previous books awards for historical accuracy. With a movie deal in the works, her editor was anxious to get more titles out there, anticipating a demand for more material. Decky was in no rush. The research was the best part. It was the hunt for information that gave Decky the most satisfaction.

There were a few emails from the graduate students she hired to do research in the State Archive in Raleigh. The students worked part time for Decky, pulling files and documents, scanning them into the computer and emailing them to Decky. They also helped with her Genealogy business. What started as a project for her mother had turned into an obsession. Once finished with her family's tree, if one is ever finished, Decky started looking up family trees for friends. The family research business had been spawned from the number of requests for information she received. Some people do crosswords to relax. Decky did genealogy.

Spam dumped, emails returned, Decky Googled Charlie. She wasn't investigating Charlie. She wanted to know everything about her. That whole, 'Where have you been all my life?' thing. They were about the same age, so had experienced the world much the same. Decky, however, was on the progressive east coast, while Charlie grew up on the buckle of the Bible belt. Experience made you who you were. What experiences had Charlie had? It was what Decky did. Truly to understand them, Decky studied people and events, in their historical and social context.

Dr. Charlene Ann Warren had a few hits. Decky checked out the listing for Who's Who of College and University Professors. It basically contained information she already knew. She scrolled down the page to several listings in The News Star, a newspaper out of Monroe, Louisiana. The first article she read was from 1995. Dr. Warren, it seemed, was hired as the new head softball coach that year at a small local college . Charlie had not mentioned that fact. Along with her coaching duties, she would join the Mathematics faculty. She had been a graduate assistant at Duke University and then an assistant coach at a small State College in Oklahoma for the two years prior to taking this job, her first as a head coach. Decky looked for a picture, but found none.

There were several articles in the archives with quotes from Coach Warren. The team, it appeared, made marked strides during the first two years of Charlie's tenure. All of the articles were positive. Then an odd date stuck out at the bottom of the list. Most of the articles had been either early fall or spring and into summer. This listing was for January 10, 1997. Decky clicked on the link.

"Coach Resigns," read the headline. To everyone's surprise, the highly successful Coach, Dr. Charlene Warren, was stepping down as head coach of the women's softball team. No reason was given for the apparent sudden decision. Former player and current assistant coach, Lynne Haskins, would take Charlie's place as head coach. Dr. Warren would remain on the university faculty in the mathematics department. At the bottom was a link to the photo that had accompanied the article.

Decky clicked the link and saw a younger Charlie, hand shielding her eyes, squinting up at another woman, to whom she appeared to be listening. She was smiling. The hand not shielding her eyes was touching the other woman on the forearm. The caption explained that this was Coach Warren discussing strategy with then assistant, Coach Haskins. Decky examined the picture closely. Charlie was damn cute. She hadn't aged that much in the ten years since this picture was taken. Yet, there was something about her eyes that was different. She had that fresh look of confidence youth gives you. No fear, no pain lines. Decky recognized that look. You had it until life knocked the breath out of you for the first time.

Something stirred in Decky's chest. She was drawn again and again to the spot on the picture where Charlie's hand rested on the other woman's arm. She had been so preoccupied with Charlie, she hadn't really looked at the other woman. The assistant coach was taller than Charlie, taller than Decky, she thought. Maybe five ten, and even though the picture was black and white, the woman's skin was obviously deeply tanned. Her hair hung out the back of her cap in a dark ponytail. This girl was very attractive. She was a dark Cajun beauty with a little Angelina Jolie on the side.

Decky felt a pain in her chest and recognized it as jealousy. How could she be jealous of someone Charlie knew ten years ago? She decided, after a few minutes of staring at the picture, she was jealous that it wasn't her in the picture with Charlie. She longed for all those years before now, when they could have been together. She had to laugh at herself.

"Oh girl, you got it bad this time don't you," she said aloud.

She printed off a copy of the picture, closed the window, and shut down the laptop. She'd surprise Charlie with it later. It was seven o'clock. Decky decided to go downstairs and fix something to eat, so when Charlie woke up, it would be ready. If she could manage the little bar cart, she would bring it to her in bed. Decky crutched past the bed on the way downstairs. She stopped to look at Charlie.

Charlie was curled into a fetal position, lost in a dream, a tiny smile on her lips. Decky watched her sleep for a moment. She wanted to kiss those lips. She shouldn't wake her, and Decky was sure that if she kissed Charlie she would definitely be driven to wake her. Finally, Decky overcame the urge to touch her and went downstairs.

Forty-five minutes later, Decky was pushing the bar cart out of the elevator. She had not been quite honest earlier. She could cook. She just didn't like to clean up afterwards. The problem was she only liked to cook certain specialty items, most of them requiring numerous saucepans and gadgets.

Tonight she had prepared strawberry crepes. It was one of Zack's favorites, so Decky always had plenty of ingredients around. First, after making the crepes, she spread some melted chocolate on one side of them. She placed a line of overlapping strawberries down the center of each crepe and rolled them up. She capped the whole thing off with whipped topping and more chocolate drizzled over the entire plate, with a few blueberries sprinkled about. She added a few mint leaves. Decky didn't really like mint leaves, but she liked pretty food. Being theatrical, presentation was everything.

Using the cart as a crutch, Decky made her way over to the bed. She sat down on the edge of the bed close to Charlie and gently brushed the hair from her face.

She whispered, "Charlie. Hey, Charlie. Wake up honey, you need to eat something and then you can go back to sleep, okay? Charlie."

Charlie's eyes popped open. They darted around the room and then settled on Decky. Again, Decky noticed how deep blue they were. Wide eyed, but saying nothing, Charlie continued to look at Decky as if she was trying to remember who she was.

"Charlie... hey there. I need you to wake up."

Charlie blinked, then as if she had suddenly regained consciousness, she leaned up and said, "Oh, hey. Man, I was gone. Wow! What is that? It looks great and I'm hungry. How did you know? Wait a minute. You can cook?"

"A few things. Mostly stuff that isn't good for you," Decky added.

"Good for you or not, that smells divine. I can't believe you did all this on one leg."

"Oh, that's just one of my unique talents," Decky replied.

"I think I like your unique talents. I can't wait to learn more." Charlie kissed Decky on the cheek, jumped out of bed, and ran into the bathroom. "I'll be back in a minute. I'm going to grab a shirt while I'm in here, is that okay?"

"Drats, foiled again. It was my evil plan to keep you prisoner here, naked and helpless."

From inside the bathroom, Charlie answered, "What makes you think I couldn't escape? I would, you know. Then I would run naked down the road screaming your name."

The scenario played out in Decky's mind. "Please, help yourself to whatever you need."

"Scared you, huh?" Charlie came out of the bathroom in an oversized tee shirt. She jumped back in bed. "Let's eat."

Decky sat on the edge of the bed, while Charlie balanced her plate on her knees. They talked and laughed through the meal. Decky was careful not to mention her mother and Charlie stayed away from the subject. When the plates had been cleared away, Decky reached under the cart.

"Now, I am going to let you in on my secret formula, guaranteed to prevent or stop a hangover." She produced a pitcher of Bloody Mary mix and poured them both drinks. "I call it a health drink because I use V-8."

Charlie took a sip of her drink. "Hmmm. That's good. I guess I will have to add bartender to my list of your unique talents. What else don't I know about you?"

"It's better if you just let the talent naturally reveal itself when needed. It's more impressive that way."

"So, I'm in for more surprises. We talked about this." Charlie was laughing when she said it, which put Decky at ease, but she felt she needed to change the subject. Decky remembered the picture.

"I Googled you," Decky said, as she hopped over to where the picture was lying by her laptop.

Decky didn't see the mood of Charlie's expression had changed until she turned back around.

"It wasn't anything creepy. I just want to know who you were, or are, everything about you. Chalk it up to my natural born curiosity."

Charlie tried to be lighthearted. "Were you making sure I wasn't only after your money?"

"You can have it. I'll just make more," Decky kidded.

Charlie saw the picture in Decky's hand. She sat up straighter in the bed and pulled the covers up close. Decky observed this behavior, the defensive posturing, but it registered a half a second too late. She had already handed the picture to Charlie.

Looking at the picture, Charlie sighed. "That was a long time ago."

Decky sat back down on the edge of the bed. Charlie pulled her legs in closer to her chest. More signs, but still Decky went on, "I can't believe you didn't tell me you were a college softball coach. When you said your scholarship was for brains, it never crossed my mind that you were a coach. I played for Carolina. If I hadn't blown out my ankle my sophomore year, we might have met so much earlier."

Charlie seemed willing to talk about this, appearing relieved not to have to talk about the picture. "I never played for Duke, but I had always dreamed of being a coach, so I made friends with the club coaches. They took me on the staff while I was a grad assistant '91 through '93. It was a great time."

"And then you went back to Oklahoma."

"Boy, you really did your research. I'm not sure I like having all that stuff about me out there on the Internet. What else did you find out?"

"It was in an article about you, when you took the job in Louisiana. There was a little bio info."

"They have stuff that old on the Internet?" Charlie looked truly amazed.

"It was in the archives. I read a few articles while I was there. Charlie Warren was a very good coach. You really turned that team around. What was that quote, 'We like to hit and run and then run some more'?"

Charlie smirked. "Yeah, I was young and riding a huge wave of confidence. Everything I had done up to that point in life had been a positive experience. Well, there was the budget cut incident I referred to earlier." She looked down at the picture. "Still, I really didn't know there were any negatives at that point. It was all just too perfect."

"What happened, Charlie? Why did you resign?" She paused. "That article was there, too."

Charlie was still looking down at the picture. "I got involved in a relationship that complicated things. It was the easiest way out and I kept my teaching job."

"Did you have an affair with a player?"

Charlie was truly offended. "Oh, God no! That's a line I would never cross."

Decky was relieved; still she said, "I didn't think you were that kind of person."

"I knew we would talk about this sooner or later, but I was hoping for a little later." Charlie leaned forward and took a deep breath before she spoke, "When I went to Louisiana, it was a late hire. The former coach had already hired assistant coaches and since they knew the girls and the facility, I decided to keep them on. Lynne, the girl in the photo, had just graduated. She had been a favorite of the former coach and she really wanted to coach. She was good, too. We did not start a relationship right away, but before the second season was over, we were very much involved. No one knew or cared about us."

Charlie paused, taking a deep breath. "Then she convinced me to give a local girl a walk-on position on the team. She was an okay player, but there were so many better girls ahead of her and more coming in every year. When she discovered in the fall of her sophomore year, that a new freshman was coming in to take over a position she thought she should have, the trouble started."

Decky felt horrible for bringing up Charlie's past. It was obviously a painful memory.

Charlie continued, "She claimed that I made a pass at her, and because she rebuffed me, I wouldn't play her. Now, as ludicrous as that sounds, the good old boys came calling. They were just forced to fire a male coach for screwing around with the female athletes. I had already been in a similar situation where I was about to be labeled and now this. It would have been a deathblow to a female coach. I hadn't done anything, but I was involved in a lesbian relationship with a former player from that university, who happened to be my current assistant."

Decky patted Charlie's knee, understanding how hard this must be for Charlie.

"The administrator was kind. She knew this was a bad deal, but the university couldn't take the chance that the paper would start snooping around for dirt, so they made an offer. Lynne could have the head-coaching job. This was agreeable to the girl and her mother. After all, Lynne had not been accused of anything. I could take on a full load in the math department at the same salary. They just wanted the problem to go away. I can still hear the dean saying how it was best for my career and the university would repay my loyalty for sparing it another nasty investigation. A win for everyone right?"

Decky was patient. She waited for Charlie to finish.

"I chose the old 'personal reasons' excuse and resigned. Everyone was happy, especially Lynne. She was finally doing what she had always dreamed. I forgot about me for a while and enjoyed how much she loved her job. The team did well and we stayed together. I was happy and it didn't seem so bad. Before too long, I gave up my dream of ever coaching again and enjoyed being a teacher.

"We were together for ten years. There were a few bumps, but I thought everything was fine. I had a beautiful house, a job I loved, and I moved steadily up in the department. Next step, chairman. Then one day she comes in to tell me she is being investigated for having a relationship with a current player. Like my momma said, don't ask questions you don't want the answers to. I asked her if it was true and she said yes. As it turns out, she had been sleeping around on me our whole relationship. She had even been sleeping with the little bitch that cost me my coaching job, way back then. She had caused the whole thing."

"I'm sorry that happened to you. We don't have to talk about it. I know she hurt you." Decky was sorry she ever copied the picture. She hated Lynne even though she had never laid eyes on her.

"She made a fool out of me. Stupid ol' Charlene at home, thinking everything is just wonderful, while she's out fucking everything in sight."

"You trusted her." Decky tried to reassure her.

"Yes, I did trust her and look what happened. That's why I said all that before. I can't do that again. I won't do it again."

Decky placed her hand against Charlie's cheek. "You can trust me. I could never hurt you."

Charlie looked at Decky for a moment, then said softly, "You know, for some reason I believe you."

"Good, and now that we have that out of the way, don't you feel better?"

"I've been sad a long time. I don't feel sad when I'm with you, so yes, I do feel better. Throw this picture away."

Decky took the picture, balled it up, and tried for a three in the corner wastebasket. She missed.

Charlie booed.

"I was fouled," Decky exclaimed.

Charlie called her a whiner and Decky pounced on her, which set off a wrestling and tickling session, followed immediately by long, slow lovemaking. Just as Decky slipped off to sleep, she heard the jukebox in her head singing, "…She couldn't believe, that God had made a woman who would never ever leave…"

4

Decky awoke to the sweet sensation of Charlie's lips in the small of her back. Charlie moved slowly up her spine as Decky squirmed under her touch. When she could resist no longer, Decky turned over on her back. Charlie crawled up Decky's body like a cat hunting prey. She had fire in her eyes as she sat up on her knees, straddling the absolutely dumbstruck Decky.

"Good morning," Charlie said in a smoky, sexy voice. She ran her fingers up Decky's abdomen to her chest, where she slowly began to massage Decky's small firm breasts. Decky's back arched slightly as her breath caught in her throat. "I've been lying here watching you sleep. I thought maybe before we head out into the world, we might have another go at that Jacuzzi."

Decky could only nod in agreement. Speech was not possible at that moment.

The sex energized them and by eight-thirty, Decky and Charlie were fed, clothed, and headed out the front door.

"Come this way. I want to take my car. It's easier to get in and out of with these crutches. It's out in the apartment garage, at the end of the lot," Decky continued, as they walked down the front steps and across the yard, to a small one-story cottage.

"I built this little, two-bedroom to live in while the house was being constructed. That way I could be here and not rush the process. After we moved into the house, Zack and I changed it into a guesthouse slash game room. It has everything a teenager could want including a nine-foot pool table. That was my contribution. He uses it a lot for his friends to hang out. We occasionally have an extra teenager or a down and out friend hanging around. With Zack gone, it's been quiet, although it is pretty early in the summer. The relatives and their families should start arriving any day."

"Won't you need the cottage we're going to look at for all those people?" Charlie inquired.

"No, they can stay at Mom's motel. It's closer to the beach anyway."

"Your mom has a motel?"

"Well, part of one. I bought controlling interest in a motel at Corolla and a few rental cottages on the beach. She runs the motel and rentals for me. In exchange, she gets a large percentage of the profit from the motel. It gives her something to do other than concentrate on my life and it was a great investment. It keeps money in her bank account. That's a good thing, because that woman was born to shop."

Decky hit a button on the key ring she had pulled from her pocket. The garage door on the cottage opened to reveal a fully loaded silver Lexus SC 430 coupe with the top already down. The interior was saddle leather trim with brown walnut accents.

Charlie turned to Decky. "That must have been an awfully big shit pot."

#

On the way to Brenda's, they met Miss Lizzie barreling down the highway toward them. Upon recognizing Decky's car, Miss Lizzie started blinking her headlights on and off and was slowing to a stop. Dixie was hanging out the passenger side window in dog-full bliss, the wind blowing her golden hair. Decky saw what was happening and reacted quickly. She had no time to explain.

Decky hit the gas and turned to Charlie, who seemed to be trying to figure out who the idiot was in the car coming at them. Now the person had an arm out the window, waving frantically, while swerving slightly back and forth. Decky grabbed Charlie's arm to get her attention.

"Whatever you do, don't make eye contact. Just look at me and act like we're talking, which we are, so it's in the realm of possibility that we do not see her."

"Who is that?"

Decky saw Charlie see the dog more clearly and the recognition on her face from having seen pictures in Decky's house. She saw Charlie process the panic-stricken look Decky was giving her. Her mother had raised no fool. Charlie read the signs correctly. This had to be Decky's mother. Putting the facts together, Charlie started laughing at some imagined conversation the two were having.

Just before they passed the now slowly rolling vehicle with the crazy woman in it, Decky broke her gaze from Charlie and looked at her mother. She waved and smiled, as though glad to see her and mouthed, "I'll call you," into her hand, now held up to her ear like a phone. She pressed a button on the steering wheel, saying, "Call mom." Over the sound system, the phone began to ring.

The voice of a woman with a deep southern drawl said into the air, "Decky, where in the hell are you going so fast? You could have run over me. Didn't you see me?"

"I'm sorry. I was talking." Decky said, rolling her eyes at Charlie.

"I thought I would bring Dixie to you and save you the trip. Who is that in the car with you?"

"It's a new teacher from the University. I am helping her find a house. I was just going to drop her off and swing by for Dixie."

"Oh, which one? I know we hired so many this spring."

"The math teacher. Look, why don't you turn around and go back home and I'll be there in just a few minutes."

"Oh, that was a last minute hire. I couldn't believe our luck in finding such a highly qualified candidate at this late date. I hope there's nothing wrong with her. You know she just picked up and left a job she had for ten years. Her recommendations were sterling, so we decided to offer her the job. I just got the feeling we didn't have the whole story."

"Mother, you know the phone in my car is a speaker phone, she can hear you."

"Oh, good Lord. I have to go. I'll see you in a few minutes." Click, the connection was gone.

Charlie was staring at Decky with her mouth open. Decky grinned helplessly.

"Well, you survived your first tangle with Lizzie. How do you feel?"

"Like I've just been violated. She shouldn't be talking about me to you like that. I mean that isn't very professional." Charlie was visually stunned.

"Welcome to Lizzie's world. The only rules are the rules that apply to everyone else. They only apply to Lizzie when it works in her favor."

"So much for her not knowing we know each other."

Decky took Charlie's hand in hers. "Honey, it was going to happen sooner or later. For a first go round with Lizzie, I think it was fairly painless."

"Look at me, I'm shaking. We flew past her at sixty miles per hour and she still got to me." Charlie was looking down at her free hand. "How do you handle her?"

"Several years ago I was watching The Dog Whisperer on National Geographic. It dawned on me that what I was missing in my relationship with Lizzie were rules, boundaries, and expectations. I set about establishing those and found that if I took the emotion out of the equation, I was able to control the situation much better. I get to be my own pack leader. Of course, it's been a constant series of corrections for her. Like this for instance, her correction is, she has to go back home. She broke a rule by not calling first, so now she has consequences. Respect for other people's boundaries is a learned behavior with Lizzie, it certainly isn't instinctual."

"Maybe we should watch the show together. I may need some help."

"I have the first two seasons on DVD. You must pay very close attention, especially to the red zone cases." Decky was trying to sound serious.

"What are red zone cases?" Charlie was serious.

"The guy, Caesar, specializes in aggressive dogs, poorly trained Pits and Rots. The most vicious dogs are called red zone cases. They usually go to his dog psychology center, where he teaches them how to be good pack members. My mom has had a few stays in the people psychology center, so I figure it's almost the same thing."

"And you refer to your mother as a red zone case. This isn't going to be easy is it?"

"Nothing good comes easy," Decky replied.

"This is good, isn't it?"

"Yes, it is very, very good."

Charlie was smiling now. She pulled the hand that held hers to her mouth and bit Decky on the knuckle playfully.

"Hey, hey, I'm driving. You can't do that when I'm driving."

"What about this?" Charlie put Decky's ring finger in her mouth and then slowly pulled it out again.

Decky jerked her hand away. "You... you stay on your side of the car. No touching." Decky placed both hands on the wheel and stared straight ahead.

Charlie hung her head back and let out a throaty laugh, her hair blowing in the wind. The first notes of 'Only the Good Die Young' came over the speakers. Decky turned it up and they sang all the way to Brenda's house.

#

Decky and Charlie made plans in Brenda's driveway for the rest of the day. Decky would be back to take her to lunch and show her the cottage this afternoon. Charlie tried to get Decky to go inside with her, but Decky said no.

"I'd rather go get Lizzie out of the way. Brenda will have enough to say this evening."

"Okay, so I'll see you about noon." Charlie was standing by Decky's window. She casually placed her hand on the car close enough to run a finger inconspicuously on Decky's arm.

For the first time Decky felt it. She wanted desperately to kiss this woman, but she couldn't. They were out in public. If Decky were a man, Charlie would lean down and kiss her right on the mouth, for all to see. As it was, all they could do was steal wanting glances or brush an unseen finger across an arm.

"I know I have to leave now, but I don't want to. Isn't this silly? I feel like a teenager with a crush." Decky's eyes met Charlie's, as she recognized the same feelings flash across them.

"I know what you mean. I can't seem to let go of this car. Did you drug me?" Charlie questioned her teasingly.

"The voodoo woman did say not to use too much. Maybe I absorbed it from you through skin contact."

"I knew it! There's no way I would have slept with you within hours of meeting you without some kind of undue influence. What kind of girl would that make me?" Charlie was using her Oklahoma homecoming queen accent to feign innocence.

"I do like my women a little on the trashy side."

"I see, I suppose the neighbors will talk if they see you dropping your latest conquest out in the street. They'll call me a loose woman." Charlie batted her eyelashes.

"My kind of girl. Now, on the count of three, you let go and I'll put the car in reverse. Otherwise, we will stay like this all day."

Decky backed out and turned the car toward her mom's house. She looked back in the mirror to see Charlie standing there, wearing Decky's too large tee shirt and shorts, her hair windblown and wild.

"God, she's beautiful."

#

When Decky entered her parents' house, her father was at the kitchen table having sausage biscuits and coffee, reading the paper. Dixie met her at the door. She was wagging her tail so hard that her whole body was involved in the action. At Dixie's feet, yapping like a banshee, was Lizzie's Yorkshire terrier, whom Decky and her father referred to as "the asshole."

Waiting patiently to be noticed, Bucky, the beagle, sat up beside her father. This was her father's dog and they were known far and wide as great buddies. Her father often let Bucky sit in his lap in the truck. Paws on the wheel, Bucky would appear to be driving as they drove down the road. Her mother said they looked ridiculous. Her Daddy said he was glad the dog could drive. That way if he got off somewhere and couldn't get back, the dog could drive them home. Her mother cringed every time he told that story.

Lizzie suffered under the delusion that Decky's father ever wanted to be more than he was. He had been a coach and school principal until he retired several years ago. He was a simple man with a simple past. He liked to wear overalls and ride around in an old pickup truck. Lizzie wanted him to show everyone that he was educated, but he talked like an old wise farmer. He knew how to speak proper English and in the right settings he did, but he chose to talk like the people he came from and the ones he dealt with everyday. His speech had a Fred Thompson quality to it. Decky liked it. You could count on him.

If Robert Charles Bradshaw had a flaw, it would be his love for Lizzie. The man had the patience of Job with her. For fifty years, he had put up with more than most men could have taken, but he loved his Lizzie. Decky's mother was not always bad. Lizzie loved her children and her husband. She was loyal to a fault. R.C. – that's what everyone called her father – and Lizzie had been a striking couple in high school. He was the handsome football star, she the blond cheerleader. Life was always exciting with Lizzie. She had tons of friends and loved to throw parties. The high life was just that, one fun family.

It wasn't until later, when the depression set in and the alcohol took over, that R.C. began to have trouble with Lizzie. They saw doctors and she took anti-depressants, but the bouts got longer and deeper. She was finally diagnosed as bi-polar and Decky and her dad began to learn how to deal with it. Her brother was useless. He was as sick as his mother was, but refused to believe it. So life was just a bowl of cherries after that, with the two of them always on the rollercoaster of highs and lows, with Decky and R.C. just trying to stay out of the way and not draw attention to them.

"Hey Dad, how's it going?"

R.C. folded the paper and patted the table for Decky to come sit down. "Much better than you, it looks like. Sit down, take a load off."

Decky crutched over to the table and plopped down. Dixie followed her and put her head down on Decky's lap. "Anything interesting in the paper this morning?"

"Naw, same old thing. Looks like the fish are biting over to the beach though. Think I might head on down and wet a line for a few days. Thought I'd go with your mother when she delivers the paychecks tomorrow. I think she wants to have her cousin come down this weekend, so it just makes sense to stay awhile."

"That sounds great. Which cousin?"

"Edna and her crowd." R.C. pretended not to want to be around Edna's crowd, but he loved company and Lizzie was always happy around Edna.

Lizzie came out of the back of the house where she kept a little office. Despite her mental problems, Lizzie was a shrewd businesswoman and took care of Decky's interest with great care. She was carrying a large blue checkbook and some papers as she approached the table.

"Did you have to take that woman all the way to town? I thought you were coming in a few minutes," Lizzie started in.

"No, I dropped her off at Brenda and Chip's. You know how Brenda is when she gets to talking." Decky was lying, but sometimes it was easier.

"Well, that's nice of them to take in a new faculty member and make her feel welcome."

Lizzie laid the checkbook out in front of Decky and she started to sign the already filled out checks and forms necessary for payroll.

Unconsciously Decky answered her mother, "They all went to Duke together. They are old friends." *Shit, too much information. Don't tell her anything she doesn't need to know,* she reminded herself.

Lizzie brightened. "I'll have to talk to Brenda about her. We should have Brenda and Chip bring her over. We could all have dinner together. What do you think R.C.?"

R.C. had gone back to his paper. "Think about what?"

"We should have Brenda and Chip and the new math professor from the university over for dinner. She's an old friend of theirs. They went to Duke together. What did you say her name was, Decky?"

"Charlie, I mean Dr. Charlene Warren. She goes by Charlie to her friends." *Damn, don't sound so familiar. She'll start digging for information.*

R.C., who adored Brenda and Chip, spoke up, "I think that would be a good idea. We haven't had a good dinner party in a long time. You'd come too, Decky?"

"Sure, I wouldn't want to miss it." Charlie was going to kill her.

"I'll call Brenda and set it up. Do you know if she's at home?" Lizzie was headed for the phone.

Almost too quickly, Decky said, "No, she isn't home. She left when I did. I think she went over to the University for the day. I'll see her tonight and tell her to call you."

Lizzie stopped and returned to the table. "What's going on tonight? It's Tuesday, you don't play ball on Tuesday."

Decky had no choice; she had to answer. "Just a few of us getting together for dinner."

Lizzie was placing checks in envelopes as Decky finished them. To the untrained eye, she appeared to be nonchalantly making chitchat, but Decky knew better. The wheels were turning in that little white head; Lizzie was on a mission to find out everything. She could not be stopped.

"That's nice. Who's going to be there?"

Decky tried a deflective move. "Just some friends of theirs, I'm not really sure who all will be there."

"Well, I do hope you will wear something nice, instead of an old tee-shirt and shorts. Dress up sometimes. You are such a pretty girl, but you dress like a tomboy. You need to dress like a lady more often, it wouldn't hurt."

The deflection had worked. Lizzie was off on Decky's way of dressing, her hair, and the fact that she didn't wear a bra or makeup. This was good for at least thirty minutes of discussion and by then the checks would be signed and she could flee. R. C. decided to take the dogs for a walk. He had heard it all before.

Lizzie wrapped up a half an hour later, right on schedule. "I don't know how you expect to find a man, when you dress like one."

Decky finished the last check and handed it to her mother. "Momma, if I wanted a man, I'd have one. And he would like me in tee-shirts and jeans."

Decky stood up and kissed her mother on the cheek. On the way out she said, "I hear Edna is coming down. Dad says he's going with you tomorrow and you're staying till Sunday?" Decky had learned from the best how to get information without appearing to pry.

Lizzie followed her out to the car. "Yes, we'll be leaving in the morning. You should come with us. Get out of the house."

Decky looked at the crutches and thought to herself, *Thank God.*

"I wouldn't be much fun on these. I'll catch them next time. Give Edna a kiss for me."

Dixie hopped into the passenger seat without being asked.

Lizzie started up again. "I can't believe you let that dog sit in that car like that."

Dixie looked at Lizzie as if she had heard her and was offended at being called a dog.

"I told you mom, she's not a dog, she's a little girl."

Laughing, she backed out, waved to her father, and let out a huge sigh of relief. She and Charlie had at least five days before they had to deal with Lizzie again, if all went as planned. Charlie wouldn't even have to meet Lizzie at the faculty luncheon. Things looked promising, but in the back of her mind, she kept her guard up. You could just never tell when Lizzie was involved.

#

Decky drove into town, about a thirty-minute drive. She gathered supplies, ran some errands, and headed back to her house. She rushed around, if one can rush around on crutches, preparing everything for the afternoon. She wanted to surprise Charlie, going about her work almost giddily. She watched the clock and counted the minutes until she would see Charlie again. She had it bad, she knew it, and right this minute she loved it.

At precisely noon, Decky pulled up in Brenda's driveway. Charlie bounded out of the house, as if she had been watching for her. They both beamed when they saw each other. Charlie jumped in the seat beside Decky.

"I was waiting for you. I thought you'd never get here. Brenda has been asking all sorts of questions. I couldn't wait to get out of there."

"Like what kind of questions?" Decky asked.

"Like which one of us is the boy?"

"She didn't."

Charlie laughed. "Yes she did."

"Oh my God, I hope Chip didn't hear her." Decky was laughing now. "What did you say?"

"I started to explain that it didn't work like that, but I just said we were still working that out." Decky laughed, as Charlie continued, "She's never asked me anything like that before. She is really having fun with this."

Decky headed the car for home, still listening as Charlie went on, "She even asked me if you were good in bed. I couldn't believe it!"

Decky didn't miss a beat. "So, what did you tell her?"

"I said you were fucking fantastic!"

#

"I thought we were going to get some lunch and go see the cottage," Charlie said as Decky turned down the road to her house.

"We are, just taking a different vehicle."

Decky parked the car in the garage and pointed with her crutch for Charlie to go around the side of the house. Dixie came bounding down the back stairway as they rounded the corner. The dog led the way as they made their way down to the water's edge.

They stopped in the boathouse to pick up the picnic basket and cooler Decky had the twins bring down for her. The twins were great. She would call them on the cell phone she had given them, let them know what she needed, and they would get it done. No questions asked. Of course, she lined their pockets and let them play with all her cool stuff.

The boathouse contained room for a Boston Whaler, a small sunfish sailboat, and a small sailing skiff. The walls held multiple sailboards and fishing gear, miscellaneous skis and water toys. There was a smaller boat barn near the shore, which contained canoes and jet skies.

Charlie picked up the cooler and looked around. "Got enough toys?"

Decky explained that she didn't want Zack involved in drugs and other teenage pursuits, so she surrounded him with things to keep him outside, active, at home, and she might add, very popular.

The twins had also pulled the Boston Whaler out of the boathouse earlier. It was gassed up and ready to go, tied to the end of the dock. Charlie loaded the picnic basket and cooler in the boat and helped Decky down from the dock. Dixie jumped up on the bow seat, ready for the trip.

"I wish I had brought my swimsuit," Charlie said, settling down on one of the seats.

"Look in the picnic basket," Decky responded while cranking the boat.

Charlie looked in the picnic basket. She pulled out a tiny, very sexy bikini. Holding it up, she looked at Decky with one eyebrow raised. "You've got to be kidding."

Decky burst out laughing. "I thought you might say that when I bought it this morning. Look a little deeper; I put a few more conservative choices at the bottom. I was hoping not to need them."

Charlie settled on a one-piece black suit. She sat down on the bottom of the boat and gave Decky and Dixie quite the show as she slipped the tight suit over her body. It was all Decky could do to not stop the boat right there and have at it, but she kept going, aiming the boat down the shoreline.

Charlie opened the picnic basket, removing two plastic champagne flutes and a bowl of strawberries that had been dipped in chocolate. Decky paced the boat for a smooth ride, then opened the cooler and removed a bottle of Champagne. It looked expensive and it was.

"You must have been a very busy girl this morning, or do you just have expensive champagne and gourmet strawberries lying around?" Charlie was stretched out on her side on the bench seat, propped up on one elbow. Dixie came over and nuzzled her face.

"She wants the chocolate. My mother spoils her." Decky pointed Dixie back to the front of the boat and she obeyed, but not without casting one last look at the strawberries.

"By the way, how was Lizzie?" Charlie said, and then bit the end off a strawberry.

"She pried a few things out of me, but the good news is she's leaving for the beach in the morning and won't be back until Sunday,"

Charlie lowered her voice. "What kind of things did she pry out of you?"

"Didn't you hear what I said? She won't be at the faculty luncheon. That should be a relief." Decky really did not want to spoil the mood.

"That is a relief, but I think you're holding something back. Come on, spit it out. I can't exactly run away, we're in a friggin' boat."

Decky decided to get it out quickly, hoping it would blow over just as fast. "She found out you were an old friend of Brenda and Chip's and I'm supposed to arrange a dinner party at Lizzie's for you and your friends, me included."

"Tell her I don't eat, at least not in public. Tell her I have a real phobia about it."

"I can't do that. Then she'd make it her mission in life to cure you." Decky was being honest.

"Will that be before or after she finds out I'm sleeping with her daughter? I'm afraid she might poison me."

"She doesn't have to know the details of our friendship."

"You keep telling yourself that. The first time she sees us together, she'll know. From what Brenda says, we have flashing red signs on our foreheads saying, 'Lesbians in heat. Watch out!' Everybody's going to know."

Decky was happy to see that Charlie was smiling. It took a sense of humor to live with Lizzie. She just hoped Charlie's would stand up to the challenge.

"I can hold her off. Tell her you're getting settled in. She'll buy that for a while, but she'll consider it rude if you never come. I know, you should send her a thank you card for the invitation and ask for a rain check. That will go a long way with her. It's a very old South thing to do. She'll think you're civilized at least."

"I am civilized. You'll find I clean up pretty good. You can dress me up and take me anywhere, just not to your mother's house. Do you people keep guns?"

"Of course we have guns." Decky was teasing her now. "Momma never goes anywhere without one. We live in the South, where we treasure our right to own and bear arms. We are all gun toting rednecks and proud of it. Momma's a real crack shot too."

"I guess that's not so much different from home, but my mother would never carry a gun. She always has a man around to do that sort of thing. Besides I thought your mother was a certified bi-polar psychiatric patient."

"There are some innate rights afforded to all Americans, even the mentally unstable. Besides she doesn't think there's anything wrong with her, and that's exactly what she told the nice policeman that tried to remove it from her purse, after she waved it at some tourist who parked a camper in her front yard."

"That would have made me mad, too."

"Mad, not homicidal. You see, with her it's varying degrees of extremes. What you call a psychotic break down, she would call a slight overreaction."

"Do you think you could hide the bullets, pull the firing pin or something?" Charlie ducked down. "She doesn't have a rifle with a scope does she?"

"No, she's more a shoot you between the eyes kind of gal."

Charlie fell off the bench. They laughed hard and long. Decky hadn't laughed this much in years. It felt good. She slowed the boat and pulled up next to a dock leading to a small cottage on stilts. It was located in a blind cove. There were other houses around the shoreline, but this cottage sat on a piece of land jutting out into the cove, tall trees isolating it from view.

A small skiff sat upside down under the decking. The sides of the cottage were covered in old gray shingles, so popular on the Outer Banks of North Carolina. It was just a box on stilts, more a vacation house than a home. The driveway looked rutted out from old traffic and spring rains. A small aluminum shed sat to one side of the property, near the tall pine trees that lined the back of the lot toward the road. An old bulkhead followed the shoreline, trying to keep the Currituck Sound at bay.

"If you don't mind, I don't think I'll try to make that haul up to the cottage." She fished around in her pocket, then handed Charlie the key. "I'll just wait here. Take your time. Oh, the alarm code is BASE."

"It has an alarm system. That's unusual way out here isn't it?" Charlie started out of the boat. Dixie followed.

"It just makes noise and calls me on the phone if someone breaks in. We had a little trouble with some friends of Zack's having a few parties without permission. I didn't want the cops coming every time one of them got a little stupid."

"Well, at least I would have fair warning before your mother could get through the door."

Decky winked. "Now you're thinking."

Charlie went down the dock and up the steps of the cottage under Decky's watchful eyes. Dixie found something to sniff under the deck. Decky's gaze followed Charlie's shadow on the ceiling of the cottage, as she walked from room to room. She soon reemerged with a big smile and trotted down the dock to where Decky waited. Dixie looked up, and followed suit.

Charlie and Dixie jumped down into the boat. Charlie went straight to Decky and hugged her. Dixie took the opportunity to steal a strawberry and return to the bow.

"It's perfect. Just the right size and the view is fantastic." Charlie sat down again and looked back at the cottage. "You're right, it's not a permanent residence, but it would be fine until I find something else. You're sure you want to do this?"

"Yes, I do. I want you to be close to me and I figure this is about as close as you're willing to come right now." Decky poured them more champagne.

"How much do you want to lease it? Charge what you would normally ask. No special deals."

"You don't want to be a kept woman? My concubine?" Decky's dimple was showing.

Charlie took a sip from her glass. "As much as I would like to, I can't take advantage of your inability to resist my feminine wiles, decide what you want and I'll pay it. No arguments."

"We'll talk about it later. Right now, I want to take you somewhere." Decky started the boat.

Decky drove the boat across the Sound towards Corolla. They stopped just off small Mary's Island, more of a sandbar with a few trees. Decky anchored the boat and pointed out the

Currituck Lighthouse over on the main barrier island. They sat and watched sailboats moving along the Intracoastal Waterway that cuts through Currituck Sound, heading north and south.

Decky told Charlie stories about growing up here in "Sportsman's Paradise," as the welcome sign out on the county line called it. She told her of the great flocks of Canadian and Snow geese that used to cover the Sound every season. The hunters still came every year, but the flocks of birds didn't come in large numbers anymore.

She told her about the time she went hunting with her boyfriend in a freezing duck blind, only to have him accidentally shoot a swan. How they had driven back to shore in the boat and snuck the dead swan into his truck. How they were so scared the game warden or her boyfriend's father was going to catch them with the illegal bird, which by the way was a two thousand dollar fine. They rushed home, cooked it, and had damn near eaten all the evidence before his momma got home from work.

Decky told Charlie about the history of Currituck County and the barrier islands that daisy chained down the coast of North Carolina. She talked about the early English settlement on Roanoke Island, further south. How the settlers had come in 1587 long before Jamestown. When the supply ships returned three years later, what had been a thriving settlement had disappeared, leaving only the word "Croatoan" carved in a tree. The vanished settlers became known as the "Lost Colony." Decky promised to take Charlie to see the outdoor drama depicting the plight of the colonists, at the Waterside Theatre in Manteo.

There were so many things to show Charlie, so much time to make up. Decky talked about being baptized in the Sound, about Easter morning sunrise services over the water, about learning to water ski and surf. She recalled how badly she had wanted out of this little county when she was young, and how she was drawn back to it like a moth to a flame, after college and a broken heart.

Charlie commented only occasionally, but mostly she just listened. When Decky told of the broken heart, Charlie wanted to hear more.

"Who broke your heart, your ex-husband?"

"Oh, good Lord, no! I married him on the rebound from the love of my life. I knew it at the time, but I couldn't help myself. I call it the dark time, a time when I temporarily lost my mind. I got Zack out of the deal, so it worked out okay."

"Then who was the love of your life?" Charlie wasn't giving up.

"I started dating William Thomas Dowdy, the third, or Trey, as he was called, my senior year of high school. I had dated a few guys, you know high school dating, the on and off relationships. Trey was a year younger than I was. I had never paid much attention to him until we were in a play together that spring. I had always dated athletes.

"Trey was totally different, sensitive and gentle. I fell head over heels, I mean gone. We stayed together, with a few hiccups here and there, all the way through my senior year at Carolina. By then he was there, majoring in theatre too. We didn't live together. I stayed with some ball friends of mine and he lived in the frat house. With our production schedules, classes, my playing sports, and his fraternity we were away from each other a lot. We had separate lives; I guess that's what I'm trying to say."

Decky stopped and took a deep breath. She didn't like remembering what happened next.

"That spring, just before graduation and one month after he had given me an engagement ring, I was helping Trey move out of the frat house. He had gotten a summer-stock job in

Greensboro, and we were moving in together for the first time that summer.

"While Trey went to get more boxes, I came across a shoebox in his closet with letters from a recent lover. I read them. I shouldn't have. They weren't signed, but it was evident from the content that my rival was a guy. He was in the chorus of the musical Trey was about to star in and a good friend of mine as well. I had been excited that he was coming with Trey and me for the summer. I was devastated. When he came back, he saw me with the letters. He couldn't lie, I was holding the evidence."

"Oh, my God, what did you do?" Charlie's face was twisted with Decky's pain.

"I screamed, I cussed, I cried, I lost my mind. He actually told me he would try to change. It was just a phase, he loved me; he would give it all up if I wouldn't leave him. I accused him of needing a cover for his family, and a surrogate for the precious William Thomas Dowdy, the fourth, he was destined to sire. As it turns out, I was absolutely correct. He now has a wife and two kids and at least one male companion, 'best friend,' around all the time, who helps out on the farm and at the feed store he inherited. I don't know what bothers me the most, the fact that he's still lying to everyone, or all that wasted time and emotion loving him."

Charlie asked quietly, "Nobody knows, about him I mean? You didn't tell anyone?"

"No, I only talked to one other person about it, my friend Jackie. I was embarrassed. For a long time I blamed myself. There had to be something wrong with me. My mother told me so repeatedly. She loved Trey." Decky finished her champagne and reached for the bottle again. "He was the perfect son-in-law candidate. Good looking, son of a prosperous farmer and businessman, along with the fact that when he sang he could melt your heart."

"She doesn't know why you didn't marry him? Why didn't you tell her the truth about him?" Charlie was coming to Decky's aid. Albeit much too late, she was trying.

"What? And have to hear about how a real woman could have changed him back? Please, I didn't need that. It was bad enough. I chose instead to say that he wasn't the man I thought he was and leave it at that."

"Well, that kind of said it all." Charlie tried to lighten the mood.

"I spent the next year drunk, feeling sorry for myself, and sobered up married to a sweet guy, but he was an alcoholic just the same. Soon there I was with a baby on my hip and a momma's boy asleep on the couch. I remember my wedding day, not because it's a special memory, but because it was so surreal. Trey actually showed up at the wedding. He begged me not to get married, said he had gotten over his phase. I told him I didn't share my toys well with others, especially the man who would be my husband." Decky paused, taking a sip of champagne.

"My father sensed something, because on the way down the aisle he said we could turn around and get in the car. He promised not to let Momma hit me more than once. Lizzie had planned – no I should say, orchestrated the production of my wedding and spent lots of money. I was afraid even R.C. couldn't stop Lizzie if I walked back down that aisle, so I went ahead with it. Trey got drunk at the reception and actually cried. I was drunk and wound up pregnant. It was all so straight out of the movies."

"How long were you married?"

Decky was emerging from the pain of her memories. "Just over two years, then I got smart, got a job, and struck out on my own with Zack in tow. I put myself through Grad school. Then I got a job at one of the Chapel Hill high schools, teaching drama and the rest I think you know."

"But how did you get back here?"

"When I sold the first book and it did okay, I bought the land, thinking I would build on it someday after I retired. When the next book sold, I started thinking about writing full time. Then the movie rights sold and the decision was much easier to make. I came here to heal. This place is like vitamins to my soul. I can breathe here. You know, it's not true what they say, you can go home again."

"I for one am glad you did. Now, if we can dispense with all the drama for a minute. I have to go to the bathroom." Charlie stood up and headed for the stern.

"If you're going to jump in, I warn you it isn't very deep. Don't dive. I had to have a tooth capped from hitting my head on the bottom when I was twelve."

Charlie stepped over onto the stern ladder and lowered herself over the edge. Decky could no longer see her. She called out to the water, "How's the water? Has it warmed up? It's still early and we had a cool spring."

There was no response, only a little splashing. A wet object came flying onto the boat and landed at Decky's feet with a splat. Dixie came from the bow to check it out. She sniffed at what turned out to be the bathing suit Charlie had been wearing and looked up at Decky.

"Hold the fort, Dix," Decky said, patting the dog on the head, "I think there's a damsel in distress I need to attend to."

Dixie enjoyed some time alone with her strawberries.

#

Decky and Dixie dropped Charlie off at Brenda's around six. Decky promised to be back in an hour, which relieved

Charlie. She didn't want to be alone with Brenda's questions any longer than was absolutely necessary. Decky stood in her walk-in closet now, staring at the clothes hanging there. She had already gone through several outfits and still was undecided.

She wasn't doing this because her mother had said to dress nice. She wanted to look nice for Charlie. Besides, Lizzie's idea of "dress nice" was much different from Decky's. Finally, she settled on white cotton, drawstring, wide leg pants from J. Crew and a navy blue, three-quarter sleeve, summer weight, cashmere crew neck. She put in some simple pearl earrings. She dabbed Ralph Lauren Romance perfume in multiple places then ran her fingers through her hair once more. She turned from the mirror, addressing Dixie.

"Well, what do you think, better than a tee-shirt and jeans?"

Dixie cocked her head then got up and left the bathroom.

"I guess that's a yes."

Dixie took the stairs and was waiting when Decky stepped out of the elevator on the main floor. Decky locked the doors and checked Dixie's bowls. She lowered the plasma screen and turned on the nature channel. Dixie hopped up on the couch.

"Now, watch some TV, don't eat too much, and I'll be back in a couple of hours." Decky put her hand out and Dixie slapped her five with her paw. "Good girl."

Decky selected a red and a white wine to take, because she didn't know what Brenda was cooking. She found a bag with a handle she could carry with the crutches and off she went. She was a little nervous. She hadn't been around other people with Charlie since Sunday and many things had changed in that time.

Chip was in the driveway when Decky arrived. He was taking out the trash. Good ol' Chip, he helped Decky with the bag of wine and into the house. He never questioned her about

Charlie at all. He knew Brenda would be taking care of the inquisition and Decky was grateful that he was choosing to stay out of it. Just as they entered the house, Chip stopped Decky. She appreciated his struggle to say the right thing.

"Decky, I want you to know we love you both. Brenda's a little worried that Charlie might be moving too fast. After what she's just been through, we don't want to see either of you get hurt."

"I promise you the last thing I will ever do is hurt Charlie."

Chip nodded. "Just take care of you too, okay."

"Thanks, buddy." Brenda was a lucky man. Decky knew very few guys with Chip's ability to accept women as equals and true friends. He was one of the good guys.

Chip slapped Decky on the back. "Nice catch by the way. Brenda says you're the envy of all the girls. Something about you getting to the new meat, before the old hawks had a chance."

Decky and Chip were laughing when they stepped out onto the deck. Charlie and Brenda were already seated with cocktails. To Decky's surprise, no one else was present.

"Well, I see the gimp made it," Brenda called out. "And look at you, all cleaned up, earrings and all." She stood up to hug Decky. "Wow, you smell good enough to eat."

There was a beat, and then Brenda added, "I did not just say that, did I?"

The four of them burst into spasms of laughter.

"Chip, I think we need drinks all around. You go fix us something special, the girls and I need to chat. That's a good boy." Brenda patted Chip on the butt as he went to do her bidding. Chip wore the pants in the family, but Brenda zipped them up. They were very cute together.

Decky sat down in the chair next to Charlie's, both of them glowing from the day's sun. They smiled at each other, too nervous to touch. Decky simply said, "Hi."

"Oh hell, go ahead and kiss her, you know you're dying to." Brenda chuckled.

Now feeling obligated, Decky leaned over and gave Charlie a soft kiss on the cheek. Charlie took Decky's hand in hers.

"Relax Decky, she doesn't bite, we're just a few drinks ahead of you. She can't hold her liquor. Be nice Brenda, she's a little nervous."

"I am being nice. Any fool could see the look on that girl's face when she walked in here just now. She wanted to kiss you the moment she laid eyes on you. Am I right, Decky? Tell the truth and let the Lord love ya'!"

"Amen sister, you got that right," Decky answered.

Decky was relaxing, the awkwardness of the moment beginning to fade. It was being replaced by the sheer joy of sharing this newfound bliss with someone who wouldn't judge them. She wanted to scream from the rooftops, look at my beautiful girl, look what I found, thank you God. For now, a friend who cared about them and accepted this relationship would have to do. Brenda was treating them as if it was the most natural thing in the world, and it was.

Chip returned with Sea Breezes for Charlie and Decky. He placed a cup of steaming coffee in front of Brenda.

"Honey, you drink the coffee, and then after we eat you can have some more booze. Dinner will be ready in fifteen minutes." He went back in the kitchen, reemerging quickly with a plate of thick mahi mahi steaks, heading for the grill.

The three of them chatted about Charlie moving into Decky's cottage. Brenda was so happy to have Charlie back. Decky could tell they had been really good friends long ago.

She thoroughly enjoyed the comfortable way Charlie played straight man to the comedienne Brenda.

Dinner was delicious. Chip had covered the mahi mahi with fresh pineapple rum glaze. Corn on the cob, pasta salad, and fresh tomatoes rounded out the menu. They drank the wine and then some more coffee, talking like two old married couples. This was such a pleasant evening Decky hated to see it end. When Brenda yawned, Charlie excused herself to pack a bag. Nothing had been said, but everyone in attendance just assumed that Charlie was going home with Decky.

Brenda walked Decky out to her car, where she stood outside the driver's side door. Decky remembered to tell her about Lizzie's dinner invitation.

"I was home all day. I wonder why she didn't call and ask me herself."

Decky blushed. "I told her you weren't home."

Brenda chuckled. "Not ready to burn that bridge yet, are we?"

"Shit Brenda, you know Lizzie's going to have a cow."

"I do not envy you that task my dear." Brenda paused. She had something to say. She squatted down in that familiar coach's stance so that she and Decky were eye to eye.

"Before you go coming out to the whole world, you make sure this is what you want. Be careful with your heart, Decky." Brenda reached out and touched Decky on the arm. "Don't misunderstand; nothing would make me happier than to see the two of you together. Charlie is a great girl and I love her dearly. I love you too, so I'm pulling for you. She told me you talked about Lynne. Did she tell you everything? Do you know how low she got before we talked her into moving out here? It got really bad, Decky. Lynne almost killed that woman. I don't know if she's really ready for you."

Decky showed Brenda her dimple. "Oh believe me, she's way beyond ready."

"Be serious, you got your first piece of pussy and you can't be reasonable. You lesbians are all alike, you think like men, with your crotches."

They laughed together.

"No, but seriously, Decky, she's still got some loose ends to tie up back in Louisiana, if you know what I mean. Lynne will be back next week, to bring Charlie's cat. That business is not finished by a long shot. I've seen Lynne in action. She's a piece of work."

"You say she's coming back. Lynne has been here?" Decky's chest tightened.

"I thought you knew that's who Charlie took to the airport Sunday. She helped drive Charlie's car cross-country. I thought Charlie told you."

"She told me what that woman did to her. She said it was over, that Lynne had moved on with some young thing."

"That young thing dumped Lynne the minute she lost her job for screwing her. Lynne came back hat in hand and has been trying to straighten things out with Charlie."

Brenda saw in her face what Decky was thinking. "I'm so sorry darling – "

Brenda cut off her sentence when Charlie came out of the house, travel bag in hand.

"What are you two talking so seriously about?" Charlie edged into the seat beside Decky.

Decky didn't answer her. Brenda rescued her by answering, "Oh, rehab time in the training room at the U, for that ankle. Call me Decky. I'll set up some time for you. You girls be safe going home. Love y'all."

Brenda blew a kiss and backed up the driveway toward the door, watching them leave. Decky cranked the car and pulled away. Charlie put her hand in Decky's lap. Decky couldn't get rid of the lump in her throat. She didn't want to talk. She turned up the music and drove into the darkness. Reba sang, "so you lie, buy a little time, and I go along…"

\#

They made small talk getting into the house. They went upstairs to change clothes. Decky had gone outside onto the deck with Dixie, after slipping into her customary sleeping outfit of tee shirt and gray cotton shorts. She left Charlie upstairs to put her things away and change. She was leaning on the railing drinking a bottle of water when she heard Charlie come out onto the deck behind her.

She turned around to find Charlie in a white knit eyelet-trim chemise. The sun today had made her skin even more golden. Her hair looked like she had run her fingers through it, but it was still disheveled from the ride home in the convertible. As hard as she tried, Decky could not control the pangs of longing. Charlie just kept taking her breath away, over and over.

Charlie smiled up at her and then bent to pet Dixie. If she knew something was wrong she didn't let on. Decky watched, as Dixie was able to get a complete back scratch, by doing her best smile and wag gag. Decky's girls were cooing over each other. Then was Charlie really hers? Why had she not told her Lynne was here, that it really wasn't over between them? That wasn't a small detail you just forget to add to the story. Decky hadn't had a cigarette in fifteen years, but she sure wanted one now.

Decky could hear Charlie's words in her head from earlier. Don't ask questions you don't want the answers to. Since she couldn't think of what to say, she just watched Charlie and Dixie. When she had finished petting Dixie, Charlie approached Decky. She wrapped her arms around Decky's waist, laying her head down on her chest, and hugged Decky to her. Decky kept her elbows on the railing where she was leaning. After a moment, Charlie stepped back.

"What did Brenda say to you? You were fine until you went to the car with her. You haven't said hardly two words since then."

A wave of anger welled up in Decky that she never saw coming.

She answered in a flat voice, "She just filled in a few details you left out of your history. A few pertinent facts, which may or may not directly affect me. I'm just trying to figure out why you thought you had to lie to me." The anger was now clearly evident in her voice. "After all that trust bullshit – –"

Charlie cut her off, "I have never lied to you, ever. Everything I told you is the truth."

Decky laughed with a smirk. "A lie of omission is still a lie. Didn't they teach you that out in Oklahoma?"

"What are you talking about?" Charlie was becoming increasingly defensive.

Decky dug deeper. "Think hard. Don't you think there are a few facts that I should have known going into this?"

Charlie was hurt and she lashed back, "I don't know, you seemed pretty intent on getting me into bed without knowing too many details."

"Well, it wasn't that hard," Decky quipped. She meant for the words to sting and they did.

Charlie took another step back from Decky. "For God's sake, Decky, what did Brenda say to you?"

"Why didn't you tell me Lynne was here, that she's coming back? I was under the impression that you were done with that." Decky had been so angry, she didn't realize she was standing on her busted ankle until a sharp pain shot up her leg. She winced.

Charlie came to her and even though she was angry, Decky let Charlie help her down into a chair. She stood over Decky with her hands on her hips.

"Rule number three: you are not allowed to be angry with me until you have spoken to me about your concerns. You just wasted a lot of energy being mad about something that does not matter to you or me."

Decky was weak from the pain and emotion. She looked up at Charlie. "How can that not matter to us? To me? What if you change your mind? Maybe she comes back into town and says the right things. Where does that leave us?"

Charlie got down on her knees in between Decky's legs. "As God is my witness, I am done with Lynne. You don't have to hit me over the head more than once before I wake up. She made her bed. She can wallow in it for all I care. My bucket is full. I do have to finish dividing up our lives, from the last ten years, but after that, she is a fading memory."

Decky was smiling now.

Charlie looked puzzled, but pleased. "What are you thinking Decky Bradshaw? You look like a Cheshire cat."

"You knew that line was from my favorite book." Decky sat up closer to Charlie.

Taking the cue, Charlie scooted up further into Decky's spread legs. "What line?"

"As God is my witness. That's from Gone with the Wind. Scarlet says 'As God is my witness, I'll never go hungry again.'"

Charlie leaned in and whispered on Decky's lips, "I know what she meant."

They kissed with a passion that unlocked new levels of intimacy between them. They were becoming one. Walls built by life's experiences melted away. Doubts became no more. Decky knew for sure, she would love this woman the rest of her life. No doubt about it.

Later, when they went upstairs to bed, Dixie was already laid up on her pillow waiting for Decky.

"Uh, oh. I forgot to tell her you were staying."

Dixie looked at Decky and then at Charlie.

"Sorry girl, you've lost your spot."

Dixie cocked her head and then slowly got off the bed and into the over-stuffed loveseat across the room.

"She likes you. I guess you can stay," Decky said, pulling back the covers.

Charlie slid into the bed and pulled Decky down on top of her. "Now let me show you what I had in mind when I packed this sexy nightgown."

5

For the next two days, Decky and Charlie played house. They spent part of the time getting the cottage ready for Charlie to move in. Decky called the twins. She needed the cottage cleaned out of furniture and Charlie's things moved from storage to the cottage. She offered prime dollars for the twins to round up all the teenage young bucks to get 'er done.

On Thursday morning, they met the boys at the cottage. There were ten of the county's lanky, deeply tanned, washboard abbed young men sitting on the dock dangling their feet when Decky pulled up in the boat. Charlie had been dropped off at Brenda's to retrieve her car and the things she had left there.

"Howdy boys!" One of the twins, she wasn't sure which, hopped on the boat and threw the bowline to his brother. Decky tossed the stern line to another boy. Dixie, who absolutely loved boys, was out of the boat making the rounds before the lines were tied. She wagged her entire body and smiled as she passed each outstretched hand, then turned back for another pass. Everybody loved Dixie. Decky got out of the boat, with a little help. As Dixie passed her on the way down the dock, running after the boys up ahead, Decky whispered to her, "Slut." Dixie looked at her, grinned, and skipped after the boys.

Most of the boys headed for the U-Haul parked at the base of the steps. Two apparent representatives for the group bracketed Decky on her left and right.

"Decky, man, we can't believe you are renting out the party pad," the one on the right said.

"Yeah, where are we going to hang out now," said the other.

"How about at home? Your parents will appreciate it." Decky grabbed a lawn chair, which one of the boys took as he followed her.

"My mother begs me to find somewhere else to be. She says she has enough to do without having to clean up after a bunch of nasty boys."

"I never cleaned up after you," Decky said, pointing where she wanted the chair.

The shorter of the two boys squeaked out, through adolescent vocal chords in the middle of big changes, "That's because you said we couldn't come back, if we didn't clean up, and take care of your stuff."

"Maybe your mother should try that at home."

The other boys had opened the back door of the truck and were nearing the bottom of the steps where Decky had decided to set up command. Josh, one of Zack's friends, who was older than the rest, stopped at the base of the steps.

"So Zack's gone to Alaska and then off to Boston. It's the end of an era. I sure had some good times here. Who'd you rent it to anyway?"

"A new math professor at the University."

"Well I can tell it's a lady from the stuff we moved. How old is she?"

Decky acted as if she had to think about it. "Thirty-eight, I think."

"Boys, this is a sad day," Josh said to the young men, who were all now listening. "The party pad is being turned over to an old-lady math teacher. Let us bow our heads for a moment of silence."

They all removed the ever-present ball caps and bowed their heads in mock prayer. As if on cue, Charlie entered the property, bumping through the ruts in the lane. She was driving a BMW 335i convertible stuffed with suitcases and some potted plants. She saw Decky, waved and smiled, then brought the car to a halt and got out.

She turned her back to Decky and the now gaping lads. She was wearing an old tee shirt with the sleeves and neck cut out and running shorts. She leaned over into the backseat to retrieve something and an audible gasp came from the crowd. Decky wasn't sure if she had participated, but no one noticed.

"Jesus Christ," one of the boys said.

Another added, "That don't look like no old lady math teacher to me!"

The youngest one said, "Man, I'm going to start studying so I can take Math in college."

Decky was enjoying this. Josh tapped his hand on the stair railing. "Boys, a smart woman, who looks like that and obviously has money is a dangerous thing. Damn exciting, but dangerous."

"Damn she's hot," slipped from somebody's lips.

"Yes, she is," Decky replied and immediately regretted it. The boys all turned to look at her. She tried to cover. "Well, I'm not blind and she is attractive. Now, go on and get that stuff unloaded. I'm paying you by the hour."

Charlie approached the group. She smiled at the boys. "I really thank you all for helping out."

The boys nodded acceptance and continued their work. Charlie stopped by Decky's chair. Dixie, who was now a sopping wet dog, sidled up and rubbed her body against Charlie's leg.

"Hey sweetheart, have you been swimming?"

"She doesn't swim, she wades. Good thing the sound is so shallow."

"I thought retrievers loved the water."

"Dixie is not a retriever, she is a princess. They may look alike, but they are very different breeds."

"And a very pretty princess at that. I see you have made yourself comfortable. You want some water or anything? I think I can find the box with glasses."

"No, I'm fine. There's water in the cooler over there. Hey," she grabbed Charlie's arm in a conspiratorial way, "you can't come up here dressed like that around these boys, not to mention me."

"Dressed like what? It's just an old tee shirt and shorts. I am hot and sweaty."

"Didn't you see the way they were looking at you?"

"Don't be silly, they were looking at the car. I shouldn't have bought it, but I sold the house for much more than I had asked for. It is sexy isn't it?"

"They might think the car is hot, but you are way sexier than that car."

"There is nothing sexy about the way I look."

"Oh, but I beg to differ and there are ten boys running around here that would agree with me."

"My God, you people are hopeless. Is everybody in this county some kind of sex crazed maniac?"

"No, that's just me, the rest are suffering from raging hormones."

"Do I need to go put on my old robe so I can get moved in?"

"No, on second thought, I think your outfit might actually move things along. They'll be up and down those steps so fast, just to get a look at you, we'll have this done in no time."

"Well, I'll keep this little outfit around then, in case I should ever need any heavy lifting. I'm going up now. You coming?" Charlie started up the steps.

"No, I'm going to hang out here with Dixie. I'll come up after the traffic slows down."

Decky waited until Charlie was busy upstairs and then set her plan in motion. Earlier she had arranged for the boys to pick up a new sleigh bed and mattress set from town. When Charlie's old bed came off the truck, she instructed the boys to set the mattresses on the old bonfire pit by the water. The frame, head, and footboards were placed in the aluminum shed, just in case they turned out to be family heirlooms.

She waited until the boys had taken the new bed up to Charlie's room then produced a can of lighter fluid, with which she proceeded to soak the mattresses. She stood poised lighter in hand until the moment Charlie stepped out on the deck.

"Decky, there's been some mistake. This is not my bed in here." Charlie came out on the deck. She began to take in the situation unfolding on the ground below her. "Decky Bradshaw, what in the hell are you doing?"

The boys began to join Charlie on the deck. They did not understand what was going on, but they knew a big fire and possible explosion was imminent. They wanted in.

Decky lit the piece of paper she had been holding and tossed it on the mattresses. With a whoosh, the whole thing went up in flames.

"Charlene Warren, your demons have been exorcised. You may now proceed to a happier life."

The boys were shouting and slapping hands. There's nothing like a fire to a boy, no matter how old he got. Charlie made her way down the steps and over the lawn where Decky stood, just out of reach of the flames.

"You know you are insane don't you?"

Decky grinned. "The voodoo princess said this would help."

"Well, I appreciate your heartfelt efforts on my behalf, however, I gave my old mattresses to Good Will months ago. Those were new."

Decky and Charlie began laughing. The boys laughed too, even though they could not hear what had been said.

The rest of the day went well. By early evening, the U-Haul was gone and everything was in its place except for some boxes here and there. Decky and Charlie were sitting out by the now smoldering mound of mattresses and discarded boxes.

"I know exactly what would make this day perfect," Decky said, smiling at Charlie.

Rubbing her calves, Charlie mumbled, "An elevator."

"Well, that would come in handy later, but right now, how about we roast some marshmallows over these coals and make S'mores."

"I can't believe you burned those mattresses." Charlie giggled.

"It seemed like a good idea at the time." Decky was a little embarrassed.

"I'm just glad you didn't burn up my grandma's headboard." Charlie giggled some more.

Decky pulled the S'more ingredients out of the cooler between them. She had even procured some hangers.

Charlie watched Decky put the marshmallows on the wire. She was tired and could not suppress the giggles. She gasped out, "Well, on the positive side, this is the most expensive bon fire I've ever been to." The giggles took over. Charlie laughed so hard she fell out of her chair.

Dixie came over and started kissing Charlie all over her face, which made Charlie giggle even more.

Decky laughed at the two of them, then said, "Easy there princess, that's my girl."

#

Decky did make it up the steps. When they had finally showered and crawled into bed, they had been too exhausted to do anything but sleep. They woke early. Charlie rushed Decky out the door claiming she would never make it to her meeting if she let her stay. Promising to go straight to Decky's after she finished with school business, Charlie walked Decky and Dixie down to the boat.

Charlie stayed on the dock until Decky was out of sight. Decky knew this because she had turned repeatedly, looking back, a pain in her chest. How long would this pain last? Would she feel it every time she parted from Charlie for the rest of their lives? Would the longing subside? It was going to have to, if she were ever going to get back to all the things she had put aside when Charlie came into her life.

That morning, Decky actually got some work done and even managed to get in a workout. She had been getting a workout, just not in the gym. She grinned to herself. Around noon, she dug around in some old CDs and located a dust-covered case. She looked at Dixie. "Made in 1988. The last time I listened to this I was still in Chapel Hill, I think. I got a feeling it will sound a bit different now."

She popped the CD in the player, turned up the volume and went off to the kitchen with Dixie for a quick lunch. Melissa Etheridge came out loud and clear. "Come on, close your eyes, imagine me there. She's got similar features, with longer hair..." Decky caught herself stool dancing and singing along.

"Yep, I got a whole new perspective on this now."

Dixie barked, putting her paw on Decky's leg. Decky handed over the bread edges she had peeled off. Dixie gobbled them down, checked again for the possibility of more, and then headed outside for her afternoon inspection of the grounds.

Decky took a book, containing some research she was already supposed to have looked at, over to the couch. She tried to read the book, but Melissa wouldn't let her. Decky played little videos in her mind for each song. This wasn't unusual for her. She liked songs that told stories. Reba was one of her favorites. Melissa's stories were not like Reba's at all. In her mind, Decky saw the longing, the pain, the rage, as Melissa poured out her soul. Only the characters in her video were Lynne and Charlie. Decky and Charlie didn't have any pain and angst in their past, so she followed the end of Lynne and Charlie's relationship in vivid color, in her mind.

By the time Melissa sang the last lines of 'Somebody Bring Me Some Water' Decky could take it no more. She used the remote control to change the music to Jimmy Buffet to lighten the mood.

Where is Charlie? When will she be here? Why did Lynne have to bring the cat? Couldn't she to put it in a box and next day air it? Stop talking to yourself. Pick up the book and read.

Decky had to command herself to do something constructive. The book didn't work so she and Dixie went down to the dock and worked on her next plan. The last plan hadn't fared so well, although she had pulled it off in the end with the S'mores. The second thing Decky marked in her book of women's behavior was that they could be bought with chocolate.

Around four o'clock, Decky heard footsteps on the dock, high-heeled steps. Alan Jackson sang "…it's five o'clock somewhere," on the radio, which was perfect because Decky was sprawled out in a lounge chair, fishing pole in one hand, and a Corona with lime in the other. The sun was sinking behind the person coming toward her. Even the sunglasses did not cut the glare. Decky shielded her eyes to see Dixie escorting Charlie down the dock.

Charlie was dressed in a black, summer, sleeveless dress. She wore pearls around her neck, which appeared to glow against her tan skin. The dress was the kind every woman had in her closet, but not every woman looked like Charlie in it. She came straight over to Decky, kicked her black heels under the chair, and planted a big kiss on Decky's forehead. She sat down in Decky's lap, took the beer, and drank it down. Decky still had not said a word.

"Decky, you really have to work on this being stunned by my presence." Charlie looked good and she knew it.

"Well, every time I see you, you look like a different person. You're not like evil triplets or something, are you?"

"Different faces for different places. You'll learn how to adapt." Charlie slid her dress off one shoulder. "God it's hot."

Decky had a bite. The pole shook and then bent as the line was being pulled out. It was the sound of the little reel feeding out line that caught her attention.

"I got a fish on. You want to reel him in?" She handed the rod to Charlie.

Charlie took the rod enthusiastically. "I love to fish. I fished all the time growing up. Wow, this thing is fighting."

"Might be a little bass," Decky said.

Charlie stood up and moved to get a better angle on the fish. She reeled the line quickly against the straining creature.

Suddenly, and as Decky saw it, without warning, Charlie screamed, "BASS, MY ASS!"

What happened next was somewhat of a blur. Charlie came by Decky's chair on a dead run. She still had the pole grasped tightly in her hands. Behind her trailed fishing line with a short fat green eel attached to the end. Dixie hopped behind the eel barking all the way. Every time Charlie turned around, she saw the eel and just ran faster. The stunned eel bumped along the dock behind her as Charlie tore ass for land.

Decky scrambled to her feet, grabbed her crutches, and set out after the two scared animals, not knowing who was more frightened, the eel or Charlie. She called after Charlie, "Drop the pole! Just drop the pole!"

Charlie screamed back, "It's the only weapon I have."

"Stop running, it won't hurt you."

"I know all about eels. I've seen them bite the hands off divers on TV. Remember 'The Deep'!"

"Jacqueline Bisset, wet tee shirt, yes I remember 'The Deep'."

"Not the tits, the eel, you idiot."

Decky had been hustling up the dock, but she was laughing so hard she just fell over. Charlie stopped running. Decky wasn't moving. Charlie carefully placed the rod on the dock and warily made her way back toward Decky and the eel, which was now wrapping itself in fishing line, as Dixie pawed at it. Charlie approached the creature, giving it a wide berth, then sped over to Decky. When she was close enough, she could see Decky's shoulders moving, as if she were sobbing. She bent down and rolled Decky over.

Decky was laughing so hard she couldn't speak. Tears ran down her cheeks.

Charlie hit her on the shoulder. "Damn you. I thought you were hurt."

Decky gasped, "I am. I can't breathe."

"Stop laughing at me. What in the hell is that doing in that water?"

"It lives there. I thought you were a fisherman." Decky was able to take short shallow breaths, but the muscles in her abs were still in spasm.

"They don't have shit that looks like that in the ponds in Oklahoma." Suddenly struck with a realization, she hit Decky on the arm again.

"You let me swim in that water, and I was naked. Oh my God!"

Charlie did a little gross-out dance.

They burst into sheets of laughter, ebbing and subsiding with the memory of their first fishing expedition together. Decky would never forget this moment or this woman.

#

During supper, Charlie's cell phone rang. Charlie looked at the caller I.D. "I have to take this, I'll be right back."

Decky and Dixie finished their plate, they always shared, long before Charlie reentered the room.

"Bet that's cold now. You should put it in the microwave. Cold lobster bisque is not my favorite."

Charlie sat back down. "Oh, I think I've had enough."

"Are you sure? You didn't eat that much. Do you want something else?"

Charlie started clearing the dishes. "No, I don't have much of an appetite, must have eaten too much at the meeting."

Decky knew that was a lie. Nobody eats at those luncheons. *The phone call, you idiot.* Decky finally came to an understanding of what had just happened.

"That was her, wasn't it?"

"Yes."

Decky went to the sink where Charlie was rinsing the dishes and putting them in the washer.

"What did she want?" Decky told herself she wasn't angry, a little jealous maybe. She told herself she only wanted to know what had upset Charlie and how she could fix it. She told herself that she would give Charlie the space she needed to finish this thing. She told herself she wouldn't involve herself in that part of Charlie's life. It was none of her business. It had nothing to do with her. She could tell herself anything. Her heart knew it wasn't true.

"She was checking on the medication dosage for Miss Kitty and finalizing travel plans."

"You don't look like that's all." Decky hated that Charlie wouldn't look at her.

"Really, that's all." Charlie said it, but Decky didn't buy it for a second.

"I don't believe you. You can talk about it. Maybe I can help." Decky reached out and stopped Charlie from placing the next plate in the washer.

Charlie looked up. "Don't you understand, I don't want to talk about it. I don't want to think it over, hash it out – I want it done, finished!" Charlie slammed the plate to the floor.

Decky pushed the door to the washer closed and stepped up to Charlie. "Hey, hey...I'm on your side. Nobody wants Lynne out of your life more than me."

Charlie was angry. She found a broom and dustpan to clean up the glass. As she did this, she talked rapidly. "I don't want you on my side. I don't want you involved in this. You have to promise me to behave while she is here. Just stay out of it, if you know what's good for you."

"Is that some kind of warning or a threat? What am I supposed to do, hide? She is coming here tomorrow, whether I like it or not, and for the record, I don't. You act like this when she calls you on the phone. What will you be like when she's here in person?"

Charlie put the broken plate in the trash. "She just said something that made me angry, that's all. No big deal, okay. Can we please drop it?"

"What did she say? Tell me."

"Can't you leave it be, please?" Charlie was pleading with her now. "I don't want to tell you, isn't that enough?"

Decky persisted, "I thought we discussed lies of omission."

"She said she loved me! There, are you satisfied?"

"And that upset you enough to break a plate? Should I be worried here?"

"Decky, Lynne doesn't know what love is. She is lonely and scared and she wants to run home to momma. Kitchen's closed, momma's moved on."

"Then why did you get so mad?"

"Because she thinks she does. Because she thinks for a second that I could forgive and forget. That right there says she has no clue who I really am. It only proves she never loved me in the first place, because she hasn't the faintest idea what love is."

"Are you mad at Lynne or mad at yourself for falling for it?"

Charlie did not hesitate. "Myself. How could I be such a poor judge of character? How in the hell did I get myself in this mess to begin with? I was young and successful, and then I did the stupidest thing. Somewhere along the line, I lost me."

"I think I found you."

The emotion of the moment beginning to subside, Charlie put her arms around Decky.

"I am so glad you did. I love you, Decky."

"I love you too, and I promise you, I do know what that means."

Charlie smiled up at her. "Prove it."

Decky grinned again. "You sure you don't want me to meet her at the airport, grab the cat, and put her ass back on the next plane out of town? I would do that."

Charlie laughed. "I bet you would."

Decky could see Charlie wanted her to kiss her, but she teased her some more. "Even better, you can call her back and tell her we're sending a private jet for the cat."

"Shut up and kiss me."

Decky did as she was told. She then took Charlie by the hand and led her to the elevator.

"Are you taking me back to the Jacuzzi?" Charlie said playfully

"Well, now that's an idea for later, but first I have a surprise for you."

"It doesn't involve fire does it?"

"Yes, it does but it doesn't involve any of your personal belongings."

Decky lead Charlie out of the house, toward the dock. The evil eel had long since been disposed of, but Charlie walked a little more warily anyway. Decky's ankle was feeling better, the moon and the stars were shining. It was a perfect early June evening.

The water was slick black all around them when Decky finally pulled the boat to a stop and anchored in the middle of Currituck Sound. Charlie sat up a little. "I know you don't expect me to get in that water with you. Not now that I know what lives in there."

"No, this does not involve you getting in the water. Close your eyes."

Decky had made Dixie stay behind. She had whispered to her what was about to happen and Dixie agreed it was best if she stayed on the shore and watched. Decky uncovered a box she had hidden in the front of the boat.

"I'm not sure I like having my eyes closed this long. I mean, I've only known you a few days. This could be the culmination of some psycho horror movie. You know, people screaming at the screen, 'Open your eyes, she has an ax'."

Decky called from the bow, "Don't open them yet, I forgot to sharpen the blade."

Charlie laughed, but kept her eyes shut. Decky worked a minute more and then returned to Charlie. She sat down beside Charlie and pulled her up onto her lap, cradling Charlie in her arms. "You can open your eyes now."

Charlie opened her eyes. She looked at Decky and then all around the boat. "Okay, what's the surprise?"

Decky leaned back and pulled Charlie's head down on her chest so they were both looking up at the stars. "Wait for it."

Just then, the little floating platform Decky had dropped over the side exploded in a torrent of fireworks. They watched the bursts of color erupt in the sky above them. The water around the boat reflected the sky as it exploded time and time again. It was beautiful.

When the fireworks had played out, Charlie turned so she was facing Decky again.

"Decky, you are a dream come true. Do you know that?"

"I want to make all your dreams come true Charlie, every last one of them."

"Well, I do have this dream about making love under the stars in a boat."

Decky took Charlie's chin in her hand. "Your wish is my command."

They fell into the bottom of the boat. They had not made love in fourteen hours, a record for them at this point in their relationship. They tore at each other's clothes frantically. Soon their bodies were bathed in moonlight. The only sounds were heavy breathing and the gentle lapping of the swell from a distant boat on the waterway.

At first, Decky thought she was seeing things. Then she knew she wasn't. A light was shining on the boat and growing brighter. Charlie was involved heavily with one of Decky's breasts when Decky grabbed her by the sides of the head. There was no time to waste.

"Charlie, oh God, somebody's coming. Put your clothes on."

Charlie didn't need to be told twice. She was grabbing clothes before Decky had gotten all the words out. Luckily, they were not heavily clothed to begin with. They both were wearing tee shirts and shorts. Decky couldn't find her underwear, so she just slid the shorts on. As soon as she had the tee shirt over her head, she was up and at the wheel.

Decky could see the approaching boat was much closer than she thought. If she tried to run now it would look strange. Instead, she grabbed a beer out of the cooler, popped the top, and kicked back as if she had not a care in the world. Charlie, finally dressed, slid up onto the seat, and following Decky's lead, grabbed a beer.

Decky saw that the boat was not a game warden or the coast guard. She breathed a sigh of relief. Firework shows were not exactly legal, not without a license, she was sure. Then just as she was about to relax, she saw who it was.

Alan Jr., that's what everyone called him. No one ever said just Alan or even Alan Spencer, Jr., which was his full name. Alan Jr. and Decky had been an item in high school on and off until Decky met Trey. Alan Jr. had taken it hard, but they moved on and went about their separate lives. When Decky had moved back home, Alan Jr. started coming around again.

He was also divorced. They dated a few times, but Decky decided she would rather have him as a friend.

Alan Jr. had a way of popping up at Decky's. He never stayed long. He would say he was just checking up on her. She didn't mind. He had always been a sweetheart, so she figured he was just trying to be nice. Right now though, she wasn't real happy about seeing him.

"Hey, Decky," she heard him call across the water after he shut off his engine and drifted toward them. "I knew that was you when I saw the fireworks. Is everything okay?"

"Yeah Alan Jr., everything's fine. Just having some fun."

Alan Jr.'s boat was now parallel with Decky's. He shined his flashlight on Decky and then moved it over to Charlie, who shielded her eyes. "Who you got there?"

"Alan Jr., this is Charlene Warren. She just moved here. Charlene, this is Alan Jr., an old friend."

Alan Jr. moved the flashlight over the entire boat and back to Decky. He studied her for a minute. "Well, I guess if you are okay, I'll let you get back to whatever you were doing."

"Thanks for checking on me. That was sweet. See you soon."

Decky watched carefully as Alan Jr. started his boat and drove away. When she was sure he could no longer see them, she doubled over laughing. Charlie was laughing too.

"I'm glad you are laughing now," Charlie said, fighting the fit of laughter, "because I hate to tell you this, but I believe I am wearing your underwear and those would be mine hanging off the throttle."

6

Charlie had to leave early the next morning. The airport was an hour and a half away. Miss Kitty's flight arrived at 9:00 a.m. Decky had taken to calling it Miss Kitty's flight, so she wouldn't have to say Lynne's name. Charlie could tell her, as many times as she liked, that it was over between she and Lynne. Decky was going to see for herself soon enough.

Decky had never been this jealous in her life. Even when Trey had betrayed her, she wasn't jealous. She was hurt and angry, but not jealous. The green monster was rearing its ugly head, eating every thought process in Decky's brain. Except the ones focused on the fact the woman she loved was on the way to the airport, to pick up the woman she had once loved. It even sounded complicated.

Decky could only watch as Charlie scurried around the bedroom. Decky was lying propped up on her elbow in the bed. She had on only a sheet draped around her waist. "I wish someone were going with you. It's a long drive."

"With Miss Kitty's case, it would be a tight squeeze for anyone else to ride with us." She checked herself in the mirror and then slid up into the bed beside Decky. She looked deep into Decky eyes. "Don't worry. It will all be over soon and we can go on with our lives."

"Remember when you asked if you could trust me? Well, I'm asking you now. Can I trust you with my heart, Charlie, really trust you?"

"I have fallen completely, madly, inexplicably head over heels in love with you Decky. I have never felt so alive in my life. I see myself rocking on the porch with you when I am old and gray. So, yes, you can trust me today, tomorrow, and the rest of my days, with your heart and soul."

Decky grinned. "I have been a terrible influence on you."

"Why is that?"

"Because you, Dr. Warren, are turning into a shameless, hopeless romantic."

Decky pulled Charlie under her with one swift movement. She kissed her hard on the lips.

"Decky, if we start this now, I'll have to speed to get there on time."

Decky wasn't to be stopped. "I'll pay the ticket."

#

During the morning, Decky and Dixie helped Brenda set up for the big party coming up that evening. This party, the annual Hawaiian luau, had been planned for months and just happened to coincide with Lynne's arrival. Brenda and Decky started calling it Lynne's going away party. The women disliked Lynne, even though neither knew her too well, but they both loved Charlie.

Brenda and Decky were almost the same age, but Brenda had always assumed a motherly role in their relationship. She was like a big sister. Brenda was pulling leis off of Dixie, who was serving as a lei caddy, and hanging them from the branches of a small tree.

"Decky, the only time I have ever seen you lose your temper was when you were protecting a teammate or your son.

You can't protect Charlie. She has to do this on her own. I know little about Lynne, but the little I've seen spells trouble. This is going to get ugly. You have to promise me that no matter what she says or does, you will let Charlie deal with this."

"Charlie told you to talk to me, didn't she?"

"She did call on her way out this morning. She is worried about you." Brenda hung some more luau grass around the deck as she talked. "She doesn't want Lynne to provoke you, she's like that, Lynne, I mean."

"What, like a fist fight? Jesus, are we twelve?" Decky was a lot more at ease than she thought she'd be. She guessed the talk she had with Charlie this morning had relaxed her or maybe it was the sex. "I trust Charlie. She'll do what she has to. It'll be all right."

Brenda looked hard at Decky. "You know Lynne's gorgeous don't you?"

"I've only seen a grainy black and white from the net."

"You can ask Chip. I swear she looks like Angelina Jolie. She's got legs for days and those eyes are unbelievable. All the guys were always so jealous of Charlie. At reunions, they would bet to see who brought the prettiest girl to the party. Charlie won every year, after she started bringing Lynne with her."

Decky was fighting the green monster with all her willpower. "Looks can be deceiving."

Brenda looked impressed with Decky's reaction. Decky thought that maybe she would actually be able to pull this off. She was an actress after all. Brenda walked over to where Decky was setting up the Karaoke machine, a party favorite. Everyone had to perform. The trick was they drew names and you had to sing whatever the person that had your name chose for you. It had always been the highlight of the party for Decky.

Brenda continued their conversation. "Just remember, Charlie is a grown woman and she's been dealing with Lynne for years."

"What do you want me to say, Brenda, that I promise not to get involved? I am involved. You and Charlie seem to forget, I have a stake in this, too."

"I want you to say you'll stay in control no matter what happens."

"Okay, but you're starting to scare me. What in the hell is she going to do, come in here, knock Charlie over the head with a club and take her away? God, I thought I was home free and now you're telling me there are lesbian cavemen, too."

Brenda laughed. "Okay, I will leave you alone, but you have to promise to leave that knight in shining armor complex at home. I guarantee the damsel will take care of herself."

"Well, that's all hooked up. I guess I better go feed my great white steed and put him out to pasture since I won't be needing him tonight."

"Decky, have I ever told you, you are a smart ass?"

"Many times."

#

Decky went home and swam a mile. She had to think. Zack still had to be called. She couldn't let him find out from someone else, and after tonight a lot more people were going to know. Cell phones not only made it easier to keep in touch, it made it easier to gossip. Now with all the new technology she could end up on the Internet, starring at her own worst moment video. She and Charlie could be up on somebody's MySpace before the party was over. The caption would read, "New lesbian discovered in the county."

Then there was Lizzie. Decky had been so focused on Charlie, she hadn't thought too much about her mother. She would be back tomorrow and Decky was going to have to deal with her sooner or later. She decided on later and pushed that issue to the back of her mind. It was easy to do.

Trying not to see Charlie and Lynne together in her mind only made it harder for Decky. There they were in a grainy black and white photograph. She swam harder and faster. What if Lynne got off that plane and Charlie couldn't remember why she was mad at her? Maybe she would sweep her off her feet all over again. It happens every day. People make promises they can't keep. 'I'll never leave you' and 'I will love you forever' were repeated daily, while broken promises came as often.

Decky tried so hard to hear Charlie's words again. She had said "...completely, madly, inexplicably head over heels in love with you Decky." *I have to trust her.* Decky made up her mind. *I have to trust her.* Just keep saying that over and over, Decky told herself. The phrase began to repeat itself in rhythm with her strokes. It pushed her, drove her, until she came out of the lap pool spent and winded.

Dixie met her on the second floor, just in from the morning inspection of the perimeter.

"Everything okay out there soldier?" She played with Dixie for a minute, then Decky fixed some lunch. She took her lunch, some ice bags, and a large bottle of water over to the couch. Propped up with the TV on, Decky tried not to watch the clock. The little voice said, "It's 11 o'clock, do you know where your girlfriend is?"

Dixie was on one end of the couch about to take her midday nap. Decky settled on an old 'Thin Man' movie and hoped the time would fly.

#

Decky was lost in a deep sleep, when she heard Charlie's voice through the fog.

"Decky, wake up, honey."

She smiled through her sleep. She became fully conscious when Charlie kissed her on the lips. She grabbed Charlie, pulling her down on to the couch. She hugged Charlie tight to her body.

"God, I'm glad to see you," Decky whispered into Charlie's ear.

Charlie hugged her back. "Maybe I should go away more often."

Decky pushed Charlie up so she could see her face. "No, never again. Dixie and I don't know what to do with ourselves. By the way, nice guard dog duty there, Princess."

Dixie sniffed the air, got off the couch, came over, and kissed Charlie in the face.

"See, she missed you too."

When the rush of being together again wore off, Charlie asked Decky to come out on the deck, so they could sit at the table. She bought some fresh peaches on the way back, at one of the many roadside stands that lined the highway. She must have stopped for crème too. She brought two bowls out to the table.

After they had eaten a few bites, Charlie spoke up. "I'm going to tell you what happened so you don't have to wonder. Just let me tell it, no questions. I promise to tell you everything. I just don't want to analyze it."

Decky heard *"you have to trust her"* echo through her brain. "I trust you Charlie." It was the right thing to say.

Charlie told Decky how she had gotten to the airport a little late, thanks to her. She found Miss Kitty and Lynne waiting on the curb. Lynne was hungry, so they stopped on the way back at a burger joint and ate in the car, because of the cat. Charlie told Lynne about Decky. She said it was absolutely liberating. Lynne seemed to take it okay, but Charlie wasn't sure, because Lynne had been very quiet after that. She had surprised Lynne by dropping her off at a bed and breakfast just up the road, instead of Brenda's. Lynne would be attending the party tonight. Brenda would be sending someone for her later.

"And that's it," Charlie was winding down. "I took Miss Kitty to her new house. Once I had her settled, I flew over here to find you passed out with the dog, on the couch."

"That's it then. I'm proud of you. You sound like you handled it as well as could be expected." Decky was jumping up and down inside, but tried to play it cool. The green monster was cowering in the corner. *That's my girl!*

#

Charlie didn't have a Hawaiian shirt she could lay her hands on before the party. Decky explained that this was mandatory, so they drove down to the Cotton Gin and bought complementary colored shirts. Decky, always the consummate scene designer, wanted them to look good together, not match but not clash either. Decky chose a tropical flower theme of bright greens, yellows, and reds on a dark blue background for herself. For Charlie, they chose a red background with flowers of green, yellow, and blue.

They had gone into the dressing room together to try on the shirts. They stood and looked at themselves in the mirror.

"That looks great on you," Charlie was studying Decky. "That blue really sets off your eyes."

"So far I haven't seen anything that looks bad on or off of you." Decky giggled. Here they were doing what women did every day, trying on clothes together. No one thought twice when they went in the dressing room together. Decky found it exhilarated her to be in public, sneaking a look or a slight brush of the other's skin. She had almost grabbed Charlie's hand on the way in. Charlie, ever on the lookout, had admonished her with her eyes and mouthed, "Behave," to Decky when no one was looking.

Here alone in this room Decky was overcome with the urge to kiss Charlie. She did. It was thrilling being bad, if this was bad, it felt pretty good to Decky. Charlie cooperated for a minute or two, and then she pushed Decky back.

"I told you to behave. Come on, we'll be late."

Decky tweaked one of Charlie's nipples. "I don't mind being late, we can make an entrance."

"Stop that," Charlie said, as she slapped Decky's hand away playfully. "Oh, I feel quite sure that our entrance will be noted by all in attendance, no matter what time we get there."

Decky started unbuttoning the shirt Charlie had been trying on. Charlie resisted until Decky ran her finger down the middle of Charlie's chest, following a line down to the button on her pants. Charlie was now under Decky's spell. She started unbuttoning Decky's shirt. Decky, who had been enjoying undressing Charlie, suddenly realized that the tide was turning and Charlie now had her in a panic.

She grabbed Charlie's hands. "You can't do that."

"Why not?" Charlie asked.

"You know exactly why not. It's too much. I might not be able to control myself. We might start banging around on the walls in here. I don't know what will happen, but I do know you cannot do that."

"So, I see you can drive me crazy, but I am not allowed to do that to you." She tickled Decky's chest with one of her fingers that Decky did not have in a death grip.

Decky squirmed under her touch. "Okay, okay, I will behave."

"I thought you might see it my way, if you knew what you were doing to me. It's not that I don't want to play these little games with you. It's the fact that I can't control myself either. So, behave yourself and we'll go back to the house and take care of this problem."

"I'll behave, I swear. Just back up."

#

Decky got dressed at her house and then they went to check on Miss Kitty and for Charlie to dress. Dixie was not impressed with the little scrawny black and white cat. It obviously had no social skills. Whenever Dixie tried to smell of it, it would grow to twice its normal size. It had even spit at her. Finding that following the creature through the house became tedious, she plopped down on the rug and caught a quick nap.

At 8:15, Decky put the Expedition in park, on the road leading to Brenda's house. There were already so many people there, she had to park about fifty yards from the driveway. Dixie, who was sitting on the backseat, sprang up on all fours. She wagged her tail and looked out the window. Oh, how she did love parties. All those hands to worship the princess, not to mention the food.

Charlie looked at Dixie's excited expression. "Well, I see somebody is ready for a party. I love the bandana, nice touch." Decky hated it when people put clothes on dogs, but several years ago, she had made Dixie a bandana out of an old Hawaiian print shirt.

"Yeah, ol' Dix here is a party animal. You should see her dance."

Decky had her hand on the door handle about to open it, when Charlie placed her hand on her other arm. "Wait a minute, before we go in."

Decky turned and patted Charlie's hand. "Are you all right with this? We don't have to go in, although I think Dixie might be disappointed."

"This is not about me. This is about you, Decky. Those people may have thought you were gay before, but there's a big difference in thinking you know something, and seeing the proof. There won't be any doubt when we walk in there, not in anybody's mind. So, you make sure you are really ready to take this step. There will be no turning back."

Decky scoffed at her. "These people have known me forever. They're not going to change the way they feel about me, one way or the other, just because now I'm with you."

"I've been there and you are kidding yourself. Not all your straight friends, who accept others as gay, will treat you the same. Some will feel betrayed by you. Beware of the 'did you ever think about me that way' question. It is a double-edged sword. If you assure them that you never felt that way about them, then they get upset because you didn't find them attractive or some stupid thing like that."

Decky listened with a slight smile. Charlie was trying to protect her. It was really sweet.

Charlie kept going, "Then there are the gay friends that tell you they've always known something about you that you are positive you did not know yourself. Or they'll start hitting on you the moment you walk in the door."

Decky was grinning. "Those broads in there have been hitting on me for years, so that's nothing new."

"Yeah, but now they think they might actually have a chance."

"Sorry, I am spoken for, aren't I?" Decky teased.

"All right baby girl, welcome to the new world."

Decky leaned over for a kiss, but was thwarted by a large golden head and brown nose. There would be none of that. Dixie was grunting and pawing at Decky.

"Okay, we better go in. The party princess is getting the urge to get her groove on."

Decky followed behind Charlie and Dixie, making their way to the door. She was thinking with all the other things that could go wrong at this party, Charlie's thoughts had been of her. Charlie was headed into a party among mostly strangers, where she would be introducing her new lover to her old lover, who didn't seem to be too happy about it. Chapters were closing for Charlie and new ones were being written every day. That she cared more about how Decky would survive this mess, said a lot about the kind of woman she really was.

That's a fine lady you've found there. You hang on for dear life. She is worth fighting for.

Decky's little voice had even fallen in love with Charlie, too.

Dixie led the way through the groups of people scattered about the house on the way to the backyard. Charlie had been right. People were looking at her differently. Knowing smiles were exchanged, as one gay woman after another gave her a silent nod of approval, a welcome to the club look. Jesus, did Brenda broadcast this on a loudspeaker at the ballpark? She had forgotten to check for the red flashing sign's appearance on her brow before getting out of the car. The damn thing must have been as bright as Rudolph's nose or the lesbian hotline had gone on high alert. She wondered who had brought the toaster for Charlie.

She also observed a different attitude from the hunk when she passed him in the kitchen on the way out, as he was coming in from outside. He looked Charlie up and down, not inconspicuously, but being sure Decky saw him. He looked at

Decky and smirked. Okay, chalk up one for the people who weren't going to play nice. As she passed him, she leaned in and whispered so only he could hear, "You can look, but don't touch." As soon as she said it, she was astounded at herself. Was she angry because he judged her or because he looked at Charlie that way?

Before she had a chance to answer herself, Brenda appeared, making a big fuss and drawing even more attention to them. The way Brenda was acting, and due to the fact that she had pulled Charlie close and whispered something in her ear, she knew the meeting was imminent. Charlie nodded and looked back to where the grill was positioned in the yard. There, surrounded by men and women alike, was Angelina. At least it sure looked like it from where Decky stood.

The men were obviously attracted and the young lesbians were practically drooling. The older lesbians and straight folks however were starting to point at Decky and then over to Lynne. The ones that didn't know what was happening were quickly caught up. Decky unconsciously reached for Charlie's hand. It wasn't there.

Charlie was walking out ahead of her, heading straight for Lynne. Charlie strode confidently through all the prying eyes. If Decky hadn't been so focused on the green monster that just seized her heart, she would have admired Charlie's audacity. Charlie knew full well these people were watching her. She knew they wanted drama and expected it. She was showing them how a lady handles situations like this.

Brenda showed up with a Margarita. "Here drink this and stop staring. You look dumbstruck, not your best look by the way."

Decky took a big drink, but her eyes never left the scene unfolding in front of her. Although Brenda had told Decky to stop staring, she too was fully involved in surveillance of the situation. Dixie had followed Charlie, not because she necessarily wanted to see what Charlie was doing, she smelled grilling beef. When Charlie stopped in front of Chip to accept a kiss on the cheek, Dixie stepped between Lynne and Charlie.

Brenda whispered over the rim of her Margarita, "Good dog."

Lynne leaned down and patted Dixie on the butt. Dixie responded by doing her best princess wag. Decky said under her breath, turning to Brenda, "Shit, she's touching my dog."

Brenda had not stopped watching Lynne. "Better yet, now she's kissing your girlfriend."

Decky's head snapped back around so fast she heard her neck pop. Lynne had followed Chip's lead and was now leaning down to apply a kiss on Charlie's cheek. Decky flushed fire red. She knew it too.

Brenda was looking at her. "Breathe honey, deep cleansing breaths." She demonstrated the process for Decky.

Lynne had Charlie's hand in hers and she was smiling down at her. She laughed at something Charlie said and patted the dog again. Decky spit out, "Traitor!"

"Who, Charlie or the dog?"

Brenda was enjoying this a little more than she should have been, in Decky's estimation. It was obvious for whom she was pulling, but Brenda did take pleasure in a little drama now and then, drama that was about to happen, because Charlie and Lynne were heading straight for them. Charlie was leading Lynne through the crowd. Lynne reached and caught Charlie's hand as if afraid she'd get lost without touching her. Decky thought differently. Lynne was making her play right here, right now.

A dog trainer would call this posturing or signs of dominant behavior, the way male dogs mark their territory and possessions. The voice in Decky's head screamed in a jealous rage, *"Mine! Mine!"* Decky turned up the Margarita glass and slammed the rest down her throat. She handed the empty glass to Brenda, saying, "I think we're going to have to switch to shots if this keeps up."

"I think you are probably right." Brenda didn't wait for Charlie and Lynne to make it all the way to where Decky was standing. She immediately went towards the bar behind them. This left Decky standing alone propped up on crutches at one end of the deck. The crowd parted like the Red Sea and quieted. Brenda popped back up beside Decky. She handed her a double shot of tequila with a lime wedge on the rim. Decky took the lime wedge out, swallowed the entire contents, and dropped the wedge back in the glass.

"I think I'm going to need another."

Brenda took the glass, but didn't move. She just handed Decky the shot glass she had brought for herself and had not yet consumed. This was too good. No way was Brenda going to miss this.

Decky caught Darlene and Brandi out of the corner of her eye. They were staring wide-eyed, mouths open, in utter silence. Decky had thought about what she was going to say, but right this minute she had no words, none at all. Her brain was mush. The green monster was having a party.

Charlie was close enough for eye contact now and she was boring a hole in Decky. She was sending Decky subliminal messages with the crease in her forehead, but Decky couldn't make it out. Was it sorry, made a mistake or hang in there, we're almost done?

The expression on Charlie's face changed. She looked like a woman who had made up her mind. Decky hoped she'd like the decision. In one stride with a little turn at the end, Charlie pulled out of Lynne's hand, stepped up beside Decky, and looped her arm around the crutch and into the crook of her elbow.

"Decky, this is Lynne Haskins. Lynne, I would like you to meet Decky Bradshaw."

Lynne smiled easily. Ooo, she was good. No strain on her face, nothing to indicate she was uncomfortable, but Decky knew better. Lynne was an actress, nothing more, nothing less. Decky had seen her kind before. Her momma always says, "Pretty is, as pretty does." In that case, this was ugly and about to get horrific. Decky could see it, even if no one else could.

This woman was a knock out. "Absolutely gorgeous," as Brenda had said. Decky had to agree, but Lynne had the quality of a Bond woman. Decky knew, sooner or later, Lynne would try to stab her in the back. Lynne had made up her mind to fight for Charlie. The eyes gave her away. No, this woman was not going softly into that good night. Decky gripped her crutches tightly.

In a voice just as smoky as her body, Lynne spoke to Decky, "I'd shake your hand, but you look like you need them. Hurt your ankle?"

Decky had to resist the Bill Engvall implications of the situation. Her ankle was black, blue, and a few other colors. She was not wearing shoes because it was so swollen; obviously, her ankle was the problem. *No, I just like to rest my feet from time to time. Here's your sign, bitch.*

"Yeah, just a sprain." Decky's manners took over, "It's a pleasure to meet you."

Charlie must have been pleased, because she squeezed Decky's arm ever so slightly. Okay, point one for me, Decky thought.

Brenda chimed in, just as she was headed back to the bar for more shots, "Bet you two have a lot in common."

Charlie followed Brenda with her eyes and gave her a look that caused Brenda to respond, in mock innocence, "What? Softball. What did you think I meant?"

Decky suppressed a nervous laugh. Charlie pinched her arm. Good ol' Brenda, always there to break up any seriousness at parties.

"Oh, do you coach? I'm sorry, I don't know much about you. Charlie didn't have time to fill in the details." Lynne still had the sickly sweet smile on her face.

Fire one. Not much of a shot in Decky's book. *Yeah, dumbass, I got this ankle tripping over my clipboard.* She said only, "No, I play."

Charlie beamed with pride adding, "Decky is a writer."

"Oh, really? How exciting." Lynne was pouring on the charm. "Are you famous? Should I have known your name?"

Charlie didn't give Decky a chance to answer. "Hollywood is making a movie out of her second novel."

Decky could see that Charlie was enjoying showing off her new girl and it made her warm inside, or the tequila just hit bottom. Brenda appeared with a tray filled with shot glasses, a saucer of salt, and a bowl of lime wedges.

"Yes, Decky here is our resident celebrity. You should see her house. She designed it herself." Brenda was laying it on thick. "I can't wait to sell her story to the tabloids when the movie comes out. Speaking of coming out, when will we see the next best seller?"

All the flattery embarrassed Decky, but she appreciated that Charlie and Brenda were telling Lynne what she was up against.

Being a washed up coach and potential fast food manager doesn't look so good now, does it, pretty girl?

Decky answered Brenda's question, "Well, with Charlie around, I haven't been doing much writing. Soon, I hope."

"Shots anyone?" Brenda presented the tray.

Charlie waved her off. Decky saw an opening and went for it. She fished around in her pocket and handed Charlie her keys. "I guess you're driving home, honey." Decky then took another shooter and downed it on the spot.

Lynne followed suit.

"Now, we party," Brenda yelled out.

The once gawking crowd, a little disappointed at no bloodshed, responded to Brenda's declarations with whoops and hollers and quickly went back to partying. They assumed the worst was over. Decky, however, was wary. This wasn't over by a long shot.

#

The party moved on into the evening. Chip had rescued Decky and Charlie from Lynne, by taking Lynne away to look at his grass. To Decky's relief, Lynne did not return to the group she and Charlie were sitting with. She was able to relax, but kept a watchful eye out for the intruder. For that's what Lynne was doing, intruding on Decky's new life.

Brenda continued to stop by frequently with fresh shots. Decky was not a big drinker. In fact, she and Charlie had consumed more alcohol in a week than she had in the previous months. However, there had been a time in her life when she could set 'em up and knock 'em down with the best of them. She was beginning to feel no pain when the CD player sang out, "Now, I've had the time of my life..." from Dirty Dancing. Couples of all shapes and sizes started dancing. Decky asked Charlie to dance.

"You can't dance on those crutches and I can't dance period."

Decky was buzzed no doubt. She stood up, grabbed a crutch with one hand and Charlie's hand with the other. "You forget I've danced with you once already."

Charlie resisted. "But that was in private."

"Close your eyes and pretend they aren't here." Decky indicated the crowd.

Charlie gave in. Decky placed her arm in the small of Charlie's back, pulled her close, and began to sway to the music. The song soon sped up, but the two of them kept slow dancing. All around them, dancers showed off their best dirty dancing moves. It didn't matter to Decky and Charlie. They had a rhythm of their own.

The song ended and they started back to their seats. The next song started. This time it was a slow love song, Faith Hill singing "Breathe." Decky loved that song, but she had to sit down. Lynne appeared out of nowhere.

"They're playing our song. One last dance for old time's sake?" She was moving Charlie toward the dance floor before Charlie could respond.

Brenda arrived just in time to see what had happened. She sat down in Charlie's chair. "Well damn, if she isn't a piece of work." She handed Decky another shot.

"Charlie could have said no." Decky slammed the shot and grabbed another off the tray in Brenda's lap.

"No, she couldn't. I saw that bitch swoop down on her. The poor girl didn't have a chance."

Decky sat up a little straighter. "Damn I loved that song. Now, it's ruined. I'll see this every time I hear it. Tonight Faith takes a flying leap off the deck as soon as I get home."

Lynne wasn't so much dancing with Charlie as she was mauling her, at least from Decky's perspective. Lynne was caressing Charlie's back and pulling her in tighter and tighter.

She seemed to be whispering in Charlie's ear. Decky drank the shot in her hand, but this time Brenda pulled the tray away.

"No, that's enough. If you want more, you have to eat. You are drunk, I can tell, and you are getting angry. Just relax. Lynne is making her last play. Two outs, bases loaded, one strike left. Charlie's got game. She can take her."

Then without warning, Charlie pushed Lynne off her. She turned toward Decky, but before she could take a step, Lynne grabbed her and spun her around. Decky was coming out of the chair, when Lynne tried to kiss Charlie. Brenda grabbed Decky's arm and pulled her back down in the chair, saying, "Sit! Wait for it. Here it comes."

Charlie tore away from Lynne. By this time, everybody was watching. Once she had sufficient space between them, she shouted, "Stop it! You're drunk." She was furious. Charlie turned on her heel and came back to Decky. Since Brenda was in Charlie's chair, Charlie sat down on Decky's lap.

Decky put her arms around Charlie, who was vibrating with anger. "Are you okay? Do you want to leave?"

"No, I want to do this." She put both hands on Decky's face, pulled her to her, and kissed her so hard it hurt, right in front of God and everybody.

Decky emerged from the kiss breathless and grinning. The crowd roared approval and Lynne exited into the house. Three or four women took off after her, no doubt in search of some 'sympathy' sex. Decky couldn't care less. She had everything she ever wanted right there in her lap, and unlike Lynne, she would never let her go.

Somebody shouted, "Karaoke!"

Brenda jumped up, almost upsetting the tray. "Let's draw some names."

Everybody started cheering and rearranging furniture. The dance floor became the stage. Charlie grabbed some food for the two of them and they ate, while the preparations were made.

Charlie sat in Decky's lap with her arms draped around Decky's shoulders. Once all the names had been drawn, each person picked a song for the person whose name they had drawn. This was hysterically funny as various participants slaughtered song after song. Brenda's rendition of 'Fancy' nearly brought the house down. Then it was Decky's turn. The crowd started chanting, "DECKY. DECKY."

Charlie, who had no idea what was happening, looked at Decky. "I think your fans are calling you." She stood up so that Decky could take her place on stage. Brenda assumed M. C. duties.

"Ladies and gentlemen, the club BC presents to you, live and on crutches...we've seen that before haven't we?" There was agreement from the crowd. "...anyway, making her first appearance since crossing over to the dark side..."

The crowd erupted in catcalls and whistles. Decky accepted the ribbing by bowing to the crowd.

"Settle down girls. I hear Decky's been looking for the toaster, so whoever brought it please give it to her before she leaves."

The young lesbian, who sat down by Charlie in the empty chair, said, "I don't get it, what does that mean?"

Charlie didn't take her eyes off Decky. Decky knew this, because every time she glanced at Charlie she was beaming up at her. Decky was definitely in her element. She had a performer's presence, an electricity that attracted an audience. Decky was just as attracted to the audience and played to them while Brenda went on.

"Wait, we have an innocent here. Would one of you please teach this child some lesbian history? Honey, do you know about Ellen coming out on TV? She's shaking her head no…oh, dear Lord, I'm not a lesbian and at least I watched the show."

Ripples of laughter filtered through the crowd. Decky talked to Darlene and Brandi, who would serve as the backup vocalists. Decky figured they must be back together, because Brandi had the nose ring back in. Brenda went on.

"I drew Decky's name and have chosen a selection I think you will like. You all know Decky's mother, right?

Someone shouted, "Good luck with that!" Charlie cringed.

"I have suggested she just sing this song to ol' Lizzie, so here she is the one and only, and I do mean only because the rest of us suck. Especially you Katie, yes you the girl in the yellow, oh honey don't quit your day job." Brenda backed away from the front of the stage. "Miss Decky Bradshaw, with backup vocals from Darlene and Brandi. Here they are with a new rendition of the Judd's hit, 'Mama He's Crazy'."

The music started. Decky took the microphone and began to sing, playing to the audience, but mostly singing to Charlie. There were whistles and calls from the crowd. Decky circled Charlie's chair, drawing her into the scene. Decky could no longer feel her ankle so she had dispensed with the crutches. Charlie watched Decky's every move. She evidently liked what she saw. Decky played to her more and more as the song went on.

Decky finished the song on her knees at Charlie's feet with a huge grin. The crowd erupted. Charlie beamed at Decky, then kissed and hugged her. She whispered to Decky, "You can really sing. I mean really sing."

"I was truly inspired." Decky kissed Charlie. She pulled her closer and said softly, "Hey, Charlie?"

"Yes."

"Can I ask you something?" They were still embracing.

"Anything?"

"Could you help me get up off this floor, I think the tequila is wearing off."

Charlie laughed and with help from Brenda they got Decky back to her feet. Decky really had to go to the bathroom. Grabbing her crutches, she told Charlie to stay there with Brenda and she would be right back.

There was someone in the closest bathroom, so she made her way to the back of the house to use the one at the end of the hall. When Decky came out of the bathroom, Lynne was waiting in the darkened hallway.

"So you think you're in love with Charlie?"

Decky was drunk and in pain. She really didn't want a confrontation, but here it was.

"Yes, I'm in love with Charlie."

"I understand that this is the first woman you've ever been with. How do you know this isn't just your first affair?"

"Lynne, you don't know me, so I'll just say that affair is a term you are much more familiar with than I am. I'm not like you, not at all, maybe that's why she's with me and not you." Decky was getting warm in the face.

"Charlie's been with you what, six days? You're going to stand there and compare that to ten years. You don't know her."

"Evidently you don't or you would know she has no intention of being made a fool of ever again."

Lynne smirked at Decky. "Do you have any idea how many times she's said that in ten years? Plenty. She never stayed gone long."

"Would you listen to yourself? You tore her down and took away her self-confidence. You hurt her and you act as if you forgot to take the trash out or something. Jesus, you are a self-centered bitch, as far as I can tell. She is much better off without you."

Decky thought she saw someone at the end of the hall. She looked around Lynne to see who it was. It was Brandi. Brandi appeared to size up the situation, then turned tail and ran.

"I won't give up without a fight." Lynne wasn't threatening, more like menacing.

"She's worth fighting for. Have you thought that if you had put this much effort into your relationship, we wouldn't be standing here having this conversation?"

Decky saw Charlie at the end of the hallway. Lynne had her back turned and didn't see her. Charlie started toward them, but when Lynne started to speak, she stopped and listened.

"What the hell do you know about my relationship with Charlie? All you know is you got your first piece of ass. This too shall pass. Remember, I have been with Charlie for ten years. I know that when all the emotion of this – whatever you two are doing – blows over, she'll freeze up on you like an iceberg. Why do you think I slept around on her? So when you're done with the frigid bitch, just send her home. I think I can take it from there."

Decky didn't think. There was no time. She balled up her fist and knocked the living shit out of Lynne. Lynne flew backwards off her feet, landing with a thud. Blood started spurting from her face. "I think you broke my fuckin' nose!"

Decky stepped forward and placed the one remaining crutch on Lynne's chest, holding her down. She had forgotten Charlie was standing there. Decky glared down at Lynne with mother bear ferociousness. "If you ever come near her again, your nose won't be the only thing broken. Do you understand? Whether she is with me or not, she sure deserves better than you, you arrogant ass."

A noise from the hall broke the spell Decky was under. She looked up, but never took the crutch off Lynne's chest. She saw Charlie, who looked so stunned she might pass out, surrounded by Brenda and twenty or so of the biggest women at the party. It appeared Brandi had sounded the alarm loud and long.

Decky casually removed the crutch from Lynne's chest. "Brenda, I think your guest has had too much to drink and I do believe she is bleeding on your new carpet."

"Oh, hell. Damn it, girls get in there and get her off my carpet. Take her out in the front yard. Take her home. Who gives a damn? Just get her out of here."

Decky thought she actually saw a few of the lesbians' eyes brighten. Brenda was right, they did think with their crotches.

Decky moved out of the way, while the still bleeding Lynne was helped off the floor. As they took her past Charlie, Lynne said through bloody hands, "Do you see what she did to me? She's a maniac. I didn't do anything."

Charlie looked hard at Lynne. "I heard what you said."

Lynne countered, "What, what did you hear?"

Charlie simply said, "Enough."

Lynne was not to be thwarted. "Come on Charlie, you know I didn't mean it."

Brandi pushed Lynne toward the front door. "Oh, would you just shut the fuck up."

Bloodshed over, the remaining onlookers left Charlie and Decky alone in the hallway. Decky was leaning against the wall, trying to hold her ankle off the floor. She had stepped full force into that punch right down on her ankle. She looked at Charlie who had tears in her eyes.

"I'm sorry. I don't know what happened. One minute I was standing there trying to reason with her, and then I just lost it. I really am sorry. Please don't be mad."

"All my life, I waited for a knight in shining armor just like in the picture books we read as girls, but I thought after my honor had been restored, I would be carried off on a white horse. Who knew it would be a woman with one bad leg and no horse?"

"I'll buy you a horse." Decky was beginning to grin now, her dimple showing.

"I don't want a horse, but two legs would be nice. I mean, I would like to be carried to bed sometime."

Decky started hopping for her other crutch. "We have to leave, now! Come on Dixie."

Dixie too had heard the alarm sounded, and had left her pile of rib bones to stand with Charlie when the whole thing had gone down.

Charlie was startled. "Why, what's wrong?"

Decky bent down and grabbed the other crutch. When she looked up, she was smiling broadly. "Nothing's wrong, I just have to start rehabbing this ankle right away."

Charlie sighed with relief, when she realized Decky was teasing her. "What's your hurry?"

"I have this lady friend and I promised to make all her dreams come true. She wants to be carried to bed, so I have to get my feet back under me, and there's no time to lose."

Charlie slid under Decky's shoulder to help her walk. "Right now, I'd settle for an elevator ride."

PART II

Hurricane Lizzie

…don't be fooled by the eye of the storm.

7

Decky and Charlie slept late. When Decky tried to sit up, she immediately fell back into her pillow. She grabbed the sides of her head, afraid the contents might burst out of her eyes if she opened them. Her movements awakened Charlie and Dixie. She could feel Charlie moving beside her and she could hear Dixie doing her morning, "I need to go out," tap dance beside the bed. Both activities were normally unobtrusive, but this morning was quite different. With every movement of Charlie's body, Decky's brain slammed into the sides of her skull, and the tapping sounded like the opening of 42nd Street with the volume on max.

"Oh, Jesus." She wasn't just saying it. Decky was really calling on anyone who could make the throbbing stop. She pulled her knees up and recalled quite suddenly that her ankle felt like a swollen eggplant and looked a lot like one, too. When she put her legs back down too quickly, the movement reverberated through her body, multiplying her symptoms.

"Morning, Sugar Ray," Charlie said into Decky's chest, as she lightly laid her head down, giving Decky a soft squeeze.

Decky only moaned and rolled her head on the pillow, still with palms pressed tightly against her temples. The rolling caused another moan, this one longer and louder.

Charlie was now just inches from her face, coming in for closer inspection of her potential patient. Decky knew this because she could hear Charlie's breathing over her.

"It could be worse, Decky. You could have eaten the worm." She was enjoying this.

Decky pleaded with a hoarse, dry voice, "Oh, please don't make me laugh, it might kill me."

"Open your eyes."

"I can't, my eyes might pop out from the pressure," Decky refused.

Charlie ran her finger along the knuckles on Decky's right hand. The image of Lynne's face, when Decky swung at her, popped on the viewer in Decky's head. Then the hit and follow-through came fast, as Charlie pressed on her swollen knuckles. Decky saw it over and over in her mind in rapid succession.

"I think you bruised your knuckles, can you move your fingers?" Charlie said, while trying to pry Decky's hand away from her head.

Decky wiggled the fingers of her right hand. "Don't pull it off. It's the only thing keeping my brain inside."

"Stay right here. I'll go get something to make you feel better." Charlie scooted off the bed.

"Easy, easy. Don't shake the bed too much." Decky dropped her hands to settle the bed, then remembering her head, quickly returned them to their previous position.

She assumed Charlie left, because she could hear Dixie's claws clicking, descending the stairs. How she had gotten into this condition played out in her mind. Some of it was a little hazy and after Charlie put her in the car to go home was a complete mystery. She had no idea how she got upstairs or where her clothes were. Taking a chance, she squinted, opening one eye.

When her brain didn't explode, she slowly opened both eyes and stared at the ceiling. Her eyes crawled around the room and settled on the painting above the staircase. It was painted to appear as though the stairs continued indefinitely into darkness. Decky longed to mount the stairs and start climbing. She had punched a woman in front of God knows how many people. Everyone in the county would know all the gory details by Sunday evening, excluding the facts, to be determined later.

Lizzie was due back, so today would be the day the shit hit the fan, she was sure. It would take a skilled gossip like Lizzie an hour, at the most, to catch wind of this. Maybe she could avoid a confrontation by hiding at Charlie's house. She definitely had to call Zack. She knew he was going to be fine with the Charlie part of the equation, but finding out from one of his friends about his mom punching someone, would not make him happy.

Her relationship with Zack was built on trust and personal responsibility. He was required to be responsible for his own actions, own up to mistakes and poor decision-making, and never lie to his mother. He expected the same from his mom. It had been just the two of them, so she had to be father, mother, and best friend. They had to look out for each other and be responsible with each other's dreams and fears. She had to be accountable now. She owed him that, he was such a cool young man.

They were due for their weekly phone call this evening, but she was afraid to wait. She may have seen a cell phone or two in the crowd of onlookers at the end of the hall. There could be pictures. The throbbing in her brain was subsiding slightly. She tried to sit up again and was pleased to actually make it this time. Her ankle stuck out from under the sheet. The gold sheets accented the shades of deep purple, green, and blue displayed on her skin.

She looked at her knuckles and massaged them. Decky may have been embarrassed to have such a personal incident happen in front of so many people. She wasn't, however, sorry. Charlie had not been mad at her for losing her temper. In fact, she had been pleased at her hero knight. Something about buying Charlie a horse flashed in her mind.

Decky found the crutches propped on the wall beside the bed. She didn't remember putting them there, but she was glad they were. She went to the bathroom, brushed her teeth, and washed her face. She was back in the bed by the time Charlie returned with a bed tray, which she set down in front of Decky.

"I know it doesn't look like much, but in my experience it has worked well. First, I want you to take this Zantac and Advil with ice water. Then you are going to eat at least one piece of dry toast with this small glass of orange juice. You have to be careful with the juice. You get too much acid in your stomach and we're right back where we started."

Decky followed Charlie's instructions as they were being given.

Charlie continued, "After you finish the toast, you can have a pop if you like. You need to get up and sit out on the deck. You need to replenish your fluid, sugar, and oxygen levels in order to come back from a bout with Jose Cuervo. Been there, done that."

Dixie jumped up on the bed with the Sunday News and Observer in her mouth. She had been doing this routine on her own since discovering that if the paper came in the house, food would soon be served. It was a Sunday morning ritual she enjoyed immensely, sitting for hours, looking at the paper, munching on a long glorious breakfast. She had waited downstairs, but when she didn't smell bacon, she had gone in search of answers.

Decky, who had been munching on dry toast as instructed, took a sip of orange juice and said, "Okay, if we're going to sit on the deck, you have to do three things."

Charlie had taken the paper from Dixie and hugged her. "Good girl." Dixie smiled and did the princess wag. She had fallen in love with Charlie, too.

Charlie gave her attention back to Decky. "Okay, what three things?"

"First, I really would prefer to do it fully clothed and second, I'm going to need sunglasses, dark ones."

Charlie laughed. "Okay, that's reasonable. What's the third thing? I know it's not sex, because that might kill you."

"You have to cook the newspaper delivery girl some bacon.

#

Decky called Zack from her cell phone, after getting settled on the deck. Charlie took the princess down to prepare her breakfast, only after admonishing Decky for feeding the dog outside of standard veterinary recommendations. The conversation with Zack had gone well. She was sure he would have questions later, but he was the kind of kid who mulled things over for a while before making decisions. She had not asked him, nor had he offered to speak to Charlie. Decky thought he should meet her in person, so Charlie and Decky would fly up to Alaska later this month.

Charlie brought eggs and bacon with more toast and offered Decky a Dr. Pepper. "I found this in the back of your refrigerator. The fizz might help with the fog and the sugar can't hurt. Did you know alcohol can lower your sugar levels? I brought a Gatorade for you, too. It replenishes electrolytes."

Decky put down the paper she had begun to read. "I thought you taught math?"

"I do, but I minored in HPER with an emphasis in coaching, lots of health classes. Brenda and I actually did a class demonstration on how to recover from a hangover. She, of course, was the person with the hangover and I had to do all the talking."

Decky picked food off of Charlie's plate with the extra fork Charlie had given her. They shared the breakfast and read the paper until Decky needed a nap. She had to replenish her energy levels too, because Miss Lizzie's arrival was eminent. Charlie needed to go to the cottage to check on Miss Kitty.

"Wait, I'll go with you. I would sleep better at your house anyway. Lizzie would never think to look there, unless she gets it out of Brenda or the twins. She is not above bribery."

Charlie had not met Lizzie. She had only heard vague references to mental problems and personality disorders. That is why she said, "Decky, I can't believe you are a thirty-seven year old woman hiding from your mother. I know it is hard to disappoint them and that's what it comes down to. Our parents' dreams for us did not include this type of sleeping arrangement. It's better to just get it over with."

Decky was amused at her naiveté. "How would you know? You haven't told your parents."

"It's different. My parents don't want to know. From what you have said, your mother has made it her business to know all there is to know about everybody. She is going to come calling."

Decky knew this was true, still she persevered. "I am making the responsible decision not to have this confrontation and it will be a confrontation, you can bet your sweet ass on that, while I am in this wounded condition. I wouldn't be able to get away from her when the objects start flying."

"So you think it's a better idea to let her track you to my house. The proverbial scene of the crime?" Charlie was gathering the breakfast things.

"Look, I know her methods. She will get home and call her friend Bobbie. Maybe Bobbie hasn't heard anything yet, maybe she has. Anyway, she will tell my mother as soon as she finds out. Now, that can be on the cell phone or after she gets home. Either way she hangs up with Bobbie and tries to call me, at every number she has. She then will get in her car and come straight over here. If I'm with you, she will not be able to find me. She will question the twins, who will tell her I left in a BMW. She doesn't know your car, but she will find someone who does. She will go straight to Brenda's. Brenda will resist, but the force of Lizzie will prevail. She will then come to the cottage, where at least, if I can get down the stairs, I will be able to swim away."

Charlie stopped on the stairs. "You mean you would bail on me and leave me to deal with her?"

"If you are there by yourself, what can she say? You say, you haven't seen me and 'my, how do such rumors get started'? You play innocent. Don't, however, make eye contact."

"You want me to lie to your mother? The woman whose name will be on my check."

"It's okay. It won't hold up in court, everyone will agree it was in self-defense. Fear of an eminent life threat."

"Is she really that bad, Decky? Joking aside, how bad is this going to get?"

"They have tornados out in Oklahoma, don't they? Well we have hurricanes. They are both destructive. However, I give it to the hurricane, because it can spawn its own tornados and last at least a week. Around here people call my mother

Hurricane Lizzie, behind her back. So, if I were you, I'd take storm precautions right away."

The phone rang. Charlie panicked. "My God, that could be her. Don't answer it." Her eyes darted about the room. "You don't have a video phone in here do you?"

"It's okay. I'm not going to answer it."

"Good. I'm leaving before she gets here. I'll take my car. You can get there any way you want, but I'm headed for neutral territory."

Dixie took off after Charlie down the stairs. Decky called after them, "See, even the dog knows it's time to run, she's leaving with you."

#

Blam, Blam, Blam. Something was disturbing Decky's sleep. Blam, Blam, Blam. The sound of someone kicking the storm door at Charlie's cottage tried to filter through heavy, deep waves of sleep. She kept trying to wake up, but she couldn't. She could see the surface and she was swimming hard, but the sleep kept pulling her down. The blam, blam switched to rapping on the window above her head.

"Decky Bradshaw! I know you are in there. Let me in or I'm going to break down the damn door. What in the hell is wrong with you? I know what you…" Lizzie's voice faded as she went down the walls of the house banging on every window, still screaming to be let in.

Oh shit! Charlie was also awake and holding a finger on her lips, pleading with her eyes for Decky not to make a sound. It was dark outside. Decky would not have gone to sleep, if she had known Charlie wasn't going to stand guard. Now they were naked in Charlie's bed without mode of escape. Why hadn't she installed that damn escape ladder? Her mother would break the door down or at least throw a deck chair through a window. There was no time to explain. She just hoped Charlie would follow her lead.

Decky jumped up, grabbed the clothes she had dropped on the floor, and started dressing quickly. When she saw that Charlie's underwear were there too, she threw them at her and kept moving. Charlie looked like a deer in the headlights, her wide eyes searching the room. Making a quick decision, Charlie took only her underwear and climbed into the armoire, attempting to shut the door behind her. Decky thought it was a good strategy. That's how she would play this. Charlie wasn't there.

Finally clothed, Decky grabbed the crutches and stepped out into the large room that ran the length of the house facing the water. She was standing just outside Charlie's bedroom door. There was a back door not five feet from her. Although the fear was acting as a wonderful painkiller, she didn't think she could get up any speed. The kitchen area in front of her contained weapons. She would have to keep Lizzie out of this area of the house, at all costs.

Decky stood there at one end of the large room, while Lizzie continued to scream at her through the door. Decky only moved toward the locked door when she saw Lizzie grab a cast iron deck chair and head for the picture window behind the couch. Before leaving the bedroom door, she looked back and saw Charlie peeking out, totally immersed in trying to get the door of the armoire to close and stay shut. She made eye contact and asked Charlie to be quiet with a wave her hand.

When Decky finally opened the door, Lizzie hit the room like a crazed, wounded animal. "I know about you and your little LESBIAN friend!" She drew the word lesbian out, adding z's for affect. It sounded like l-e-z-z-z-bian to Decky. It had a connotation to it that indicated right away where Lizzie stood on this matter.

Dixie had watched the whole thing evolve from the deck, where she had been lounging when Lizzie drove up. Decky was sure that Dixie had led Lizzie happily to the door. Dixie evidently knew better than to follow Lizzie into the house. She was now sitting in a deck chair watching through the picture window, to get a better view of the action inside.

Just as Lizzie started for Decky, Miss Kitty made her entrance, by scrambling out from under the couch at Lizzie's feet. Lizzie thought something had her. She screamed and leapt onto the couch. Miss Kitty ran past Decky and into the bedroom. She was twice her normal size and frightened out of her mind. Decky heard the armoire door squeak open and close again. At least they were together. Decky was out here on her own.

The absurdity of the situation hit Decky and she started to grin. She tried desperately not to, but it was hopeless. Her mother was dancing around on the couch, still vibrating with anger. Her girlfriend was naked and hiding in the armoire with her cat. Her dog was enjoying the show from a safe distance. It was all just too much.

"Have you lost your damn mind? I did not raise you like this. What in the hell is wrong with you?" Lizzie was still on the couch, but gaining momentum.

"You need to calm down," Decky said, still unable to stop grinning.

"You had better wipe that smile off your face right this minute."

Decky bit her lip. It didn't help, but at least she was making an effort.

"I am going to slap your ass into Tidewater Psychiatric Institute so fast it will make your head spin. They can fix you. No daughter of mine is going to be sleeping around like trash. I don't care if that woman does have a PHD in mathematics."

From the bedroom, much to Decky's horror, she heard Charlie say, "It's an EDD in Administration."

Lizzie flew off the couch. She was experiencing the same phenomenon that had just seized Miss Kitty. She seemed to blow up to twice her size, as she tried to get past Decky to the source of the voice. Decky backed up as best she could, dancing in front of her mother to block her path. Over her shoulder, she said to the bedroom door, "Would you shut up? You're not helping."

Lizzie snatched a crutch away from Decky, almost toppling her. She waved the crutch around still trying to enter the bedroom. Although happy that she was no longer Lizzie's target, she couldn't let Lizzie get to Charlie. She grabbed the crutch her mother was waving around and held it down in front of them. She had to hold very tight.

"Momma, that's enough. You need to go."

This redirected Lizzie's anger to Decky.

"I will not be made a fool of. You will not embarrass your father and me this way. I can't believe there isn't something mentally wrong with you. It's common and trashy and you will not behave this way. Is that understood?"

Still clinging to the crutch, Decky spoke as calmly as she could, "Mother, I am not a child. I am sorry this has upset you, but this has nothing to do with you."

"Nothing to do with me? It has everything to do with me. What kind of mother will people think I am? I should have never let you play softball in the first place."

"I did not do this because you let me play softball. Why are you acting like this? You have friends with gay children. You adore Toby at the burger place and he's going through a sex change."

"They are not my children. You are, and you will not be part of this family, if you don't straighten up and fly right."

Decky let anger slip into her voice. "Then I won't be a part of your life. Would that make you happy?"

Lizzie let go of the crutch. She took two steps back from Decky and then with the coldest look Decky had ever seen, she said, "You are going to burn in hell for this."

Then it was over. Lizzie left without another word. When Decky was sure the coast was clear, she went back to the bedroom. The house was silent once again. She looked at the armoire. In the ever so small opening, where the door would not close all the way, were Charlie's fingertips digging into the wood. She was still trying to hold the door shut when Decky pried it open.

There, huddled together, were a naked Charlie, underwear in one hand, and a really freaked out cat between her legs.

"She's gone. Get dressed. We're leaving."

Charlie did as she was told, still shaken and a bit confused. "Where are we going?"

"We don't have a lot of time."

Charlie looked even more frightened, if that was possible. "What do you mean?"

"That was Lizzie sober. We just have time to make it to my house. Grab the cat and let's move, now!"

Charlie dressed, went to get the cat carrier, and rounded up Miss Kitty, who was still in shock and happy to be back in a familiar environment.

Charlie asked Decky, as she followed her slow progress down the steps, "Why are we going to your house, won't she just come there?"

"Yes, she will, but I have something there you don't have here."

"What?"

Decky jumped into the driver's side while Charlie and Dixie got into the Expedition. She looked at Charlie and said very seriously, "Bullet proof glass."

#

They didn't talk much on the way to Decky's house. Charlie bit the tip of her index finger. Her feet were up on the seat, knees pulled in close to her body. She didn't look scared anymore. She looked like she was solving a problem far away on a classroom chalkboard.

When Decky wasn't looking at Charlie, she was watching the road for any sign of danger. The last time Decky was going to roast in hell was when she got a tattoo. It was just a small rose on her ankle, very elegant. Now it was barely visible through the scars from past surgeries. Her mother had freaked. First, she'd gone and associated herself with Carney trash, which is what her mother called theatre people, by changing from pre-law to theatre in college. Then Decky got a tattoo in the spring of her senior year.

Decky had gone home on the Friday after getting the tattoo. Her mother had somehow found out about it and was waiting at the county line when Decky crossed it. She had followed Decky home with her headlights flashing on and off, honking the horn and swerving the car, all the time screaming at how Decky had better get her ass home. Decky could not hear her mother over the road noise and honking horn, but she could definitely read her lips.

Lizzie had threatened to have skin grafts taken from Decky's ass to cover it up. Decky had to wear socks to church whenever Lizzie was around. Going to church had been her father's idea. He had two strong willed women living in the same house. Decky had attended church from birth to college; after that she had only made it at Christmas and Easter.

With Decky's lack of church attendance, playing ball, or doing theatre on Sundays, and now the tattoo, Lizzie had had enough. Decky's mother said that she would burn in hell and refused to speak to her. It would have been fine with Decky, if when her mother refused to speak to someone, she really did it. What Lizzie really meant was she refused to speak civilly to her. R.C. had suggested to Decky that she go to church more often when she was at home, to try and ride out the storm. It helped, and Lizzie finally forgot about the tattoo and moved on to other things.

This time, Decky thought, was different. The look in Lizzie's eyes meant war. She would work every angle on this one. First, there would be Zack. Thank God, he was grown or Social Services would be waiting on the doorstep when they pulled up. Lizzie would call them anyway to see if the dog could be rescued.

She would threaten Charlie's job, but they had already talked to Brenda about that. She told Charlie and Decky that the administration had faced this issue under previous circumstances and chosen to leave it alone. It seems the U's attorney advised them of a major lawsuit loss based on the U's non-discrimination policy and all was swept away. The same would go for Charlie and Decky, even more so, since Charlie could accuse Lizzie of using her position to break the law, which is one definition of discrimination.

That didn't mean Lizzie couldn't make life hell for Charlie. The administration may back Charlie, but she would be judged and sides would be taken. Administrators hate controversy and Lizzie could stir it up with the best of them. Those who hated gay people in general could be rallied to Lizzie's cause, no doubt. It could get ugly. She only hoped that she could shield Charlie, as much as possible, from Lizzie's wrath.

Decky checked her messages when she got in the house. The first message was from Brenda. Lynne had been deposited at the airport and in a perfect world would be gone forever. Decky hadn't thought about Lynne in hours. She flexed her right hand. Next were a series of calls from her mother that began with a call that morning relaying their arrival home. Within the next message it was evident Lizzie had talked to Bobbie. From then on, the calls became abusive and Decky simply deleted them.

There was a frantic call from Brenda warning them of Lizzie's arrival and an apology for telling her where they were. Zack called. He said Lizzie had called him a few minutes ago and he was just glad he was in Alaska. He wished her luck and said he loved her. The last call was Brenda, again apologizing, and offering Charlie sanctuary until the hurricane had passed.

While Decky listened to the messages, Charlie went down to the mudroom to retrieve an old rubber pan Decky had suggested they use as a litter box for Miss Kitty. The house was surrounded by sand, so Charlie filled the pan, and prepared food, water, and bathroom privacy for Miss Kitty. When Decky was off the phone, they let Miss Kitty out of her crate.

Miss Kitty was a small black and white cat, with a big attitude. Not a bad attitude, more a queenly manor. Dixie, who was the only royalty in the house up until now, sniffed at Miss Kitty. She must have associated the smell with Charlie. She walked over, sat down at Charlie's feet, and moved her eyebrows up and down. She seemed to be asking whether this was a necessity. She glanced over at Decky.

"She's staying, get used to it," Decky said to Dixie's upturned face.

Miss Kitty in turn, ran straight for the couch and began sharpening her claws on the cushions. Dixie followed her and barked when Miss Kitty started scratching. Miss Kitty stopped and got comfortable on the back of the couch. Dixie assumed her normal spot on the end of the couch, and they both appeared to have decided to share the space.

Charlie smiled and held Decky's hand as she watched the two animals on the couch. Charlie spoke to Dixie, "I need to warn you Dixie, this may all be a ruse. She's been known to play tricks like hiding behind doors and springing out after you."

Decky added, "Well, in the spirit of full disclosure, Dixie has been known to eat cat food, so it will all even out."

Charlie wanted to take a shower and Decky needed a swim. Decky craved the swimming. It relieved stress and let loose all kinds of wonderful chemicals in her body. She was addicted to it. She needed it now. Decky also needed the exercise to work the alcohol completely out of her system, and she needed to think.

Decky swam like a woman possessed. She swam the first laps in anger. Her mother was judging her. Decky was the same person that her mother knew yesterday. What was so different about Decky that her mother had acted that way? Why couldn't she sit down and discuss this reasonably?

Decky would tell her mother she did not expect her to accept Charlie as a member of the family, just a member of Decky's family, Charlie, Zack, Dixie, and now Miss Kitty. She would tell her they could agree to disagree, much like the tattoo. Decky and Charlie did not have to be around her mother, after all Decky had been avoiding Lizzie as a vocation for years. It would be much better if her mother were not so invested in Decky's life. Decky had been glad when Zack was born, because it gave her mother someone else to concentrate on.

It was all about Lizzie. Lizzie would be telling herself she was trying to help Decky. She would tell herself Decky was in need of mental help. She would tell herself anything except the fact her daughter was gay. Well, she is going to have to learn to deal with it, Decky thought. If this was finally the straw that breaks the back of Decky's relationship with her mother, then so be it. She did not want to hurt her mother, but she was not going to let Lizzie ruin everything. Not now, when she had Charlie, the one thing she knew she had been missing her whole life.

Decky swam for the sorrow of loss. She could never go back to the way things had been. At the party last night, all had been accepting of Decky's new lifestyle, for the most part. After all, this was a lesbian friendly environment; however, she did notice that some people treated her differently than before. Decky felt no differently about them. Why should she? Nothing had changed, other than she was now involved in a relationship with Charlie. That really had nothing to do with anyone except the two of them.

Fortunately, Decky did not care what other people thought of her. She liked herself. She had never sought or needed approval from others to be happy. She was comfortable in her own skin. Decky had made unfortunate decisions, but she learned from them and moved on. Unlike Lizzie, Decky did not hold on forever to every misfortune or tragedy. If she got over Trey, she could get over anything.

Decky did not want her relationship with Charlie to cause her son any hardship. She would take extra care to insure he was protected. Decky recognized it would be hard on her father. He would have to try and hold Lizzie together without Decky's help. She would call him tomorrow night, when she knew her mother would be at her Eastern Star meeting. Decky understood in her heart, he would love her no matter what. He was just like that.

Decky was sorry her mother had chosen to dive full throttle into a downward bi-polar drama. She would work this to death and finally have a psychotic episode, where she would embarrass herself to no end. Lizzie would then slink off, sorry for her behavior, until the next thing set her off. From here out it was anybody's guess how it would go down. Decky could count on one thing for sure. The reaction would be directly proportional to the amount of alcohol Lizzie consumed between now and the moment she lost her mind.

Decky swam until her arms and legs became too heavy to lift anymore. The swim helped her ankle. She had placed one of many braces she had collected over the years on the ankle before the swim. It felt good to use her leg fully. Decky climbed out of the lap pool. Then she went to the bar where she created an ice bag. Returning to the Jacuzzi, she climbed in the warm bubbling water, propped up her ankle up on the side with the ice bag covering it, and cooled down.

She was reclining there, lost in thought, when Charlie descended the stairs.

"Decky, we've been touring the house with Miss Kitty."

Charlie, holding a struggling Miss Kitty, was following Dixie down the stairs. The cat had all four legs flying in different directions. Then Decky witnessed an incredible feat. The cat actually spun her back legs around and kicked off of Charlie's chest. While her back legs were doing this, her front legs and head were facing the other way. It was like a wild game of twister. Dixie was mystified.

"I see she's really enjoying it." Decky was finally relaxing. It had to be Charlie's presence, because how bad could life be with her by Decky's side.

#

After preparing a meal and eating it, the two tired women retired to the bedroom. Miss Kitty proceeded to make herself comfortable in the center of the bed. The 'queen on her throne' look drove Dixie nuts. There was only one royal in this house and Dixie was sure it was she. Dixie jumped on the bed, did three circles around the cat, and then chose Decky's pillow for her perch.

Decky and Charlie left the animals to work it out among themselves. Decky sat down in one of the oversized chairs with ottoman, making it the size of a twin bed. Charlie fixed Decky a bucket of ice for the ankle, which Decky dipped in and out of, while they watched the news. They did not talk much. Charlie fell asleep in the chair, her head resting on Decky's chest. It felt like the calm before the storm.

Decky had locked the house up tight. Not knowing what Lizzie's next move would be was always unsettling. She could only hope Lizzie's reaction would be kept in the family, but she knew her mother would divide the entire community. Lizzie would have to be assured by everyone she came in contact with, that she was acting exactly as she should be. Lizzie would discuss Decky's personal life with the postman, the pharmacist, the garbage man, etc. Decky had to be prepared, but for what?

The gunshot crashed into a window downstairs. It was a gunshot. No doubt about it. Charlie didn't so much hear the shot as experience the aftermath. Decky was on her feet in a split second. She elbowed Charlie in the chest on the way up, nearly sending Charlie crashing to the floor. Decky grabbed the crutches, heading for the elevator.

Charlie stood up with that baby, wide-eyed look, so familiar to Decky now. "Decky, what is it? What's happening?"

Decky did not look back. "Stay here," was all she said.

Decky stopped at a small desk, removing a nine-millimeter, and placing it in the waistband of her pants.

Charlie, who had now come fully awake, grabbed Decky's arm. "Decky, stop! What is it?"

Decky turned to her. "I don't know, Charlie. I think I heard a gunshot, but I'm not sure." She lied. "Stay here with Dixie. Don't let her follow me. I don't need to have to worry about the two of you right now."

Charlie dropped Decky's arm and headed straight for the telephone.

"Charlie, don't call the police. If it is Lizzie, I don't want her leaving here in handcuffs. I would never hear the end of it."

"You don't want your mother in handcuffs, but you might shoot her? What kind of logic is that? Don't go out there."

"I have to. Stay here. I mean it. You are my only witness, I need you alive." She grinned at Charlie.

Charlie put the receiver down back into the charger. Decky wasn't grinning on the inside. She had to leave before Charlie saw she was trembling. This was it: Showdown at the Hurricane Lizzie Corral.

"Of course, if she gets around me you guys are on your own. Take my cell phone down the deck stairs and call the twins. They know what to do."

Charlie located Decky's phone with her eyes and then followed Decky's gaze to the outside doors to the deck, all the time sizing up the situation. She had evidently decided to follow Decky's instructions.

Just before Decky's head disappeared out of view, as she descended in the elevator, she called up to Charlie, "Make sure she's in the house before you leave. You don't want to run up on her in the dark outside. It's pretty scary."

Decky had only been trying to alleviate some of Charlie's fears by joking. The truth was she was frightened for Charlie. In the right circumstances, Decky was sure her mother would shoot either Decky or Charlie, even herself. Lizzie could be really demented. Decky tried to tell herself her mother could not escape her mental condition, but from her observations, Decky didn't think her mother tried to help herself either.

Decky approached the foyer area carefully. The motion detectors had illuminated the front yard. Through the front door glass, she could see Lizzie aiming a pistol at yet another window. Decky went to the door and opened it.

"Momma, what are you doing?" Decky said this calmly, not wanting to inflame the situation anymore than it already was.

"I know that harlot is in there. I went to the cottage, so I know she's in there."

Decky thought that was what Lizzie said anyway. It was hard to tell. The liquor accent made it difficult to understand her.

"Momma, this is between you and me. Charlie has nothing to do with this." Decky was attempting to draw her mother's attention away from Charlie and on to herself.

"That dyke must have drugged you. There is no way a daughter of mine would do something this...this dissssguuusting!"

Lizzie was waving the pistol, using it to punctuate her tirade. Decky swayed on the crutches with each pass of the barrel. Lizzie was fit to be tied, literally. Decky could swear that Lizzie's eyes were glowing. She was stark raving mad this time. Decky had seen this drunken personality distortion only once before. Under normal circumstances, although easy to anger, Lizzie would handle adversity as a woman full of southern grace and charm. She would refuse to have anything to do with you, but talk about you behind your back and generally try to make your life miserable. However, on one occasion, many years ago, Lizzie had been pushed to the limits with her sister-in-law on R.C.'s side.

R.C.'s brother was a major asshole and married to "the slut." The slut had made a pass at R.C. "The slut," having been rebuffed by Decky's father, made the mistake of talking badly about R.C., in front on an already angry Lizzie. Decky had been young, but she clearly remembered the look of rage on Lizzie's face, when she pulled the grate from the bottom of the refrigerator and proceeded to pummel "the slut" until R.C. arrived and interceded.

Lizzie, upon sobering up, went into a deep depression, because she had not acted like a lady. She was exceedingly sorry, even though Decky told her over and over she had done the exact same thing Decky would have done. Now that the same anger was being leveled at her and Charlie, Decky wasn't so sure she should have encouraged her mother.

"Get out of my way. I'm going in there and send that bitch packing." Lizzie was coming up the steps now.

A new sensation overtook Decky. Up until this moment, she had dealt with her mother with sadness for Lizzie's disability. Decky fully understood the depths of her mother's illness. She had talked with doctors and researched bi-polar disease. She had been able to trace the depression in her mother's family, through medical records, during her genealogy research. Suicide, alcoholism, post partum depression, psychiatric treatments; they were all there. Lizzie had a chemical imbalance, which she could no more control than the color of her eyes.

The new sensation was an anger born out of the threat to the woman in the house, whom Decky loved more than life itself. That was it. Lizzie was going to have to kill her before she let her get to Charlie. No question about it. Lizzie had crossed a line.

"Momma, I'm going to ask you nicely to get back in your car and leave." Decky said this, as she leaned her crutches on the railing, and using the rail for support, hopped down one step closer to her mother.

Lizzie was stunned by the look on Decky's face. Decky could see it in her mother's eyes. Lizzie hesitated, then unbelievably got angrier. She continued up the steps.

"Are you threatening me?" Lizzie demanded. "I'll make you wish you were never born."

The bridge had been crossed and left burning like Atlanta. The relationship between Decky and her mother was about to cross into new territory. A place where Decky no longer put the fact that this was her mother, the woman who birthed her, a woman who was sick and needed help, before what she said next.

In a calm, deep voice Decky spoke, "You're going to have to shoot me, if you think for one minute you are going to get past me. However, and let me make this very clear, when you shoot you had better kill me. You will not get a second shot."

Lizzie stopped dead in her tracks. She took a long look at Decky's face. Lizzie seemed to be trying to decide what to do next, when R.C.'s truck headlights bounced into view. He was barreling down the lane straight for them.

Decky's father was out of the truck before it came to a complete stop. His arrival had distracted Lizzie. Decky heard a noise behind her, but she did not take her eyes off of Lizzie. R.C. stopped short of the steps.

"Elizabeth Bradshaw! You come down those steps this instant!"

Decky noted her father was using his most educated authoritarian voice.

Lizzie turned on R.C. "Are you going to let her get away with this? Tell her she can't do this!"

R.C. never looked at Decky. "Decky is a grown woman. Neither of us has any say in how she lives her life. It has nothing to do with us."

Lizzie was not to be outdone. "Nothing to do with us? What will people think about us? I did not raise a gay daughter!"

"It makes absolutely no difference what anyone says about us. We are not responsible for Decky's decisions. As I said, she is a grown woman."

"It's your fault!" Lizzie screamed at him. "You turned her into a boy with all those sports. You did this."

R.C. remained calm. "I doubt seriously that either one of us had anything to do with this."

Lizzie turned back to Decky. "You do this and you can kiss your father and me goodbye. I won't have a lesbian in my family. I won't have it!"

Lizzie was waving the pistol again.

When R.C. spoke this time he was not asking, he ordered her, as he would have a child who was misbehaving, "Elizabeth, get in the truck, now!"

Lizzie hesitated, only a fraction of a second. As she passed R.C. at the bottom of the steps, he took the gun out of her hand. Lizzie did not look back.

Decky hopped down the steps toward her father. "Thank you. She's really gone off the deep end on this one."

R.C. spoke in a much calmer voice still with the serious quality of his order to Lizzie, "Decky, I don't agree with your choices, but I'm sure you didn't expect me to. You are still my daughter and I love you. That is really all that matters. I will try to talk to your mother, but I don't think this is going to blow over very fast."

"No, I don't imagine it will. Thank you, Daddy. I love you, too. I know this is hard on you. I hate that it has made momma so crazy, and I know this is going to make your life hell. I did not choose this. It chose me. I hope one day you'll understand."

"I'm sorry I let her get away. I fell asleep watching the race." Decky's father loved NASCAR, but was famous for falling asleep during the middle of the race. He would wake up at the end every time. He had some kind of weird built-in alarm. "We'll talk later. I better get your mother home. I'll get the car tomorrow. I'll bring some boards over to cover that window. At least she only shot out the one."

"Don't worry about the window, dad. You just lock up all the guns and take that pistol away from her." Decky smiled and hugged her father.

Decky went back up the steps. She was thinking about what her father had said and gathering her crutches. She did not look up until she was almost to the door. Charlie was peeking out from behind the door. She looked utterly terrified. Decky went into the house and closed the door before she spoke.

"Come here." Decky held out her arms and gathered in the trembling Charlie.

Charlie said into Decky's chest, "Oh my God, I thought she was going to shoot you."

Decky replied, "Me too!"

Charlie pushed away from Decky's chest, but stayed in her arms. It was then that Decky saw her cell phone in Charlie's hand.

"Thank God, I called the twins. You were right. All I said was that your mother was here and she had a gun. The one that answered said okay real quick and hung up. I guess they knew to get your dad."

"I'll have to give them a bonus this week." Decky was trying to lighten the mood, but it didn't work.

Charlie looked deeply into Decky's eyes. "I thought I was going to lose you. I actually stood behind that door and thought, I have just found the best thing that ever happened to me. I can't lose her now. I prayed to God please to let me have you. I don't want to live without you Decky, not another minute."

Decky hugged Charlie to her. "You don't have to. Not another minute."

The mood suddenly changed. Charlie pushed Decky away and hit her with the hand holding the cell phone.

"Have you lost your mind? Why did you open the door? Why didn't you just call your father? You scared me to death." Charlie was off to the kitchen on a tirade.

Decky could hear Dixie barking upstairs. Charlie had evidently locked her in the bathroom.

Decky defended herself only slightly. Now that the adrenaline was subsiding, she realized how dangerous the whole situation had been. Her mother could have shot her. It was a thought Decky did not want to dwell on.

"I'm sorry, Charlie," Decky said, following her to the kitchen. "I just opened the door and went out there. I didn't think she would really shoot me." She lied.

"That woman is insane! You don't know what she'll do!" Charlie was wrapped up in the anger felt after a big scare.

Decky tried again to calm the situation. "It's over now. Nobody got hurt. I think that was the worst of it. At least Lizzie's already maxed out. The rest of this should be easier."

Charlie was not calming down, not yet. She jerked open the refrigerator, grabbing a bottle of water. She unscrewed the top, violently slamming the door, and took a big drink.

"If you knew this was the kind of reaction you were going to get from your mother, then why in the hell did you do this? Didn't you think about this at all?"

Decky told the truth. "No, I didn't think about this. I saw you. I touched you. That was all that mattered. It's all that matters now. I choose you, Charlie. I choose to love you no matter what anybody thinks. I choose to live with you forever, if you'll have me. Nothing will ever come between us. We will survive this. I've known from day one that if you were with me, nothing anybody said or did would ever change the way I feel about you."

Charlie answered quietly, "But that's your mother."

"I know that. I still don't care. I'm sorry she's hurting, but I can't live my life according to what Lizzie wants. I have done that enough. She will either get over this or not. All that matters is you. I only need you, and of course Zack and Dixie. I can live without Lizzie, if that's what it takes to love you."

"I don't want you to wake up one day mad at me for ruining your relationship with your mother." Charlie's eyes were studying Decky, as if trying to see the future.

"Please, Charlie, understand this for once and for all. Lizzie ruins her own relationships. I could never blame you for any of this. I did this. Me, just me. I made this decision. I went after you. You didn't even notice me."

"How do you know I didn't notice you?" Charlie was relaxing.

Decky began to relax too. She grinned at Charlie. "You never said you noticed me."

"Oh, I noticed you all right. I noticed your ass. You wiggled it so cute before each pitch."

Decky grabbed a water bottle out of the refrigerator, as she played along. "How could you see my ass, your dug out was on the other side of the field.

"When I came to the game late, I stood outside the fence and watched for a batter or two. I was impressed with your ass the minute I saw it."

"But that was the second day. I saw you first." Decky left the bottle on the counter and went into the area leading to the stairs down to the mudroom. She entered a small closet and removed an orthopedic boot. She listened as Charlie answered her.

"I saw you the day before, when we were warming up. It seemed like every time I looked at you, you were looking at me. So I decided to check out this chick that was definitely checking me out."

Holding the boot, Decky came back to the kitchen. "Was I that obvious?"

Charlie was enjoying this now. "Oh honey, you were practically drooling and of course there was the fact that you seemed dumbstruck in my presence. I thought it was cute."

Decky sat down on one of the stools. She started putting the boot on, pulling all the Velcro straps tight. "I was not drooling. I wasn't even gay at the time."

Charlie laughed. "Don't kid yourself. Straight women don't look at other women like that."

Decky had finally adjusted all the straps on the boot. She stood up gently and tested her ankle. Then she looked at Charlie. "How was I looking at you?"

"Like you wanted to ravish my body."

"Oh, you mean like this." Decky moved toward Charlie. She left the crutches behind.

Charlie smiled up at her. "Yes, exactly like that."

The kiss released all the emotion of the recent events. They kissed away all the fear and anger. They kissed passionately until Dixie's barking became so persistent Charlie went to let her out.

Decky busied herself cleaning up the shards of glass from Lizzie's assault on the window. The glass had held, but shattered, sending slivers to the floor. Decky was enjoying the freedom afforded to her by the boot. The ankle still hurt, but she was glad to be hindered no more by the crutches. Charlie and Dixie bounded down the stairs just as Decky was pouring the swept up particles into the trash.

"I think Dixie is upset she missed all the action," Charlie said, hopping down from the last stair, Miss Kitty on her trail. "Miss Kitty, however, is not used to gunfire. Look at her eyes."

The small cat's eyes were wide and frightened. Her feet hit the floor and she bounded for the top of the couch, where she surveyed the environment for more trouble.

"I think Dixie thrives on Lizzie's tirades. She seems so happy afterward." Decky rubbed Dixie's head. "Thought it better to let you sit this one out, princess. I'll tell you all the details later."

Dixie accepted the proposal and moved on over to her food bowl to top off for the evening. Decky and Charlie made coffee, decaf. They didn't need the caffeine. The buzz from the excitement was enough to keep them awake talking into the night. Decky made Charlie promise to stay with her for a while.

"Won't that just make your mother more angry?"

"Lizzie is as angry as she can get, I think. I would feel better if you were here with me at night. When you're at the U, you'll have to watch your back. She's not above coming to visit you at your office."

"To my office? Are you kidding me? If she's worried about what people think, why on earth would she come to my office?" Charlie's eyes were getting wider as she spoke.

"Lizzie's brain doesn't work like that. Right now, you are the prey. She is a focused hunter. She will not rest until she meets you face to face. When she can't get to you at home, she will go there."

"If she comes to my office, I will refuse to have that conversation there. She can't cause a commotion if I don't let her draw me into one. I will appeal to her southern manners to keep this a private matter."

Decky laughed. "You are using reason. That will not work. Lizzie gets tunnel vision. She will stalk her prey and attack as soon as it is in her sights. She won't care who's listening, because in her mind everybody is on her side anyway."

"What exactly do you suggest I do?"

"Vary your schedule. Take different routes to and from classes. Make office hours by appointment only. It's summer, everybody does it." Decky was serious, but she grinned to try and make this easier for Charlie to deal with.

"How have you lived your life like this? I mean, I know I come from Ozzie and Harriet land, but this is way off the charts of dysfunctional families."

"I learned to adapt the stories I told her, to disguise the real truth. Not lying, per se, just filtering. Like with Trey, she didn't need to know the truth. She would have set about ruining his life. I didn't want that to happen."

"And you couldn't have hidden us away from her, is that what you're saying?"

"Not after I just slugged your ex-girlfriend in front of half the county."

They both laughed.

"Okay, but what if she corners me in my office?" Charlie asked when the laughter subsided.

"Walk as quickly to your car as possible. It will minimize the damage. Get in the car and come straight home. Don't speed, but don't stop if she follows you. Call me on the cell phone. I will call R.C. to intercept her. She drives like a bat out of hell, so be careful."

"You're serious, aren't you?" Charlie looked slightly amused, but more worried. "What do I do if she starts shooting?"

"R.C. is locking up all the guns. He'll call around to the local shops and alert the clerks not to sell Lizzie another one. He has a little routine he does when she gets like this. Sort of blocking avenues of destruction she may take. He's been doing this a long time. He's gotten very good, learned from his mistakes. He should have never shown Lizzie how to hot-wire a car. He learned that the hard way."

Charlie yawned. "How have you turned out so well? I mean from what I can tell you're pretty sane."

Decky took the cue and stood up stretching. "Survival instincts I guess and the Boy Scout code."

Charlie held Decky's hand, as Decky turned off the lights downstairs. She stopped Decky in the dark.

"You mean, always be prepared."

Decky nodded her head. "Yep, why do you think I put on the boot?"

8

The next morning, Charlie drove Decky's car to the cottage, grabbed as many clothes as she could, her materials for school, and headed to campus. Decky had decided her car would be safer, since Lizzie would be focused on the BMW, and there were a couple of other Lexus that looked like Decky's on campus.

Once Decky was alone, she called Brenda. The grapevine was in full bloom and had already gotten the news of Lizzie's little shoot 'em up. The twins, though loyal, had a mother that was thrilled to pass on every move Decky made to anyone who listened. She was one of Lizzie's primary sources.

Brenda was laughing hysterically on the other end of the phone, while Decky relayed her version of what had happened.

"It isn't funny, Brenda. She could have killed one or both of us."

"Oh, I'm not laughing at what she did. I'm laughing at how different the story is than what's going around."

"What, what did you hear?" Decky knew this would be entertaining.

"I heard she shot out everyone of those expensive windows of yours, while you, on crutches, and R.C. chased her around the yard. You didn't get control of her until she tried to reload." Brenda was cackling so hard, Decky had to wait to answer.

"Jesus, people need to get lives of their own," Decky finally said. "I'm starring in my own soap opera, 'Days of Decky's Life'."

Brenda's laughter finally subsided enough to say, "It really is fun to watch Lizzie go off. I mean it's funny for those of us that don't have to participate, this time."

"Oh, you just wait. She hasn't gotten around to you yet. Remember you are the one that recommended Charlie for the job. Your time will come."

Brenda stopped laughing. "I guess the dinner plans have been cancelled."

The two women laughed and promised to get together again soon. Decky called the twins to put plywood over the window her mother had shattered. She then called the manufacturer to order a replacement. Feeling much more comfortable in the boot, she went to the dock after her work out. She made sure to take her cell phone with her in case Charlie called. As she passed the spot where the eel had come to rest, she laughed aloud, as the whole thing played out in her mind again. It was funnier every time she thought about it.

Decky spent the rest of the morning cleaning the Whaler. Dixie grabbed the hose, spraying Decky with it, which started a fight for the hose that ended with the two soaked from head to tail. After the boat was clean and gassed up again, she stored it in the boathouse.

Decky decided to take Charlie for a ride in the Hunter day-sailor when she got home from work. She would go up to the house and pack a basket with wine and cheese, some grapes and bread, with oil and balsamic vinegar dip. She loved making baskets to take on the boat. It was a thing she did with pride. Probably the only Martha Stewart type thing she did, but she did like Martha's eye for detail.

She was thinking about what to put in the basket and whether she needed to go to the store for more supplies, when she heard the boat approaching. She was in the process of paddling the sailboat out of the boathouse. Alan Jr. was pulling up by the time she was able to tie up the sailboat to the dock. He didn't come all the way in and tie up as usual. He idled off the end of the dock and stared at Decky.

"Hey Alan Jr., you been out fishing?" Decky could see rods sticking out the back of the boat. Alan Jr. was known to take a day off and go fishing for that prize bass on a regular basis. He was known for his abilities as a guide. Decky had encouraged him to start a guide business. He didn't need to die old and poor on a farm, but he didn't listen. He said his father, grandfather, and great grandfather had farmed that piece of land and he intended to do the same.

"No, I wasn't fishing, just driving around thinking. I hear Lizzie took a shot at you. What'd you do this time?" He was still looking at Decky with an unfamiliar glare. It was unsettling, but this was Alan Jr. She'd been a good friend to him and he had been there when she needed him.

"Lizzie did not take a shot at me. She only shot out one of the windows in the house. People will make up the damnedest stories." Decky tried to evade the question of why her mother had shot at the house.

"You must have really done something this time. I've heard a rumor, but I don't think it's true." Alan Jr. was finally getting around to it.

Decky prepared for the inevitable. "Exactly what rumor are you referring to? There are so many people who seem concerned about what goes on in my life, I'm sure it will be entertaining."

"I heard you'd gone and got yourself a girlfriend. Wouldn't be that woman I saw you with the other night? The one that's moved into your cottage?"

Decky was offended by his stare and his tone. "Well, Lizzie's got nothing on you. You seem to have quite a bit of information yourself. Are you asking me as a friend or are you here to get more information for the Decky Bradshaw rumor hotline?"

"I want to hear it from you. I want to know if what they're saying is true. Are you fucking a woman now?"

He was angry. She could see it. It wasn't pretty. She knew he cared about her, maybe too much, but what she saw now was a twisted face of, what was it, hate?

"I respect you enough not to lie to you. I hope you will respect me enough to accept the answer. Yes, I am having a relationship with a woman."

"Just like that, you go gay. Have you been gay all this time? Were you trying to make a fool out of me, Decky?" He was screaming at her now.

"Alan, this has nothing to do with you. We are just friends. That's all we were ever going to be." Decky could not understand why he was so angry. She had made it quite clear to him that she was not in any way interested in a romantic relationship.

Alan Jr. slammed the boat into drive and sped away. Charlie had said people would act differently. Decky could accept that, but she was shocked at how her sleeping arrangements seemed to be distressing Alan Jr. in such a personal manner. It didn't have anything to do with anybody other than Decky and Charlie, as far as she was concerned. She was still Decky, the same person she had always been, maybe even better.

Now she was in love. She was happy. Why couldn't they just be happy that she had finally found someone to love and love her back? How in the hell did Alan Jr., her mother, or anyone else think they had a right to judge her? Alan Jr. felt like a fool because he loved Decky. She assumed he would have thought no different if it was a man Decky fell in love with. Only, for some reason, he appeared to think this somehow reflected on his manhood.

"That is absolutely ridiculous," Decky said aloud to Dixie, as the two of them headed to the house for lunch. Decky tried not to think about the incidents with her mother and Alan, Jr. Not thinking about it did not work. She went to her thinking place and swam until the visions of Lizzie with the gun and Alan's angry face moved to an appropriate spot, in the back of her mind. The rest of the swim was devoted to the plan for the sailboat ride. Maybe she should hide the gun on the boat, before Charlie got there. Decky was beginning to see that whatever reaction people had to lesbians, it was very unpredictable.

"Be prepared," she said to Dixie, when she got out of the lap pool.

#

Decky waited anxiously from the moment she had expected Charlie, until she finally pulled up. Decky didn't wait for her to come in. She met Charlie at the car.

"How was your first day?" Decky hoped all had gone well.

"No sightings of Lizzie." Charlie grabbed an armload of things out of the trunk.

Decky breathed a sigh of relief. "So, it went okay then?"

"Yes, my classes are full. Evidently the news hasn't hit the student body yet and the faculty members I did see, if they knew, were polite enough not to let me know they did."

"Great! Are you ready to play then?" Decky was excited to have Charlie back home. It thrilled her that Charlie's day had gone well. Maybe this wasn't going to be so bad after all.

"I have to get this stuff inside. I figured if Miss Kitty and I were living here, we would need a few things."

"I'll help you, and then you are going on a sail boat ride with a former sailing instructor."

"Another hidden talent. My but you do have varied taste."

"Varied taste." Decky chuckled. "You know, since I've been gay, everything has two meanings. I think about things differently. I find humor in ordinary words. Varied taste. That just about says it all doesn't it?"

Charlie laughed at Decky, calling over her shoulder, as she ascended the steps, "That has nothing to do with being gay, you are just horny."

The car unpacked and Charlie's things stowed away, Decky led Charlie down to the sailboat. She explained what all the parts were and what they did, as she prepared to launch the boat. Decky raised the mast and set the sails. Charlie loved it from the moment the wind caught the sails.

Decky showed Charlie how to steer the boat, and watched at her childlike joy, when she completed her first tack. Charlie had just avoided getting smacked in the head by the boom as it swung past her. She was so delighted with the whole process that Decky relaxed and let Charlie wind her way back and forth along the Sound. She gave suggestions now and again, but allowed Charlie to fall in love with sailing, as Decky had done as a child.

After about an hour, Charlie turned the boat into the wind. They dropped the sail and drifted for a while. Decky opened the picnic basket, producing a silk tablecloth. She took out the wine and cheese, added the Greek bread and vinegar and oil dip along with the grapes. They floated along, eating while they talked about Charlie's day.

"So, I think I'm going to be happy here. I was worried after being in one place for so long, but I think the move has been good for me. I am more energized. I remembered why I loved to teach." Charlie said, between bites of cheese.

"I'm glad you're happy." Decky *was* glad she was happy. She would do everything in her power to keep Charlie happy forever. It made her feel so complete inside to be here with her, laughing, enjoying the sheer joy of each other's company.

"Oh, by the way, this morning when I was leaving, I saw this truck parked out on the road near the entrance to your driveway. There was no one in it. I didn't think anything of it at the time, but when I came home, it was still there. Only it had moved to the other side of the road and there was a guy sitting in it this time."

Decky tried not to let her voice show any concern. "What color was it?"

"Bright red. That's why I noticed it in the first place. It's really red."

"That's just Alan Jr. He keeps a boat at one of the docks down the other lane." Decky didn't want to tell Charlie about earlier, but she would have to. *No lies of omission, remember.*

Charlie continued, "I didn't get a good look at him the other night on the boat. I didn't recognize him."

"He stopped by today while I was getting the sailboat ready. He had heard about us of course. He wasn't very happy."

Charlie was interested. "What did he say?"

Decky explained how Alan Jr. had somehow decided this was a blow to his manhood. "He actually said I had made a fool out of him."

Charlie looked concerned for Alan Jr. "Do you think he'll be all right? Did you break his heart?"

Decky thought about it. "I never gave him one reason to think there was a chance for the two of us to have more than a friendly relationship. If he's hurt, he's suffering under some false hope of his own making and of course a completely blown out of proportion male ego."

Charlie was compassionate. "I hope he gets over you soon. I hope it doesn't hurt him, too badly. No one should have to suffer a broken heart."

Decky smiled at Charlie. The fact that she could empathize with someone else's pain made her even more beautiful to Decky. The more she found out about Charlie, the more she liked her. She had loved her from the first second she kissed her, but she really liked Charlie, too. She was the kind of person she would have hung out with. Maybe in another life they would have been great friends, but in this life, Charlie was the love of her life and quickly becoming her best friend.

They sailed for the remainder of the afternoon. They even swung by the dock and picked up Dixie, who had been watching their every move from shore. Decky told Charlie about the first woman she had ever taken out on a sailboat.

"You mean I'm not the first woman you've been sailing with?"

"I've been sailing with other girls, sure, but not a woman, except for this one other time."

Decky started grinning at the memory. It had taken on a completely different look now that she was with Charlie. Decky began the story, "One year at Four-H camp, down on the coast, near Wilmington, I became infatuated with one of the female swimming instructors. Looking on it now, I was gay all the way back then, but I didn't know what it was. I just knew I was excited and wanted to be around her. The camp had sailboats, but not like this one. The ones we used were like the sunfish, with a flat deck and centerboard."

Decky chuckled at the memory of what came next. "I was so proud of the fact that I was able to talk this woman into taking a ride on a sailboat with me. I call her a woman, but she was really probably a college student. I took off with this pretty coed, leaning back against the mast facing me. Things went great for a little while. She was smiling and seemed to be enjoying herself. I was too, until it happened."

Decky blushed red. It was the same blush she felt when the plan to burn the mattresses had gone awry.

Charlie was grinning at Decky. "Another plan bit the dust, huh?"

Decky began sheepishly, "Well, I had that little sunfish clipping down the cove the camp was on. We were moving pretty fast for that kind of boat. Then with a loud cracking sound, we hit the oyster bar, just under the surface. It wasn't marked. I didn't see it."

"Did the boat sink?"

"No, it was worse. The boat hull itself had skimmed over on the surface, but the centerboard had been forced up violently. The coed happened to be sitting so that when the boat slammed to such a sudden stop, she slid into the centerboard, crotch first. I was horrified. I tried to tell her how sorry I was, but she insisted that we go back to shore immediately. She held her crotch the whole way back and never said another word."

Charlie was now whipping herself, laughing so hard at the story.

Decky continued, "That wasn't the end of it, by a long shot. Once we got to shore, she sat on the edge of the boat. I'm sure she was trying to figure out if there was any permanent damage to her vital parts. I kept saying how sorry I was right up to the point when I dropped the boom on her head. I could have died right there. I dropped the rope I was still holding and ran like the wind."

Charlie was able to gasp out, "Did you see her again?"

"Yes, later at dinner she called me outside of the mess hall. She told me it was okay, she knew it was an accident. She cautioned me to be more careful of underwater hazards and left it at that. She had no way of knowing that I was absolutely crushed, with no idea why I felt the way I did. I stayed away from her the rest of the week."

Decky joined Charlie in laughter. Decky thought about all the little crushes she had on different females growing up. It all made a lot more sense now.

Charlie commented on the way in, "Well, I for one am glad you only hit on straight girls. If you had come up on the right kind of lesbian, under the right circumstances, your life would have been a lot different."

"Yeah, Lizzie would have put me in a straight jacket and hand delivered me to Tidewater Psychiatric Institute, making them promise not to let me out until I was cured. Cured, meaning not gay."

Charlie chided, "You would have been stud lesbian of the community, who are you trying to kid? You would've gone through the crowd around here and half the ones in the next county by your early twenties, if it took that long."

Decky pretended to be offended, pretended because it was probably true. "I think I might have been a bit more selective than that. I've seen some lesbians that scare the shit out of me."

"Okay, maybe you would have only screwed the pretty ones, but you definitely are a sex maniac. If you had known about this back then, you would have been a legend." Charlie wasn't letting up.

Decky pulled the sailboat into the boathouse and secured it. She got out of the boat, offering Charlie her hand. "I guess you're lucky I didn't become a lesbian sooner. Now you can experience my climb to legendary-lesbian lover status up close and personal."

Not missing a beat Charlie replied, "It better remain real personal or I'll have to show you what we do to cheaters out on the Panhandle."

Decky grinned. "Yeah, and what's that?"

Charlie started for the house. "Your momma's not the only one who knows how to use a gun."

#

Decky, Charlie, and Miss Kitty were on the couch, stuffed to the gills with steak, baked potato, and salad. Dixie burped and lay down at Decky's feet, scoured T-bone across her paws. A black and white Nancy Drew movie was playing on the TV screen.

"I ate too much. I have to exercise or my stomach is going to burst. Come on, go swimming with me." Decky tried to pry Charlie up from the couch.

Charlie was watching the movie. "No, I have to figure out if it's the business manager or old farmer Gray. It'll drive me nuts if I don't know for sure. Go ahead. I'll come down in a minute."

Decky left Charlie to solve the mystery, while she and Dixie ventured downstairs. Decky set the timer on the treadmill for Dixie, which the dog dearly loved, and started swimming laps. Since meeting Charlie, Decky had eaten more food and consumed more alcohol than she had in years. Her body was starting to fight back. She had to get back to some kind of a routine, soon.

Decky swam until her stomach felt better and the overstuffed feeling had dissipated. She made the turn at the far end of the lap pool and headed back to the other end. She wore goggles when she swam laps, not so she could see, but because the water bothered her eyes. The goggles did allow her to keep a close eye on where exactly she was in the pool.

Decky checked to see how far she was from the end of the pool. She almost took water in her lungs when she saw first feet, and then followed the legs to the golden triangle, there just below the surface. She pulled up short and stood up. There before her was a very naked Charlie.

"I watched you for a while, and then when you didn't stop I thought I would see if I could get your attention." Charlie had a mischievous smile on her face.

Decky took off the goggles. "You have my complete attention."

"I was just wondering, does that hot tub on the bedroom balcony work?"

Decky thought she could see where this was going, so she got out of the pool and headed for the steps. "Yep, it works."

Charlie was following her out of the pool, looking a little curious as to why Decky would get out of a pool with her naked and still in it. "I thought we might try it out when you got done down here."

Decky threw a towel at her, grabbed one for herself, slipped into the boot, and stepped into the elevator. "Life is good!"

Charlie stepped in front of the elevator, still confused. "What are you talking about?"

Decky grinned and showed Charlie that dimple. "I am in an orthopedic boot about to race a naked woman to the third floor and I have an elevator." Decky shut the folding iron door. "Life is definitely good!"

9

Decky laid awake, silently watching Charlie dress for work. She loved to watch Charlie flit around the room fixing her hair, tying her shoes. Decky thought Charlie dressed comfortably, yet very professional. She was one of those women that looked good in cotton or silk, with or without makeup. Today Charlie wore a white cotton sleeveless shirt with pressed khakis. She looked fresh, even though the night before had been a long one.

Charlie checked herself one more time in the mirror.

"You look cute as a button." Decky finally spoke.

"You need to get out of that bed, if you're taking me to get my car. I don't like leaving it at the cottage. And I am not going to be afraid of your mother." Charlie was emphatic on this point.

Decky knew there was no point arguing. Charlie had made up her mind and told Decky so, the minute she awoke.

"Okay, Charlie, I'm up. I'll take a quick shower and we can head out."

"I'll go start the coffee. You want anything to eat, toast or something quick?"

"No, I'll just have yogurt. That should hold me for a while."
Decky skipped past Charlie to the bathroom. Charlie slapped
her on the butt as she went by.

"Get a move on there, little doggie."

Decky called to Charlie, as she disappeared into the
bathroom, "Is that one of those cowboy things I have to get
used to?"

Charlie exited down the stairs, but not before adding, "At
least I haven't crawled in bed with my boots on."

She was gone before Decky could tell her that actually
sounded hot to her, but the words Charlie and bed together
sounded hot to Decky anyway. Decky showered, jumped into a
tee shirt and shorts, and joined the rest of the family in the
kitchen. Charlie had just poured Decky a cup of coffee when
the phone rang.

Decky absent-mindedly answered the phone, because for
the moment her defenses were down. She was still imagining
the boot scenario. "Hello."

A male voice was on the line. "I'd rather see a cow back up
to a stump than two lesbians."

Decky's facial expression must have changed. Charlie
stopped talking to the cat and watched Decky.

"Who is this?" It was the only thing Decky could think to
say.

The phone line went dead. The other party hung up.

"What was that all about?" Charlie asked.

"Nothing, wrong number I guess." Decky hung up the
receiver. She checked caller I. D., but the number was
unavailable.

Charlie would not let it go. "That didn't look like a wrong
number. Your face went white as a sheet."

Decky hid her face behind the coffee cup. "I just didn't understand them at first, that's all. Let's go. You don't want to be late."

Charlie did not look pleased, but she gathered her things and followed Decky and Dixie out the door. Charlie told Decky she would be home around 1 p.m. Decky had errands to run in town. They would meet back at the house for a late lunch. Unbeknownst to Charlie, Decky had a new plan.

Just before she got out of the Expedition, Charlie turned to Decky. "I know that wasn't a wrong number. Decky, I'm in this too. You can't protect me all the time. I'm a big girl. I can take care of myself."

Decky smiled. "I know you can, but I can protect you from the trivial bull shit, stuff that isn't important. I promise to keep you informed of all the important things, okay?"

"Was that a threatening phone call, yes or no?" Charlie was speaking in her teacher voice. Decky felt like a student late with homework.

"No." Decky was being honest. The person had made no threats.

"Okay, I'll see you at lunch then." Charlie hopped out on the ground and headed for her car.

Decky backed up and pulled around so their driver side doors were facing each other. "Hey! Didn't you forget something?"

Charlie looked around. She couldn't see that anything was missing. She even looked at her shoes. Nope, she had forgotten nothing. She shrugged at Decky.

"You forgot to kiss Dixie goodbye. She's really hurt. I mean I can get by without a kiss, but the princess is a very sensitive young lady."

Charlie walked over to the back window, where Dixie was hanging out as far as the window would let her. Decky couldn't roll them all the way down, because Dixie had taken a flying leap out the back window once, while Decky was driving. Thank God, she had only been going twenty miles an hour at the time.

"You have a wonderful day there, princess." Charlie kissed Dixie right on the lips, and then started back to her car.

"Hey! What about me?" Decky pleaded out the window.

Charlie smiled slyly and turned around. "Thought you said you could get by without it?"

"I lied."

#

Decky drove into town. She first went to the builder's supply that would be receiving her replacement window and handling the install. She made sure the same guys that installed the other windows would be on the crew, paid for everything, and headed to Birdsong's, the old hunting and fishing store downtown.

This was one of those old stores found in little towns all over, until Bass Pro Shops put most of them out of business. The bells jingled on the door and the wooden floor squeaked as Decky entered. The walls were lined with shelves containing farming, hunting, and fishing apparel. One corner held waders and boots of all sizes. Decky really liked the tiny pair of waders in the window. She always pictured a "little man" and his dad hunting for the first time when she saw them.

Decky had been coming to this store as long as she could remember. Sometimes on Saturday mornings, she and R.C. had sat for hours, rehashing the Friday night football games with the locals. Everyone who worked here knew Decky and she knew all of them like family. Decky wanted to buy Charlie her very own fishing rod and this was the only place to do it.

You couldn't belong here until you had a rod or gun from Birdsong's. It was part of her new plan.

Decky went over to the rods and reels section. She could see that Mr. Birdsong was busy with some men in the back corner by the cold pot-bellied stove. They were there either to do business or brag on a fish. Either way, Decky didn't want to disturb them. Decky knew what she wanted and could find it on her own. She practically had the merchandise memorized.

Decky chose an eight-foot-six-inch Fenwick, inshore rod, adding a Daiwa Steed reel. She gathered line and a few new casting lures. After she had completed her fishing gear selections, she made her way over to the counter.

Mr. Birdsong waved to her from the back of the store. "I'll be right there."

Decky waved him off. "Stay there. I have a few more things to get."

Mr. Birdsong smiled at her and went back to his conversation. A few of the men standing in the back turned to look at her. One actually sniffed the air, wrinkled up his nose, and turned back around. Decky told herself it was nothing. Maybe just a personal tick the guy had. She went over to the wader's section. Charlie would need a pair of these when Decky took her flounder gigging at Oregon Inlet.

Flounder gigging was a favorite activity of Decky's. In the marshy section of the Inlet, you could walk around at night with a lantern and gig the flounder by tracing their outlines in the sand, or when the two eyes, located on the same side of its head, shined up in the light. Decky didn't frog gig. She wouldn't eat frog legs. She didn't kill anything she couldn't eat. Most of the time, she released the fish she caught, unless she planned to cook them. Decky loved flounder and she loved to catch them this way. It made it a game.

Today was a different kind of fishing. Decky found a vest and hat for Charlie and carried them along with the waders up to the counter. Mr. Birdsong met her there. They chatted, small talk about her mother and father. Decky bought Charlie a lifetime fishing license. Mr. Birdsong totaled her purchases and ran her card. While she waited, he went to get some paper to wrap the rod. The men in the back broke up their morning bragging session and exited one after the other, shouting a farewell to Mr. Birdsong. The last to leave was the man who had sniffed the air.

Now Decky could see who it was. It was Trey's uncle. She hadn't seen him in a while, so she had not recognized him earlier. He came very close to Decky. So close that she pressed her stomach to the counter to let him by.

"I know what you are," he said under his breath so she could hear him. Then he left.

Decky was stunned. The venom in the man's voice was so clear. What did he have to do with anything? How did her life impinge on his? It didn't, but there it was. Hate. Hate for this thing she was now. Labeled as not natural. Abhorrent to normal society. The normal society that got to decide what was "normal" for everyone else. The holier than thou bunch. *Fuck 'em.*

She knew Mr. Birdsong had heard the man the minute she saw his face. What would he say? He had watched her grow up. Surely, he wouldn't let something like this change the way he had always treated her. She told herself it wasn't shame she was feeling, but it sure felt like it. Decky was not ashamed of the way she felt about Charlie.

"I'm sorry he said that, Decky. What you're doing don't sit well with most folks around here. You can hope it'll blow over when they find somebody else to talk about." Mr. Birdsong at least was not judging her. Even if he was, he was keeping it to himself. Decky wished everybody else would too.

"I'm sorry too, Mr. Birdsong." Decky picked up her packages from the counter.

Mr. Birdsong came around the counter to open the door for her. Before opening the door, he stopped, blocking Decky's path. Here it comes, Decky thought, but what he said was not what she expected.

"Decky, you remember my oldest boy, Jack?"

Decky nodded yes.

"He went off to college and he never came back here. I know why, although he has never told me. He couldn't live his life here. I miss him, but I wouldn't have him live here. I would be afraid for him. I'm afraid for you too, Decky. It only takes one person in a place like this to rile up the wrong kind of people. Your momma has been all over this town and the surrounding counties, if not in person, by phone or email. Everybody knows, Decky."

"What does everybody think they know? I have a new friend. The rest is nobody's business." Decky was overwhelmed with the audacity of people.

"You are right. It is nobody's business, but sometimes being right is the worst thing you can be. If you can't reason with a person, being right doesn't mean a damn thing. Be careful, Decky. You are not a nobody around here. People know who you are, where you live. You don't know this side of life. You've always been liked and loved. You don't know the evil that exists in some people, self-righteous people."

"I appreciate your talking to me, Mr. Birdsong. I'll be careful. Remember, I might have been liked and loved, but I did grow up with Lizzie. That should get me a few points."

Decky hugged him, with her packages banging in to him. As they parted, Decky said, "Hey, tell Jack hello for me the next time you talk to him."

#

Decky went home, packed the boat, and waited. She swam laps, worked out with weights, did some work on the book, caught up on email, but all she was really doing was waiting. When the time came, she fixed lunch and waited some more. Decky needed Charlie. Charlie made none of the other things matter. Time ticked by slowly and the anxiousness in her chest grew.

Decky did not want to think about what her mother had done. She definitely did not want to think about Trey's uncle. She couldn't let herself think about Mr. Birdsong's warning. It was too frightening. She had known Lizzie would freak out, but why did her being with Charlie fill so many people with hate? That's what it was, pure malicious hate. Had Decky really been that naïve? Charlie had to come home soon. Decky was becoming more and more paranoid by the minute.

When she could stand it no longer, she called Zack. Zack, of course, was not answering so she left a long rambling message. Then she called back to tell him to ignore the previous message, explaining Lizzie was making her crazy. At least Zack would understand. No one else in the world could understand Lizzie, unless they had seen it for themselves. It was beyond others' ability to comprehend. The closest thing people could relate to Lizzie was a crazed sitcom mom. However, there was nothing funny about Lizzie when you were on the shit end of her stick.

Decky was about to call Brenda when she and Dixie heard a car door slam. She checked Dixie's tail. If it was up and wagging everything was safe; if it was between her legs and she was looking for a way out, she knew it was Lizzie. Dixie had an uncanny way of knowing when Lizzie was on a warpath and she definitely knew the sound of Lizzie's car. Dixie's tail was up and in full princess swing. She beat Decky to the door.

Decky had to wait in line until the greeting of the princess had been completed. Then she had to wait while Miss Kitty did donuts in the floor and whined until she had been thoroughly petted. Finally, Charlie made it to Decky, where Decky grabbed her and hugged her tight.

"Whoa! You're squeezing the air out of me." Charlie coughed.

"God, I missed you. I think you should quit your job and stay with me all the time. I don't do that well without you. It's not as if you would be a kept woman or anything. I've thought about it. We could call you a mental health specialist and I could pay you. Then you wouldn't feel like a hooker."

Charlie set her briefcase and some papers on the table in the foyer. She was looking at Decky, trying to read her. Charlie took Decky by the hand and led her to a stool at the island. She took two bottles of water out of the fridge and then sat beside Decky.

Charlie reached for Decky's hand. "Honey, what happened today? Obviously something did. You're going to have to catch me up."

"Well, what do you want to hear first, the part about the asshole in the hunting store or the live news bulletin Lizzie has managed to circulate? You pick." Decky said this with sincerity. She was just relaying the story.

Charlie squeezed her hand. "Did somebody say something to you at the store?"

Decky was off. She told Charlie the whole story without stopping, even the part about Lizzie sounding off like a foghorn. It felt so good to tell someone, to tell Charlie. Charlie would understand. She had been gay a long time. She would know what to say to make the fear and anguish go away.

When she was finished, Decky sighed and then said, "So, how was your morning?"

Charlie smiled slightly. "Decky, nothing happened that you weren't expecting. We talked about this. You just saw it up close for the first time. Did it change anything? Did it make you sorry you did this?"

Decky popped her chin up off her chest. "Absolutely not! I wouldn't change a thing about us. I don't care what people say or do."

"Then what people say has no meaning. It can only hurt you if you let it. It isn't an easy thing to give up the image people have of you for a new one, but that's all in their heads anyway. Nothing you say or do will change the way people feel. They will feel the way they want to about you and me. You have to decide to rise above it or it will eat you alive."

Decky listened intently to every word Charlie said. Then quietly she said, "I really didn't think it would bother me what people thought. But then again, I didn't think it would bother so many people. There are gay women everywhere. I thought they'd be used to lesbians by now. I don't see people ragging on the girls at the ball park."

"That's because you haven't been to the ball park since you and I got together. You start hearing and seeing things that have always been there. You just see from a new perspective. Ask the girls. They will tell you. It happens in every town on every field. Some drunken redneck starts up and gets his buddies going. You just keep playing and hope they go away." Charlie told this from the vantage point of experience.

"I guess you were right. I am naïve." Decky felt defeated, although she hadn't been sure what game she was playing.

"No, you just look on the bright side of things. You've led a charmed life, other than Lizzie, now you have to face adversity. You will be fine, once the shock wears off and the anger sets in. Then you can have fun coming back at them with one-liners that usually go right over their heads. It's great fun. I'll show you the next chance I get. It's that stunned look on their faces, when you actually speak to them that really gets to me." Charlie made a very funny face as an example.

Decky laughed and begged Charlie never to make that face again. Decky felt so much better, she was hungry again. She had thought she would not be able to eat lunch, but now that Charlie was here, things were looking up. What Charlie said made sense. Other people did not make you feel. You felt what you allowed yourself to feel. Right now, she felt like eating and then taking her girl out for some bass fishing. God, she hoped Charlie didn't catch another eel.

#

Once lunch was done and Charlie had changed clothes, Decky gave her the vest and fishing hat. The hat had a long bill, which looked cute in a goofy kind of way on Charlie's little head. Charlie balked a little on the fishing idea, still fearful of what else might lurk in the Sound waters. Decky promised they would only use top water gear aimed at catching plain old bass, no exotic species.

"Okay, I'll go, but if anything I can't recognize gets on my hook, you have to be the boy and get it off."

Decky laughed at her and took her hand. "I'll be your hero. I promise."

Once on the boat, Decky showed Charlie the new rod and reel. Charlie really was a fisherman. She had the line loaded and was taking practice castings before Decky got the boat away from the dock. Dixie assumed her station in the bow.

"Reel it in Jimmy Houston, we're going to my favorite fishing hole."

With that, they were off, flying over the water with the spray from the small swells splashing over them. Decky had never opened the boat up for Charlie, but when she hit the channel, she roared both engines into full throttle and watched Charlie as she grinned from ear to ear. This was Decky's kind of girl all right.

Decky slowed the boat and pulled into a secluded cove. No houses were in sight and the way the cove was shielded from the wind made the surface slick. The bugs and frogs sang loudly, echoing across the water. Decky dropped a trolling motor into position and maneuvered the boat to a good spot. An old tree had fallen in the water, its branches extending above and below the surface. The bottom near the tree was prime bedding sand for bass.

"You can usually catch a few in here. Every now and then one of those big mommas gets on your line. That's when this light tackle becomes really fun."

Charlie cast her lure expertly at the base of the tree. "I love this rod and reel. It's like the one I used at home, but seriously, you have to stop spending money on me. I have money of my own."

Decky cast her lure away from Charlie's, but still near the tree. "I don't buy you things to make you feel good. I buy them because it makes me feel good. Don't deny me my little pleasures. I have so few."

Charlie responded, "Oh, I think you've been getting plenty of pleasure lately."

Decky just grinned.

They fished for several hours, moving around the small cove. Charlie and Decky both caught a couple of small bass and released them. The fight with the little fish was entertaining on the lightweight rods. The rod would bend and dance with every movement of the fish.

Dixie always enjoyed the way the bass would splash out of the water. Although she didn't swim, so much as wade, she did enjoy the aquatic life around here. She never did understand why Decky had freaked out when she wallowed in the dead fish she found on the shoreline. It had smelled so pretty to Dixie, apparently.

Charlie's shoulders started to burn. She had not spent as much time outside as Decky and had forgotten sunscreen. Decky dug around in the boat and located the bottle she kept around for Zack. Although he was as tan as Decky, he was much fairer skinned, and needed sunscreen if he stayed out for a long time.

Decky was applying the sunscreen to Charlie's shoulders when Alan Jr.'s boat slowly made its way into the cove. A thought flashed in Decky's mind. *Had that been Alan Jr.'s voice on the phone this morning?* It was hard to tell. It had sounded muffled, as if something were over the mouthpiece of the phone. Decky stopped putting the lotion on Charlie. Something felt different about seeing Alan Jr. This time she felt fear.

Decky did not take her eyes off Alan Jr.'s boat, while she used the trolling motor to aim the boat out of the cove. He was not alone. She could see two or three male heads in the back of the approaching boat. From the sounds emanating from the stern, the men in the boat had been drinking.

One of them stood up when they got closer. Decky recognized him. It was one of Alan Jr.'s friends, Tommy Mercer. Decky knew him as a teenager. He was a drunk then and he was no different now.

"Hey there, Decky," Tommy slurred. "Who's your new friend?"

"How are you, Tommy? It's been a long time." Decky deflected his question.

It must have been the tone in Decky's voice that alerted Charlie to a problem. She continued to fish, but Decky could see the tightening of Charlie's neck muscles. The other men, including Alan Jr., were not saying anything, but they were definitely prodding Tommy along.

"Jr. here tells me you're batting for the other team now. Ain't you a little old to be takin' up muff diving?"

Alan Jr.'s boat erupted in laughter and backslapping.

One of the other guys spoke up, "Naw, Decky ain't switched teams. She just needs a real man to set her straight, so to speak. What's the matter, Jr. here ain't man enough for you?"

Tommy jumped in, "I got your man right here." He grabbed his crotch. "That looks like a mighty fine piece of ass you got there. Any chance I can get in on that?"

Decky was pissed. She would have shot him if she had a gun, but she didn't. Instead, Decky lifted the trolling motor out of the water and headed for the steering console. To her dismay, she heard Charlie starting to speak. Charlie had reeled in her line and placed her rod in the ski well along the side. She was standing facing the boat full of men when Decky realized what was happening.

"Decky here told me that there were lots of different kinds of people around these parts, different from what I grew up with in Oklahoma. I'll be glad when I meet them, because from where I stand, you have exactly the same beer bellied, redneck assholes we have at home. Been there done that, so if you'll excuse us, we'll be leaving now."

Decky took her cue and floored the boat, as much as she could in the shallow cove. She looked back to see all of the men with the exact look Charlie had described. They were stunned. Charlie grinned back at Decky.

"See, I told you so."

#

That night Decky and Charlie decided to go down to Hatteras Island, after Charlie got off work Thursday afternoon. She would not have class on Friday, because summer classes met only two days a week. Being out of the county seemed like a good idea to both of them.

Decky had a cottage at Rodanthe, which she kept for her and Zack, so they could go to the beach whenever they liked. She never rented it, because she never knew when she would get the urge to go walk in the sand or surf fish.

Into the night, Decky entertained Charlie with tails of the Outer Banks. Decky wanted to show Charlie everything. She knew it was impossible in one three-day weekend, but she would take her down to see the Cape Hatteras Lighthouse. They would leave early Friday morning, see the lighthouse in Buxton, and then drive down to Hatteras Village to catch the ferry to Ocracoke.

The Cape Hatteras Lighthouse had a special place in Decky's heart. She had climbed it enumerable times as a child, flying kites off the top on a fishing rod and other unrestricted activities. Now that the light had been moved, because of the dwindling shoreline, you couldn't just run around in it like a wild child. Built in 1870, it was still the tallest lighthouse in the nation, standing watch over the Graveyard of the Atlantic, as this treacherous area of the ocean was known. Sharing this icon with Charlie would delight Decky.

Decky explained how Edward Teach, better known as the famous pirate Blackbeard, had his head chopped off just outside the harbor at Ocracoke. Legend says his body swam around the boat three times looking for his head then sank to the bottom.

Decky talked about the Civil War, how her ancestors had come all the way from Raleigh to fight in a battle on Roanoke Island, only to be taken prisoner as they stepped on the shore. How they had then been held in Elizabeth City, until pardoned. Decky talked about blockade running through the dangerous shoals. She told Charlie how the locals had surrendered without much of a fight on Hatteras and Ocracoke Islands, allowing the damn Yankees to occupy both forts that guarded the valuable Hatteras Inlet.

Charlie was enthralled. Decky showed her pictures in books and lectured on coastal history from the 1500's through World War II, when the Germans came ashore as spies or ship wrecked submariners. One group of spies had lived right there in Buxton, unnoticed by the locals. Decky would show Charlie all the German memorabilia at the Lighthouse museum. There was also the new museum down in Hatteras Village where you caught the ferry.

Decky was so excited, Charlie didn't interrupt her except to have her expound on a particular fact or place. It wasn't until Charlie yawned, that Decky looked at the clock. She had been talking since they sat down after supper and it was now 10 o'clock.

"I'm sorry. I didn't realize it was so late. I do this when I write, too. I will write for eighteen hours nonstop, take a nap, and go again. I have a tendency to tell you everything I know about a place. I find history irresistible."

"I am fascinated. Oklahoma is only 100 years old. Our history goes back to the ice ages, but we didn't really participate in the Civil War and certainly not the Revolution. It's all very exciting and I want to see all of it, but I am tired from the sun and I just can't let you get started again." Charlie teased Decky. "You forget I know how obsessed you can be over something you find irresistible, and I have a job to go to, while you may sleep-in if you like."

Decky feigned hurt. "I have a job. I just have a bit of a different schedule than most people."

Charlie quipped as she started up the stairs, "One of us has to appear normal, so we can keep your mother from sending you to the crazy farm, and there's no chance in hell it's going to be you."

Charlie ran, because Decky was no longer on crutches.

10

Charlie was rested enough to wake Decky early. They showered together and generally played grab ass for part of the morning. They played like newlyweds, engrossed in each other's hopes and dreams. They read the Wednesday paper, not talking, but occasionally touching the other. Charlie finally got dressed for work and left Decky feeling as though this was the way life should be, the way life would be with Charlie.

Caught up in the glow, Decky set about cleaning house. She hated to clean house. It was never going to be clean enough for Lizzie, so why try, but she liked her house to be clean. It looked so nice that way. She usually had her mom send one of the girls from the motel over to help her. Most of the girls lived on this side of the beach and did not work every day at the motel. They liked the money Decky paid and Decky liked the company. It made work so much easier and not to mention faster.

Today Decky didn't need company. She was her own company. Miss Kitty and Dixie watched her as she moved from room to room, singing at the top of her lungs to a CD she had made of her favorite cry in your beer music. She wasn't sad, not in the least. Decky loved to sing those songs, and now that she knew what the songs were crying about, the loss of real love, they became much more dramatic. Some of the high notes scared the animals into different parts of the house.

Decky laughed at them, but kept on singing through the morning, as she cleaned three floors of a too big house. She was finally finished after wiping down the equipment in the gym. In the salty air, everything had to be wiped down regularly to slow down the inevitable rust. Decky put away the cleaning supplies and stripped down to nothing. She plopped herself in the Jacuzzi with a bottle of water, proud of her accomplishment. She really did have a job, she thought, keeping this big ass house together.

Miss Kitty led Dixie down the stairs. She appeared to have been chosen to give Decky a message. She walked back and forth in front of Decky, just out of reach, meowing repeatedly with this voice that squeaked out in almost syllables. Decky tried to understand, but it was just impossible. What in the hell did this cat want?

Decky looked to Dixie for help. "What's she saying girl? Help me Dixie-wan-Kenobi, you're my only hope."

Dixie cocked her head and raised her eyebrows. She was just as dumbstruck as Decky. Decky decided Miss Kitty wanted her to follow her, so she picked up her dirty clothes, threw them into the laundry room, grabbed a robe, and following Miss Kitty's lead, entered the elevator.

Evidently, Miss Kitty had figured out how the thing worked and was now prepared to be carried like the queen she was to the next floor. Dixie, not to be outdone, climbed in and then jumped out again. Decky figured Dixie remembered the first and only ride she had ever taken on the contraption. She had hated it. Now she made her way around to the stairs. Decky closed the door and up they went, the queen and her servant.

Dixie had beaten them up the stairs and did a kind of Na-na-na-na-naaa dance outside the elevator. Miss Kitty exited the elevator, as if she did not notice Dixie. She started the squeaky meows again and tiptoed quickly into the couch area. Decky and Dixie followed her, both somewhat afraid of what Miss Kitty may be leading them toward.

Miss Kitty was doing circles in front of the couch. The squeaking, "Maa, maa," became louder and more rapid. Decky could not see anything out of the ordinary. There was a pair of socks on the couch that she thought she had left on the bed upstairs. Miss Kitty suddenly jumped on the couch and pounced on the socks. She killed the socks repeatedly while showing Decky the best of her vocal qualities. Decky and Dixie had never seen anything like it. Charlie would have to explain this behavior. Miss Kitty didn't stop making noise until Decky petted her on the head and took the socks.

"Good job! Killed those nasty socks. We're saved!" Decky said to the purring animal. Dixie was excited too, although she didn't know what the big deal was. If she messed with Decky's socks, she got in trouble. Decky must have felt sorry for the little black and white furry thing. It was obviously mental.

After dressing upstairs, she came down and put on the socks Miss Kitty had killed for her. She had worn a much smaller brace this morning, but now she put the boot back on. Too much, too soon and she'd undo the healing already taking place. She didn't have to be as careful with the boot.

Decky fixed everyone lunch. She had a salad, Dixie had her regular food with her monthly medicines enclosed, and Miss Kitty had a can of her cat food up on the counter, away from Dixie's prying nose.

Lunch accomplished, the three of them settled in to do some research. Decky felt so happy, she might write a little this afternoon. If the muse should strike she was energized enough to accommodate her. Decky had just become engrossed in a particular passage when the phone rang. Decky checked the caller I.D. It was her father's cell phone. She had given it to him so he could get through to her when she was avoiding her mother.

"Hey, Dad. How's it going?" She forgot momentarily that his life probably hadn't been as peaceful as hers had lately.

"Oh, fair to partly cloudy. Got some checks here from your mother, she said just sign where she highlighted. She also said if you needed to see the checkbook balanced, she would send that along too."

"I see this is going to leak over into the business side of things. I thought she would at least leave that out." Decky had only hoped, she had known there wasn't much of chance her mother would miss this opportunity to play the martyr.

"I'm trying to stay neutral here, if you know what I mean. Can I come over there or would you rather meet somewhere else?" R.C. actually sounded serious.

"Daddy, you come over here anytime you want. You are always welcome. I'll see you in a few minutes."

"All right then, I'll see you soon."

R.C. arrived just as the pot of coffee Decky had put on finished filling up. R.C. knocked on the glass in the front door. He always did this; he never rang the bell. Decky shouted for him to come on in. Dixie barked a greeting at R.C., for which she received lots of scratches and pets.

Decky and R.C. had their coffee out on the deck while Decky signed the checks.

"You know Dad, we could set this up electronically and I would never have to sign another check."

"Your mother doesn't trust the bank to take care of your money. Somebody could steal your codes or whatever and clean you out."

"The bank would have to repay the money if they allowed it to be stolen. It's actually safer than having a checkbook lying around." Decky had tried to win him over before. It was hard for his generation to trust electronic banking. He liked to see his cash.

"If you are going to keep lettin' your mother do the books, then you have to let her do it her way. Just like you want her to let you do things your way. Get my meanin'?"

"I get it, Dad." She handed him the signed checks and papers in a manila envelope. "Hey, I'm taking Charlie down to the Rodanthe cottage Thursday night. Drive by a couple of times, here and at the Sound cottage, will ya'? Keep an eye on the place for me, okay."

R.C. must have seen something in Decky's face. "Have you been having any trouble?"

Decky didn't want her father to worry, so she played it off. "No, not really, Alan Jr.'s been a real redneck asshole, but that's all."

"Why, what did he do?" R. C.'s expression had changed. He didn't have to agree with Decky's lifestyle, but she was still his daughter. Anger flashed in his eyes.

"Oh, he just showed his ass the other day, nothing for you to come rushing in to defend me for. Just keep an eye on things. I would appreciate it." Decky did her best to impede him from any further discussion about it. She introduced him to Miss Kitty, who did a dance for him all around his feet. He forgot all about the anger and played with the cat, which caused Dixie nearly to knock him over to get attention, too. Soon he was at the door.

"Decky, you be careful. You let me know if Alan, Jr. gives you any more trouble. I'll take care of that."

"Thank you, Dad. I love you. I love momma, too, for whatever it's worth." Decky meant it.

"I know you do. I'll keep a watch out while you're gone. Take care." R.C. left and Decky went back to reading.

Around the time Decky expected Charlie to be home, the phone rang. She recognized Charlie's number and answered it.

"Hey, I was just starting to look forward to your arrival." Decky said, in the happy voice she had all day.

Charlie's voice came on the other end, "That's why I'm calling. Brenda and Chip want me to go out to dinner tonight with some colleagues at the U. I think I need to do this. I will need all the friends I can get if your mother creates a bigger scandal than she already has."

Decky was crushed. She tried not to let it show in her reply. "That sounds like fun. You should go. Meet some new people."

Charlie sounded relieved. "Brenda said you had been holding me hostage long enough. It was time for me to get out in the world."

Decky hated Brenda. She would tell her so the next time she saw her. "What time do you think you'll be home?" *Brenda would die.*

"I'm not sure. We have to wait for Chip, so Brenda and I were going to do a little shopping and meet him later. Are you sure it's okay?"

Decky was so jealous, she started to laugh at herself. Charlie could go shopping with Brenda and out to eat with new friends. Decky wasn't so much jealous as disappointed at having to wait longer to see Charlie again, but she loved Charlie and she needed to do this. "Yeah, we're great. Remind me to tell you what Miss Kitty did, later."

"She didn't mess up anything did she?" Charlie sounded as if that was a real possibility. This was a little tidbit she may have left out.

"No, she killed a pair of socks." Decky was thinking about the cat doing real damage to something.

"Oh, she does that. Just take it away from her. She usually doesn't steal more than a pair a day. I've never been able to figure it out. She certainly wouldn't kill a mouse, she's afraid of them."

"Your cat is afraid of mice?" Decky laughed.

"Well, like you said, Dixie isn't a dog. What makes you think Miss Kitty is a cat?" Charlie was laughing too.

"Have a good time. Call me, so I know when you're coming home. I love you."

"Yes, well, I'll call you later and get that information to you." Decky knew someone had walked within hearing range of Charlie. Here it was again. Hide so no one can see.

"Bye." Charlie hung up.

Decky sulked for a while and then went for a swim. She had not been the least bit lonely until she met Charlie. Now every time she was away, Decky felt terribly alone. She had always been able to entertain herself. Now she wanted to entertain Charlie. Jesus, Decky, grow up. She was chastising herself. The woman has to go to work and she is allowed to have friends other than you. This is not third-grade when you could only have one friend.

Decky finished her laps and a heavy work out. She still couldn't run, so she rode the stationary bike until her legs and lungs gave out. She took a shower, put on comfortable clothes and did what she did before she met Charlie. She crawled up on the couch with her laptop and two cases of current research materials. Once again, Decky was lost somewhere in history, learning about other people's lives, and forgetting about her own.

The phone rang at 6 o'clock. Decky had been immersed in her work for four hours. It was Charlie. Maybe she was on her way home.

"Hey, I didn't realize what time it was until the phone rang. What's up?"

"You miss me that much, huh? Brenda and I are heading to meet Chip now. I wanted to call and tell you it will probably be nearly nine before I get home." Charlie sounded like she was having a good time.

"Okay, but be careful coming home. I do miss you. I'm actually lonely." Decky was serious.

"Oh poor thing, can't find anything to do in that big house filled with all those toys."

Decky crooned into the phone, "I can't live, if living is without you…"

Charlie found this exceedingly funny. "You are insane. I'll be careful. I'm not going to drink anything since I have to drive back. I wouldn't want one of your momma's buddies down at the sheriff's department to have an excuse to lock me up."

"That's my girl. Keep thinking, stay one step ahead of her. I love you, hurry home."

This time Charlie said it, "I love you, too."

Decky could hear Brenda doing her best gagging routine in the background. "Tell Brenda I love her, too."

Decky did not want to go back to the research, so she put everything away and went down to the boathouse. The boathouse had a live well, a refrigerator for beer, and a freezer for bait. She grabbed some frozen chicken wings and a net. She pulled the chicken out of the bag and placing it inside the net, she dropped it in the water so the chicken could thaw, but not be carried away by critters. Well, not until she was prepared to catch them.

Decky found the ball of string and cut some sections of about ten feet. She got a lidded bucket from under a shelf, recovered the chicken and the net, and went in search of her prey. Decky could have just set some crab pots, but this was so much more fun. It took skill and patience. Decky had perfected her technique since childhood.

She tied the still frozen wings, easier to break apart now after a few minutes in the warm shallow water, to the lengths of string. Today was a good day for crabbing. The water was clear. The crabs here were not as big or as salty as the ones on the ocean side, but they were just as good. A little more work because of their size, but then they were free and she had a great deal of fun catching them.

Decky and Dixie set out several lines around the dock. The crabs would pull on the string attached to the chicken. Crabs had this thing where they couldn't just stay there and eat something. They had to back away with it rapidly. If you tugged on the string, they just held on tighter. You then scooped up crab and chicken with the net. This only worked because the crab was too stubborn to let go. Kind of like Lizzie, Decky thought.

They caught two-dozen good-sized crabs, gave the remainder of the chicken to the survivors, and put away everything. It was now 8:00 p.m. and the sun was beginning to go down. Decky started a crab boil in the kitchen with a little vinegar, Old Bay seasoning, and a beer. While she waited for the water to boil, Decky went upstairs to take a shower. She didn't hear the phone ring.

Decky didn't realize she had missed Charlie's call, until a few minutes after she dropped the crabs in the boiling water. She had picked up her phone to take it with her onto the deck, where she was preparing the table for some serious crab eating. When she set the phone down on the newspaper-covered table, she saw the message light was blinking. She checked the missed calls list to see who had called. It was Charlie. Decky called the number to retrieve her messages.

Charlie said she was on her way home, it was 8:20, but first she had to stop for gas and at the cottage. She wanted to get some things for the trip to Rodanthe. Decky hung up and wished she had answered. She would have told Charlie to come on home. She would pick up anything Charlie needed from the cottage while Charlie was at work tomorrow morning. Decky tried to call her back, but Charlie must have been on the causeway. The cell reception there sucked. She left a message, but the message would only go through after she reconnected with her network. Decky doubted she would look at her phone while she was driving.

Decky went back to cooking the crabs. They were ready, so she drained the pot and put the crabs on the deck to cool. She prepared some butter and cocktail sauce. She put several beers in a bucket with ice and set it on the table with red and white checked giant napkins. She gave it the Martha Stewart seal of approval. Now all she needed was the girl. She was humming a tune from Gypsy, "...all I need now is the girl," when the phone rang again.

Alarm bells went off in Decky's head. The phone was ringing the special tone she had given the alarm system at the cottage. She answered and waited for the recorded message. There were several depending on the nature of the alarm. After the recorded voice identified the property address, the message continued, "The property at this address has lost power. The backup battery system is not responding. An unauthorized entrance is suspected."

Decky hung up. She tried Charlie's cell phone. Charlie should have been able to hear the phone ringing. She had to be at the cottage by now. Decky called the landline at the cottage, still no answer. Maybe Charlie had forgotten about the alarm. Maybe the power was out when she got there, and she just walked in without punching in the code. She was probably on her way over here now, embarrassed by the whole thing.

Decky clung to these hopes only momentarily. Something was wrong. She could feel it in her gut. She had learned not to ignore her gut. She grabbed her gun and Dixie and hit the door to the garage in full stride. She had run down the stairs, unconscious of her ankle. She let Dixie in the back and jumped into the driver's seat. The big SUV roared to life. Decky barely waited long enough for the roof to clear the still rising door. She turned the SUV around toward the road and floored it, throwing cones and pine needles along with a rooster tail of sand all over the front steps.

It was only five minutes to the cottage. It felt like it was taking forever. She felt the SUV ride around the final curve on two wheels. The tires squalled, as she braked to make the turn down the sandy lane. The three houses she passed on the lane had power. She could see the people moving around in them through the lighted windows. Her heart beat even faster. Her hopes of this being a simple power outage or forgotten alarm were vanishing quickly.

She flipped the phone open and speed dialed the twins. Her father would be asleep in his easy chair. The twins were her best hope.

"Conrad?" Decky said excitedly into the phone, when one of the boys answered.

"No, Travis."

"Whichever one you are, listen to me. Something's wrong at the cottage." Decky wanted his full attention.

"The one we moved the math teacher into?"

"Yes! Get my dad! Go over there and wake him up if you have to!"

"Where are you?"

"I'm pulling into the drive now. Move it!"

She slammed the phone closed and threw it on the passenger seat. Decky hit the ruts in the driveway going full bore. She and Dixie bounced around in the cab of the SUV like rag dolls, but somehow Decky hung onto the wheel. She had not bothered with the seatbelt, so was unhindered when she threw open the door and leapt out, Dixie hot on her heels. There was Charlie's car. No lights were visible on the property except for the streetlight at the back of the lot. It was on a line that ran from the road.

Something was definitely wrong. It was too quiet. The audible alarm was not sounding; the interior strobes were not flashing. The alarm had been disabled. Decky ran up the steps as fast as she could. The boot was heavy and each step sent a stab of pain through Decky, which under normal circumstances would have stopped her. Decky ignored the pain and pumped up the steps with all her resolve.

Reaching the front door, she turned the handle. It was locked.

"Charlie, are you in there? Are you all right?" Decky was frantic now.

No sounds came from inside the cottage. No lights shown except for slivers of light from the streetlight slicing through the blinds and the almost full moon. Decky walked around the deck, peeking in the windows, calling Charlie's name with the painful realization that something was terribly wrong here. When she arrived at the back door, she tried the handle, again locked. Why hadn't she brought the spare keys? Why hadn't she brought a flashlight?

She peered in the little windows on the back door. The curtain Charlie had added made it hard to see. Decky looked at the kitchen floor shining in the beam of light coming through the door of the bedroom. The window curtains must be open in there. She was just turning to go look through the bedroom windows, when her eye followed the beam of light toward the corner cabinets. She saw her feet first.

Charlie was on the floor, sitting tightly up against the cabinets in the corner. Decky could barely see her. Charlie saw Decky. She leaned forward, more into the light. It was then that Decky saw the white gag across Charlie's face… and the blood. Charlie's hands were tied behind her back, her feet tied at the ankles. Her blouse was torn and streaked with blood. She wasn't wearing any pants. Her eyes were wide with fear. She was trying to tell Decky something, but Decky didn't wait to figure out what was happening.

Decky pulled the pistol out of the waistband of her pants. She shattered the window by the lock, stuck her arm in through the hanging shards of glass, and turned the lock. She pulled her now bleeding arm out of the window, and burst into the cottage. She stopped with her back to the bedroom door, which blocked the light from Charlie. She was trying to see Charlie again in the dark, when she saw her, struggling to get up on her knees.

"Oh God. Charlie. Oh my God." Decky tried willing herself to move, but she just stood there with her arms out to her sides, the gun hanging loosely in her right hand. Suddenly, her knees gave out. Her whole world came crashing in around her. Slowly she came toward Charlie, sliding across the floor on her shins. Her survival instincts left her. She set the gun down and with trembling hands reached to untie the gag on Charlie's mouth. She never made it.

The blow to the back of her head wasn't enough to knock her out, but it did knock her down. She tried to reach for the gun, but it was too late. A large male hand, holding her gun, disappeared out of view just as she reached for it. Decky, sick with dizziness, couldn't make out the face of the man standing over her. It was too dark. The man backed up in front of the open back door, his face still in shadow. Decky thought for a second he was going to run, but then he started to laugh.

"Welcome to the party, Decky. Now it's every man's wet dream, two women at the same time. Although it would be nice if you'd cooperate a little better than your friend here, I just got done tying her up when you pulled up. She's a feisty little critter."

Decky's eyes were still swimming in her head. The ringing in her ears sounded like a train's whistle. She couldn't tell who this was, but she thought she recognized the voice, the part of his voice she could still hear, while the train passed through the station in her head.

"What the fuck are you doing?" Decky was trying desperately to regain her footing. The boot made it all that much harder.

The man laughed again. "I thought I made that quite clear. I intend to fuck the queer right out of both of you."

Decky regained her senses all at once. Not quite all at once, but quick enough to have caught that last sentence in full volume. Decky rose off the floor with some unknown strength. A noise from the back door startled the man. He turned his head to see what the noise was. It was then that Decky saw his face in the moonlight. It was the man from the boat. The one she hadn't known, the one egging Tommy on. He kept the gun on Decky as he scanned the darkness outside the door.

The man reached out to shut the door, taking his eyes away from outside and back onto Decky. He should have looked a little longer. Dixie dove at the door, knocking the man back against the frame of the bedroom door. Decky made her move. She ran at the man as hard as she could.

They bounced off the frame of the bedroom door and fell toward the main room. The gun flew from the man's hand, skidding across the linoleum floor toward the middle of the

233

room. This guy was big and strong. He threw Decky off of him with no real problem. He was actually enjoying this. He turned toward the gun and started to crawl after it. Dixie clamped onto one of the man's arms. She was determined not to let go, until the man managed to kick her in the ribs. Dixie whelped in pain as she hit the floor.

Decky once again lunged at the man, landing on her chest instead of his back. He quickly stood up, scooping the gun up as he did. He aimed the gun at Dixie, who was preparing another attack.

Decky screamed, "No, Dixie! Come here."

Dixie obeyed. The man followed Dixie with the gun. Decky sat up on her knees, as Dixie approached, limping. Decky patted her on the head. "Good girl, now go around there with Charlie, that's a good girl."

Dixie did as she was told. Decky waited until she heard Dixie's claws over near where she assumed Charlie still was. She wasn't sure anymore.

"If you think for one goddamned minute that I am going to let you hurt Charlie any more, you had better go ahead and kill me."

"Oh Decky, I'm going to kill you... but first, you are going to suck my dick, while your girlfriend there watches. And if I feel one sliver of a tooth, I will blow your head off, and then fuck your girl until I get tired. Then I am going to kill her and your goddamned dog." He had Decky by the hair, on her knees in front of him. The other hand had the pistol stuck in Decky's temple.

"Kill me now then motherfucker. Will that make you a man?" Decky was in an unfathomable rage. "Kill me now you low life piece of shit!"

Decky was spraying blood from a punch she'd taken, as she spoke.

"No, I'm going to play with you first. I have the gun, my rules." He let go of Decky's hair and undid his jeans with one hand. He took his dick in his hand. "Yeah, a little bit of this will straighten you girls right on out. You'll probably thank me when we get done."

"Shoot me! You limp dick asshole. I bet you need that gun to get it up?" Decky spit blood on the hand holding his limp member.

Something flashed across the man's face in the dark. He slapped Decky and put the gun under chin. He reached for his dick.

At that moment, the sharp report of a rifle exploded in the air. Glass went everywhere. The picture window shattered to reveal R.C., still holding the rifle on the man. It wasn't necessary. The shot had penetrated the man's brain and dropped him instantly. He crumpled to the floor in front of Decky. Dixie limped out from behind the counter and lay down next to Decky. Decky kissed Dixie, whispering, "Thank you."

It wasn't until R.C. climbed through the window that Decky got up. She swayed on her feet, but made her way around the counter to where the terrified Charlie waited, not knowing what had happened. When she saw Decky, she began to sob uncontrollably. So did Decky. She removed the bindings from Charlie's hands and feet along with the bloody gag. Charlie's left eye was swelling shut, her cheek already beginning to change color. Her lips were cut and bruised. Blood trickled from her nose. She'd had the holy shit beaten out of her.

Neither of them said anything. They just sat there on the cold linoleum holding each other, while Dixie watched over them. R.C. had come around the counter and seen the carnage. He said to someone, "Call an ambulance, call two. Get the sheriff. Don't stand there, do it now!"

Decky's father was suddenly all over them. He took Charlie from Decky. He laid her down on a blanket he had grabbed off the bed. He hovered over Charlie, all the time talking to both women.

"Decky. Rebecca! Are you okay? Where are you hurt?"

Decky didn't hurt. She was numb. She could only stare at her father as he worked on Charlie. He checked her pulse. He listened to her chest. He checked her eyes and spoke gently to her. "I'm Decky's father. You're going to be okay. The ambulance is coming." When he pulled her shirt open, he tried to hide the grimace.

Charlie managed a painful crooked smile. "Getting a little fresh there aren't you, R.C.?"

"I suppose that's some of that Midwestern sense of humor my daughter is so fond of. I'm going to put this comforter on you so you don't go into shock. You have to stay awake for me, okay. Decky talk to her."

Decky didn't move. She couldn't. She had nothing left.

R. C. covered Charlie up and turned his attentions to Decky. He checked her all over for injuries, feeling the bump on the back of her head. He looked around and saw a softball bat on the floor by the door. "Good thing you have such a hard head."

He checked her pupils. Then taking her face in both of his hands, he pulled her face up to his and looked into her eyes.

"Decky I just saw you fight for this woman, and for yourself. You have to dig deep now. If she's worth dying for, you have to help her now. Love's a powerful thing honey. You got to wake up now. She needs you."

Decky came around, slowly at first, then more quickly. She started talking to Charlie. She made Charlie tell her about all her brothers and sisters. Even though it hurt to talk, Charlie answered all of Decky's questions, until the first ambulance squad arrived. These were local volunteers, but highly skilled.

They only paused briefly over the dead man lying in the floor. Assessing the victims, they chose to take Charlie, which was the right decision. Decky stood up as the stretcher sprang up from the floor. She kissed Charlie on the forehead, the only place that didn't look injured.

"I'm right behind you. Stay awake. I'm right behind you." Decky's heart cracked in two when Charlie's fingertips left hers. How did this happen? All she did was fall in love with another human being, not a woman, not a lesbian, but a human being and not a thing to be hated. Why had this happened to them? They were so happy. Why couldn't everyone just leave them alone?

The sheriff's cars arrived en masse. A few stragglers came later, but the majority of the sheriff's department arrived at the same time as the sheriff. A dead man in a lesbian's cottage was evidently the biggest crime of all of their careers. They set about marking off the crime scene, taking pictures, and questioning the witnesses. Satisfied for the time being that R.C. and Decky posed no threat to anyone else, they let Decky go with the second ambulance squad.

Decky leaned on R.C. coming down the steps, because she refused to let them put her on a stretcher. Her father told her he would wake up the vet to look at Dixie and keep her with him overnight. The hunky ambulance driver was carrying the princess down the steps. Dixie looked at everyone as if they should pet the conquering hero, and of course, they did.

It wasn't until Decky reached the ground that she saw her. There was Lizzie talking to one of the deputies. R.C. didn't react quickly enough to stop Decky from heading for Lizzie with a head of steam.

"Are you satisfied now? Are you happy? Did you see what he did to her? Is that what you wanted?"

R.C. came up behind Decky and grabbed her by the waist. He couldn't hold her, as she continued toward Lizzie. Lizzie was frozen to the ground. The deputy took a step back from Lizzie as Decky drew within inches of her.

"You did this, you meddling old witch. You and your goddamned pride! Stay away from me, stay away from us. You did this and I will never forgive you!"

As R.C. and the hunky ambulance driver tackled Decky and put her in the ambulance, Decky screamed at her mother, "Why couldn't you just let me be happy? Why did you have to make this about you?"

Decky was played out. She fell back on the stretcher sobbing and finally let the worried EMT look at her wounds. R.C. said he would call Chip and Brenda to go to the hospital, while he took care of Dixie. Decky closed her eyes and tried to see Charlie, Charlie before the man had found her here, alone. How could Decky have let this happen to Charlie? Would she ever forgive her? Would she ever feel safe with Decky again? Then everything went black.

PART III

In front of god and everybody...

11

Decky regained consciousness in the emergency room entrance, when the big doors swooshed open. The excited noise inside contradicted the singing rain frogs outside on the grounds. She had people's hands all over her, all talking at once. Her eyes were being probed with light. She tried to find Charlie with her eyes, but she couldn't focus. She tried to say her name, but no one was listening.

Decky was rushed off for a CT scan. She fell asleep again in the machine. When she awoke, she was in a hospital gown, in a bed, with her ankle in a cast and her head throbbing so intensely that she quickly closed her eyes again. *What had Charlie said, she needed fresh air and liquids – Charlie!* Where was Charlie? How was Charlie? She opened her eyes, ignoring the pain, searching for the call button. Finding it down by her hand, she picked it up and held the button down until someone came to the side of her bed.

A nurse, Decky recognized as a player on one of the local teams, answered her page. "I'm glad to see you're awake. You had us worried there for a while. Turns out, your head is pretty thick where he hit you with that bat."

"Where is the woman who came in with me? Charlie... Charlene Warren, where is she?"

Decky grabbed the sides of her head. It hurt to talk.

"Let me get you something for that headache. I can't give you much though, you have a concussion."

Decky let go of her head. She looked at the nurse, reaching out to stop her hand from straightening the sheet and blanket covering Decky.

"Charlene Warren, is she okay? I have to know, now! Please." Decky stared at the nurse as tears welled up in her eyes.

"Decky, I heard what you did. Those deputies down the hall don't know how you two women and a dog fought that man off until your daddy got there. You're not next of kin, but if you're willing to die for her, then I reckon I can go find out how she is."

"Thank you." Decky sighed in relief.

The nurse left with a promise to come back soon, bringing news of Charlie's condition and pain meds for Decky's ankle and head. Decky wasn't sure why her ankle was in a cast, but she knew it was beginning to come back to life from the local anesthetic someone obviously used. She must have been really out of it. The evening flashed by, on the viewer behind Decky's eyes. She settled on the look of terror on Charlie's face.

When she no longer thought she could stand seeing that image one more second, a noise distracted her. She opened her eyes. It was Alan Jr. holding a grimy farm cap in his hands. He shuffled only a few feet into the room. He never looked up from the floor.

"I heard what Tommy's friend did to you and that other woman. I'm sorry, Decky. I wish I could take it all back. You have the right to love anybody you want to. I just wanted to let you know how sorry I am."

Alan Jr. didn't wait for a response from Decky. He just turned around and left. Decky was still staring out the door when Brenda's face popped into the doorframe.

"They told me you were awake. Are you okay? Do you need anything?" Brenda wanted to hug Decky, but refrained when Decky waved her off. Decky didn't want to know how many other places hurt. Her head and ankle were enough. Decky wanted only one thing from Brenda.

"How's Charlie? Where is she?"

"Decky, Charlie's pretty banged up. There was some internal bleeding. He thumped on her like a punching bag. She's out of surgery and everything looks fine. It was just a small bleed from a cracked rib. She's in the room behind yours. You are both in this special care unit."

Brenda patted her hand as tears rolled down Decky's face.

"She's never going to forgive me for getting her into this mess," Decky cried.

Brenda let out a little laugh. "Honey, every time that girl's eyes have been open, she's asking about you. I don't think you are going to be able to get rid of her that easy."

Decky brightened. "Can I see her?"

Brenda assumed the role of mother again. "Not right now. She needs to rest and so do you. You've been through a lot and you are both lucky to be alive. God Bless the NRA and R.C. Bradshaw!"

Decky relaxed a little. Charlie was okay. She was hurt, but she still loved Decky. They would get through this. Together they could do anything. She took the pain meds when the nurse brought them and drifted off to sleep.

#

She awoke again in the wee hours of the morning. The activity in the hall had quieted down. A pair of crutches leaned against the table beside the bed. A note was tied to them.

"Thought you might need these. Dixie is okay, just bruised ribs and a sprained ankle. Must run in the family. I'll see you tomorrow. Love, Dad".

Decky's head and ankle throbbed in unison as she made her way to the bathroom. She didn't ask anyone if she could get up, she was afraid they would bring a bedpan. She stood in front of the mirror, examining the bruises developing under both eyes. Her lip was swollen. There were a few other scrapes and dings, but she looked better than she felt. Her ribs ached. She thought about Charlie in the next room.

Decky was overcome with pangs when she thought of Charlie waking up scared and alone. She slipped her head out the door. No one was in the hallway. The nurses were all talking at the nurses' station several doors down. Decky slipped into the hall and into Charlie's room unnoticed. As unnoticed as a hospital gowned woman, with her ass hanging out, on crutches could be. She went to the side of the bed where a chair was positioned. Brenda had probably sat with Charlie so she wouldn't be alone. Decky would have to thank Brenda for being there for Charlie when she couldn't.

Charlie looked better only because there was no blood all over her. Someone had washed her face and arms; her clothes had been taken as evidence. Her hair still contained dried blood in places. Decky fell down into the chair. She put her head on the side of Charlie's bed and cried. She tried to be quiet, but her shaking must have awakened Charlie. Decky felt Charlie's hand on the back of her head, gently stroking the huge knot left there by the bat.

"Brenda says... your hard head... saved your life." She was hard to understand through the split lips and swollen cheeks, but Decky followed her perfectly.

"That's what they tell me. I hear you're pretty tough, too." Decky took Charlie's hand in hers.

"I guess – we'll be postponing – that trip to Rodanthe." Charlie tried to smile.

Decky squeezed Charlie's hand. "I'm so sorry, Charlie."

Charlie was trying to help Decky get through this. "It's okay, sweetheart. We can reschedule it for recovery time. I've always wanted to go to the shore to recover, like rich folk do."

"I'm sorry I let this happen to you. Can you ever feel safe with me again? Can you trust me to take care of you?" Decky was at rock bottom, a place she had never been before, not even with Trey.

"Decky, look at me. You did not do this. You are my knight in shining armor. Didn't you know that? Instead of a horse, you brought a dog, but you saved me. You saved us both."

"If my dad hadn't come –"

"But he did come – because you called for him. You knew you needed him. You saved me from a crazed maniac. I am yours from now until the end of time. You can bet your sweet tight ass on that." Charlie laughed and it hurt her. She squeezed Decky's hand again. "I love you, Decky Bradshaw, more than life itself."

Decky laid her head down next to Charlie's leg. She cried softly for a while, and then leaned back in the chair, propped her ankle up on the end of Charlie's bed, and fell asleep still holding Charlie's hand. A little while later, she heard someone enter the room. Decky did not open her eyes. The person seemed to stop and take in the two women. She heard the person go to the other side of the bed to check Charlie. Then the person put a blanket over Decky and let her sleep.

#

When the nurses came in the morning, they escorted Decky back to her room and took Charlie down for a sonogram or ultrasound, Decky couldn't remember which. They were checking for more bleeding before taking her off the special care floor. Decky was being moved to a private room. She asked about the prospect of a double room for her and Charlie. When she was told it would not be possible, she told the lady behind the clipboard that she would pay anything, just make it happen. The woman agreed to try.

Charlie came back from the test with great results. She could move into the room that had "suddenly" opened for the two of them. They would be together even if it wasn't at home. Decky called R.C. to check on Dixie. She was being treated like the hero and princess that she was, and loving every minute of it. Decky told her father to stay with Dixie. She was sure they would be let out of the hospital tomorrow, and then he could bring Dixie home and visit with her.

They hadn't talked about what had happened. It had all been such a rush, neither of them had time to discuss the events that led up to R.C. pulling the trigger. Decky was glad her father shot first and asked questions later. She was also glad he was such a good shot. Decky thought about what she would say to him, when she had the chance. Thank you did not cover the range of emotions she had experienced in the last twenty-four hours.

Decky had been moved into the new room when the orthopedic surgeon came to see her. She had previous surgery on her ankle to repair ligament damage. The screws from this repair had remained in place, but the ligaments they held to the bone had ruptured. A new surgery, requiring much more extensive repair, would be needed. He suggested she make arrangements with her own doctors in Chapel Hill. He said she should remain in the cast until doing so, to prevent any further damage to an already beleaguered joint.

The doctor ordered an I.V. with saline, to replace fluids Decky had lost. He also okayed some pain meds introduced intravenously. She was in the clear on the brain injury, but they would hold her one more night. Decky thought about her throbbing ankle. She would eventually need ankle replacement surgery in old age, but for now Decky would repair, rehab, and pray it would hold up a little longer.

Maybe by then they would have bionic ankles. The pain meds kicked in and she was lost in dreams of flying around the bases with a bionic prosthesis, faster, stronger, better than before. The sound effects from the bionic woman played as she beat throw after throw. N-n-n-n-n-a. Safe!

"Hey Decky, we brought you a roommate." A jolly nurse, much like Kitty on "That 70's Show," was wheeling Charlie into the room with the help of two orderlies. "My name is Mary Jo. You girls just push that call button if you need anything. It seems I have been hired as a private nurse just for you two. Isn't that sweet? Somebody must really love you."

Mary Jo talked non-stop until she left the room. She made sure everything was just right, and then left to see about lunch. When Mary Jo finally left them alone, Decky and Charlie remained quiet for a moment. Then they looked at each other and burst out laughing. This made both of them wince in pain, so they breathed shallow breaths until they had regained their composure.

Decky had requested her bed be on Charlie's right side, so Charlie wouldn't have to try to see her through the swollen left one. Decky lay on her left side with a pillow between her legs to support her ankle. She could see Charlie, but not touch her. It was much better than separate rooms. After lunch Decky listened, while Charlie, who was now speaking much easier, told her what had happened at the cottage, before she got there.

It had all begun back at the restaurant. The man from the boat the day before was sitting at the bar. Charlie hadn't noticed him until he came over to the table to speak to one of the other guests. He was being introduced around the table, and when he got to Charlie, he recognized her. He said nothing, but he glared at her as he walked away from the table. His last name was Bagley. She didn't remember the first.

"He saw me leave. He must have followed me out. I didn't notice I was being followed, but I did stop for gas. How else would he have been able to beat me to the cottage?"

Decky responded, "Alan Jr., must have shown him where it was. Did I tell you he came by to apologize?"

"What did you say to him?"

"Nothing. He didn't give me a chance to say anything. He walked in, said he was sorry, and left."

Charlie, who Decky was learning could find something good about anybody, said, "He loves you, Decky. He was just hurt. He didn't mean for any of this to happen."

Charlie went back to the story, not giving Decky enough time to argue that Alan Jr. was certainly partially responsible for their current physical condition, even if he didn't mean for it to happen.

"I noticed the lights were off right away. I knew I had left a few on to make it look occupied. Besides, the outside motion light did not come on when I pulled up and parked. I didn't think anything of it. It was probably a fuse or something. I thought it was strange that the alarm was not on, because you had shown me the backup battery. All of those warning bells, and I just went right on in."

Decky reassured her, "You couldn't have known he was in there."

"This is the stuff you scream at the movie screen. Don't go in there, you idiot. It's dark and scary and you have been warned."

Decky laughed and winced again. She might as well laugh as cry. She didn't think she had any tears left.

"After I shut the door behind me, I went to the bedroom to get my flashlight. I keep it by the bed. He was on me before I knew what was happening. We fought, but he was so big and he knocked me loopy. He yanked my pants off but I kicked him in the face. That's when you drove up I guess, because he stopped, like he heard something. He tied me up and gagged me in the kitchen. I thought he was going to kill you. I tried to warn you, but I couldn't talk."

"I probably should not have set the gun down on the floor. Not the smartest thing I've ever done." Decky again felt a wave of guilt wash over her.

"I know. We really have to work on that being stunned in my presence thing." Charlie laughed and winced, which made Decky laugh and wince. They went back to the shallow breathing.

They napped and talked the rest of the day. After supper, Brenda stopped by with a report that Miss Kitty had been retrieved from Decky's and was now Chip's best friend. Charlie was on official medical leave until she felt better, which could be August as far as the administration was concerned. They were afraid Lizzie's association with the U could be tied somehow to this whole thing and wanted no part of a lawsuit.

Decky's house was locked up tighter than a tick. The crime scene tape was now down at the cottage and the local ladies had cleaned it. It was spotless, not to mention that now the local ladies knew everything Charlie had at the cottage. There were no secrets in a small place like this. Brenda assured them everyone was praying for them and very angry that this had happened. She kissed them both and went home to break up the love affair between her husband and the little queen taking up residence in her house.

R.C. came by even though Decky had told him not to. He was officially introduced to Charlie and she thanked him for saving their lives. He mentioned he imagined her daddy would have done the same. He gave Decky another update on Dixie. She was living it up on the couch in the den as they spoke, he surmised.

R.C. sat on the edge of Decky's bed so he could see both women. His tone became serious. "I had a visit from the sheriff today. Seems this man's name was Jim Bagley, from over near Chowan. His folks have old money."

Charlie cocked an eyebrow in question.

R.C. explained, "Old money comes with power new money only dreams of. This Jim Bagley has been accused of this sort of thing before, been arrested more than once on sexual assault charges. The sheriff said the word was the family bought him out of it. Witnesses left town, the prosecuting DA refused to press charges."

Decky was incredulous. He had done this before and he was walking the streets. She looked over at Charlie, whose expression she thought surely mirrored her own.

R.C. went on. "Well, the Bagley family has decided charges should be pressed against the three of us. The same DA that dismissed the charges against the Bagley man agrees. My lawyer says that both the Bagleys and the county are trying to head off a civil case holding them responsible for allowing Jim Bagley to walk free, knowing he was a sexual predator."

"You bet your sweet ass I'm going to sue them. Those bastards knew he was dangerous and they let him out of their sight. What idiots!" Decky grabbed her head. She had raised the volume just a little too much.

Charlie took over where Decky left off. "How does blaming us relieve them of culpability in this? What possible motive could we have?"

R.C. cleared his throat. "Now, remember, this is just a cover story to save their hides. It seems you, Charlie, met Mr. Bagley at the restaurant earlier in the evening. You invited him home to your cottage…"

"What!" Decky and Charlie said at the same time, followed immediately by a simultaneous, "Bull shit!"

R.C. raised his hand. "I know, I know, just listen. Be quiet and let me finish. Charlie, after allegedly bringing him to her house, agreed to some sexual bondage play. Charlie would agree to this because of her lifestyle as a homosexual. Decky, meanwhile, drives over to the cottage. Sees through the bedroom window what is happening and in a jealous rage broke in. She attacked you, Charlie, then pulled a gun on Mr. Bagley, when he tried to stop her. He had just wrestled the gun from Decky and was attempting to save his own life when I shot him, misunderstanding the situation."

Decky was crazy with anger. *What in the hell was wrong with these people?* "What about the fact that the wires were cut and the alarm disabled? Did I do that on my way up the steps?"

R.C. said quietly, "No, I supposedly did that after the shooting, before the sheriff was called. They claim it was to give you, Decky, an alibi. There is such a short time between when the alarm went off and when the shooting occurred, it is possible for that to have happened."

Charlie tried to help, "But the twins, she called the twins. They came and got you didn't they?"

R.C. sighed. "They figure Decky called them after the shooting and I let them find me at home. Then we called the police after I arrived back at the cottage. If we had done it that way, and been quick about it, it's conceivable."

"Too bad Dixie can't be a witness." Charlie was trying to find a lighter side to this mess.

Decky remembered something from that night. R.C. had called out to someone. "You told somebody to call 911. Someone else was there. Who was it?"

"Your mother."

R.C. then explained that the prosecutor of record wanted all the facts out in a public venue, to insure no one would ever accuse him of not investigating the incident thoroughly. Therefore, there was going to be a preliminary hearing to weigh evidence and decide if it was a lawful death.

In the meantime, Decky and Charlie would have to appear at the jail to be processed. He had already been there. He assured them it was only a formality. They would be on their own recognizance until the hearing. He said he would be by in the morning to take them home. The doctor had told him it would be all right.

Decky and Charlie were left alone again. They stared at the ceiling for a while, not knowing how to respond to such ludicrous accusations.

Finally, Charlie said, "Well, look on the bright side, after this we won't have to worry about being careful in public. Everybody in the whole world will know about us by the time the hearing's over."

12

By the time Decky and Charlie were picked up at the hospital, Decky had already called the lawyer she used for local business, and asked him to meet them at the courthouse. He would do for the formality of receiving the charges and arranging their release. They were duly surrendered, charged, fingerprinted, and released.

When they arrived at home, Brenda was waiting for them. She had Miss Kitty with her, who she now called the demon child. She was carrying on, busying herself around the bedroom, making sure her patients were comfortable and prepared for anything. If they needed ice or water, it was right there. Ice bags were in a cooler, to be switched out at a moment's notice. Prescriptions filled and at the ready, food waiting downstairs. All laptops, phones, and remotes within reach. Brenda was a born mother. Maybe she *had* been a nurse in a former life.

Decky drew the line when she saw Brenda getting out of the elevator with a bedpan.

"Get away from me with that."

Brenda laughed. "Don't be silly, it isn't for you. It's for Charlie."

Charlie was stricken. "Get away from me you crazy woman. I can fucking walk. She's the one who can't walk. Make her piss in the pan." Charlie was absolutely firm on this. She was leaving Decky high and dry, and not looking back.

Brenda doubled over with laughter. "Look at you two. Squirming like children. It's not for you to piss in." She had to stop to catch her breath. "Charlie, it's from school. Remember, when Chip got hurt and we stole the bedpan and slid down the hills in the snow. I found it in the garage. I thought it would be a hoot."

Charlie visibly sighed. Decky was even more relieved. She had thought there was a possibility that Brenda was actually going to force Decky use the pan, after Charlie's argument. The facts were there.

Brenda was still laughing. "It was a hoot, at least from my point of view. Decky, I put the number of a very good defense attorney there on your nightstand. You should call her. She's out of Durham."

Decky picked up the card. "How do you think the locals would react to an outside attorney coming down here? Don't you think it would make it worse?"

Brenda spruced a flower arrangement she had made all by herself out of weeds. "Maybe I should explain further. Charlie, do you remember that cute little second baseman from the J.V. team, the one that looked like Jodie Foster?"

"Yes, is she an attorney?"

Brenda moved on to fluff the pillows in the chairs around the room. The woman really could not sit still. "Her name is Molly Kincaid. She is a lesbian and extremely good at her job."

Charlie really thought this was a bad idea. "Brenda, you are nuts. A lesbian lawyer! What in the hell made you think that was a good idea?"

Decky in the meantime had opened her laptop and located Ms. Kincaid's webpage. She elbowed Charlie, which hurt Charlie, who retaliated. When the pain subsided for both of them, they looked at the web page together. Ms. Kincaid, as the page often referred to her, was a high profile, murder case, defense attorney. She had never lost a case and was referred to as the 'Matlock' of southern, female defense attorneys.

Decky read aloud, "Charming juries with her perky smile and southern drawl; make no mistake Ms. Kincaid is an intelligent attorney and a fierce opponent. Law Review, 2006."

Charlie stared at the picture. "Damn, little Molly grew up. Who knew? She's gorgeous."

Decky grabbed the laptop. "Don't drool on the electronics."

"What, I'm not allowed to appreciate a pretty girl now?" Charlie was laughing at Decky.

"Okay, you can look, but no touching." Charlie was playing. Decky was serious.

Brenda laughed at both of them. "Ah isn't that cute. Decky's jealous."

"I'm not jealous, I'm wounded and feeling vulnerable."

Charlie went back to the lawyer. "Brenda, do you really think she would come down here for something this trivial?"

"As soon as I found out they were charging you, I called Molly. I explained the situation to her. Molly was livid. She said she would clear time on her calendar. She loves to get back at the good ol' boys anytime, anywhere, was what she said. So, she's waiting for your call. She also said to tell you hello, Charlie. She remembered you."

"Call her, Decky." When Decky hesitated, Charlie followed with, "Give me the phone, I'll do it."

"No, I'll do it. Just wait a minute."

Charlie was not to be put off. "Are you going to pass on Molly, because I think she's cute?"

Decky put her good foot on the floor. "No, I just need a minute. I have to go to the bathroom and Brenda is still holding that bedpan. I'm afraid she will decide I have to use it."

#

Brenda spent the night in Zack's room. She was up and down all night checking on her patients, waking them up to ask them if they needed anything. Decky finally begged her to let them sleep and the final four hours had been uninterrupted.

Decky rode the elevator down to the main floor, joining Brenda and Charlie for breakfast. Brenda had Decky's Polaroid digital camera in her hands and the two women were trying to figure out how to use it.

"What are you two cooking up now?" Decky inquired.

Charlie came over to Decky and kissed her on the cheek. Decky thought it was so sweet considering Charlie looked worse. The swelling had gone down, which made the bruises show even more colorfully. Charlie looked like she had been several rounds with Tyson.

"Molly called Brenda on her cell. She said we need to take pictures everyday of the progression of the bruising. We missed yesterday, but they took photos at the hospital."

Decky tried to remember. "I don't remember anybody taking pictures of me at the hospital."

Charlie evidently had a vivid memory. "A couple of deputies came in and had the nurses strip me down so they could take pictures. They told me they had already taken yours, even though you were still out of it."

Decky was horrified. She had grown up with most of the deputies and the thought of them seeing her naked, not only naked, but helpless, made her cringe.

Brenda, now positive she had figured the thing out, came around to the side of the island Decky was sitting on. "Okay Decky, strip. You want to do this out on the deck?"

"No, I do not want to go strip naked on the deck and get accused of public indecency next, and what do you mean, strip?"

Brenda replied, "Well, the lighting is better out there. You have to strip so we can show all your bruises. Don't be silly. I've seen plenty of naked women. Hell, I've seen you naked. There was the skinny-dipping episode last summer. You certainly were no shrinking violet back then."

"Yeah, well that was before." Decky sounded like a child.

Charlie enjoyed this, while Brenda toyed with Decky.

"What, do you think you look any different, because you're sleeping with Charlie? I assure you that you still have all the same parts."

"Who's going to see these pictures?" Decky wasn't giving in, not yet.

Brenda answered her very seriously. "Everybody in the county, I suppose. You know they will probably print them on the front page of the paper, with those black strips over the private areas."

For a second they had her. Decky bit hook, line, and sinker. Her mind was racing with the images of her naked body staring out at her in all the newspapers in the county. Farmers were opening the paper with shocked looks. Little boys huddled together to see the naked lady. Suddenly, Brenda and Charlie could hold the laughter in no longer. They laughed so hard Charlie had to sit down and hold her ribs in place.

Decky finally agreed to the pictures, reluctantly. Charlie, however, was happy to have her pictures taken. She had the battle scars to prove what had happened to her and she wasn't afraid to let anyone see it. She wanted everyone to know how brutal this guy had been. She wanted no question in anybody's mind that he intended to kill them, a fact she was as sure of as the sun coming up every morning. Decky agreed with her totally.

Decky had spoken with Molly, making arrangements to meet her Monday, in Durham. Decky had to see her surgeon in Chapel Hill. Brenda would drive them up Sunday night. They would stay in a hotel, see the surgeon in the morning, and Molly in the afternoon. Molly had been exactly what Decky expected on the phone. Very intelligent, cunning, and thorough, covered with the cutest southern drawl. She could see how people would be drawn into a false sense of security around Molly.

Molly was all business underneath the seemingly innocent exterior. She already had the existing court documents faxed to her. She had reviewed the release papers assuring Decky they were safe from being locked up on the prosecutor's whim. The charges were, well, laughable. Molly was going to have a field day with this case. It was once again a chance to nail a bunch of good ol' boys and Molly dearly loved to make them howl to be let up.

Decky felt much better after the phone call. If Molly's reaction was any indication of how this thing was going to go, Decky thought she might even enjoy the show. She had no doubt in her mind that the right thing had been done. She was sorry R.C. had been drawn into this, but he just seemed to accept it as part of the process. When he stopped by Saturday afternoon, Decky told R.C. about Molly. He agreed to let her represent him also. Decky felt her life had turned into a made for TV movie on the Lifetime network. She just hoped the good guys would win again.

#

The rest of the day and most of Sunday morning were spent covered in ice bags and resting. They had ventured into the Jacuzzi with Decky's cast taped up in a trash bag and Charlie's incision covered as well. The water massaged their sore muscles. Even if Decky couldn't swim, she needed the water on her skin. Water was like a vitamin to her. More pictures were taken on Sunday before they took off for Chapel Hill. R.C. picked up Dixie. They decided to drive the SUV, so Decky could keep her foot up on the backseat.

They stopped by the emergency room at the hospital to have Charlie's incision checked before leaving town. The same doctor who had treated them on Wednesday night was there. He examined Charlie's incision and her other wounds. He seemed pleased the two women were doing so well. To Decky, he appeared to be amazed at the beating they had both taken and lived through it.

Decky settled into the back seat surrounded by pillows. She couldn't really keep up with the conversation in the front seat. Brenda and Charlie talked about things she knew nothing about, and although she wanted to know everything Charlie had ever experienced, the ride began to make her sleepy. Decky took another Loratab and drifted off to sleep.

They took a side trip off the highway into Wilson. Decky had to introduce Charlie to the best Carolina barbecue in the south. The barbecue at Parker's was vinegar based sauce and chopped pork for which the Carolinas were known. There was a huge debate over who made the best. In Decky's mind, nothing beat Parker's.

They ate family style, with large portions brought in big bowls to the table, just like at home. The menu included barbecue, slaw, red potatoes, Brunswick stew, fried chicken, cornbread sticks, and pitchers of sweet iced tea. Even though her lips had not totally healed, Charlie ate with gusto and agreed with the other two women that this was heavenly.

People stared at the two bruised women. They looked like car accident victims. Decky didn't care; she loved Parker's. After filling up, Decky ordered some cornbread sticks and more barbecue to take with them. They even bought a gallon of the sweet tea, because Charlie had liked it so well.

Decky checked them in to adjoining rooms at the Carolina Inn. The trip had exhausted the three women. After a snack on the cornbread sticks and barbecue, they all retired to bed. Really alone for the first time in days, Decky and Charlie talked, lying facing each other on the pillows. Decky didn't remember falling asleep. She woke alone in the bed. The sun was shining and the shower was running. Decky hobbled over to the bathroom door. Charlie must have heard her, because she peeked from behind the shower curtain.

"Good morning, sleepy head. Care to join me?"

Decky looked down at the cast and vowed to have that thing off by the time she left the doctor's office. She must be getting better, Decky thought. She was thinking about sex for the first time in days.

"I can't come in there with this on. I'll just wash up over here in the sink. Do you think you could wash my hair, if I lean down over the tub?"

"Sure, hand me a cup from the sink." Charlie cut the shower off. Evidently, she was finished with her shower.

Decky knelt down on the floor mat after taking off her tee shirt. "I hate feeling like this. This cast comes off today."

Charlie, ever the more mature of the two, suggested Decky listen to her doctor before making any rash decisions.

"I probably know as much as he does about my ankle at this point. I know whether I need a cast or not." Decky was quite serious. She thought she could have a medical degree by now.

"I think you need some breakfast. You are a little edgy this morning." Charlie teased her.

"I'm sorry. I have a lot on my mind and this cast is driving me crazy. I hate it. A boot works just as well." Decky really hated casts.

She and a friend had cut one off of Decky once, because the itching drove her to it. Her mother had been pissed and taken her to have a new one put on right away. Lizzie had been in the back of Decky's mind since the charges were filed. Would Lizzie be so angry at Decky that she would lie? Decky didn't think so since R.C. was involved, but still she wasn't sure how angry Lizzie was at what Decky had said to her, after the attack. Decky did not remember most of the scene, but what she did remember she could never take back. She hoped Molly wouldn't want her to. She meant every word.

In Decky's eyes, Lizzie's meddling had alerted scum like Jim Bagley to the situation. If Lizzie had kept her mouth shut, nobody would have been the wiser. Decky was forgetting the whole incident with Lynne and the party. She was focused on Lizzie as the culprit and she could not be swayed. Decky didn't even blame Alan Jr. anymore. At least he was sorry.

Lizzie was probably fuming at Decky for involving her family in such a huge scandal. Not only was her husband being charged, Lizzie was going to have to testify in front of the whole county. Lizzie was probably fit to be tied.

Decky's visit to the doctor went pretty much as she had expected. The doctor had cut the cast off, x-rayed the ankle several times, ran her through an MRI, and declared surgery necessary to repair the damage. He scheduled surgery for a couple of weeks away, to give Decky time to recuperate and deal with the trial.

He had listened as Decky told him what had happened. He was a friend by now, since they had known each other so long.

He was flabbergasted at the way Decky and Charlie were being treated. He felt so badly, he even let Decky talk him into a boot instead of a cast, but she had to stay on the crutches until the swelling went down.

They arrived in Durham a little before lunch. On the way to meet Molly, Brenda drove around the Duke campus, reminiscing with Charlie and showing Decky different haunts and scenes of youthful escapades. Brenda told the story of this particularly mean group of girls who had antagonized their little group back then. Charlie began to turn red. Decky knew this was going to be a good one.

"Well, there were six of us in this little mustang. Patty, our too large to be driving this mustang D.H., spotted the mean girls. We called them 'the bitches' at the time."

Charlie started to giggle, sending waves of pain through her rib cage. Decky could see her trying desperately not to all out laugh, but this story was bringing back images, of which Decky could only guess.

Brenda continued, "So, Patty spots the bitches, points, and proceeds to drive the car up onto the sidewalk the bitches happened to occupy at the time. The bitches, seeing this, take off in the opposite direction, still on the sidewalk. It finally dawned on them that the longer they stayed on the sidewalk, the closer the car got, and they took to the hedge."

Decky by this time had joined Charlie in her attempts not to laugh too hard, but Brenda wasn't finished.

"Later in the vice president's office that same day, he looked at me and said, 'You I can't do anything to because you have straight A's and you were in the backseat. You, on the other hand,' referring to our friend Charlie here, 'were in the front seat. Apparently, from reading witness statements, cheering the driver on.'"

Charlie gasped. "I didn't!"

Brenda waved her off. "The vice-president was not impressed with Charlie's denial, he said, 'Charlene, what would your daddy say if I called him and told him a bunch of wild girls had chased you down the sidewalk in an automobile?' Our aforementioned friend said in her best Okie twang, 'He'd probably want to know what I had done to make 'em so mad.'"

Charlie and Decky both were in the full throws of painful laughter. It hurt, but it felt good to laugh like that for a moment. Decky would think of it later as a moment they all went back to a time of innocence, before life happened.

Decky finally managed, "What happened to you?"

Charlie, finally able to talk again, answered, "I had to work extra hours in the training room. When I'm healed, I'll tell you about the fish in their bathtub."

They ate lunch at the Magnolia Grill, which stirred even more memories. Decky enjoyed seeing the light in Charlie's eyes, as the memories flooded out. It resembled the younger Charlie from the newspaper photo so many years ago. Lunch went by so freely, Decky almost forgot about what they were facing. Too soon, the ugliness would reenter their blissful life.

Molly Kincaid's main office was located in an old home. Decky knew she would like her immediately upon seeing the bright yellow and white trimmed fully restored Victorian. Decky liked anybody who respected history. This house reflected Molly's belief in just that. Molly, Decky learned later, also maintained an office with her firm, near the courthouse downtown, but enjoyed working here so much more. Electronics made that possible.

Another thing Decky liked about Molly was the way she had incorporated every electronic device necessary to compete in today's global market, yet kept the ambience of the old south intact. Decky was glad to see they would be able to videoconference and send and receive documents with ease. A lawyer in your living room wasn't a bad thing at a time like this.

The three women were escorted straight into Molly's office. Decky couldn't believe the resemblance to Jodie Foster. She could have walked right out of 'The Panic Room,' right down to the cute little dimple. She even had that self-assured air Ms. Foster exuded. Decky had always adored Jodie Foster.

After Brenda and Charlie caught up with Molly, the attention turned to the case against them. Molly asked Brenda to wait in the outer room, while they discussed the details. Even though Charlie and Decky had nothing to say to Molly that they wouldn't say in front of Brenda, Molly assured them it was necessary for attorney client privilege to remain intact.

The details of the event were examined from both women's perspectives, Charlie telling what had happened before Decky arrived and Decky filling in the parts Charlie was unable to see while behind the counter. Decky gave contact information for the twins and R.C. She reluctantly handed over Lizzie's cell number, too.

"About your mother," Molly began. Decky was watching in amazement, as Molly's mouth actually moved like Jodie's when she uses a southern accent. Molly snapped her out of it with the word mother.

"Your mother is the only person you haven't spoken about. Did she actually see the shooting?" Molly was writing on a legal pad.

Decky answered quietly, her eyes cast to the floor, "I don't know what she saw. I haven't spoken to her."

"You know she was there, but you haven't spoken to her. Is there a problem I should know about?" Molly was looking at Decky. Decky could feel Molly's eyes on her while she was still counting the colors in the Oriental rug under her chair.

Decky finally looked up after she heard Charlie sigh. "My mother and I have a unique relationship. We have spent our lives talking and not talking. She has ideas about how I should live my life and, for that matter, everyone else in the world. She ran her mouth about my relationship with Charlie and I see that as the inciting incident. I told her so that night. I wasn't nice about it. I haven't spoken to her since."

"I will talk to her. I understand about the mom who flips out when you're gay and do not fit the image she has for you. Let's just say, I am experienced in that area. The only other thing I wanted to cover with you is a name I see here on the potential witness list that you haven't mentioned. She is not with any of the responding agencies, I checked. The name is Lynne Haskins."

Charlie bolted upright in the chair. "She doesn't even live here!"

Decky followed suit. "She was back in Louisiana when this happened as far as we know."

Molly was intrigued. Anybody that could make these two react like this might be a problem. "Who is she?"

Decky and Charlie relayed the whole story. How they met. The party. The punch. The whole sordid mess. When Molly learned Brenda had seen the whole thing she asked her to rejoin them.

Brenda was as shocked as Decky and Charlie had been. "I can't believe that bitch has reared her ugly head again. I thought we were done with her."

Molly sized up the situation. She must have seen how uptight Charlie and especially Decky were behaving. "I've dealt with her kind before, she'll be no problem. But still, I think you should have sent the private jet for the cat. Write that down for future reference."

They thought she was serious for a second, then Decky caught the grin on Molly's face and relaxed into painful laughter. Charlie joined her. A huge wave of relief swept over the room.

Except Brenda, who looked at Decky and said, "I didn't know you had a private jet!"

More laughter was followed by arrangements for Molly to come down and view the "crime scene," so to speak. She would interview R.C., the twins, and Lizzie. Decky felt so much better, when they left Molly's office, she offered to drive the first leg of the trip home. The boot made moving around so much easier and the pain had dissipated some. She was good for at least sixty miles she was sure.

For an hour, they sang to the radio at the top of their lungs. Charlie and Brenda stopped occasionally to listen as Decky sang some of the ballads. After Brenda started driving again, they talked some about the things that Molly had said. Decky knew this wasn't going to be a walk in the park. It certainly wasn't going to be comfortable airing her private life in front of everyone she knew and some she didn't.

Charlie decided she would call her sister with the details and let her choose how and what to tell her parents. Brenda had suggested it was such an interesting story FOX or CNN might run it. Molly had spoken with the University Systems Board of Governor's attorney. Molly related that the attorney would not only prevent any action to be taken in regard to Charlie's job, but that he offered to be of service in any way possible. At least there were some people not living in the dark ages.

The trip home went quickly even though they took the long way around, at Decky's insistence. Decky pointed out landmarks and historical homes as they passed. She had Brenda veer off the main road at Plymouth to show Charlie houses with cannon balls lodged in chimneys from wars past. Charlie was impressed with the history, but not the smell. Plymouth's two pulp mills made the air smell like rotten eggs on a bad day. This was a bad day.

They drove past Fort Raleigh National Park, where Decky told Charlie about The Lost Colony, and how the outdoor drama performed there tells its story. It also contained an Elizabethan Garden of extraordinary beauty, in which Decky had been married on a hot June day, Brenda pointed out. Decky talked about new discoveries being made on a daily basis within the various architectural digs in the area, including one on Hatteras Island that may lead to more clues about the fate of the colonists.

They drove through downtown Manteo to get a glimpse of the Elizabeth II, a composite design replica of a 16th-century ship, named after one of the vessels that sailed the ocean when Sir Walter Raleigh first brought colonists to Roanoke Island in 1587. Again, Decky promised to take Charlie to see all of this up-close as soon as they were well enough.

They stopped at Daniel's restaurant where Decky introduced Charlie to fried shrimp sandwiches. Then they were back on the road approaching the Wright Brothers' Memorial. In Kitty Hawk, the Wright Brothers had changed the world forever in 1903, by completing the first successful sustained powered flights in a heavier-than-air machine. Decky pointed out the monument rising high from atop a hill. The Wright Brothers' Beacon was designed and built by the U.S. Lighthouse Service, as a lighthouse for airplanes. It had been off for years until re-lighted in 1998.

They crossed the Wright Memorial Bridge over the Sound back into Currituck County. They were almost home. They stopped for gas in Grandy. Decky and Charlie did not get out of the car. Decky noted several people she knew stare and point at them. Decky was anxious to be out from under the harsh lights of the pumps.

For a while, they had been three friends touring the roads. Now they were back under the prying eyes of a divided community. This was undoubtedly a divided community because as some people smiled and waved at her, one of the women in a group of trailer trash clearly mouthed "Dyke" at Decky, as they left the parking lot.

Decky was elated to be home when she finally exited the elevator on the main floor. Miss Kitty had met them downstairs, with loud cries that only meant one thing. There were dead socks somewhere in the house. Decky found them when she plopped down on the couch.

Decky called out to Charlie, who was in the kitchen, "I think there must have been a mass uprising of socks while we were away. How does she get them out of the drawer is my only question?"

"The girl has skills." Charlie said, handing Decky pills and a bottle of water.

Charlie had started keeping up with Decky's pain meds when Decky couldn't remember when she had taken the last one. It was probably for the best. Brenda decided she would go home to Chip, after Charlie convinced her they were able to take care of themselves now. She had hated giving up her nurse duties and promised to be back the next day to check on them.

Charlie went to change and brought Decky something comfortable to wear, so she wouldn't have to go upstairs. Decky checked her email, while Charlie called her sister. She heard Charlie laugh, so she knew the phone call was going well. There was a message from her editor. The local news hounds were calling her for a statement and she wanted to know what to say. Decky replied with only two words, "No comment," and passed on her attorney's contact info. Let them work it out, Decky thought.

Most of her email messages were from people she barely knew, or spam, and were immediately deleted. Decky jotted a few notes to well-wishers she truly cared about. She was on Birdsong's email list, so there was a note from Mr. Birdsong wishing her a speedy recovery. Mr. Birdsong went down on Decky's list of the good guys.

She had been compiling a list in her head of the good guys and bad guys. On one side were the people you could count on and on the other were the ones she knew were against her. No matter what the truth was, those people wouldn't care. Then there were the gray area people. The ones she wasn't sure about. She had discovered that people's reactions to her being a lesbian could not be predicted. Now that she was a lesbian murder defendant, she was sure at least some of them had been swayed to the bad guy's category.

Decky had read John Grisham's 'Innocent Man' last year. She had followed the North Carolina Center on Actual Innocence cases, as one wrongfully accused person after another was released from prison. The fact that the justice system did work in the end delighted Decky. The fact that they went to prison in the first place scared the shit out of her. She had to remember to make a donation to the center.

Charlie finished her call. She sat down in the chair across from Decky, letting out an immense breath of air.

"Are you glad that's over? How did it go?" Decky asked, shutting the laptop.

"I just started at the beginning. By the time I got to you popping Lynne in the nose she was laughing so hard I had to stop and let her catch her breath. She said, 'Good job!' by the way."

Decky made herself comfortable. This was obviously going to be a long story. "I think I like your sister."

"Well, you have a fan. She said I should have done it years ago. It softened her up for the rest of the story. Franny was much calmer than I expected. She said she would handle the family and for me to concentrate on getting better. She offered to come out here, but I told her no, that would definitely set off alarm bells at home, in the middle of summer league baseball. She has two boys."

"I heard you laugh. I was hoping it was going well."

Charlie smiled. "She said I should walk around with a sign that says I have six very large, older brothers. She thought it might frighten future attackers."

Decky thought of a better reason. *The fact that the last guy who attacked you is dead ought to take care of that.* She said instead, "I'll have to remember that."

Charlie went on for a while about her conversation with Franny. It was obvious the sisters had few secrets. Decky had wished for a relationship like that with a sibling, but seeing how her brother was the only candidate, she settled for a series of best friends.

Decky's closest friend in the world was off in Africa shooting a documentary. Decky had known Jackie since college. They had never lived near each other after school, but visited and kept in touch with each other's lives. Jackie was bisexual, which Decky never thought about one way or the other. Theirs was a true best friendship. They could pick up from anywhere, anytime, as if no time had passed. Decky couldn't wait for Charlie to meet Jackie.

"Well, that's over," Charlie was saying.

Decky realized she had drifted away from the conversation to think about Jackie. Decky drifted away from conversations often. It was usually when someone said something that triggered her onto another "I hadn't thought of that," moment. Maybe she should be tested for A.D.D. She could totally identify with Dory from 'Finding Nemo.' There she went again.

"Charlie, I'm tired. I can't concentrate. Can we go to bed?"

"Are you sure this isn't some ploy to get me in the bed, now that we're alone?" Charlie teased.

"No, but I have thought about it. The thought of our ribs bumping together just doesn't appeal to me, but I'm working on another Jacuzzi plan."

Charlie helped Decky up from the couch. "Your plans have been interesting so far. Let's see, you burned up my brand new mattresses, almost got us caught naked by your friend Alan Jr., and we met those nice gentlemen on the boat. I can't wait to see what you come up with next."

13

The next two days went by quickly. Decky changed into a brace and swam with floats on her ankles. This allowed her to let her legs glide behind her while working out her upper body. The swimming began the healing process in her aching muscles. Range of motion returned and her spirits began to lift. Charlie worked out lightly, but was unable to really do much more than stretch. She spent most of the time in the Jacuzzi, while Decky swam.

As soon as Brenda left after her daily check in, Decky enacted her latest plan. They were alone, and feeling a little better. Decky put on some soft music, lit the candles, and turned down the lights. She didn't bring alcohol to the Jacuzzi, Charlie had forbidden alcohol and pain meds, something about her background in first aid and not wanting to have to use it. Instead, she made some fruit smoothies and served them in plastic hurricane glasses. Decky had a thing about glass in the pool area. It was a beautiful evening and they watched the sunlight disappear turning the sky rich colors of blue and pink.

Just as Decky was about to make her move, a screeching Miss Kitty came flying down the steps. Right behind her was the princess, who although limping had managed to escape outside, only to return with a gift of a marsh rat for her family.

Dixie paraded around the floor, proud of her recent acquisition. Decky was usually calm in most situations, but not ones involving rodents. She screamed and tried to get out of the Jacuzzi. Unable to do this without crutches, she determined the best course of action was to dive. Dive deep and fast.

Decky went underwater still holding the smoothie. From under the surface, she could see movement, but the water was moving too, she couldn't make out what was happening. She would have to surface soon; she was running out of air. Maybe a quick breath and a peek at the scene above were in order. When Decky surfaced, she saw Charlie standing out of the Jacuzzi holding a very dead rat by the tail. Decky wasn't sure if Charlie had killed it, but she really didn't want to know.

"Is my big strong girl afraid of rodents? You and Miss Kitty, my word!" Charlie said, with her hand on her hip.

Miss Kitty was still screeching, but now she was atop the bar. The cat obviously had the same aversion as Decky to the nasty creatures. Dixie was sitting like a good girl, but eyeing the rat. If Charlie made a mistake, it would be hers again.

Decky warned, "Watch out! She'll take it back. She does that. And then you have to chase her and hope to God the thing is dead by the time you get it from her."

Charlie grinned at Decky. "You really are frightened aren't you?"

"Yes, some people are afraid of heights. I am afraid of rodents, squirrels too. They're just big rats with fluffy tails."

Charlie had Decky in a position Decky didn't like much, in her complete control. Charlie started to allow the rat to sway slightly toward Decky. To which, Decky swayed like a fighter on the ropes. Charlie must have felt sorry for her. Decky truly hated rodents. Charlie went over behind the bar and dropped the rat in a plastic bag. She then carried the bag out to the garage bin.

Decky beamed from the tropical stained Jacuzzi, surrounded by pink foam and bits of fruit, "You are my hero. Thank you Lord, I got a girl who will take care of the rodents. How lucky was that?"

#

The twins came over and cleaned out the Jacuzzi on Tuesday. After they left, Decky and Charlie sat down and worked on their statements for Molly. She had asked them to write down exactly what they had seen and done the entire day Wednesday. They were not to compare stories. Perceptual differences made stories more believable. They were to write this on legal pads, make only one copy, and give it to Molly in person. She was thorough.

Decky also wrote Zack a detailed email keeping him up to date on all the activities at home. She told him to stay in Alaska, when she called to tell him what had happened. He seemed relieved not to have to deal with the chaos surrounding his mother. First, she calls to tell him at thirty-seven she decided she was gay. Then she called to tell him in succession: she had come out basically in front of everyone at Brenda's party, she had been in a lesbian brawl, his grandmother had shot at her house, and then to top it all off she was now accused of murder, along with his grandfather. His grandmother was a key witness and his future was up in the air. He gladly stayed in Alaska.

During the afternoon on Tuesday, they prepared Zack's room for Molly, with the help of Brenda. Well, Brenda did it and Decky watched. Charlie helped when she could. Brenda essentially changed Zack's room into a guest room, including new curtains and comforter on Decky's credit card. Brenda loved to spend other people's money.

All of Zack's things were moved into the giant closet across the hall. Decky got the first look at what it would be like when Zack moved out. She decided she would always let it be his room, until he was ready to give it up. The office was cleaned and readied for Molly's arrival. Brenda would pick her up at the Maple airport in the morning.

Brenda laughed as she went out the door. "That ought to get the locals going, a corporate jet. I hope it has big tits painted on the side."

Molly and Brenda arrived back at the house just in time for the brunch Decky and Charlie had prepared. Molly looked around Decky's house, escorted by Brenda, who loved to brag on everything in it. It sometimes embarrassed Decky, but she was proud of it too. It was a dream she had. She made it come true. How cool was that?

Molly came back to the kitchen island where Decky and Charlie were already seated. She was dressed casually. Well, as casually as you can be in a thousand dollar outfit. Decky didn't know what it really cost, but she couldn't wait to see what she wore to court.

"Get out! This is the coolest house I have ever seen." Some of Molly's professionalism had worn off. She felt comfortable here. Decky relaxed even more. "I am so glad I decided to stay here instead of a hotel. I even have my own office. Decky you are a genius."

"I had a lot of engineering help and professional builders.." Decky tried to be humble.

As Brenda and Molly joined the others at the island, Molly said, "I read your book by the way, the second one. I can't wait to read the first one. Are they similar?"

Decky was flattered. She felt the blush coming on. "They are similar in subject matter but entirely different people, more the working class side of my father's family. They were the men and women who tamed this territory right around here. They dragged the chains to map out the land and built the first roads, dug the canals, drained the land."

"That sounds fascinating. I can't wait to read it." Molly added.

"I'll get you a copy. I'm sure there's one in the house somewhere." Decky gushed.

"Charlie, you have won yourself a very rare kind, the southern gentlewoman writer, only yours is quite the handy woman to have around."

Decky felt the full force of the blush hit her forehead. It was the first time anybody had ever said Charlie was lucky to have her. Hell, Decky even thought she was lucky to have Charlie, but someone thought Charlie the winner here. Decky was not attracted to Molly. It was the words that made her blush, because it made Charlie feel better about having jumped into this with Decky, without a lifejacket. Any points she could get at this juncture could only help.

Decky was really pleased when Charlie leaned over and kissed Decky on the cheek. "I know. I can't believe how lucky I am and she doesn't even smoke a pipe."

"I know one thing," Molly said between bites of fruit, "after seeing this house, we might have to renegotiate my fee."

After brunch, they all loaded into the SUV and struck out for the cottage. Decky described everything she did on Wednesday night. They chose not to let her recreate the speed she had been traveling, explaining her leg was in far worse shape now. Decky thought they were all chicken.

When they bumped into the opening revealing the cottage, Decky hit the brakes. Someone had painted LEZZIE on the back of the cottage with red spray paint.

Brenda said from the backseat, "That is fucking amazing."

"What?" the other three asked in quiet unison, still looking at the red paint glaring at them.

"Those little cock suckers actually got it together enough to get a ladder and everything. I am fucking amazed anyone who would do that would have the actual brainpower to pull it off. It must have taken several cases of beer to work up to this bright idea."

Molly jumped out the passenger side door. She reached back into the floor, retrieving her brief case. Out of it, she pulled a digital camera. She did all this in a hurry, as if the paint would disappear. "What time is it?" she asked.

Decky looked on the dashboard clock. "12:30"

Molly was now focusing the viewfinder on the back of the cottage. "I want to make sure the time and date stamp is correct. This is great. It perfectly depicts the attitude of the community. We'll have to call the sheriff and have him do an official report. These pictures will document the existence of the graffiti at this time and date, if they are slow to respond."

Decky exchanged glances with Charlie, who was in the backseat. Molly was on the ball. They smiled at each other. The shock of the graffiti had worn off by the time the Expedition pulled up to the bottom of the steps. Decky didn't want to have to walk any further than necessary. Brenda walked Molly over to where the wires had been cut, while Charlie helped Decky up the steps.

Decky and Charlie had not been to the cottage since the night it happened. Neither of them said a word, as they waited out on the deck for the others to join them. Images of that night flashed in Decky's head. Noises played loudly on her eardrums even though it was quiet there, out of the wind. Decky looked at Charlie. She was seeing it all again, too. Decky put her arm around Charlie and waited there quietly. Nothing she could say would change the way either one felt, it was best to let it pass.

Brenda came noisily up the steps, leading Molly, talking non-stop about the idiots in this part of the world. It was wide spread illiteracy that she thought caused the whole thing, even though some of the brightest people in North Carolina had come from the coastal area or had ties to it. Decky had friends from high school that now taught at Duke, Columbia, and Berkley. Brenda insisted if she could teach them all to read, she could cure the bigots of the world. Decky thought maybe they read too much and understood too little.

When Molly joined them, Decky led the way inside. The picture window had been boarded-over, probably by R.C. and the twins. She hadn't even thought about having it done. They couldn't turn on the lights, but the ever-prepared Brenda produced a flashlight. The shadows cast through the rooms gave it an even eerier feeling. Charlie walked them through everything that happened before Decky broke in the kitchen door.

They both told the next part, because Decky hadn't seen the guy walk up behind her. It was interesting hearing Charlie's perspective. Even though they had gone over it before, Charlie told the story with more detail this time. Decky was proud of her. Charlie was not emotionally attached to this place. She had no fear. She had been assaulted and someone was going to pay.

Decky finished up her side of the events after Charlie had been left behind the counter. She told Molly she never saw her father and had no idea anybody was there. Molly had called R.C. earlier and asked him to join them. They had talked on the phone, but it was their first face-to-face meeting. Once he arrived, Molly quickly charmed R.C. He told how the twins had awakened him from a nap in his chair.

"They came up, banging on the door. One of them said something about stealing his mother's car. When they finally told me Decky might be in trouble I grabbed my rifle, it's always by the front door. Lizzie wouldn't take no for an answer, so we piled in the truck and came over here. I could hear commotion when I came up the steps. I could hear Decky there screaming at somebody. I didn't make out what she was saying, until I hit the top of the steps. I saw the back of a man through the door. It was only a shadow, but I knew it was a man. I stepped around to the picture window. I could see Decky's face and the gun in the light from outside. I leveled my gun on the shadow's head and pulled the trigger. I didn't know Lizzie had followed me until I heard her gasp. She had seen everything. She must have been right behind me the whole time, but I was focused on the task at hand."

Molly was impressed. "We're all glad you pulled that trigger Mr. Bradshaw. You did a heroic thing. You tell your story like that on the witness stand and no one will blame you for what you did."

"Ma'am, I did not want to shoot that boy, but under the circumstances I did not see a way around it, and call me R.C., everybody does."

"Okay, R.C. what happened next?"

All three who had participated in the events relayed all they could remember from their own perspective. Charlie had been taken away much sooner than Decky. Decky talked about being questioned and released to the hospital. She told what she could remember of her fight with Lizzie. Not all her memories of Wednesday night were lucid, but some moments with Lizzie were very clear.

They moved down to the dock just to show Molly how beautiful the Sound was. Molly listened and observed them all carefully. She sat them down on the bench near the end of the dock, next to the cleaning table. Thankfully, anybody using the cutting surface lately had cleaned it well and the stink was only a pleasant memory for Decky. This was part of life here, in sportsman's paradise.

Molly walked back and forth in front of them. She only stopped moving when she was making a point, and only wanted comments when she asked for them. She was summarizing for the jury. Decky was enthralled. Molly wasn't, however, talking to the criminal jury. She was presenting her civil case.

"Look at all you've lost. This beautiful place will never be the same. It is lost to you all, forever. You'll sell it if you can, but no one wants a house where such a tragedy took place. What family wants to live in a cottage where someone attempted to murder two women and then was killed on the premises? You will not be able to get full price, even if you can sell it. You'll probably burn it down and make a vacant lot out of it. A piece of valuable real-estate damaged irrecoverably."

The idea of a bon fire appealed to Decky at the moment. Just burn it to the ground. She'd never spend another night there.

Molly turned to Decky's father. "R.C., you have been forced to take a human life, because the county and his family allowed a sexual predator to go free. Why was he here and not back in his own county? Because his parents paid for him to play in Currituck, to avoid yet another investigation."

Decky didn't know this. Molly was good. She had done her homework.

Molly stopped in front of Charlie. "Your reputation has been soiled. You have been through a tremendous shock. Who knows how this will shape your career in the future?" She moved on to Decky. "What kind of influence will this have on your book sales? There may never be a movie and certainly not another movie deal."

Decky didn't like the sound of that. She listened even more closely to Molly.

"These people allowed a predator into your community. They will pay like the tobacco companies to get out of this one. It will never see the light of day in a courtroom. They'll settle. You just have to decide how much more comfortable you want to be for the rest of your lives. We have them by the balls, excuse me R.C., they don't stand a chance."

Decky was glad her attorney was so convinced they would win a civil suit, but what worried her most was prison time. She had money. What she didn't want was a big old lesbian girlfriend in the pen.

"Molly, I appreciate your enthusiasm, but what I want is to not go to prison. Of course, I don't speak for Dad and Charlie, but I'd really like not to go to prison."

Molly assured them that no one was going to prison. This case was absurd. The District Attorney thought so. He had told Molly unofficially that someone up the food chain felt the need to clear the air. The D.A. had picked an assistant to prosecute the case, not the one involved in the previous Bagley litigations. The less significance he felt they gave the case, the better. Who knew how deep the Bagley pockets were? It was hard to tell with old money.

Still, in the unlikely event the case made it to Superior Court, he said he would refuse to prosecute it. He had a conflict of interest, due to the ongoing internal investigation of the past cases and how they were handled. This was just some politician in Raleigh repaying an old debt to the family, nothing more. The Bagleys were just too proud to admit their son was a sexual deviant.

Molly went on, "This is merely a formality that you have been forced into. The fact the family and an official in the D.A.'s office are involved in influencing the bringing of the charges makes them even more culpable in the civil case. This will not be comfortable for any of you. Your personal lives will be put out there for all to see. That's what they're banking on, public opinion, and your being afraid to come out in public as a lesbian. Public opinion has no place in a courtroom and I intend to keep it out."

Charlie chuckled. "Tell that to prosecutors in the O.J. case."

"No matter what they dredge up, it will not mitigate the fact this man broke into your home and tried to kill you. We have witnesses to your behavior at the restaurant Charlie, thanks to Brenda. The twins will testify about the phone call. The alarm company will supply records indicating time of the power loss. Charlie has a receipt from the gas station. This coincides with the time frame we have developed for the assault and, if it becomes necessary to involve her, we have Mrs. Bradshaw."

Decky brightened visibly at the possibility that Lizzie would not be needed to testify. She was more positive than ever that Molly was the right attorney for the job. If she could keep Lizzie off the stand, Decky would double what she was paying her.

The meeting on the dock adjourned. Molly asked R.C. to give her a lift to the courthouse. She needed to speak to the sheriff and a familiar face was always nice to have along. Decky doubted seriously that Molly needed any help with sheriff's and deputies from places like this. She had made her fortune busting their cases. Molly climbed right up in the seat of the truck with Bucky and off they went.

Decky, Charlie, and Brenda returned to Decky's house. Decky called the sheriff's office to report the vandalism at the cottage. Brenda ran to the store for steaks to cook on the grill. Chip would be coming over to take care of dinner. He was a great cook and Decky looked forward to having a meal prepared in her house, by a chef like Chip.

Decky and Charlie used the quiet time, when it was just the two of them, to crawl into bed and take a nap. When they awoke an hour and a half later, Miss Kitty and Dixie were curled up in the bed with them.

Decky smiled at Charlie. "One big happy family."

#

Chip cooked the steaks to perfection, crusted with Cognac pepper. He added twice-baked potatoes to the menu and, on the side, a beautiful green garden salad. Chip gave credit for the salad to Brenda; after all, she had picked out the vegetables at the roadside stand. They ate out on the deck and no one mentioned the case at all. The pall having lifted for a while, it was a pleasant evening between old and new friends.

After the meal, Brenda and Chip cleaned up the dishes and excused themselves to go home. This left Decky and Charlie to entertain their guest. Molly was most interested in them personally, how they met, everything about the last two weeks. She claimed it was so she would not be surprised in court, but after listening to the story she said, "It just fascinates me how you two got together. It's a fairy tale, well except for the ex, the fight, the mother, and the dead body. It really is quite sweet."

They all laughed, and then Molly asked Decky, "Are you prepared to come out of the closet in open court? It will then be a matter of public record."

Decky snorted. "I don't think I can get much further out of the closet at this point."

"What people suspect does not hold up in court. You would have to be caught in the act of a sexual nature, with a woman, in order for the court to recognize anything other than an admission from you. Being a suspected lesbian is much different than seeing it on a court document, a public court document, I might add."

Charlie added her thoughts on the matter. "I guess that puts you right up there with Rita Mae. You will forever be known as 'the lesbian writer' instead of simply a writer."

"Too bad I didn't screw somebody famous. I could write a loosely based fictional account of the affair and make a fortune." Decky thought this was funny, so did the other two.

"Really, I'm set. If I never sell another book, I'll get by. I just want to be proven innocent, no matter what I have to say under oath. As I said, I just really don't want to go to prison. I've been having nightmares about large women fighting over whose bitch I was going to be."

Charlie asked, "Where am I in these dreams?"

"They fought over you already, now it's my turn." Decky said seriously. She was really having these thoughts. It was making her crazy.

Molly went over the court dates and appearances. The date had been set two weeks to the day from the incident. Molly had been able to rush things through due to her contacts in the DA's office. Everyone wanted this over and done with.

Charlie finally asked the question, the same one Decky had been mulling about in her brain. How did Molly know the DA so well? It appeared to be more than a professional arrangement.

Molly grinned. "I played on a traveling team with his daughter for years. He's a really nice guy."

The rest of the evening was spent talking about the house, Charlie living in Louisiana and growing up in Oklahoma. They even told Molly the eel story. They turned in from the full day and all went to sleep soundly. Decky and Charlie felt better than they had in a long time about the situation in which they found themselves. Still, Decky said a little prayer before she drifted off to sleep.

14

Molly left the next day. She would return Monday before the hearing. In the meantime, Decky and Charlie worked on getting better, getting healthy, and getting to know each other. Molly had told them to lie low, so they did. Sunday marked their three-week anniversary, which Decky remembered with a necklace holding a small, silver dolphin charm for Charlie. Brenda had gotten it at the Cotton Gin after Decky described what she wanted.

When Molly returned on Monday, Decky and Charlie picked her up, at the Maple airport, on the way back from having Charlie's stitches removed. It made Charlie's wounds look red and raw in places. Molly spent the time between her arrival and the court date prepping Decky and Charlie, along with all the other witnesses she intended to call. Decky saw the list. It contained a few names from the party, in addition to the names Decky expected to see, and a few she did not know. God, I hope it doesn't go that far. It's bad enough already, Decky thought.

Brenda came by Tuesday night, bringing a fresh strawberry pie. Chip had been busy. They ate the pie while Brenda repeated all the gossip she had picked up at the grocery store and the market.

"You won't believe it girls. The lesbians are on page two of the scandal sheet. It seems that a very famous actress has been seen arriving and departing from the Maple airport. Jodie Foster is in town scouting locations."

The women shared a laugh.

Charlie added, "I wish I was Jodie Foster. She keeps her private life locked up tighter than a tick."

Decky noted that since Molly had come, they all spoke in more pronounced southern accents. It was fun to listen. The sweet southern drawl rolled off their tongues like songs. It was a live version of the Ya Ya Sisterhood. They laughed and talked into the night. When they went to bed, Decky and Charlie made love for the first time since the incident. It was soft, tender, and much needed. It freed tensions that so needed to be released. They slept soundly all night with Decky spooned in Charlie's arms. Tomorrow was indeed another day.

#

When the clerk came in and spoke with the bailiff, he called for quiet in the packed courtroom. It was the largest courtroom in the new courthouse. Even so, the room was overflowing into the hall. The historic jail and courthouse, just down the road, had been turned into offices and a museum. The bailiff asked for quiet again.

"Please stand, this special hearing is now in session, the Honorable Judge Richard Barker presiding."

The judge took his seat, the Bailiff asked everyone to be seated, and the judge banged the court into session. Decky peered around the courtroom. There were a lot of gray area people, most she knew, some she didn't. The contingent present for Charlie and Decky included Chip, sweet old Mr. Birdsong, and the young men that moved Charlie into the cottage, having also recently removed some graffiti with pleasure. The twins, Brenda, and anyone else expected to testify were being held out in the hallway.

Darlene and Brandi sat with Mother Margie and a few women from the team. The other people sitting squarely on Charlie and Decky's side were the lesbians of the community that were out and proud of it. Two of their own were in trouble and they had rallied. Some were dressed nicely and had tried to show their "normal" side. Others came in full, "kiss my ass if you don't like it," lesbian attire. Decky wasn't sure whether to laugh or cry. Instead, she just smiled at the nodding heads behind them and turned her attention to the judge who was now ready to proceed.

Molly stood up when the judge addressed her. They handled some court business, while Decky thought how absolutely hot Molly was in that seven or eight thousand dollar Chanel suit. She could only imagine what the boys in the gallery were thinking. More than one person had said, "Look, Jodie Foster is their lawyer." Discussion had gone on in the gallery, as to whether or not Ms. Foster had a real law degree; after all, she did go to Yale. Decky and Charlie had listened in on some of the conversations and giggled until Molly told them to stop. It wasn't hard to hear in this room. The acoustics made even whispers audible.

On the other side of the courtroom sat the assistant district attorney, who had pushed for this proceeding, and the Bagley family. Decky recognized them from photos of the funeral that had appeared in the paper. With them were several men dressed in lawyer attire. No question these guys were here to protect the money. The rest of the courtroom filled out with onlookers.

The judge was no surprise. Brenda's contact had let them know the minute the decision was official down at the courthouse. Decky knew him. Everybody did. He was a fixture at the local schools. He supported athletics as well as Fine Arts events. He was known for his generosity to needy college students and others outside the courtroom. Inside the courtroom and in the judicial community, he was known as "the hanging judge." Decky hoped he had fond memories of her.

The prosecutor led off with an opening statement outlining the events of the evening in question, as he interpreted them. The question at hand was not whether Jim Bagley had been killed, but rather whether or not a cover up had taken place. Also in question was the motive for the murder that had been disguised to suggest the victim was at fault, as alleged by the deceased family. Did Decky, Charlie, and R.C. stage a very different scene than what had in actual fact happened? The prosecutor would present the evidence, the defense would rebut, and the judge would rule.

Molly began, "Your honor, the defendants in this case are in fact the victims of a horrific crime committed by a man, who was shot and killed in order to save the very lives of these women. What we have here is undue influence on the prosecutor, from the family of the deceased, and a rumor mill run amuck. The prosecutor admitted as much in his opening remarks. It's that simple. We will prove the defendants' innocence beyond a shadow of a doubt, not because we have to prove blamelessness, but because these women and this father deserve the truth to come out. Thank you."

Decky and Charlie exchanged looks. Molly was as hot as her suit. She had the room in the palm of her hand, at least for now.

The medical examiner reviewed not only Jim Bagley's wounds, but those of Decky and Charlie as well, for most of the morning. At least, everybody now knew that they had the shit kicked out of them. Those that didn't know Jim Bagley learned just how big he was, six foot three inches tall and weighed two hundred and fifty pounds. The M.E. also established a time of death in a range that would allow the shooting to have happened much sooner than Decky or the others had reported.

Next, a parade of law enforcement personnel began. The officers recounted everything they saw and heard that night. They identified evidence collected and entered it into the record. Pictures taken at the scene and at the hospital were also added. Copies were handed to the judge and the defense table. Decky blushed uncontrollably. Just as she suspected, she had gone to school with the deputies that took the pictures.

Then Decky blushed with anger when she saw the pictures of Charlie. She wanted to cry, but these were tears of anger. Decky thought about standing up and shouting at the family, "See what your precious son did to her." Charlie must have read her mind and took the pictures away. Molly did not object to any of the testimony. She did ask the M.E. if it were possible that the shooting happened when the defendants said it did. He had answered that yes, it was possible.

The most damning piece of evidence was a total shock to Decky. Her gun had not been loaded. It had an empty clip inside. Decky remembered sliding the empty clip in the gun the last time Zack had a lot of friends at the house. She never wanted a kid to find her gun, not to mention her loaded gun. She must have forgotten to put the full clip back in. When she flew out of her house that night, Decky had not stopped to look. It must not have been loaded when she met the crazed Lizzie on her porch, either. *God, how stupid! Pulling an unloaded gun in a crisis, not once, but twice.*

The twins were called in succession just before lunch. The prosecutor attempted to get each teen to indicate R.C. had not been asleep, but had actually been waiting for them. He even brought up the fact that they had used their mother's car without permission, at Decky's request. In fact, they were employees of Ms. Bradshaw and would say anything to keep the money flowing. When it was her turn, Molly asked the boys just one question. Are you telling the truth? They both answered with an emphatic, "Yes!" Molly knew when a boy was lying. This judge knew it, too.

Lunch was a quick step over to the ancient grocery store across from the old courthouse. The problem was all the other people were doing the same thing. R.C. went in and brought out a box of drinks and snacks. No one really had an appetite. Decky ate only to keep her sugar levels up. In times of stress, her sugar sometimes bottomed out and she became either out of it or obnoxious, no in-between.

People openly discussed the case around them on the lawn of the old courthouse, going over the evidence among themselves, but loud enough to be heard. Molly talked on her cell phone, during most of lunch. Decky did not have a chance to ask her how she thought it was going. They ate and returned to the courthouse with nothing better to do.

Upon returning, Decky was startled to see both her mother and Lynne Haskins waiting with the prospective witnesses. Molly led them to the other end of the hall.

"That is an old prosecutorial trick. Let you see what's coming. Get you off guard. Do not worry about their testimony. I will handle it. You two stay cool, and R.C. just keep looking handsome down there."

Molly was in control or so she thought, Decky said to herself. Lizzie was impossible to read and, judging by the look that she was giving Decky, Lynne was bearing a huge grudge, displayed prominently on her shoulder. Brenda was also in the witness area, boring holes in the back of Lynne's head with her eyes. Decky recognized Brenda's attempt to give Lynne the evil eye. She found it amusing and pointed it out to Charlie. Their laughter caused everyone to look at them. Thank God, Molly came to get them to go back in.

Mr. Birdsong stopped Decky and hugged her. He whispered, "Jack sends his best. He says you are a brave woman. I tend to agree."

Decky could only say thank you before she had to rush to her seat. Lynne was the first witness called. Molly objected, but the prosecutor said it went to the motive and state of mind of one of the defendants, namely Decky. Lynne recounted her memory of the party, the break up and the punch. Her memory was a bit skewed. Decky took all of her energy not to ball up her fist. She had never known it to be so stressful to try to relax. Her future rested on Molly's ability to tear this bitch apart.

Molly began the annihilation with the first question. "Where were you on the night in question?"

Lynne replied, "In Monroe, Louisiana."

Molly followed the answer with a quick, "I have no further questions your honor."

Decky was shocked when Molly dismissed Lynne. What happened to, "I've dealt with her kind before." Decky searched Molly's eyes as she returned to the table. Molly winked at her. She actually winked. Decky was sure others saw it. What could she mean? She hadn't asked Lynne what she had said to make Decky hit her. She hadn't proven Lynne was the piece of work she really was. All these people saw was the poor Angelina Jolie look alike, who was attacked, unprovoked. Charlie whispered to her, "Be still."

Brenda was next. The prosecutor had her tell all about the party, the night at the restaurant, and her relationship with Charlie, starting in college. Brenda was on her best behavior. She answered his questions with thoughtful consideration, speaking in her most educated sounding voice. It was a little odd to see Brenda so subdued and proper, but it was not to be. Alas, the old Brenda reared her ugly head. She had just instructed the Prosecutor, "Please, call me Brenda."

"Brenda, is it true that you left your husband and home to care for and live with the two female defendants, when they were released from the hospital?"

Brenda answered sweetly, proud of her nursing the two back to health, "Yes, I stayed with them night and day for several days."

"Are you involved in anything or have you been involved in anything of a sexual nature with these defendants?"

Molly objected, but Brenda begged to answer. She lowered her eyes on the prosecutor and said, so everyone could hear clearly, "If you are asking me if I am a lesbian, I remind you that I happen to be married to that blonde hunk there in the first row. However, if I was not married and I chose to love a woman, then I could not think of any two women I would be more proud to have love me back. Is that what you wanted to know?"

Decky was so proud of Brenda, she wanted to clap. A few of the lesbians in the gallery did, but were quickly silenced by a sharp rap of the gavel. The prosecutor decided to leave Brenda alone after that. Molly rose and Brenda smiled at her.

"Brenda, may I call you Brenda?" Molly was so professional

Brenda replied with glee, "Of course honey, we're old friends."

Now Decky wanted to strangle Brenda. *Just answer the damn questions and only the questions.* How many times had Molly said that to all of them?

"Brenda, you testified earlier that you, your husband, and a few other friends, including Ms. Warren, had dinner at a restaurant and bar in town, on the night in question. Did you at any time see Ms. Warren speak with the deceased, other than when he was introduced at your table?"

"No, Charlie never talked to him after that, or before, for that matter."

Molly went for the point she was trying to make. "How do you know Ms. Warren never spoke to the deceased in private?"

Brenda realized the point Molly was trying to make. "Because I was with her from early afternoon, just after she got out of class until she left to go home from the restaurant. I even went to the potty with her. She didn't know where it was."

Molly saw a chance for Brenda to shine. "And what did you do all afternoon?"

Brenda didn't miss a beat. "What all girls do with time on their hands and credit cards in their pockets, we went shopping."

Even the judge laughed. Brenda was dismissed and blew kisses to Decky, Charlie, and R. C., as she passed them. Since she had now testified, Brenda slipped into the row with Chip, making everyone squeeze in.

The next witness was Tommy Mercer. Tommy had tried to clean up for the hearing. He had shaved and cut his hair, but the suit he was wearing was purchased several cases of beer ago. His stomach protruded through his jacket, straining against his shirt buttons. The shirt did not fasten at the neck. His tie was the only thing holding the collar closed, and not very well.

Tommy gave his version of events on the boat the afternoon he and his friends had found them rubbing lotion on each other, half-naked. He had only offered to help rub the lotion on them. This drew a giggle from the crowd, which the hanging judge found offensive, proven by the tone of his gavel and the scowl on his face.

Tommy happily relayed how his friend Jim had only tried to introduce himself when the foul-mouthed little one had called them assholes and Decky sped away in her boat. Nothing else was said on the boat and they just had some more beer and went swimming in the channel.

Now it was Molly's turn. This time she approached the small lectern and asked permission to move it closer to the witness. She positioned it where the gallery could see her profile, in front of the judge's bench. She carried a yellow legal pad full of notes with her.

"The deceased was a friend of yours. In fact, wasn't it you that introduced him to the other men in the boat?"

"Yes, Jim was a friend of mine. I did show him around a bit, because he had just moved here."

"How long have you known the deceased?"

Tommy had to think. "Roughly fifteen years, or there abouts. We met doing community service."

Molly took the chance the prosecutor was asleep. Jim Bagley's criminal past had not been introduced into evidence.

"Are you aware of the past sexual assault charges that were levied against your friend, you admit to knowing roughly fifteen years?"

"Objection!" shot from the prosecutors mouth so quickly, he almost choked. The attorneys approached the bench. After several tense moments, the attorneys returned to their original places.

The judge addressed the court. "It is the court's decision that the witness may answer. Since the character of the defendants has been brought into question, the decedent's character may also be examined. Mr. Mercer you will answer the question."

Tommy looked like a man alone on an island. He searched the Bagley family and the bank of lawyers in front of him for what to say.

The judge spoke. He could definitely spot a liar. "I remind you that you, sir, are under oath."

Tommy sighed and said under his breath, "Yes, I knew."

Molly wasn't about to let the answer go unheard in the back row. "I'm sorry, you need to speak up. Please repeat your answer."

Tommy was done covering for his friend. "Yes, I knew Jim was a pervert. I just never thought he'd go that far."

The prosecutor looked like he wanted to crawl under the table. Molly took a long poignant look into the gallery. The horde had to be quieted again. This time the judge threatened to clear the room. Molly didn't need Tommy to recant his testimony about what happened on the boat. The damage had been done. He had said exactly what Molly wanted him to say. She was finished with him.

The prosecutor huddled with the lawyers on the other side of the aisle. He stood up and called the assistant district attorney, who had repeatedly dropped the charges against Jim Bagley, to the stand. He testified that insufficient evidence had been the reason for the dropping all of the charges, after the several initial arrests of Mr. Bagley. The prosecutor must have thought that would be the end of it, but he had never tangled with Molly.

Molly approached the lectern again with a different pad full of notes. "I have only a few questions for you sir. First, you have political aspirations, don't you? In fact, you are running for District Attorney next year. Is that correct?"

"I don't see what that has –" The prosecution took the cue and objected.

Molly answered the objection with, "It goes to credibility of the witness your honor."

"I'll allow it," the judge said. Decky was beginning to think Molly had charmed the judge. So far, so good on the objections.

"Yes, I am running a campaign for District Attorney."

Molly smiled and said in that sweet southern drawl, "I only have one more question," she paused, allowing a wave of anticipation to circulate the room, "Who are the largest contributors to your campaign? Just name the top three. That will be fine."

"I don't recall," came the answer.

Molly pulled out some papers that had been earlier placed in the back of the legal pad. "Oh, that's okay," she said, handing the witness, the prosecutor, and the judge a copy of the paper she was now holding. "It is a matter of public record, and as you see here, I have your fundraising statistics. Let me help you recall. Looking at the document, and refreshing your memory, am I correct in finding that Mr. and Mrs. Bagley along with their son, James Bagley, and Bagley Enterprises are the top three contributors to your upcoming campaign?"

The man on the stand went white. He was about to admit to tampering on the stand and he knew it. He finally said in a defeated voice, "Yes, you are correct."

Done. Molly was ready to move on. The next witness was a man Decky did not recognize. His name was one she had not recognized on the witness list. Don Stedman looked like what he probably was, a day laboring drunk, who hung out at the bar. Still young enough to change, he looked much older around the eyes. Too many years ago, he lost his hope in a bottle.

Don testified that he was in the bar when Charlie came up and stood beside him. He had heard her ask the now dead man if he would like to follow her home for some rough sex. He remembered, because he would have gone, if the guy had said no. The prosecutor seemed gun shy to let Don talk anymore. He turned the witness over to the defense.

Molly left the table with no pad in hand. Once again charming, she questioned Don, "Mr. Stedman, if you could, would you tell me what the defendant in question was wearing the night you saw her in the bar, 'standing right beside you,' I believe you said?"

Don froze. He had nothing. Finally, he recovered enough to say he didn't remember.

"But Mr. Stedman, you testified that this really hot chick came and stood right beside you and offered rough sex to the man next to you." Molly backed away from the table pointing at Charlie, "Are you telling the court that this extremely attractive woman stood beside you and you cannot remember what she was wearing? Why Mr. Stedman, boys around home would be talking about that down to the last detail for days, if it had happened to them."

"Objection!"

"Sustained. Is there a question, Ms. Kincaid?" The judge asked Molly.

"Withdrawn. I don't need to question this witness any further." Molly was setting them up and mowing them down.

The prosecution asked that Molly's last remarks be stricken from the record. It didn't matter. Everyone had heard them clearly.

The prosecution rested. The summation was rendered next. Decky thought the man was scared he wouldn't get another chance to tell people why they were even there to begin with. He went back over the evidence that pointed to guilt on the part of the defendants. Decky had been proven through testimony to be a dangerous, jealous lesbian, and prone to violence. Charlie was seen in the bar offering perverted sex to the victim. Decky's father had only helped cover it up, after misunderstanding the situation and shooting the victim.

The victim had in fact been invited to the home and in a jealous rage, Decky had attacked first Charlie and then Mr. Bagley. R.C. had reacted to what he had seen as his daughter in danger, but was she really? The timeline afforded Decky the time to send R.C. back home and call the twins, before calling the police. It had been a woman's voice on the 911 call. It sounded an awful lot like Decky Bradshaw, not her mother. Last but not least, the most important fact, the gun being held on Decky was not loaded. She was never in danger. She knew it and that's why she had to cover it up. Charlie had gone along for the money and her father had gone along out of misguided fatherly loyalty.

Molly did not ask for the customary dismissal of all charges, at that time. She had promised the girls their day in court and they would have it. The judge appeared to want to complete witness statements today. Molly only had four witnesses listed. He called a recess of ten minutes and warned everyone to be back on time.

Decky, Charlie, and R.C. left Molly at the defense table shuffling papers and stepped out into the hallway. Decky needed some fresh air. They ended up on a bench outside facing the water, their backs turned to the door. The wind was blowing in off the Sound. If Decky closed her eyes, she could pretend she was at home. Charlie's voice brought her back to reality.

"Decky, no matter what your mother thinks about us, she won't let her husband go to jail for something he did not do."

R.C. excused himself, to speak to someone.

"I still blame her for all of this. I don't care what she says."

Charlie was calm and patient, but she spoke her mind. "Your mother did no more cause this than you or I did. You did not consider her feelings at all. You let her find out about us from the rumor mill. You never once have considered how that had to make her feel. She was hurt Decky, but I can't believe your mother wants anything, but to see you safe and happy. Give her time."

Decky had been intently studying a patch of clover the whole time Charlie was talking. She lifted her eyes and saw her mother standing behind Charlie. Lizzie turned around and went back into the courthouse. Decky didn't tell Charlie that Lizzie had been there. How much had she heard of what Charlie had said? What had she heard Decky say? R.C. came to get them at that moment and they went back to the defense table.

Molly had set up an easel. It had an eleven by seventeen blank sheet of paper covering other pages underneath. Charlie was the first witness called. Upon taking the stand, Molly asked Charlie to tell the judge what had happened that night, beginning with the dinner in town. Charlie told the story as she had so many times. She saw Jim Bagley at the restaurant when he came to the table, to speak to an acquaintance of his. She remembered him from the boating incident, and by the way, that had happened nothing like Tommy had testified. Jim Bagley had recognized her too, though he said nothing at the time. She simply forgot about him. She saw him at the bar when she was leaving. She stopped to get gas. She went to the cottage and he attacked her. When Charlie stopped, Molly gestured to Charlie to continue. She obliged, telling in graphic detail exactly what happened to her before Decky came in and what happened to them both, up until she heard the gun shot.

"Ms. Warren, is this the gas receipt from the night in question?"

"Yes, that's the one. It is time stamped."

"Let the record show the receipt time stamp reads exactly twenty-five minutes before the deputy testified the alarm company called Ms. Bradshaw at eight forty-eight p.m."

Molly stepped over to the easel. She removed the top piece of paper, revealing a close up of Charlie's face on the night of the beating. She asked Charlie if she remembered when and where the photograph was taken. Charlie answered her. The two of them went through a series of photos of Charlie in the same manner.

The bruises were horrible and the cuts grotesque. Decky hadn't seen them so vividly before. She must have only seen the Charlie underneath the bruises. She had not wanted to see all the damage on the surface. A tear rolled down her cheek. She let it fall on her silk shirt, unable to move, her eyes fixed on the photos.

Molly turned Charlie over to the prosecution. He seemed un-interested in the night of the attack. He began by questioning Charlie about her and Decky's behavior at the party. When he got to the incident with Lynne, his motive was clear.

"Ms. Warren, did you see Ms. Bradshaw strike Lynne Haskins that night?"

Charlie started to reply, "Yes, but she –"

He cut her off. "Just answer yes or no, Ms. Warren. Now on the occasion of your moving into the cottage, did Ms. Bradshaw burn any of your property?"

"Yes," Charlie had learned her lesson.

"Did she in fact burn your mattresses believing them to be the ones you had slept on with Lynne Haskins?" He was twisting everything.

"Yes," Charlie looked helpless.

"Let's address another area. You were living in the residence of Ms. Bradshaw at the time of the alleged attack. Is that correct?"

"What do you mean living with her?" Charlie was fighting back.

"Sleeping in her bed, with her, to make it clear."

"Yes."

"You had clothing and personal items along with your cat there at Ms. Bradshaw's residence. Why did you stop at the cottage late at night by yourself? Why enter a dark cottage alone? Why not wait until the next day? Is it because nothing was wrong with the lights and you planned to meet Mr. Bagley there for sex?"

Molly stood up to object, but Charlie handled it just fine. "Which question would you like me to answer yes or no to?"

"Withdrawn."

"Now Ms. Warren, what if anything did you see in the living room area just prior to the shot being fired?"

"I was behind a counter, I couldn't see."

"So you could not see what was actually happening on the other side of the counter?"

"No." Charlie wanted to say so much. Decky could see it on her face.

"Have you paid Ms. Bradshaw any money on the cottage? Is there a rental agreement or lease?"

"No."

"Ms. Bradshaw has in fact spent quite a bit of money on you in the previous month?"

"Yes."

Decky thought how stupid she had been for spending so much money on Charlie. Then she remembered why she had done it and wasn't one bit sorry. She wanted to spend money on Charlie. Charlie didn't need anything she couldn't buy herself. Decky bought things that brought joy to them both.

"One last question, did you have sex with Lynne Haskins when she was in town a week before the party?"

Charlie was out of the chair. She stood up as tall as her five foot three inch frame could stretch. Out of all the things Charlie had been accused of, this one made her furious.

"I most certainly did not!"

The prosecutor rested. Molly began redirect.

"Ms. Warren, what kind of car do you drive?"

Charlie looked confused, but answered, "A 2007 BMW 335i convertible."

Molly acted impressed. "That's a really nice car. Did you purchase this car before you met Ms. Bradshaw?"

Charlie caught on quickly. "Yes, I purchased it with part of my savings and some of the proceeds from the sale of my home in Louisiana."

"Ms. Warren, why did you go to the cottage that night?" Molly was allowing Charlie to say the things she wanted to.

"I went there because we were going to the beach the next day, and I needed some things that were still packed away at the cottage."

"Now, the prosecutor asked you if you saw anything of the fight, just before the gun went off. You said no. Could you tell us if you heard anything?"

"Dixie, the dog, jumped on the backdoor causing the man to fall against the doorframe, then Decky went for him. He easily slammed her into the other part of the room where I could not see. I heard Dixie growl. I heard slamming and banging around. Then I heard the man scream. I heard Dixie yelp and whimper. The next thing I remember that really sticks out is Decky telling Dixie to stop attacking and come behind the counter. Decky told the man he would have to kill her if he wanted to get to me. He told her he was going to kill her, but first he was going to make her –" Charlie paused.

Molly was gentle when she asked Charlie to go on.

Charlie swallowed hard and looked right at Decky during the rest of her testimony. "He told her he was going to make her suck his …dick, while I watched, his words not mine. Then he said when he was through with Decky he was going to fuck me and kill us all, including the dog."

"One last question, why do you think Decky Bradshaw told him he would have to kill her first before he could get to you again? You had known each other less than two weeks, at the time."

Charlie was still looking at Decky. "Because, she is an honorable person who would lay down her life for others and because she loves me."

Molly turned to the judge. "I'm done with this witness your honor. The defense calls R.C. Bradshaw to the stand."

Charlie stood and retook her seat beside Decky. Decky said nothing, just took Charlie's hand and held it tightly.

R.C. walked head held high to the witness stand. Molly had him tell a little about himself. When he had finished a short biography, Molly began to weave her tale.

"So you have lived in the Albemarle area all of your life, except for the time you were in college, is that correct?"

R.C. was giving her his full attention. They might as well have been in the room alone. He was a smart man. He knew not to look around the room, not unless he wanted to. He answered the question with one word, as he had been told to do.

"Yes."

"You were a math teacher and coach before becoming a school principal, I believe you said." She knew exactly what he had said. "You ought to be pretty good with maps, distances, and time, with that background. I ask you then, how long does it take to get from the gas station, where Ms. Warren stopped, to the cottage she recently moved into?"

"That drive can take you thirty to thirty-five minutes. It would vary according to speed, but that's about average."

Molly showed him the gas receipt. "Do you see the time stamp on this receipt and would you read it to the court?"

R.C. put his reading glasses on. This caused chuckles from the gallery. He looked out over the top of his glasses at the crowd, with that principal's stare. The gallery again became quiet. "It says here eight twenty-three p.m."

"Now, we have heard testimony that the alarm company called your daughter at eight forty-eight p.m., exactly twenty-five minutes after the time stamped on the gas receipt. We have also seen evidence, namely your daughter's phone records, showing a call to the twins, as they are so fondly called." A rumble of laughter waved through the gallery. "The twins were called at eight fifty-six p.m., eight minutes after the alarm call. At what time did the twins arrive at your house?"

"It was two minutes after nine. I have a habit of looking at the clock," he explained.

"What time did you arrive at the cottage?"

"Well, that particular time I wasn't watching the clock. I suppose it took me ten minutes to get there. About nine twelve, I reckon."

"Mr. Bradshaw, we heard testimony that the 911 call came in at nine seventeen p.m. Who made the call?"

R. C. straightened in the chair. He cast his eyes amongst the spectators. He dared anybody to make a sound with his eyes. He knew Lizzie was a source of much grief and ridicule, but she was his. "My wife, Elizabeth Bradshaw."

"Now, Mr. Bradshaw, the prosecution has agreed that you shot the deceased, in what you thought was the defense of your daughter. You are being accused of a cover-up. Is there anything you think the prosecutor overlooked, other than the timeline, which we will get to in a minute, a missed piece of evidence maybe?"

"Yes, there is one thing. Do you have a picture of the decedent on your easel there?"

Of course, Molly had a blow up of the decedent and another even closer shot of his crotch.

R.C. leaned forward. "You see that man has his pants unzipped and his, pardon me, penis in his hand. That is called the death grip. A bullet to the right part of the brain and the person will grip whatever they have in their hand, at the time of the shot. He must have been about to do something with it when I shot him."

There was an audible gasp in the gallery.

"With your experience as a math teacher, could you take the times we have discussed here and feasibly have Ms. Warren arrive at the cottage before the alarm was cut?"

"Not unless she's a NASCAR driver and the Smokies were asleep, which isn't often."

Decky could hear people mumbling in agreement. That kind of drive on winding roads is just not possible, not for a normal person in a normal, albeit hot, car. Charlie had just moved here. No way had she made that drive in less than thirty minutes. The judge had driven these roads his whole life. He had to know it was almost impossible for Charlie to make that run.

Decky had also been doing some adding. If she hadn't stopped to call Charlie's cell phone, or the house phone she might have beaten Charlie to the cottage. She could have prevented this. It was only a three-minute window between the times Charlie probably arrived at the cottage and when Decky called the twins. She was that close.

Decky came back to the courtroom from her ruminations on how three minutes had changed their lives, when she heard her full name being called. The Rebecca usually meant she was in trouble, so she always snapped to attention when she heard it. She realized she had been called to the stand. The prosecutor had decided not to question R.C.

Charlie whispered, "Stay calm."

Decky flashed the image of Charlie on her tiptoes denying she had slept with Lynne the week before they got together. Charlie sure kept her cool all right.

Molly began before Decky could settle in to the fear that now gripped her heart. This was it, the decisive moment.

"Ms. Bradshaw, everybody around here knows you as Decky, may I call you that?"

Decky was southern through and through. Even though the woman who was questioning was now her friend, Molly was in a position of authority. Decky's answer reflected this. "Yes, ma'am."

"Okay Decky, we have heard what happened from Ms. Warren and your father. I want you to take us through your ordeal, from the time you got the call from the alarm company, until the gunshot. Take your time."

Decky told the story. She tried not to become emotional, but she did. She told the courtroom exactly what she said to the man, while he held her at gunpoint on the floor. The gallery was transfixed. Decky was in full fury by the time she finished. The anger boiled out of her. She glared at the prosecution table.

Molly tried to redirect her. "Decky, did you know the gun wasn't loaded?"

"Hell, no!" Decky's reply had the gallery in stitches.

"Do you know how the gun came to have an empty clip in it?" Molly was trying to keep Decky focused.

"I put the clip in before school got out. My son, Zack, had an end of the year party and I didn't want one of our finest shooting a foot off. I forgot to reload it. I certainly wouldn't have knowingly carried an empty gun into a dark cottage where a bleeding woman was lying on the floor. I have better sense than that." Decky was playing the audience for all it was worth. She liked this part and she was not as angry anymore.

"Decky, now I'm going to ask you a tough question. Why did you tell him to shoot you?"

"Because, I did not want to see what he was going to do to Charlie. She might have been able to escape. She still had Dixie. I thought maybe I could buy her some time."

Molly was finished. She knew the prosecutor was going to go for Decky like a starving dog. She was counting on rebuttal testimony to put out any fires. Molly had discussed her strategy with Decky, so she knew it was coming.

"Ms. Bradshaw," the prosecutor was going to keep this formal, "Do you consider yourself a violent person?"

"No." Decky remembered yes or no answers.

"But we have heard testimony today that in a jealous rage you attacked a woman at someone else's home. How do you explain that?"

This was not a yes or no answer. She swallowed hard. "She was rude."

"She was rude? Is that all, just rude and you nearly broke her nose?"

"Yes." Back to yes or no, good, Decky thought.

"Well now, I find that hard to believe. You'll have to be more specific."

Decky couldn't help herself. "She said some things about Charlie, and if you were any kind of gentleman, you would not ask me to repeat it. If she had been a man, most people in this room would be slapping me on the back, not judging me."

This caused a stir amongst the gallery. The prosecutor changed tactics.

"You would have us believe that within eight minutes, you arrived at the cottage? You were in an orthopedic boot at the time I believe. You reacted extremely fast. Were you expecting trouble?"

"No. I drive fast. Too much NASCAR." This elicited nods from the gallery. Decky at one point or another had passed most of them.

"You had no reason to fear for your safety? Isn't it a fact, your own mother shot at your home just three nights earlier? Were you taking that gun to kill your own mother?"

"No. Are you nuts? My mother and I may have issues, but she is my mother. What kind of person are you to even imagine such a thing?" Decky thought this guy was really an idiot. He was beaten, so now he was grasping at straws.

The prosecutor looked flustered. He was losing steam. One last plunge and he might just quit.

"I'll ask the questions and I have one final one. Why would you risk your life to save a woman you barely knew? You expect us to believe that you were trying to stop her from being hurt, at the very peril of your own life? You had known her only ten days. That seems to be the hanging point here. How are we to believe that you went from being straight to gay and fell in love in ten days? It is easier to believe you attacked this man in a jealous rage." The prosecutor looked smugly at Decky. He thought he had her.

But, Decky knew what she had to say. "Mr. Prosecutor, I feel sorry for you. If it is so hard for you to believe that two people can find each other, find the missing piece, then why listen to love songs? Why read love stories? Romeo and Juliet, West Side Story; just burn the scores. Don't look at a painting of a beautiful woman, painted by her lover hundreds of years

ago. Poetry is worth no more than the paper it's printed on."
Decky was on a roll.

"Our whole lives revolve around the search for true love.
The fairy tales we read our children, Cinderella, Sleeping
Beauty are entranced in our minds, from our own childhoods.
What little girl doesn't dream of being swept off her feet?
What boy doesn't dream of being someone's hero?"

The prosecutor objected, but the judge said, "You opened
the door, too late to close it now."

Decky snuck a look at Charlie, and then finished her
answer. "No sir, I'm not the one asking you to believe
something unfathomable. I find it just as unfathomable to
believe in a world where love at first sight doesn't happen and
soul mates don't exist, for all of us. Mr. Prosecutor, I did not
go from being straight to gay. I went from being alone to in
love, it just happened to be with a woman. And if you
wouldn't give up your life to save the woman you love, then I
feel sorry for her, and quite frankly, for you too."

The courtroom erupted. The judge let it go on for just a
second. He then rapped his gavel to quiet the gallery, but he
wasn't as adamant this time. The prosecutor had given up half
way through Decky's speech.

Molly, who had been sitting, rose. "Your honor, I see no
need to redirect this witness. She may be excused."

Decky barely had the emotional energy to crutch back over
to the table. R.C. could see she was hurting and jumped up to
help her. Charlie did also. She whispered to Decky, "I knew
there was a reason I fell in love with you, the southern poet,
the hopeless romantic."

The court could see that these women were nowhere near
healed. It would be a long time coming.

Decky reached the table and grabbed Molly's arm.
"Momma doesn't have to testify does she?"

Molly grinned just like Jodie Foster with a secret. "I think you'll be pleasantly surprised." She turned to the judge. "The defense calls its final two witnesses."

The prosecutor fumbled with papers on his desk. He knew nothing of an additional witness. He let the court know with a loud objection.

Molly laughed at him. "Your honor, the one witness is being escorted by the other. We call Elizabeth and Dixie Bradshaw."

Decky turned to see Dixie leading her mother down the aisle. Dixie was petted and scratched the whole way. Everyone loved Dixie. She was the star of her own show. Decky couldn't help but smile. She gave Dixie a kiss as she came by, but did not make eye contact with her mother.

Dixie went right up on the witness stand, following Lizzie. She even allowed the judge to pet her. When Lizzie took her seat, Dixie sat where she could see the gallery and they certainly could see the princess, posed in perfect show form. Decky loved that dog.

Molly smiled and approached Lizzie. "Good afternoon, Mrs. Bradshaw. I asked you to bring Dixie with you, didn't I?"

Molly didn't have to ask another question. Lizzie was off. "Yes, well anybody can see this dog would not attack anyone unless one of her people was in danger. Everybody here knows this dog. She would never hurt a flea. A baby is safer with this dog than half the mommas in this county. This dog bit that man because he was going to hurt people she loved. Dogs don't know how to lie. They steal, but they don't lie."

The gallery was trying desperately not to make noise. There was a lot of shuffling of feet and butts grinding into the benches. Molly too, was having a hard time keeping a straight face. Decky buried her face in her hands. Charlie made her sit up.

"Decky, where do you think you got all those dramatic skills, now sit up and pay attention, she's brilliant." Charlie was unbelievably becoming a Lizzie fan. Would this day never end?

Molly finally regained her composure long enough to ask, "We have heard testimony as to what happened when your husband arrived at the cottage. You were with him, what happened from the time you pulled up?"

And they're off! Lizzie hit the starting gate before the horn sounded. She had been waiting all day to say this, and by God, everybody better listen.

"R.C. said as soon as we could see the cottage that something was bad wrong. He gets those feelings and I've come to trust them. He hit the ground running. The truck wasn't even stopped. He had his rifle and he was focused on getting up the steps. He did not know I was right behind him. I could hear Decky screaming, although I could not make out the words, I knew she was in trouble. A mother knows."

A pang shot across Decky's chest. Her mother might pull this out. She sat up straighter and listened.

"R. C. stopped at the front door, but he only paused. He was moving in on the prey. I've seen him do that hunting deer. When he moved away from the door, I could then see the shadow of a very large man. The room was a mess from what I could see, and Decky was shouting for this man to kill her. I followed R. C. around to the picture window. I saw the man slap Decky and put the gun under her chin. Then he grabbed his – male member. The next thing I knew, he is on the floor and that was that. R.C. told me to call 911 and I did. That is what happened. You can all make this out to be about whom my daughter has chosen to love, I for one will not. I may not agree with her choices, and most of you know I don't, but they are her choices and it has not one damn thing to do with that maniac that tried to kill them both."

Decky was in shock. She looked at her father who was grinning from ear to ear. The prosecutor simply said no questions. He wanted none of Lizzie. Molly rested her case. She chose not to summarize so the judge could deliver a quick decision, hopefully. The bailiff called for everyone to stand so the judge could exit. The gallery grew restless. The judge was almost out of the room, when he came back to the bench. Decky thought he must have forgotten something, but instead he sat down and asked everyone to be seated.

"I have the responsibility to the state, meaning you people, to render a judgment on whether there is sufficient evidence to bind the defendants over for trial, on the charges of conspiracy and murder. Now, I could leave here, go back to my chambers, and play solitaire on the computer, so you'd think I was reviewing this case. To tell you the truth, I don't think I have ever seen victims of a crime treated in this manner in my entire career. From where I sit, the victims are the defendants in this case and I urge them, with all due speed, to file civil cases against everyone involved in the travesty that allowed Jim Bagley walk around free among law abiding folks. Case dismissed!"

Decky was not going to prison. She was not going to prison! *Thank you, God!* Dixie barked at all the excitement. She evidently thought all the applause was for her. For the room did erupt in applause. A few people were not pleased, but were too outnumbered to matter. Decky hugged everybody after she hugged Charlie. Her ribs were not a concern, although she was reminded frequently that they still needed a little more time to heal.

Molly was as excited as everyone else. She hugged Decky. Decky looked her straight in the eyes and said, "Sue their asses off."

Molly grinned. "Then forget the fee for the criminal trial. I am going to make so much money suing these assholes it would be a drop in the bucket. I'll call you with their first offer, but I can tell you already we're not accepting it."

Slowly the crowd finally cleared. Decky saw her mother with Dixie by the door. She approached cautiously, just in case the meds her mother was obviously on had worn off.

Lizzie didn't even wait for Decky to speak. "Decky, I meant what I said. I don't agree with the lifestyle you have chosen, but I saw what you were willing to do for her and I have to say you really do love her. She's a smart girl. You should listen to her. I would never put you in harm's way. Not really."

Decky knew Lizzie was trying to rationalize the gunshot to the house.

"Momma, it's over. Let's go home. We're both sorry for things we said and did. Let's just live and let live for a while and see how it goes."

Lizzie agreed and they all left the courthouse in a stream of honking cars that followed them almost all the way home. The lesbians were queens for a day.

15

An impromptu party enveloped Decky's house. It went on into the night. There was a joyous time had by all. Even R.C. and Lizzie came for a little while. Decky enjoyed the place of prominence on the couch with Dixie and Miss Kitty. Charlie played hostess and looked beautiful doing it. Even with the bruises, she was still the most beautiful woman Decky had ever seen.

They snuck a kiss or a touch when they could. It was well past 1:00 a.m. when Brenda and Chip left, after helping straighten up and shooing away stragglers. Finally, they were alone.

Decky used the remote lighting control to turn off all the lights, except for the windows, which she made glow a light moonlight blue. She stepped out onto the deck, taking in the bright moon shining across Currituck Sound.

Charlie slipped up behind Decky. She wrapped her arms around Decky's waist, hugging her from behind. Charlie stayed there with her head resting on Decky's back. Quietly, they remained like this for a few minutes.

"I've spent most of my life in this county," Decky said, breaking the silence. "I was thinking the other day that we might have to leave here to find some serenity. I was willing to do that. Just cut the ties and go somewhere with you, where we could live in peace."

Charlie squeezed her ribs, but remained silent as Decky continued, "I think I'd miss the Sound the most. I always found my tranquility on the water. No matter what was happening on land, as long as I was out there, I could leave it behind for awhile."

Decky turned around to face Charlie. "I think we're going to be all right here. What do you think?"

"Yes, I think we're going to be fine," Charlie said with a twinkle in her eye, "but you have to promise me one thing."

"And what would that be?"

"I want a houseboat."

This was not what Decky had expected Charlie to say. She didn't know what she thought Charlie was going to say, but houseboat had never crossed her mind. She cocked her head and looked at Charlie.

"What on earth do you want with a houseboat?"

Charlie answered, "So when Lizzie goes off her meds, I can find my own serenity out on the Sound."

"What, you don't think Lizzie can drive a boat?"

Epilogue

It had all started with a touch. Decky closed the laptop. There were more adventures to come and a few since, but the first four weeks of their relationship were all she could hope to capture, in the new book she was sending her publisher.

About the Author

R. E. "Decky" Bradshaw, a native of North Carolina and a proud Tar Heel, now makes her home in Oklahoma with her wife of 25 years. Holding a Master of Performing Arts degree, Bradshaw worked in professional theatre and taught University and High School classes, leaving both professions to write full-time in 2010. She continues to be one of the best selling lesbian fiction authors on Amazon.com.

43559140R00182

Made in the USA
Middletown, DE
13 May 2017